SEEDS

Volume Three

M.M. Kin

Books by M.M. Kin

Seeds

Volume One
Volume Two
Volume Three

Upcoming Novels...

Interludes in Myth
Hivemother
Through Infinity

and more!

This has been a long journey, but well worth it. My heart goes out to Paige, Madame Thome, Elke, and last but most certainly not least Marit, who have been a cherished source of encouragement and inspiration. I would also like to thank everyone else who has given me encouragement or feedback when this book was still in progress. I could not have done it without your help and feedback, you have my undying gratitude.

I would also like to thank Lani Rush, Sophia Luo (Sorelliena), Teresa Dec and Zele Jones for their feedback and editing help, and Moranyelie Osorio Morales for the incredible cover she designed for this book.

I would like to thank everyone for reading and enjoying the previous books in this saga. I could not have done this without the support of my readers. Without further ado, the final installment of Seeds.

ROOTS

Chapter XXXIX
Chapter XL
Chapter XLI
Chapter XLII
Chapter XLIII
Chapter XLIV
Chapter XLV
Chapter XLVI

Chapter XLVII
Chapter XLVIII
Chapter XLIX

FRUITAGE

Chapter L
Chapter LI
Chapter LII
Chapter LIII
Chapter LIV
Chapter LV
Epilogue

Afterword

Chapter XXXIX

oOo

With trembling fingers, Persephone brought her hand up to her lips, feeling the faint stickiness from the remnants of the pomegranate. She started to feel her throat constrict from anxiety, much as she had when she realized that her father was dead. Honestly, the two situations – as different as they were – had one thing in common; Death had taken her father from her, and now her freedom.

No. No! It can't be! When she felt Hades's hand on her shoulder, she flinched away, her head snapping up to look at him with wide eyes that displayed a clear mixture of emotions – shock, hurt, and rapidly increasing anger. Hades's own face reflected surprise and perplexity when he noticed the sudden shift of emotion in her features.

"Seph..." His voice was calm, masking the confusion he felt, and the slowly dawning realization that slipping her the seeds was something he probably – *definitely* – should not have done. The juice stood out against her pale skin like a bloodstain, and she let out a quiet whimper as she drew her hand from her lips, her gaze flicking down to her fingertips.

Persephone couldn't breathe. It was as if an iron band had wrapped itself around her chest, and she felt light-headed. She opened her mouth to speak, but despite her best efforts, no words were uttered.

"Seph." She heard Hades say her name again – the nickname he used to show his affection for her. He dared to use that name after what he had done to her? How many seeds had she swallowed? She tried to remember. His fingers and lips had pressed seeds into her mouth... she remembered feeling something cool under her fingers... a larger hand entwining its fingers with her own as it guided her to touch whatever that thing had been... that sweet coolness that had been so refreshing after such a physically draining act. Her gaze flicked over to the offending fruit, seeing for the first time how most of its seeds were gone. It was a given that Hades had eaten most of it, but she was certain she had swallowed at least a dozen. Possibly – no, probably – more.

Persephone didn't want to believe it. She had swallowed the seeds that had tempted her for so long. She remembered the crunching of seeds between her teeth, the savory tang of the jelly sliding past her tongue and down her throat... Hades whispering lovingly into her ear as he encouraged her to swallow the seeds that would seal her fate.

Seal her fate. She was now forever bound to the Underworld.

Hades glanced at her, still perplexed by her mixture of emotions. Surely she wouldn't be having second thoughts, not after the way she had enjoyed herself so passionately, and how she had been so eager to eat the seeds. His fingers were running along her arm, and he had been about to pull her into an embrace, to initiate more lovemaking. After all, his reserve of energy far exceeded that of even the most virile mortal male, and it would provide an enjoyable distraction for both of them. All she needed was to be reminded of what he could offer her... *would* give her.

"Hades." Usually, her tone was welcoming. Now, raw pain was clear in her voice. He did not notice the signs, not at first as she came to her realization; because his eyes were roving along her breasts as he reached for her. But when she said his name, Hades stopped, picking up the unmistakable undertones in her voice.

"How could you?" With that, she started to wiggle away and climb out of bed. He reached for her, grabbing her with an expression on his face that was deceptively placid, as if nothing had happened.

"I had to," he merely said, trying to smooth things over, but that just made her more angry and offended. How *could* he try to calm her down? He knew what he had done!

"You *had* to? You sneaked these seeds into my mouth! You... you used sex to play a trick on me!" She jerked away from him, grabbing the first thing she could find on the floor. It was his cloak, and she quickly wrapped it around herself, having no desire to bother with all the pins that held up her chiton.

"You only used that cock of yours to get your seeds in me!" Her eyes blazed. Had she been in a happy mood, she would have laughed at her unintentional pun on the word 'seed'. Hades stared back. Used sex to play a trick on her? Sex had been something they *both* wanted. Hadn't she made her desire clear often enough? He frowned at her harsh accusation.

"You *gave* yourself to me. We both remember the words that came from your pretty little mouth. I gave you what you wanted!" He moved closer to her as she scooted further away, and he had to pull himself out of bed.

Even though part of him knew that what he had done was wrong, that she hadn't been fully conscious when he had offered her the seeds, he refused to feel guilty over it. What was done was done. He was confident in his power, but given how the situation on the surface world was nearing a point of no return, he had felt it prudent to ensure that she was bound to him. He had simply done what needed to be done. That was all.

But damn, he certainly hadn't expected her to be so furious. Given how close they had grown and the fact that she wanted to be with him, he had been certain that she would respond to this more positively. Perhaps even appreciatively, now that she didn't have to worry about resisting the food of the dead. She had eaten, so the pressure was off. Shouldn't she be relieved with that, given how she had gazed hungrily at the food he had set before her on multiple occasions? He had done her a favor, damnit!

When he reached for her again, she viciously slapped his hand away, and this caused him to feel hurt. After the way she had responded so eagerly to his touches, and lavished her own attentions on him, this was what she felt she had to do? Push

10

him away? Hadn't she seen the hurt in his eyes whenever she refused to eat his food?

"Just stay away from me," she whispered fiercely, looking away from him. She had to get some message to the gods above. How? Hades would never permit it. Why would he? She had eaten the food of the dead.

"You bastard." Tears welled up in her eyes and she turned away, but the ornately-framed mirror on one wall revealed her tears all too clearly. As she turned away from her reflection, she caught a glimpse of his frown.

"I am not a bastard. You need to understand! I need you so badly. Do you not see, Persephone?" he hissed, grabbing her shoulders. She jerked away from him with a yelp before placing her hands on his bare chest and shoving away sharply.

"I told you to stay away from me! You have no right to decide where I will stay!"

"Yes I do!" he growled, "You belong with me, Persephone. How can you say you would rather live with Demeter, treated like a child, never listened to or truly appreciated for the person you are?"

"I belong to no one!" she shrieked back, choosing to not respond to the rest of his statement.

The Lord of the Dead felt anger well up in his chest, though he struggled to contain it. He didn't want to yell at her. That would make things worse, but it was getting pretty hard to be civil, especially with how she was behaving. How could she be like this when she knew she belonged here? Why did she continue to deny it? What was it that made her respond well to his advances but refuse to eat the food of the dead – the food he and the other underworld deities ate every day!

"I am leaving!" Persephone huffed and went to open the door to leave, only it would not open. She yanked on the handle and jerked it, and even tried pushing instead of pulling, but it would not open any way she tried it. She growled angrily and turned around to stare at him with fire in her eyes. Before, her eyes had been a pleasant myriad of colors – mostly warm green and blue – reflecting her happiness and pleasure. Now they glinted with a fierce orange-yellow, and Hades could almost swear he even saw flecks of red in them.

"You bastard! Let me go! Let me out!" she yelled, and he stood up, towering over her and looking impressively intimidating, even scary despite his nakedness.

She started to pound on his chest angrily, looking for some outlet for the rage she felt. How dare he trick her like that! He knew she was always somewhat dazed after sharing pleasure with him and had used that to his unfair advantage! She felt his essence leak between her legs since she was now standing up and moving around, and it only infuriated her even further.

Persephone could do no real damage to him – they both knew that – but despite the fact, she continued to pound at his chest, shrieking and yelling obscenities that would have made Demeter faint if she heard them coming from her daughter's mouth. Hades did not do anything for several moments, but soon enough he scowled and grabbed her wrists, halting the blows. Of course, this did nothing to dampen the fires of her rage.

"Stop!" he ordered sternly, but she kicked at his shins, refusing to be deterred as long as she could lash out at him in any way.

"No! Let me go! You cannot keep me down here!" she screamed, clawing like a cat and kicking. Suddenly, she found herself bound by shadows all the way up to her nose, effectively muffling her shouts and stopping her from hitting or kicking. Her eyes blazed as she struggled against her shadowy binds.

It was like a flexible full body cast, keeping her standing upright and rigid. She could not move, and the more she writhed and struggled against the bonds that would not give an inch, the more her body began to ache as the shadows squeezed more firmly.

"Mnph! MPH!" She screamed into the shadows. Hades sighed, looking at her with a stern, reproachful expression. He did not want to bind her, but if she was going to carry on like this...

He had been gentle with her before whenever she had asked to go to the surface or been defiant, but now he needed to be serious. She might be feeling hurt – and he genuinely regretted that. However, she had to understand that this hadn't been done out of any hatred. He saw how happy she was down here and knew she didn't belong in her old life. She belonged with him. The seeds he had fed her – seeds that he had imbued with bit of his Dark essence – would ensure that no other god could ever have power over her.

Persephone writhed around angrily. The shadow bindings were flexible so she could wiggle like a worm. She tried to scream again, and glared at him as fiercely as she could. She tried spitting up the seeds, but of course that was to no avail.

The flesh and juice around the little seeds had long since been swallowed, and the kernels wouldn't make a difference even if she spat them out. The point of the matter was, his essence was inside of her. She was bound to him and his world forever, whether or not she liked it. He glared back, matching her anger, and strode forward, putting his hands on her bound upper arms and looking down into her eyes.

"Listen..." he growled, almost panting with anger, "I have done so much for you, Persephone. I have shown you a life so much better than the one you were living with Demeter. You have free reign of the Underworld, and Elysium, which is so much more beautiful than the little strip of land you were confined to above. You have no right to act this way, all I did was take the final step to bind you to me."

Persephone glowered at him, refusing to accept this... excuse. He hadn't asked her! She wanted to scream that he had made a decision for her, a choice she should have made herself.

That rebellion, that defiance, was something

Hades admired in her, but in this situation it was tiresome and he merely wanted her to understand. She may have made the decision herself in time, but when would that be? Months? Years? Aeons? He did not want her to live in the torment of a flavorless world, a world where one's stomach was constantly a null void, a reality of constant self-denial.

For a god of the Underworld, eating the food of the dead was by no means any sort of death sentence as it was for a mortal soul or an Olympian. When she realized and understood that, then she'd be free.

Persephone's struggle slowly ceased. She knew she couldn't fight the shadows. Her head hung limp, and she felt tears on her cheeks. Her eyes burned, and her body felt sore from the violent struggles against the shadows. Her limbs trembled, and if the shadows hadn't been holding her up, she would have collapsed.

"Persephone..." he whispered, and she slowly looked up at him, cheeks shining wetly. A soft whimper issued from behind the shadows that covered her mouth.

He brushed a hand along her lips, and the shadows seemed to melt off her head, joining the shadows that wrapped around her neck.

"No..." she whispered, looking away as he caressed her cheek.

"I love you," he replied softly, his voice almost pleading. It even almost looked as if he might cry, and she squeezed her eyes shut, ignoring the pleading she saw in his gaze. She kept her eyes closed, determined to be angry. She couldn't let his pleas soften her heart. It was tempting to just give in, since Hades could be persuasive when he wanted to. She couldn't let him win!

She shivered within her bindings as he continued to touch her face. As he did, the bindings began to relax around her body.

"Persephone, please..."

"Please what?" she asked stiffly, his light touch sending chills up and down her back. She opened her eyes to glance at him. He felt the moisture on her cheeks, and lifted his hand to taste her tears. This made her feel embarrassed, and she looked aside.

"I want you to understand why I did this..." he said. She remained stubbornly silent. Hades let out a quiet exhale as he withdrew his hands, the shadows sliding from Persephone's body.

The Queen of the Underworld slowly collapsed to her knees, leaning against the mirror as she looked up at Hades. Part of her was pleased that he seemed to actually feel so bad about what he did. If he had looked smug, acted victorious and triumphant, it would be easy to hate him forever. But as she knew already, Hades was just like any other male, having made his own mistakes and despite his regal demeanor. This mighty god had his own insecurities, however well he hid them.

She had to admit, she was surprised that he actually seemed sorry about doing this to her. Of course, that didn't excuse him from what he did.

But at least he wasn't rubbing it in with some sort of victorious declaration such as 'Now you are stuck with me forever!' or the like, which was what she might have expected after their months-long struggle over the food.

What was she supposed to do now? Was she to never see Mother again? Or to confront the god who had sired her and so casually discarded her fate?

She remained where she was for a while more, leaned against the mirror before she looked up. Hades had already settled into bed, watching her quietly. He looked morose, and she felt a tug at her heartstrings. She had to resist the urge to climb in bed with him and comfort him.

No! I'm the injured party here, not him! She wrapped her arms around her knees after adjusting the fabric around her body more neatly and comfortably.

"Come to bed. There is no point in you staying on the floor," she heard Hades say.

"No."

"Surely you prefer the comforts of our bed to the cold, hard floor."

"Leave me alone."

"Come now, love. You do not intend to spend the night there, do you?"

"Maybe." Her face was pressed against her arms, and she wished she could shut out the sound of him as effectively as she had the sight of him. He saw how distressed she was. Would it be so fucking hard for him to acknowledge what he did and even... oh, perhaps *apologize?*

"Persephone..."

"No," she cut him off sharply. "I do not want to hear your excuse. Just leave me the hell alone."

There was silence, and she relaxed slightly, thinking she had won. After he had fallen asleep, she figured she could settle on the divan next to the fireplace. There really was no reason to spend the night on the floor, but of course, she wasn't going to say that to him!

She felt a hand slide along her side and gasped softly, pulling away and opening her eyes to see Hades.

"Come now, Seph. There is no reason to make yourself uncomfortable."

"Thank you for your concern," she replied sarcastically. She was pleased and faintly amused to see that he had wrapped his chiton around his hips. Good. She wasn't in the mood to see all of him, however much she had enjoyed seeing it before.

"Do not be like that," he chided gently. She narrowed her eyes at him.

"So you are going to act like nothing happened?"

"Nothing terrible happened. I will never forget this night. How we enjoyed it. How *you* enjoyed it..."

"Don't remind me."

Hades took a deep breath. "I gave you what you needed and wanted... in more ways than one," he whispered. She scoffed at him.

"I know you wanted to taste my food. So I made it easy for you."

"Whatever assuages your guilt," she replied bitterly.

"Oh, Seph..." He shook his head, his eyes radiating sorrow. "Is what I did truly so awful?"

"I will never be able to go home!"

"This is your home." He reached for her. She snarled and backed away.

"You see fit to dictate my life! You are no better than your brother!"

Hades reeled back as if he had been dealt a physical blow, his eyes glinting with dismay and hurt. *Like Zeus?* Gaea forbid! He was nothing like his youngest brother, and Persephone knew that he did not hold the King of the Gods in high regard. He was in no way like that irresponsible womanizer!

"Do not say that..."

"It is true!" she shrieked, her eyes glinting fiercely. "Mother sought to mold my life to her purposes! My sire sought to make a decision for me without even consulting me! And now you did the same! Is there nobody I can trust!"

Hades opened his mouth, then closed it, frowning. Deep down inside, he knew she was right. But he would – could – not show her any weakness. She would simply go after any chink she sensed in his armor and attack him mercilessly if she knew he felt guilty. His expression was calm and stern as he looked down at her.

"I did what I had to do," he stated.

"Do not bother with excuses."

"I was not making an excuse. I was simply

telling it as it is," he replied firmly, refusing to be swayed by the tears on her cheeks.

"Then you delude yourself." Her tone was tart as she turned her back to him. Hades let out a low groan, seeing that if he tried to argue with her further, she would only become more stubborn. Just as she had come to know him and how to manipulate him in some ways, he had figured his own way of handling her. It didn't always work, of course, but he hoped he would make the right decision *this* time, at least.

"There is no need for you to be so upset. Perhaps a walk would clear your head." He strode to the door, unlocking it with a wave of his hand before opening it. She could run off to any place in the Underworld and he would find her.

There's no need to be upset, my ass! At least he was letting her out. Without a word, she rose to her feet and bolted out of his bedroom, retreating to the library and slamming the door before collapsing in a fresh torrent of sobs. To think that she was cursed to live forever in this realm, cut off from the world she had grown up in and loved... How could Hades do that to her, knowing how much the surface world meant to her? He claimed to care for her and want the best for her, but in what world was being deprived of the sunlight and nature best for her?

Looking down at the fabric that covered her body with a disgusted expression, she tore it off and cast it to the floor. She shouldn't be wearing any of his things!

Rather than choose one of the many exquisite

silk robes or gowns in her wardrobe, she opted for a chiton of familiar and comfortable linen in a warm and dark shade of green, choosing a cloak of a slightly darker hue. Cloe was able to fetch all of this from her own room at the dark palace, and she hastily dressed herself. Her neck and arms remained bare of adornments, because at that moment, she could not stand to feel cold metal or gems on her flesh. The jewelry and stones Hades freely lavished on her were beautiful, but they lacked the warmth and vitality of the flowers she had so often placed in her hair or on herself in her youth.

Cloe brushed all the tangles out of her hair – her passionate night with Hades had left it a rumpled mess – and pulled it back with a green sash, wrapping it around Persephone's head with its usual efficiency. Persephone shuddered as her servant's ethereal 'fingers' brushed against the back of her neck.

When the shade was done, the goddess looked at her reflection in the mirror. She looked more... natural, less like the Queen of the Underworld. The stain on her lips even made her look a bit more lively, and she sighed softly as she licked her lips, tasting the last remnant of the pomegranate.

Damn Hades. Even knowing what the food of the dead was, she wanted more seeds. She craved the dark sweetness of the jelly and the satisfying crunch of the kernels. It had felt so good going down her throat, and she ached for more. She lifted her fingers, sucking off the last traces of flavor, sticking one finger after another between her lips. There was no doubt that Hades would be all too eager to offer her a pomegranate if she asked for one.

She knew she shouldn't want any more, but gods, it had been so delicious! It tasted sweeter and more fulfilling than any pomegranate that grew in Mother's orchard. Was it like that with the rest of the food here? She remembered all too well how scrumptious everything looked and smelled on Hades's table. She yearned for a full feast, to sample all of the culinary wonders that the finest chefs among the dead had to offer. Was this because the food of the Underworld really was better, or just because she hadn't eaten for so long? After all, a starving man would find just about anything pleasing after being deprived, wouldn't he?

Persephone stilled as she thought of her last dream. How long would Mother rage on? Goodness! If Mother had indeed discovered what Zeus had done, then that would explain why she had been so angry and frightening in the dream. Did Hades know? Surely he had to, since he knew so much about the other gods. He had promised that Mother would know before the first day of winter, and apparently she already did. But he had promised nothing else. If Demeter already knew, then he wouldn't have to tell her himself, effectively nullifying his promise.

Thinking about it made her miserable. She felt so helpless and frustrated, even more so for wanting more pomegranate seeds. How was she to live like this? Eternity stretched out before her. She let out a slow sigh, closing her eyes for a moment before opening them again, staring at her reflection as Cloe hovered nearby. She had no desire to remain in the Blessed Isles.

"Take me to Lethe."

Chapter XL

Melissa was afraid of the dark, so she didn't like this place, but at least she wasn't starving anymore. She didn't feel hungry or full. Just... *empty*.

She would never forget that terrible day when everything dried up and there was nothing to harvest. Mama had promised her that she could help this year, that she could join her older brothers and sisters in gathering what the gardens and orchard had to offer. She was always the youngest and littlest, and she wasn't often allowed to do what she thought her older siblings took for granted. So when she was able to do something they did, it made her feel more grown-up.

After that day, everything changed. There was not much food left from previous harvests. Supper had been a meager portion of dried fruit and a bit of jerky. It had gotten no better than that. Because Daddy was the High Priest, he had been able to get a decent portion of food supplies from the temple for his family. However, with so many mouths to feed, even the carefully rationed extra stores ran out. In seemingly no time, everyone's rations – even Daddy's – had been cut down to just one dried date a day, and a cupful of brackish water. Rains did not come, and the river trickled down to a thin stream, drained dry when it reached the borders of Olympia due to so many people dipping into it along the way.

Weeks went by and it only got worse. Melissa felt hunger gnawing at her insides constantly, even after she had just eaten whatever food her father gave out that day. It seemed that food only made it worse, so one day she just stopped eating. She would take whatever was given her and disappear out of sight so she didn't have to eat it in front of anyone else. She didn't want to throw it away – it would be terribly wrong to throw away food at a time like this – so she hid it under her bed in her wooden toy box, where the food would sit next to her little doll and clay animals.

It was actually easier to not eat. The hunger became less worse, and then one day she had simply lay down in her bed and been unable to get up. She was too weak to lift her arms and legs, and couldn't even lift her own head. Mama had cried about it, but strangely, as the day went by, the little girl found herself unable to care about the tears. She became more and more light-headed, and then all of a sudden she was floating up. She was no longer so tired or weak, and when she turned, she saw her mother crying and holding an awfully thin little girl. She didn't register the fact that this was her, because the thing Mama held was grotesque – hollow cheeks, limp hair, skeletal limbs, looking more like a mockery of a doll than a human being...

She floated out of the room, led by some invisible pull. Images flashed before her – dry fields, a stark and cloudless sky, parched river-beds – before everything became dark. She tried to go back into the light, but she couldn't find the way out. There were others here too, and they looked weird to her. She could make out faces, arms, legs, clothing, hair, even that they were young or old or their gender, but they didn't look like creatures of flesh – more like weird moving outlines where people *should* be. Why was she here with all of these strange people – if that was what she could call them?

Melissa reached out with a hand, and saw that it wasn't solid like it should be. She could see the outline of her fingers and hand and arm.

What had happened to her? Despite the fact that she was no longer flesh and blood, and had no more heart to beat frantically to reflect her current state of distress, she still felt an overwhelming sense of anxiety and hopelessness. Where were Mama and Daddy? Where were her brothers and sisters? She wanted to cry, and felt a phantom tightness in her throat and chest as she blinked, feeling her cheeks remain dry despite her crushing sadness.

"There, there, it will be all right. Come here." This came from her right side, and she turned around to see a woman. The outlines made it harder to determine her age, but the lady looked a lot like Mama, and she seemed only a little younger. Her hair was tied back and kept off her neck with a few sashes in the fashion that most women wore, though Mama preferred a braid.

"What is this horrible place?" Melissa asked.

"Oh, it is not horrible. This is the entrance to Hades. We are just waiting for our turn to cross the Styx. It should not take long."

"Hades?" The little girl's voice expressed her dismay all too clearly, and she drew back from the woman. Daddy was the head priest at the temple, and they all worshiped Zeus. Daddy always said that Zeus was the mightiest of the gods, and those who obeyed and honored him would remain in his favor.

They had all gone to the temple at the appropriate times, held the festivals every year, sung praises to his name, and everything else that Daddy said to do. Daddy even had a small shrine to Zeus in their courtyard.

They didn't talk much about the other gods. Of course, everyone knew that Zeus had a big family – aunts and uncles, brothers and sisters, and countless children, nephews, and nieces. She knew a lot of names. Poseidon, Hera, Demeter, Apollo, Artemis, and so on. Sometimes Daddy or Mama would tell stories of the other gods, and she had to admit – though she never said it out loud to her parents – that she liked hearing about them better than she did Zeus, because she heard about Zeus so much.

She had only heard about Hades a couple of times. He was the Lord of the Realm of the Dead, and people didn't like talking about him. Some people were even afraid to paint his image on murals or vases. When she asked her parents about him, they would always shush her and tell her to not speak his name.

Since she was so young, her parents had kept her sheltered from the worst of the situation in Olympia. They didn't talk about their neighbors dying. When Melissa asked to see her friends, her parents would distract her with something else, not wanting to tell her that they had died.

"No!" Melissa gasped, "I want to go home!" The woman shook her head slowly.

"This is your home now."

"No! No*nono*!" She tried to run, but the woman took hold of her, just as if both of them were still solid.

"I wanna go home! I want my mama and daddy!" Melissa cried. Several others turned to look, but nobody came forward, letting the woman deal with the little girl, though they all looked at her sympathetically. Older people knew and understood that Death would come for everybody, but no one wanted to see a child or a youth die. Younger ones usually had a harder time dealing with their new 'life', especially children.

"Hush now, dear. Things will be better," the woman said, setting Melissa down when the girl ceased her struggles. She had thrown a few tantrums in the past, but since she was the littlest in the family, it was easy for her parents or older siblings to grab hold of her to calm her down, and she knew all too well from experience that she couldn't win as much as she kicked or screamed. She hated being little.

"No, they will not. I am dead," she replied sullenly.

"We all are. It is the fate of every living creature."

"It is not fair. Daddy said that if we worshiped and honored Zeus, he would always favor us."

The woman regarded her silently for a moment before she spoke. "Were you hungry before you died?"

"We all were, but then I stopped eating and..."

"The same thing happened to me," the older soul explained sympathetically. "It seemed that every bite I took only made me even more hungry..."

"And it became easier to just not eat," Melissa finished. Her companion nodded.

"Zeus might give out many blessings, but even he cannot command the earth. Nor can he command his sister." The woman chuckled wryly.

"What do you mean?"

"Zeus has angered Demeter by taking away her daughter. She has vowed to keep the earth barren until he gives her back."

"He should just give her back, then. Why does he not?" Melissa asked with the blunt indignation of the young.

"I wish I knew the answer, but whatever happened, he will not give her back. Many in my village now openly curse him. My husband is dead, and now so am I. My mother is very old and weak and I worry about my children and if my mother will be able to care for them. But does he care? No! He hears our prayers and pleas, yet he does nothing!"

"What a stupid man," Melissa muttered. That would have received a firm scolding and possibly even a slap from her parents; no one in the household was ever allowed to criticize Zeus. But the woman laughed and nodded.

"Not all men are, my husband was a good one. But Zeus has made plenty of mistakes in the past, and this seems to be the biggest one he has made. Yet I fear it will not be his last. And he certainly is not the only male – god or human – who has made a stupid mistake."

"Will you tell me more?" she asked. The woman smiled. A woman her age certainly knew plenty of the more randy tales and rumors of the gods, though she'd be careful what she said to this little one.

"Of course. What's your name?"

"Melissa."

"Nice to meet you. I am Thalia. Oh, look. It is already our turn to cross the Styx. Come on, you can sit on my lap."

o0o

Since it hurt to get on her knees, Hypia sat on her daughter's bed, the thin padding giving a bit of comfort to her bony behind. Having ten children hadn't been a great ordeal for her – childbirth came naturally to her – but it had thickened her figure over the years. Now, she was thinner than she had been even as a maiden being courted by Skouros. She might have been pleased with the return of her girlish figure if not for the suffering that surrounded her. Skouros had withered away, a tall and gaunt man, much of his hair and beard having fallen out. Her oldest sons and daughter – fine, strapping youths and a comely maiden all resembling their father – suffered similar ill effects.

She had been hoping that after Nikos died, she wouldn't lose another child. And now it seemed as if she might lose the rest, starting with Melissa.

Hypia gave out a soft groan as she leaned down, her back creaking as she reached for the space below the bed. There was a layer of dust – lack of energy caused by malnourishment robbed the matriarch of the usual energy she had to keep the home clean. The only time where anyone moved was to hunt for food, or if not that, something to chew on. Most of the time they simply sat around lethargically, conserving as much energy as they could.

Her fingers met smooth wood, and she pulled it out, gazing at her daughter's toy box. It was not a large one, about the length of her forearm and a little more than half that as wide. It had been her own toy box when she was little, carved for her by her father. It had been passed down to her daughters, and when the two elder daughters outgrew their toys, Melissa had been the recipient of the gift.

Hypia slid the top off the box, seeing first the little ceramic animals, smooth from years of handling. And then the doll... Her eyes widened when she slid the lid all the way off, seeing several dried dates and prunes. No one could say that Skouros did not treat his children well. He made sure that everyone got some food however meager the ration, which was more than could be said for other families where some children were left to fend for themselves, sold into slavery, or daughters abandoned in favor of sons. She had heard stories of people refusing to feed their own parents and turning out the elders.

Why didn't Melissa eat? Had she simply given up on life? As Hypia stared at the food, she knew she couldn't let it go to waste. She loved her daughter, but Melissa was dead and gone. She slid the lid back into place and tucked it under her arm, rising off the small bed, placing her hand on the wall for leverage as she felt her knees buckle.

oOo

Zeus had to hear nagging from all directions wherever he went. He heard it from his siblings, children, and even his own mother. He was pecked on at least once a day, his family acting much like the birds did in their mad scramble for the last seeds of grain and what was left of the insects in Hellas. Whenever he tried to find some quiet time for himself, someone always showed up to nag him and ruin his good time. He had tried locking the doors to his villa, but Hephaistos had simply made it so that the doors would not lock anymore, and anybody could waltz in and get right in his face any damn time they pleased.

No matter how much he tried to defend himself, the harassment did not stop. Even the nymphs that normally would come to his bed at his behest now shunned and openly disdained him. Despite his exalted position as King of the Gods, everyone treated him like a pariah, speaking to him only to demand that he give in to

Demeter's plea to have her daughter back.

Zeus took the form of an eagle and flew to the lands that lay to the east, where Demeter's wrath had not spread. At least not yet, some of the other gods warned, pointing to the ever-increasing radius of barren lands that spread out from the nexus, Olympia. Ugh, there was no reasoning with that woman!

Here, the land was warm and palm trees grew around lakes of deep azure blue set in oceans of brown and gold. Further east lay the lands of Mesopotamia, where different gods ruled over the people that resided there. Since the gods ruled over lands far more expansive than any mortal king could ever dream of, there generally was little to no dispute of territory, and the Olympians preferred the more mountainous and forested realm of Hellas to this hot and dry land. Still, it was not without its perks. Mesopotamia would not have existed if not for the twin rivers that fed the fertile region of the Levant.

He settled down in a verdant area, happy to see the lushness of his surroundings after the dearth of an almost-dead land. As he took human form, he inhaled the air, taking comfort in its warmth as he mentally compared it to the dry, frigid air of the deep winter that Demeter had blighted Hellas with.

It should take no time to find a pretty maiden to share the pleasure of his company, Zeus mused as he looked around at the tropical clime. His virility was practically a Gift on its own – he could sense females nearby. There was a rustling in the trees and foliage nearby, and he turned around, discerning the aura of several women. These auras were infused with magic much like that of nymphs, and the comely apparitions that emerged from the foliage certainly were equivalent to the nature-spirits of Hellas.

Their skin varied from light honey-brown to a more dusky tone, and their hair shone in the sunlight like polished ebony while their eyes were emerald-green surrounded by long, thick lashes. The trio was similar in appearance, but there were enough differences for Zeus to be able to discern them separately due to differences in height and proportions. The shortest one seemed to be the leader by the way she positioned herself in front of the other two. All of them were clad in misty veils of green, blue, and gold that left much of their flesh concealed, but were diaphanous enough to showcase their nubile curves.

They all smiled brilliantly at him before the leader started speaking. Her language was entirely unknown to him, and he responded in his own language. The desert nymph spoke in her own language again, her tone set in a query. Zeus shrugged apologetically, saying that he did not understand.

The dark-haired women chattered quietly amongst themselves before the tallest one shrugged, and the leader nodded her head. Zeus shot her a warm smile, knowing that his brilliant grin had its charm and usually put most women at ease. He could treat a woman very well – as long as he was interested in her, at least.

The nymphs of Hellas knew just what he had done, thanks to Demeter. How could they not, being part of nature and thus affected by the Harvest Goddess' wrath even though they were not mortal? As riverbeds dried up, the Naiads would wither and had to seek another home or perish. The Dryads and Leimoneides became as parched as their forests and meadows were. They were in no mood to entertain Zeus, especially since he was the very source of their troubles. Even the Oreades that lived high up in the mountains and the lofty Aurai of the skies felt the barrenness of the earth, because all aspects of Nature were interconnected. It was a dismaying experience being a pariah among his former playgrounds, especially since his daughter was better off with Hades than she was with any other god. Couldn't Demeter see that? When Hades made a promise, he kept it, and he had vowed that Kora would always be safe.

He shook himself free of these thoughts, intent on enjoying this lovely day with these splendid ladies. If he could have all three of them, well, that would certainly be a memorable occasion indeed. It'd been too long – at least, for him – since he had been able to woo a woman because of what his sister was doing.

The leader lifted her hand, gesturing to herself.

"Layla," she said, her voice soft and melodious, deep and almost purring.

"Layla." It didn't sound quite the same coming from his own throat, but the woman nodded before she gestured to him, raising her eyebrow. He nodded and pointed to himself, smiling faintly.

"Zeus." Always good to start off with a name, no?

Layla blinked and shared a glance with her companions before they whispered amongst themselves. Their facial expressions and quick tones did not bode well, but he had to hold back a frown, and maintained a smile, beaming at them and doing his damnedest to exude a relaxed, friendly aura.

"There is no need to worry. I bring you no harm." He knew they did not speak his language, but he hoped his tone and open mien were reassuring enough. Layla simply regarded him with a frown before she spoke again, this time to him. Her words were rapid, and she pointed at him accusingly. To his chagrin, Layla blurted out Demeter's name somewhere in her angry chatter, and the mighty King of the Olympians knew that he was defeated.

The exotic nymphs looked at him, feminine disdain all too clear in their eyes. Before Zeus could attempt to plead his case, they were gone as quickly as they had appeared, and if anything, the thick foliage around the oasis actually seemed less verdant. He couldn't even sense their presence anymore.

"Damnit!" It was going to be a very long winter if things kept on like this...

oOo

The River Nile – known as H'pi to the people of ancient Aigyptos – was the lifeline of the people of this land. Because so much of the land was desert, it was important to respect the gods of the river and use its power correctly.

Before it reached the Mediterranean on its northward journey, the river broke into a delta, creating a fertile land that extended for miles beyond the coast. From the rich soil, the people of Aigyptos harvested many exotic plants and spices, much of which was traded with Hellas for things that were scarce in this desert country.

However, the merchants that traded with the Hellenic sailors were experiencing a drop in business. A couple of moons ago, they had been trying to offer less in exchange for receiving more, and they no longer wanted exotic linens, gems, or spices. Just food – basic flour, barley, fruit, salted meat, and the like. The merchants and traders of Aigyptos were getting annoyed with the sailors that came south. Trading was not what it used to be.

Atet frowned as he stood on the pier, seeing the familiar sight of a northern ship. He thrived on trade and was willing to strike all kinds of deals, but lately, his patience had been pushed. The harvests of Aigyptos had been meager this year; enough to feed the locals but not much left over to trade to the men from the north. If the sailors wanted more foodstuffs, they had better be prepared to pay a steep price for it.

The appearance of Tyre, the ship's captain, startled Atet. His shock only increased when he saw the helmsman and oarsmen. They were all lean, but not from the rigorous exercise that came with the occupation. He held back a comment on their appearance as he noted their gaunt cheeks. Having docked the ship, the oarsmen simply sat where they were, leaning across the oars and dozing.

Having grown up poor, Atet recognized the signs of malnutrition. What was going on in Hellas? Yes, some years came with bad harvests, but that was a part of life, and one had to prepare accordingly. As he stood there listening to Tyre, he thought about the last couple of months and the shift in supply and demand. Tyre had no interest in the usual exotic offerings of Aigyptos. All he wanted was grains and whatever fruits and vegetables they could offer. And if cheese or dried meat could be spared, that would be simply wonderful, the captain said with emphasis.

Atet was about to say no, but Tyre beckoned him into a cabin. There were several wooden chests, and the captain went over to open one. The merchant's eyes widened as he saw gold and silver ingots along with certain valuable stones that could not be obtained from the sands and mines of Aigyptos. The other chests had similarly valuable items, and Atet stroked his beard. Even a sizable load of food had nowhere near as much value as what Tyre was offering him. Mentally, he weighed the profit margin to be gained from these valuables against the food Tyre was asking for.

Well. The last harvest hadn't been *bad*, after all. Just... *meager*, and besides, he had seen the crops growing over the last month, the priests said that the gods were happy. The H'pi had been generous this year with its annual deposit of the fertile silt that was needed to grow food in the harsh climate of the desert. Because the cycle of harvest and planting was different in Aigyptos due to the annual rhythm of the H'pi, the harvest here was only several months away, instead of nearly a year like it was in Hellas.

"Of course," Atet said with the smile reserved for closing a deal as he regarded the worn-looking captain. "It will take a bit of time, but I should have everything you ask for on the morrow." His command of Greek was good, a vital necessity when one traded with them, and he had no problem communicating with Tyre.

The captain almost looked as if he would collapse from sheer relief and gratitude. He collected himself quickly, but not without effort.

"Certainly. But would it be too much to ask if my crew could have some food now?"

"Oh, certainly not. Just have these chests be ready when I come back. Give me an hour." Atet replied. Inwardly, he felt shocked again. They needed some food *now*? Did this mean they had nothing left in their stores? Before he was able to work his way up to the occupation of merchant, he had spent his teenage years aboard a ship, and had a practical knowledge of being a sailor, which benefited him as a merchant. Any seaman worth his salt knew to always pack enough rations for everyone, plus more in case a storm sent the ship off course.

"I will give you what you need," Atet added solemnly, "but I need to know what is happening in Hellas. Trade has changed. And..." He glanced pointedly at Tyre's body. The captain sighed heavily, this motion seeming to drain all the energy from his body.

"The Harvest Goddess has been angered." He seemed hesitant to say anything more, and Atet decided to not press him. Like the people of Hellas, the Aigyptians – and other races – had their share of vengeful gods. His grandfather had lived through the plagues that the god of the Hebrews set upon the Aigyptians for the Hebrews' many years of slavery, and Atet remembered these stories well. His grandfather had been the second son in their family to make it past infancy, and was thus spared the death that Yahweh visited upon the firstborn sons of Aigyptos.

The merchant could not help but wonder what would make a goddess so angry she would let her people starve, or what would cause a god let his people be enslaved. The gods could be capricious, and mortals couldn't do a damned thing about it if the deities were angry enough.

o0o

It had not rained for many days, but a rainbow hung in the sky, a faint iridescent ribbon that arced its way to Olympus. Rhea looked up from her courtyard, seeing the Messenger of the Gods float down from the heavens, her aura streaming the multi-hued trail of light she left behind her.

She landed gracefully, her aura dimming so that she no longer exuded such brilliance. At the moment, her hair was its natural black color, but she was capable of changing the color any time she pleased.

"Greetings, Iris. Would you like to sit with me?" Rhea asked, gesturing to the table and the comfortable padded chairs. Iris smiled and nodded, following the older goddess to the table.

The table was set with a platter of ambrosia, stuffed olives, and pieces of fruit drizzled lightly with nectar. Despite its simplicity, it was still a far cry from what was left of the food down on Earth. There were mortals down there who would be willing to kill one another for such a meal, but the gods did not like to contemplate such matters. Various gods had gone to try to help their worshipers, attempting to use various aspects of their Gift – like making rain or creating heat – to try to coax the earth to become fruitful again as well as to comfort the mortals or keep them alive.

Rhea had tried to use her Gift over the earth, but her own ability over Nature was weak compared to her daughter, especially because rage fueled Demeter's power. She could only raise small amounts of food from the earth at once, and was able to keep a limited amount of mortals alive this way. Unfortunately, Demeter had blighted the earth so much that for Rhea, using her Gift was like having her energy literally drained dry. Every time she used her Gift, she felt exhausted afterward and needed a few days and ambrosia and nectar to rejuvenate, otherwise recovery took much longer.

She had talked to her sons, pleaded with them and cajoled them to correct their respective mistakes. Hades said his decision was made, that Zeus and Demeter had their own problems, that he would not be involved. Just like that, he left. Zeus on the other hand hemmed and hawed, going between excuses and half-hearted admissions that he was wrong. Yet he would not apologize to his own sister. His demand was that she restore the earth to its good graces before he apologized and would go to Hades himself to see about returning Kora. Of course, Demeter could only be outraged by this presumptuous offer of a bargain. And that was that, so her three children remained stubborn while Hellas starved.

She didn't know if she could influence her daughter. Zeus was the closest to her out of all her children by the sheer fact that he alone had been saved from a miserable existence in Kronos's pit. She hadn't known her husband would try to harm any children they would have when the Fates told him of his prophecy because he had refused to share it with her at first; that a child of his would overthrow him just as he had overthrown his own father. He had sliced Ouranos into so many pieces with his sickle and scattered the parts to the four winds. Naturally such a prophecy issued by the Fates themselves would send this mighty Titan into a panic.

Their first child was a girl, and Rhea thought that perhaps Kronos would not see a little girl as a threat. And then Hades had been born. Kronos cat his two young children into a pit, hidden from her with a malicious use of his Gift. Every time afterward, she tried to save her children, but Kronos would not be denied his attempted aversion of the prophecy. He could not kill his children – Gaea would know if their blood had been spilled – so he did what he thought was the next best thing.

She had searched for them, of course, but he had hidden them too well. With Zeus, she had replaced his body with one made of earth to resemble the babe before getting her husband drunk. Thus he threw a lump of dirt and stone into the pit without realizing the trick his wife had played on him.

The ordeal in the pit had affected her children profoundly, all in different ways. Zeus alone felt closest to her; her other children had grown up without her and did not have the familiarity she shared with her son. She could not help but feel bad for her youngest child, but she also had a family to take care of. She was mother, grandmother, sister, cousin, and aunt to the entire Olympian-Titan brood, and right now, most of that family was angry with Zeus.

"Iris, I have a favor to ask of you. I would like you to send a message to Demeter and ask her to come see me."

"Certainly." Most other gods would have told Rhea to not bother, that there was no use in attempting to reason with Demeter or even threaten her, but Iris was a messenger of peace. She was also the preferred messenger among the goddesses, especially those who had no care for Hermes's mischievousness.

Now that everyone knew where Demeter was, anyone was free to try to petition her. At their own risk, of course. The Harvest Goddess threatened to castrate any god who dared to ask her to just forgive Zeus, to let things be. Rhea sympathized with her daughter, having had five children taken from her and Kronos being far too powerful for her to stand up to, but she hadn't lashed out at the mortals for what her husband had done.

After sharing lunch with Rhea, Iris rose to her feet. Whenever she took flight, she glowed with all the colors of the rainbow. No matter how often Rhea saw it, she never became tired of the sight. After Iris took flight, a trail of iridescent ribbon remained, starting from where she had been standing moments before. Rhea reached out, seeing her skin take a reddish hue from the infrared side of the trail. Before the rainbow faded, she played with the other colors, seeing the play of different hues on her skin. It provided a nice albeit fleeting distraction.

oOo

Stay calm, Rhea told herself as she stared at her daughter's sullen and hostile countenance. It was all too clear that Demeter was more than prepared for confrontation.

"Welcome, daughter. Would you come and sit with me?" She gestured to the other seat, where

Iris had been sitting before.

"Just tell me why you sent Iris to fetch me!" Demeter replied bluntly, her shoulders squared. The Harvest Goddess had always been full and curvaceous, but now her body seemed hard, as if it were made of stone rather than flesh. "If you summoned me to beg me to stop my famine, then I am leaving now."

"Wait!" Rhea raised her hand. "I am not going to tell you to forgive Zeus or forget what he did. You have every right to be angry with him. I too think he acted rashly, but then you and I know that he does not make the smartest choices at times." Rhea loved her son, but she would not make excuses for his flaws or mistakes.

"Good." Demeter relaxed only just slightly. It was nice that Mother agreed with her, but she knew this was not the end of it. So she decided to cut her mother off before she had to listen to another stupid plea. How many of *those* had she heard? "I intend to stay the course unless I get my daughter back."

"At the cost of human life?"

"If Zeus really cared about his precious mortals, I would already have Kora back. Apparently he values his pride more than his worshipers. He just does not get that what he did was stupid and wrong!"

"You are right. Zeus knows you are furious, but he still does not quite understand why what he did was so terrible to you. But why make the mortals suffer for his ignorance?"

"Because Zeus is an idiot who would not even

tell me what he did in the first place until I forced it out of him. He had the nerve to let me go around worrying and wondering if my daughter was being hurt! There is no way in hell I am letting him out of this until he acknowledges what he did and apologizes."

"So it is an apology you want?" Rhea asked, placing her chin on her hand.

"A real one!" Demeter amended. It was one thing to say 'I am sorry', and another to actually mean it.

"You need and deserve one. But please, stop your blight on the earth!"

"No. If I did, Zeus would think everything was all right, and just go on as he had before!" Demeter crossed her arms, unaffected by the pleading in her mother's eyes. She had grown up without a mother, as did the other four siblings cast into the pit with her. Even after all this time, Rhea was still closest to Zeus, and at times like these, she felt jealous of her youngest brother, for he alone had grown up with a mother's love and affection. Part of her was bitter and resentful of her mother – even after all these centuries – for not being able to save her children from Kronos. She would not be like Rhea and let someone else take away her own child – her only child!

"You let your husband take away five of your children. I refuse to let history repeat itself, and I am appalled that you would be complicit with such a scheme. Some mother you are." Demeter narrowed her eyes, glaring at her mother.

Rhea was so stunned by these hurtful words

that she could only stare at her daughter. With a tight, cold smile, the Harvest Goddess spun around and left.

oOo

The Lord of the Dead lay on his bed, staring blankly at the wall, ignoring the ornate fresco that was illuminated by Elysium's light. He did not focus on his surroundings, merely allowing his mind to wander as he mused the events of this night.

He would – and could – never forget the feel of Persephone's body under his, the heated pliancy of her flesh under his hands, the sheer satisfaction that came from consummating the most physical aspect of their relationship. Having her eat the seeds was the final act that bound her to him. He had been so certain that this was a clever plan, but deep down, he knew that this decision had been in part spurred by his fear of losing her.

He knew the situation above was desperate, and a confrontation with his sister was inevitable. Yes, he knew that Demeter would be upset, but he honestly hadn't in his wildest dreams ever imagined she would react so thoroughly, destroying most of what sustained humankind in a scheme that was brilliant despite its consequences. Had she merely cursed Zeus himself, the King of the Gods would find a way to deal with that consequence, and try to hide it from the other gods. But here, everybody, whether god, mortal, or spirit, could not hide. Demeter had found the most wide-spread medium to express her rage.

Well, Persephone had eaten the food. Her fate was sealed. And if needed, he would act against Demeter. The only reason he hadn't done so yet was because it would take a truly drastic – even borderline forbidden – act to stop her and release the earth from her vicious chokehold that not even the other nature-goddesses could loosen.

It was easy to just lay the blame at Zeus's feet, since he was the one who had given his blessing to the marriage and not told Demeter about it, but who had committed the kidnapping itself? Of course, he wasn't the one lashing out at the earth. All he had done was kidnap the woman he loved.

Bah. He looked at the remnants of the pomegranate he had shared with Persephone. Well, at least the deed was done. In a way, it was an immense relief to him. He could only hope that she could come to feel the same way.

He rose from his bed, wondering where she had gone to sulk. With a wave of his arm, the shadows in the room thickened for a moment before dissipating. With them, he could find anyone anywhere within his kingdom.

Where are you, my love? When the shadows pinpointed her location, he felt his heart thud sharply in his chest. No. He knew she was angry and upset, but to want to go to Lethe... Did she intend to erase her memory? He couldn't let that happen! He shouted for Cloe, and the shade appeared with clothing for him. He would be damned if Lethe had her way with Persephone.

Chapter XLI

oOo

The obsidian trees seemed to reach towards Persephone with their taloned branches as she walked down the path disconsolately. The wild mixture of emotions surging through her left her feeling raw, and she ached for a soothing balm.

How could Hades do that to her? He knew how languid she became after sharing pleasure with him. Honestly, it was hard to react any other way to a man who was a skilled and attentive lover. She had never imagined that he would exploit her during such a vulnerable moment. She had *trusted* him!

But you said yes when he offered it to you, her conscience reminded her. She could have said no after the first seed when she realized what he was doing or spat it out, but it had been so cool and delicious that she just couldn't stop eating, enjoying the act of being fed by her lover. After over four months of eating nothing, it had been hard to resist his offering.

Trees stopped appearing along the path as the light slate hue of the sky darkened almost imperceptibly. Normally, the 'daytime' sky was as if it was merely a cloudy day in the world of the living with the sunlight filtering through the gray veil. That visual effect made the Underworld easy to see and traverse through, but now, it was as if that artificial sunlight had disappeared, though she could still see clearly. The path below her feet was no longer gritty nor dusty, it was as if an invisible hand had smoothed it out.

Ahead, she saw a structure emerging from the mist. The closer she approached it, the more it came into focus, yet there was still something blurry or undefined about its edges. She had explored enough of the gem-rich caverns of the Underworld to recognize that the structure was made of some sort of crystal, but it was hard to tell when the edges simply refused to come into clear focus.

It was an entryway made of two grand pillars standing side by side with an arch sitting on top. Beyond that, she could hear the quiet splashing and lapping of water. She looked down, noting that the path was now comprised of smooth and polished crystal. She could not tell whether the rock was black or simply transparent because there wasn't enough light.

She touched one of the pillars, gratified that it felt solid and cool under her hand. At least it confirmed for her what her vision wouldn't. When she ran her finger along one of the cut edges, it was well-defined. She looked down at her hands to make sure there wasn't anything wrong with her eyes, and was relieved to see that her hands looked the same as they always did, without any shifting of the lines. Around the base of the pillars, the shadows were thick, leaving the path and nothing else visible. The sky was darker now, giving minimal illumination.

Squaring her shoulders, Persephone strode down the path. Despite the darkness she saw surrounding her, the path was clear. As she continued walking, she noticed small pinpoints of light in the darkness, very much like stars. Whenever she saw the sky like this, it was easy to forget that she was in the Underworld, because this so closely mirrored the starlit heavens of the world of the living.

"It has been far too long since a living being passed through the Shadowed Gate!" Persephone heard someone say. She saw a slender figure approaching her, and was surprised to see a beautiful woman. Her skin was as pale as her hair was dark, and her eyes were silver-gray. Her ankle-length peplos was a smoky gray hue.

"Um. Uh." Persephone was unsure of what to say for a moment as she stared at the other woman. "I was looking for the Lethe River, and this is where I was led to..."

"You have come to the right place." The dark-haired woman circled around the Queen of the Underworld. "I sense a lot of anger and sorrow." The corners of her pretty lips turned down in a slight frown. Gently, she reached out to brush a stray lock of hair from Persephone's face. She did not speak, but she nodded in agreement. This woman's voice was soothing, and she seemed so concerned. Persephone sensed divinity, so she knew this woman was a goddess.

"Would you come with me, dear? I know just what will make you feel better."

Despite this apparent friendliness and concern this goddess showed, Persephone wasn't so naive as to just go off with someone whose name she did not know. The Underworld was not without its dangers; she had remembered her lesson from Styx all too well. She drew away from the hand that was stroking her face – a hand that was surprisingly warm.

"Who are you?"

"Lethe." The way she said it didn't sound so much the way others said it. It came out of Lethe's mouth almost like a purr combined with the whispering flow of a river. *Lyyytheee...* "And you are?"

"Persephone."

Lethe blinked before she smiled. This was no ordinary nymph or goddess. She had already known this woman was exquisite, but this was just *lovely*.

"It is so rare that I get visitors," Lethe said. Most souls simply remained where they were assigned by the Judges, so she rarely had company. A god or goddess had not come through the Shadowed Gate for several centuries. It got so lonely here, since people only came here to wash away their memories and start a new life. They would be here for a moment, and then gone the next, whisked away by eternity.

Lethe was a child of Nyx, but the circumstances of her birth was unusual. To be a god was to be immortal, especially if one was a primordial goddess like Nyx. Each pregnancy came to fruition, and mother and child always lived, unlike the gamble of childbirth for mortal women.

But when Lethe was born, she slipped from

her mother's body, unnoticed, uncared for. The child's Gift had manifested itself in her mother's womb, so it was through no fault of Nyx that the mother had unknowingly abandoned her child, forgetting the fact that she'd had a baby. Born from the shadows and the night, Lethe was to take her place in oblivion. Much like Hestia, Lethe represented a thirteenth, unofficial member of the ruling deities of the world they lived in.

She ate dreams and memories, swallowing them away into oblivion, purifying the cosmic energy that made up souls before they were sent back to the world of the living to be reincarnated. To see Lethe was to be entranced by her. She was a beautiful goddess – if people remembered her, they would say her beauty rivaled Aphrodite's – and like a Siren, she would lure one to their end.

Her appetite was constant. She lurked around on the fringes of consciousness, rich with memories but creating none for herself in this lonesome place.

Unlike everybody else, Lethe did not forget. Within her were all the memories and dreams she had eaten. She had seen countless lifetimes and the course of human history through them, playing them through her mind like an ever-shifting sequence. Lethe could peek into that oblivion and see all that it contained, but memories were a poor substitute for a real companion. Persephone was practically pulsating with vitality, and not just from her anger. The Underworld was such a dead place, literally and figuratively, and this young goddess was like an oasis in the desert, a lifespring amidst a bleak and dead landscape. And Persephone was quite the stunner. Unlike a mortal, she wouldn't disappear. She could stay here forever. She would satisfy Lethe's thirst in more ways than one...

"Come, walk with me," Lethe said, gently touching Persephone's arm.

"Where are we going?" Persephone asked as she strolled forward.

"To a place where you will feel better."

Despite the warm comfort of Lethe's presence, the younger goddess had the presence of mind to remain alert.

"Where?" Persephone pressed, refusing to be swayed by Lethe's gentle touch on her arms.

"Whatever would make you feel better, my dear. Would you like to soak in the hot spring? Or sit down on a soft divan?"

A hot bath certainly sounded nice, but Persephone opted for the furniture. Though Lethe apparently meant no harm, her instinct told Persephone to be aware of her surroundings. She had just met this woman, she wasn't about to jump into a hot pool with someone she did not know.

"Lovely. We can sit and talk," Lethe said cheerfully. The sky above her head was inky black, with countless little sparkles of light scattered across the nothingness, but there were no discernible heavenly bodies such as planets or asteroids like she saw when she visited Nyx. Before her, the crystal path widened into a plateau, the polished stone sharply giving way to velvety blackness. Two divans sat perpendicular to a table that was set out with a small banquet. Persephone stiffened as she saw the food, taking a step back.

"What is the matter?" Lethe asked, genuinely surprised.

"I... I am not hungry." That was a lie, of course. The food looked so damned appetizing, and she remembered the refreshing sweetness of the pomegranate seeds.

"Then you do not have to eat. Just sit and relax." Persephone found herself ushered toward the nearest divan. The padding was soft and firm in a way she had never felt before, as if there was water under the upholstery. It sloshed before molding comfortably against her.

"There now, do you not feel better already?" Lethe asked with a faint smile as she sat down on the other sofa. Persephone nodded slowly, leaning her head back against the cushion. It was just so comfy, and she did need some rest. She closed her eyes, folding her hands in her lap as she did so. Between the incredible sex with Hades and their heated fighting, she hadn't gotten much sleep.

She murmured softly when a hand caressed her cheek. A curvy and soft body pressed against her own as an arm snaked around her middle. She opened her eyes, seeing Lethe looking down at her adoringly. She blushed and looked away, stiffening when she realized just how closely the older goddess was holding her. She might be enraged at Hades, but this certainly didn't mean she wanted another lover!

"Lethe..."

"Hush, sweet darling. Forget your anger and pain..." Lethe's voice was thick and sweet, like sugar on honey. "Just stay here and relax with me, let me treat you right..." Her hand slid along Persephone's hip, sending a shock of relaxed pleasure through her flesh. It was alarming how nice it felt, and Persephone tried to fight through the mental haze she now realized she was trapped in. It felt as if she was floating along, submerged in a river that seemed to have the same temperature as the hot springs in the Isles of the Blessed. That stirred up a memory of Hades showing it to her, and lovingly washing her in it.

Lethe's nimble fingers drew out one of the pins on Persephone's gown, revealing some of her left arm. Removing another pin revealed the skin just above her elbow. The younger goddess had been sheltered before Hades brought her down here, but Persephone had once in a while eavesdropped on the nymphs, hearing whispers of same-sex pleasures. How Zeus was not above enjoying the company of a handsome youth, that Artemis was rumored to take lovers among her nymphs and priestesses...

The Queen of the Underworld was no longer virgin, having offered the last vestige of her innocence to her captor. She had been subjected to a myriad of dazzling pleasure from an attentive Lord. Yet this felt nice, and she felt her resistance wavering in face of the soporific attentions of the Guardian of the River of Forgetfulness.

Lethe pulled the last pin from the left side of the gown, causing the fabric to fall away, revealing the side of her chest. Her girdle prevented the material from going further, but the seductress regarded it with minimal annoyance, focusing on the exposed breast. The younger goddess arched and moaned softly, blushing even more.

"Mmm. Just relax and let me have you... you will be so happy here." Lethe looked forward to having a flesh-and-blood companion, and a powerful one at that!

Persephone sighed as she felt lips against her throat, peppering her with kisses. Her tit was being played with, tugged and rolled before heated lips wrapped around it. She was almost delirious, but in the recesses of her consciousness, she knew something was not quite right. It was nearly impossible to think straight, almost as if she was drunk. No, a hundred times worse. She felt a bit tired and light-headed on the few occasions she had been allowed to drink wine, but this overwhelming sensation was ridiculous. She shouldn't be feeling so damned happy!

Why was she so happy? Wasn't she sad and angry? Sad and angry at what? It was impossible to concentrate with Lethe's hand now sliding into her gown, her girdle already loosened. When had *that* happened?

"Lethe..." The part of her that wasn't being distracted by Lethe's actions simply wanted out of here. True, she might be curious about what being with another woman would be like, but this was definitely the wrong time and wrong place. She blinked, focusing on her surroundings. There was

57

no longer the table or any furniture. She felt a current flowing all around her – warm and comfortable. Why was she considering that? It was so hard to remember...

"You are so tense... relax." A hand was now rubbing her back, sending more waves of Lethe's mysterious relaxing effect pulsing through her nerves. Persephone frowned and shook her head, focusing on her thoughts, finding lucidity in them when she meditated in an attempt to block the sensations of Lethe's attentions. She recalled what had happened before she went to Lethe. Yes. She was sad and angry because she had eaten seeds, and had thought to come to Lethe, to think and perhaps gain some solace from the waters. She had felt so... condemned. She was now forever tied to Hades, and might never see the surface world or her mother again.

She had wanted to forget all of that. If she was stuck down here, why not forget the surface world? But as she fought Lethe's influence, she realized that this was a spur-of-the-moment decision. Wiping her memory would not make things right. It would be easy forgetting everything that had happened up until now so Hades could have a blank slate to protect and mold into his ideal image of wife...

Persephone berated herself for that now. How could she make such a silly decision, even though she was hurt and angered in a way she hadn't thought possible. She couldn't lose any of her memory! She jerked away from Lethe, gasping and struggling against the current as she tried to reach the surface. Hands grasped at her, trying to pull her back, but she fought, kicking and struggling free. A hand reached between her legs, fingers renewing the pleasure she felt as Lethe's lips nibbled along her ear.

"You are safe here, stop fighting and just lie back..."

The younger woman ignored her, trying to shove her away. She could feel Lethe attempt to wipe her memory, focusing waves of numbing pleasure on her. Persephone remained resolute, imagining the surface world, focusing on how it felt, the warm sunlight on her skin, the grass under her feet... *Lethe cannot take that away from me.*

Persephone focused her inner energy, envisioning a protective field around herself. It was inspired from her experience with Styx, as a way to better protect herself against unknown dangers. She wouldn't let Hades or Lethe win!

With a short gasp, she broke the surface, paddling over to the bank and hoisting herself out of it before Lethe could grab her again. She crawled up the gray sand, the cool air of the Underworld causing her to shiver violently as goosebumps formed, the warm droplets quickly coalescing to nearly-frozen beads on her skin.

"Come back, Persephone!" Lethe wailed, her song beautiful and eerie. Her hand brushed against the younger woman's ankle, and it was so warm, providing a touch of soothing relief to the frigid atmosphere. Persephone jerked away, scuttling further up the bank.

"Go away," she muttered fiercely, focusing on the cold and shivering as she did so. Her hair clung to her neck and back, dripping onto the sand. She had never liked cold, and ached to be toasty and comfortable, but she wasn't going to give up her memory for it! Her breath came out in steamy wisps as she wiggled her way further up the bank, trying to speak. She wanted to call for Cloe to bring her things to wear, since Lethe had stripped her entirely. To her horror, the words were frozen on her tongue as she rubbed her arms, feeling the goosebumps.

"Persephone!" She raised her head when she heard a distinctly masculine voice call out her name. Hades came within view, his cloak billowing as he closed in on her. She remained mute as his eyes moved along her body, filled with concern as they checked her for injuries. He repeated her name softly as he placed his hand on her arm, jiggling it. Her gaze met his, but still she did not speak.

He removed his cloak and scooped her up in it, wrapping her snugly as he cradled her. Upon hearing where she was, he took the shortest – and indeed fastest – route. He went the same way, teleporting to his Palace, determined to wash Lethe's water off her and make sure she was alert. She offered no resistance when he unwrapped her and lowered her into the tub, even going slack as he dunked her head under the water after telling her he was doing so. He asked her questions here and there, trying to get her to speak, but he received no responses. Her gaze was distant.

After he was satisfied that every last drop of the River of Forgetfulness were washed away, he wrapped her in a towel and carried her to the bed. The fire was larger than it usually was, sending extra heat through the room.

"Are you all right?" Hades asked as he grasped her shoulders, giving her a light shake. "Look at me, focus on me." He touched her face, trying to get her to look at him. She kept her eyes averted, evading his roving gaze. "Please."

He placed his head on her lap, looking up at her.

"Seph, I was so worried about you. You gave me a scare, disappearing off to Lethe. I am so glad you are well." He took her hand, nuzzling and kissing it. She hated that the concern was so evident in his eyes and tone. Despite being a bastard, he at least showed real concern for her well-being. She wasn't about to give him any relief despite her awareness of his distress, though.

She pushed his head off her lap and turned away from him, burying her face against a pillow. She heard a sigh before his hand touched her shoulder. A quick jerk of her shoulder was her response.

"Go away," she muttered. She was even more tired than before, and wanted to sleep so she could think of something later. No effort was made to stifle a yawn as she pulled up a blanket.

Hades could see her fatigue, so he decided to stop talking for the time being. He settled down, starting to spoon up against her only to be the recipient of an annoyed hiss and a firm shove.

"I told you to go away!"

"Duly noted." The dejection in his tone was clear as Hades slunk off the bed and retreated from the chamber. He sat on the divan in the main room, lighting a fire there. He had always liked having a fireplace or hearth lit; it gave a bit of light and cheeriness to the Underworld. Disconsolately, he fiddled with the edge of his tunic, hating how bad he felt about what he had done. He tried to tell himself that he had done it out of love and necessity, but remembering the pain in Persephone's voice and eyes served as a harsh reminder that he *had* sneaked through the promise he made for her and offered her the ethereal food during her vulnerable moment.

He wanted to deny his wicked deed and assure his male pride by saying that he had simply done what was best for her, as any loving husband would. But no matter what excuse he came up with, he always just as quickly dismissed them despite his attempts to not admit his misstep.

Like Zeus, Hades never had an easy time admitting his errors. However, unlike his younger brother, Hades didn't make nearly as many mistakes. That didn't make accepting his error any easier. He knew what he had to do – Persephone needed and deserved an apology. He swallowed thickly, squaring his shoulders as he stared at the dancing flames, drumming his fingers against the armrest of his chair.

o0o

Persephone stretched her arms above her head as she stirred awake. The large bed she was nestled in was now familiar to her after her time in the Underworld. She lay there quietly for several minutes, slowly coming out of the haze of slumber as she processed the events of late. There had been the euphoria of making love with Hades and the pain and rage when she realized she had eaten the seeds he gave her. A slow sigh escaped her lips as the consequences of this deed sunk in, and she stared up at the ceiling for several moments, thinking of how best to deal with this. Lethe wasn't the solution; that much she realized. Should she draw her strategy from her experience with the Styx, then?

She looked over, seeing Hades. He had climbed into bed after she succumbed to exhaustion. *Devious prick.* But at least he wasn't touching her, keeping himself – and his limbs – on one side of the bed.

She climbed out of the bed and retreated to her room. After some internal debate on what to wear, she chose an outfit of emerald green and rich, golden yellow. These colors reminded her of the surface world, and perhaps it would remind Hades as well.

The yellow fabric was woven with bright red and orange flowers along its edges, making a suitably festive touch to the garment. She swept her hair up in a simple fashion, securing it with a green sash. Her neck and arms were bare, reflecting her decision to go au naturel.

The door to the terrace was open, so she went outside. She had eaten the seeds, but was there still some chance she might yet see her mother? Or see the living world again? Hades insisted that she was her equal, that all she had to do was embrace their relationship. She had offered her maidenhead; didn't that indicate well enough to him that she enjoyed his company? Apparently that hadn't been good enough for him.

*When you give yourself to me, I will have **all** of you.* He had said that a while ago, and his words had caused a shiver to race up her spine. He certainly had shown her that he meant it!

She drummed a random beat with her fingers on the marble railing. Even though she hadn't decided just what she would say to Hades, she was feeling very clear-headed. She would overcome this one way or another. Sensing another presence, she looked over her shoulder to see Hades.

Persephone regarded him coolly. His hair was slightly tousled, and he had thrown on a comfortable black peplos, the hems ending at his elbows and mid-calf. He looked grand in full regalia, but he looked just as good in plain garb. He was leaning against the doorpost, staring at her with an expression that illustrated a mixture of emotions, mostly melancholy. She crossed her arms loosely, waiting for him to speak.

"Persephone... I am sorry."

She stared at him for a moment, not completely registering this information. Was he, the high and mighty Lord of the Underworld, *apologizing?*

"I never meant to hurt you. I am usually not such a rash person, but my actions regarding bringing you here and keeping you... I will admit, it's the first – and only time – I have ever loved anyone. I did what I thought was best, given the circumstances. Still, that is no excuse for what I did." He took a step closer as she maintained her silence.

"You have every right to be angry. I truly am sorry." His gaze was pleading as he looked down at her. *Damnit.* With the right gleam in his eyes, he could melt her heart, and she gave out a soft sigh. It was so damned hard to hold onto her anger or pain when he stared at her pleadingly. The more she tried to resist, the more she just wanted to throw her arms around him. She quickly looked away, collecting herself.

"Sephie..." Hades came closer and dropped to his knees, taking her hand. He did not bow before even mighty Zeus, ruler of the gods of Hellas. Yet here he was, on his knees before the woman he loved. "I humbly beg for forgiveness and hope that you find me worthy of it." The regal, powerful Lord of the Dead was simply a man who had inadvertently hurt the woman he loved, and yearning for her forgiveness as he stared up at her.

Chapter XLII

oOo

Demeter glared at her niece, irritated by the way that Aphrodite flipped her honey-blond tresses over her shoulder, smoothing an invisible wrinkle out of her fine linen and gauze gown which was the same pale and rich blue of her eyes. In her ears and around her neck, were gold and blue topaz, and the jewels were worked into her girdle as well. *Leave it to Aphrodite to primp and pamper herself before she took her turn in begging to stop the plight that had befallen Hellas*, Demeter thought sourly.

"Come now, dear aunt. Losing a child is terrible," Aphrodite offered in her graceful voice, shrugging her shoulders slightly. "But Kora is a queen! If Zeus thought she was in trouble, wouldn't he make Hades give her back? Despite Father's flaws, he does have a good heart." She smiled winningly, holding out her hands in a placating gesture. All she received was a level glare.

"Have a heart, the mortals are starving. My temples are empty. My followers call out *your* name."

"Lust cannot feed people," Demeter replied acidly. A momentary frown graced the younger goddess's features.

"Is it fair to them, or to us?"

"Was it fair to me?" the Harvest Goddess snapped as she rose to her feet, an imposing and powerful figure compared to Aphrodite's own lithe and form. "Was it fair that my daughter was stolen from me? Is it fair that I was told by Zeus that there is nothing he can do, nothing that he *will* do after he has so callously discarded her to the Underworld? Am I the only one who cares about something other than stupid and idle pleasures?"

"Kora is just one child. Well, I guess thanks to Hades, she is no longer a child..." Aphrodite hadn't said this out of malice, but pleasure – her own or others' – was never far from her mind. However, she realized an instant too late that she had just provoked Demeter further. A flash of rage passed through the older goddess' eyes before they suddenly narrowed, fixing on Aphrodite.

As far as anyone knew, Hades hadn't had any mate or affair in the past. His relationships with Minthe and Leuce had been discreet and the details unknown, and it was because of that that hundreds of years later, mortals would get the facts wrong and claim that Hades had cheated on his wife with these two when he became bored of his Queen.

"You..." Demeter growled. Aphrodite was known for the mischief and chaos she caused among gods and mortals alike. When she was bored, she thought nothing of using her Gift to create attraction between unlikely couples, or just one half of that couple. It was one thing that Demeter disapproved of strongly. Love, like life, was a rare gift to be cherished, and part of

Aphrodite's Gift was to make those she affected believe that what they felt was genuine love rather than the truth of burning lust, infatuation, and even obsession.

"You made Hades desire Kora!" she snarled, pointing an accusing finger at her niece. Aphrodite's eyes widened in unmistakable surprise for an instant before she shook her head.

"If my Gift worked on Hades, he would have stolen a bride a long time ago," Aphrodite replied, gazing at Demeter pleadingly. "Eros hit him with his arrows a few times, but Hades is impervious to my son's magic. And my Gift is nothing to him. This..." she gestured to herself as if showing off a valuable prize – and she certainly considered herself one – "does not even warrant a second glance from him." The Goddess of Love pouted prettily.

"Someone who does not respond to your constant demand for attention, how *fascinating*. Too bad he did not snatch *you* away instead of my baby." Demeter was harsh and unforgiving, budging not one inch towards her niece's cloying words or attempts at humor. Aphrodite was glad she was alone with her aunt – however enraged Demeter was – so no one could see her wilt, her face turning pale as her smile froze.

"I swear, I had nothing to do with your daughter's disappearance. And all my brothers and sisters had no involvement in it either... If you must take it out on Zeus, then surely I understand! But why punish the rest of us?"

"I tire of not being taken seriously. I give, and

give, and *give!* And what I value most was taken from me!" First Iasion and now Kora...

"Oh, but I do take you seriously!" Aphrodite pleaded, racking her brain for something she could use. If she sided against Demeter, her followers were lost. If she joined sides with Demeter, what did she have to lose? A pretty little smile replaced the frozen grin she had on her face, and she tapped her chin.

"I do know that I would feel terrible if someone took either of my sons away from me." Aphrodite said as she slowly approached the Harvest Goddess. "I would be *so* sad and angry."

Demeter glanced at her curiously. Had she actually managed to make a point with Aphrodite – the least sympathetic of the goddesses? Could Aphrodite use her abilities to rally more to Demeter's side? Before the Harvest Goddess could further consider the possibilities of an alliance, her niece's next words set her blood boiling again.

"I am happy to help you, Aunt. I will speak to Zeus myself. I can help rally what is left of Father's allies to your cause. No one should have to lose a child. But I take a risk in siding with you. I will need something in exchange, but oh, it is such a small favor... all I want is for you to restore Ares to his... full manhood."

Barely containing her rage, Demeter stared at the blonde goddess, not sure whether to be shocked or appalled at such a request. Hey, why not go for both?

"That bastard tried to *rape* my daughter. He is

much better off as is," Demeter snarled.

"Has he not been punished long enough? He has not hurt anyone!" Aphrodite pleaded. She had found other lovers, yes, but honestly, Ares was the best she had ever had. She missed his roughness and passion.

"Get out. Your followers can starve for all I care," she replied, her voice cold as the winter that had overcome much of Hellas.

"At least let me take some food..."

"Get out!" Demeter roared, her power flashing around her in an aura, rolling off her in waves as her green eyes blazed with righteous fury. "Never set foot in Eleusis again or I swear to Gaea, I *will* smite you." She would never forget how she had destroyed the last piece of Ouranos. Aphrodite was a powerful – and whole – goddess, but her Gift did not compare to Demeter's own.

As if Aphrodite sensed her aunt's thoughts, she swallowed nervously and left without another word, visibly shaken when she went back to Olympus to report her failure to Zeus.

oOo

Zeus let out a low sigh as he saw Rhea and Hestia emerge through the doorway to the Council Room. Ordinarily, this room was reserved for the Council of Twelve, but in emergency situations, senior members of the clan made an appearance. Demeter's empty throne was a conspicuous sight, and Rhea glanced at it for a moment before she and Hestia took the extra seats that had been set up for them. There was enough room at the table to accommodate a dozen more deities, and the newcomers settled in comfortably before Rhea looked at her youngest child with a stern and disappointed expression on her face. None present missed it.

When it was first discovered that Zeus had handed over Demeter's daughter to Hades, the reactions had been mixed, from disapproval to neutrality or acceptance, even endorsement. However, now there was not one single god on Olympus who could even be at least somewhat amicable toward the King of the Gods for what had happened due to the disastrous effects of Demeter's wrath. Poseidon, Apollo, and most of the other gods had sided with Zeus in the beginning, seeing nothing at all wrong with what he had done, but now they were fully aware of his folly and wished for him to correct it as soon as possible, by force if needed.

The tension in the air was palpable, and Zeus swallowed thickly as he felt a dozen pairs of eyes fixed on him, none of them encouraging.

"Do not look at me like that!" Zeus stated, trying to keep up a strong facade. "I never thought that this kind of thing would happen! Do you think I like having all the mortals suffer and die?"

"So this means that if you knew how infuriated Demeter would become, you would not have given away her daughter? Is that the *only* thing that would have stopped you from making the agreement with Hades behind her back?" Athene asked, staring at her father coolly. Zeus tried to control himself, but he bristled visibly under his oldest child's stinging words.

"I did not come here to be antagonized. I want to work out a solution, but if all you are going to do is make things difficult, then there is no point in me being here..." the King of the Gods replied, rising from his seat.

"Sit down. Right now." This came from his left, and Athene did not bother hiding a smirk as Hera stared at her husband frostily, her tone matching her words. Her lips were set in a tight line as she stared at her husband. "You have no right to complain about anything any of us might say to you. We have seen the misery in Hellas and put up with you dicking around for too long."

He tried to defy his wife, silently commanding his feet to carry him away. All he could do was lower himself back into his throne, bristling under Hera's blunt description of his actions. It sounded so odd to hear such a crude word from a woman who was usually far more refined in her speech.

"Even after all this time, do you not realize what you did was wrong? Whether or not Demeter would have wreaked her anger on Hellas has nothing to do with it," Hera added. There were some murmurs of agreement, mostly from the goddesses. The gods were pointedly silent but for Hephaistos and Dionysus. Truth be told, it did not surprise Hera that Poseidon, Apollo, or Ares didn't really *see* what was wrong with Zeus's actions other than the death of the mortals, for they truly were of his ilk. Hermes looked uncomfortable, silently drumming his fingers on the table.

The Messenger God had been thinking about Kora ever since he heard about what had happened. One thought that nagged at him was why Zeus had taken a role in this at all. He had plenty of children, from goddesses and mortal women alike. He certainly wasn't above involving himself – or rather, meddling – in important matters concerning his offspring, such as marriage. His help was often beneficial. If not for Zeus, Perseus would not now be king of Joppa, a mighty city that lay on the opposite side of the Mediterranean, yet untouched by Demeter's blight. Zeus certainly enjoyed seeing his children succeed, for it reflected on him as a father, even though he actually spent little time with each individual child – a result of having so many of them and spending so much time in the pursuit of making more.

Zeus wasn't a bad father, just an overall distant one except for the few lucky times any one child might gain his undivided attention when he was in a fatherly mood.

Now, what had Kora done to gain Zeus's attention? Especially when she was the daughter of his sister, a powerful goddess who was more than capable of taking care of her own affairs? Hermes did think it was a bit odd that Demeter wanted to raise Kora in secret. He had never seen anyone so protective of his or her child, so why did Zeus not consult his sister, much less ask permission to give the girl away to Hades?

There was a possibility that quietly nagged at

the Messenger God whenever he dwelt on that question. It was the logical guess, but at the same time it baffled Hermes.

"Perhaps I should have consulted with Demeter in that matter, but I felt she was too protective of the girl, and..."

"A good mother is protective of her children!" Hera replied firmly, giving her husband another displeased glare.

"I am not saying it's a bad thing..." Zeus said, gently waving his hands as he tried to placate his wife. "But Kora was of suitable age. I was concerned that she was being... denied opportunities in her life because Demeter was keeping her so sheltered. So when Hades asked for my blessing, I thought, why not? He promised she would be taken care of, and we all know he is a man of his word. I have explained this before, yet you are all acting like I am the bad guy here! I am not the one who is starving Hellas!"

As Hermes listened to the other gods argue, he pondered. Why be so concerned about Kora? From what Hermes saw, she was already well-cared for. She apparently didn't seem to feel a need for the company of men. And why did Hades go to Zeus? It was all obvious to Hermes when he carefully examined the facts one by one and put them together like a puzzle.

"Zeus." Rhea's voice was quiet but strong, silencing the others. "Do you not feel bad for Demeter? Not because of what is happening in Hellas, but because of how she feels? You hurt her terribly."

Zeus let out a long, slow sigh. He genuinely meant best, but he was well aware that his best intentions sometimes hurt people. He thought he was doing Hephaistos a favor by giving him Aphrodite as wife – and look at how poorly that had turned out! He always hated it when he made things worse by doing someone a favor – and his general strategy of dealing with such occurrences was to try to avoid the matter as he quietly attempted to fix whatever it was he did. Danae had been lonely and he gave her companionship, but then her father wanted to put her to death when he found out she was pregnant. She was discarded like garbage, forced into a coffin and tossed into the seas so that King Acrisius could claim that he didn't actually slay her. She had been alive and well when she left his hands, rationalized Acrisius, what fault was it if a storm or a leak claimed her life?

Zeus was satisfied that he had done right by her. She had found a new home and a good man who took her in, treated her kindly, and raised her son as his own. It was too bad that the situation with Demeter couldn't be ameliorated so easily. Demeter wanted to protect her daughter, and that was certainly understandable after what Ares had nearly done to her. But Hades promised her safety and well-being, and with her being of age, Zeus honestly thought it was best for all parties. After all, what better husband than Hades? He was honorable and taciturn, and his word was of infinitely more value than the riches of the Underworld. Demeter would never have to worry about whether her daughter was being mistreated. She loved her daughter so much, but she was terrifying when angered. He remembered all too well that fateful night so many years ago when she had discovered his trickery.

"No. I did not want to hurt her. I just gave my blessing to what I thought would be a good situation for everyone. It was never my intention to make her feel like this. If I could go back in time and change it, I would. I am sorry." It was not often that Zeus apologized, because it had never been easy for him to swallow his pride and admit that he made a mistake, even though he had made them often enough. But as the last phase rolled off his tongue, he was surprised to note that he actually felt a bit better.

"Have you told her that?" Rhea answered.

"... No."

"After everything that has been happening, it had never occurred to you to apologize to Demeter?" Hera was incredulous.

"I do not know how much help it would be at this point, but you need to apologize to your sister." Rhea let out a low sigh, rubbing her temples as she heard mutters of agreement. The last couple of months had been stressful on everyone, and this ordeal could not be over fast enough. Hestia said that the hearths throughout Hellas no longer provided as much warmth. The mortals who managed to survive famine now had the cold to contend with.

"Yes." Feeling overwhelmed, Zeus nodded. There was the possibility that an apology would assuage his sister's fears. And there was that bit about not eating any Underworld food. If Kora hadn't eaten any of the food, she could return to the surface. There was hope yet, however slim.

oOo

Demeter was silent as she and Iris arrived at Olympus. Initially, she hadn't wanted to come, but the summons had come from Zeus himself and Iris had made it clear that it was important to Zeus and that the messenger herself thought it was too. Perhaps now Zeus was ready to return her daughter!

Iris was glowing, her aura conveying a palette of mostly green, with a bit of other earthy colors here and there. Demeter knew that this display was intended to soothe her, but she was too tense to enjoy the luminous show.

Demeter was a stately sight even in her drab cloak. It was a dull gray-brown, much like the lifeless earth in Hellas. The other gods stared at her as she entered the Council room but did not take her seat. The tension was palpable, and nobody could ignore it.

Rhea rose from her seat, going to her daughter's side. She touched Demeter's arm.

"It is most fortunate that you are here. Come, sit and we can talk."

"I have no desire to sit and chat. I was invited here for a reason, and I will be told of it now or I am leaving." The Harvest Goddess pulled away from her mother. Rather than entreat Demeter further, the older earth-goddess turned toward the others, fixing her attention upon her youngest son.

"You heard her. You know what needs to be said."

The eyes around the room turned from Demeter to Zeus, and the King of the Gods felt his breath catch in his throat. This was indeed a humbling moment, but he knew he needed to speak quickly so he could get it over with and things could go back to normal, or at least closer to it.

He rose from his seat and cleared his throat, looking at his sister.

"Demeter. I am sorry." There was a terse silence around the room for an unbearable moment, and Zeus swallowed again. He could see his sister frown at him, her eyebrows furrowed in confusion.

"Ahem. What I mean is... I apologize for what I did. I regret my actions, and am sorry for the pain I caused you. I did what I thought was best, but I acted rashly. Words cannot express how aware I am of my wrongdoings or the consequences they had on everybody else. I truly... honestly... am sorry." He hung his head, looking like a chastised boy. He had meant his words, and once he started talking, it had all just poured out of his mouth with the charm that he could so easily draw upon. Out of the corner of his eye, he saw Hera nod approvingly. Rhea's features softened as she looked at him.

"Is that all?" Demeter asked coolly. He refused to let her dismissal bother him – at least, openly – and returned his gaze to her face.

"You have every right to be angry, but I meant what I said. Not a day will go by that I will not remember this. I have never been so sorry!" How could he ever forget the misery he saw on Earth? He was the mighty King of the Gods, but he couldn't even feed the mortals that worshiped him and his brethren?

"All right then." Demeter remained aloof, arms crossed under her cloak.

"Sister, you are furious with me and I understand why. I will apologize a thousand times if I have to, but please, do not punish anybody else for what I did! Why should others suffer for my own stupid mistake?" He appealed her, palms turned upward as if begging for alms.

"I am glad to hear that, Zeus. You certainly do not apologize as often as you need to."

Zeus gracefully accepted the barb sent his way, bowing his head again. Now was most certainly not the time to show any arrogance or impatience.

"I hope that you did not bring me here just to give me words," Demeter stated, her hands moving to her hips. Inwardly, he grimaced. Demeter wanted absolutely nothing less to have her daughter at her side again. He risked a fresh spate of her wrath for not having the fulfillment of her desire at hand. He could only hope that what he could give her might give everybody even the slightest measure of relief.

"There is a chance yet," Zeus explained, trying to sound as optimistic as he could without sounding too cheery, "Is it not said that those who eat the food of the dead are forever doomed to that world? Are we not all..." He gestured to the rest of the deities within the chamber, "aware that we must not eat any of the food there? Each of us tells our children that the food is a curse, to only eat the ambrosia and nectar of the gods if not the food the mortals have to offer?"

Demeter paused. It was an admonition she had imparted upon Kora. The Underworld was a gloomy enough place for any deity, but for deities of the earth, who had the Gift to manipulate life-energy, the realm of Dis was a dead place indeed. She could not use her Gift because there was nothing down there to apply it to. Heaven forbid that she ever become trapped down there! She hoped that Kora hadn't become tempted enough to eat... but even if she did, Demeter would still act. Her daughter had been kidnapped after all. Whether or not she ate the food of the dead was beyond the matter.

"Is that all you can offer?" the Harvest Goddess asked calmly, masking her fury.

"I have no control over the Underworld or its denizens. Only Hades has power over such a matter."

"So you are as impotent to fix things as ever," Demeter snarled.

"Ahem! If I might interject..." Hermes knew he was taking a risk speaking in front of Demeter, but he had been the one to replay messages to Hades from either Zeus or Demeter. Because Demeter was not on speaking terms with her brother, no one else but Hermes knew what she and Hades said to each other. There was one thing that he hadn't reported to Zeus, and the messenger god knew the time was now.

"Respected aunt, you know I only wish you the best. I have done what I could in the search for your daughter. But have you forgotten Hades's offer? He is willing to let you see Kora..."

If looks could kill, Demeter's glare would have rivaled Medusa's.

"What? Is that true?" Poseidon asked. The other gods glanced at one another in surprise and curiosity. Despite Demeter's glare, Hermes continued.

"Hades told me that he is willing to allow mother and daughter to reunite, but only if..."

"Hermes!" Demeter's voice was steely.

"Hermes has something important to tell us," Rhea said, staring pointedly at her daughter. "Go on." She nodded at her grandson.

"He said that he intends to keep her as his bride, but he is willing to allow a reunion if Demeter will accept that fact."

"Hmm." Rhea frowned, but she was surprised Demeter hadn't jumped on that chance.

"Then consent, and you will see your little girl again!" Poseidon interjected. There were several comments of agreement from the men at the table. It sounded so simple!

"Consent to a marriage I never approved of in the first place just so I can see Kora again! I am insulted that any of you would ask me to consider that!" Her features contorted in a fresh burst of fury as Rhea reached out.

"I will not ask you to decide on that. And none of them should, either!" Rhea said, her eyes roving along the faces of the others in the room as she frowned at them. She hoped Demeter would accept Hades's offer soon enough for the sake of everybody, but she understood her daughter's anger. The offer was insulting to a mother who had her daughter abducted and carried off due to the schemes of men. "Let Hermes go to the Underworld right now. He can ask if Kora has eaten any of the food, and if she has not, then Zeus will do his best to get her back... you will do that, dear son, yes?" Her tone was pointed as she glanced at Zeus, and he nodded. "And if not... well, we will talk later. Without the interference of men." A talk between the women of Olympus should yield better results than one where the casual comments of men would just provoke Demeter's wrath further.

o0o

Hermes disliked every trip to the Underworld, and hoped that this would be the last one in a long time. He remembered the spark of defiance in Kora's eyes. Demeter claimed that she knew to not eat the food of the Underworld. If she was as rebellious and spirited as ever, then he just might be returning with the daughter of the Harvest Goddess and bring an end to the starvation and cold that had a firm hold on Hellas.

But if he came back empty-handed... ooh, he

did not even want to think about it. He looked over his shoulder one last time, giving Demeter a brief nod before he shot up into the air.

Chapter XLIII

oOo

Hades wanted forgiveness, and Persephone was tempted to grant it as he looked up at her, sorrow and regret all too clear in his eyes, but his remorse did not undo what he had done. She was now bound to the Underworld, her fate forever tied to his. It weighed heavily upon her shoulders, and despite his obvious regret at hurting her, it did not necessarily mean that he truly understood just what he had done to her. He said he had been called to this place and was willing to be King of the Underworld, rather than be at the short end of a gamble between his brothers and himself. Great for Hades that he found his place, but who was he to decide where *her* place was?

"I gave of myself to you in a way we both wanted. Was that not enough for you?" Persephone asked as she looked down at him.

Hades looked away for a moment before answering. "Why did you give yourself to me? We could have continued as we had before. I was willing to wait, as much as I desired to take you fully."

Persephone was unable to speak for a moment. She had consented to sharing her time with him, after all, and she did enjoy the pleasures he had to offer. She conceded to him the first night because she was curious, and he had promised that she could keep her maidenhead, that he would not force her into anything. So she let him put her through a myriad of experiences, confident that since she would still be a virgin, her hymen intact, she could go back to the surface world and Mother would not know what she had done. It had started out as rebellion, a desire to be treated like a woman, not a child, and by a man who would respect her boundaries and stop when she asked him to. It was supposed to be safe, a way to explore her sexuality with a man she was quick to find herself attracted to. He made her a promise, and she trusted him to keep it. And he had.

There was no end to the delight he could give her, and she certainly had her own share of fun returning the favor – sans the shadowy powers that were part of his Gift, of course. She had remembered Cyane's words about using a man, not letting them gain the upper hand and getting your satisfaction from them before they tired of you. It had seemed to work well because she learned so much, the knowledge he offered not limited to the carnal arts. She should have been happy with this. So why had she decided that her virginity was no longer worth keeping?

Persephone slowly slid her hand out of his embrace and drew it to her chest.

"I offered myself since it was something I knew I would enjoy. What especially hurts about what you did is that I was enjoying your company and you knew I did. I thought... hoped that would be enough for you. Just because I miss the upper world and wish to go back to it does not mean that I never wanted to see you again. You have taught me so many things."

"I know you do enjoy yourself here. You have blossomed into a radiant goddess. Here you get the chance to experience freedom and achieve your potential..."

Persephone shook her head. As much as she had grown, as far as she had come... she knew she still had a ways to go. She could sense it, something within herself that was... *incomplete*. Despite all she had learned and accomplished here, the emptiness remained, only further emphasized by the knowledge that she was bound to a dead place.

"I am not there yet," Persephone answered humbly in all clarity. "You do not know what I can do. You just... decided my fate as if it were not my own."

"Again, I am sorry." He bowed his head before looking up at her again.

"You say that you are sorry... but you need to prove it. My forgiveness must be *earned*. I may care for you, but I need you to understand just what has happened to me and why I am so upset."

Hades rose to his feet, reaching towards her. She shook her head and backed away.

"I need to be alone. Please respect that, Aidon."

"Very well. But just know that I love you. I always have, and always will." His voice was sorrowful but rich and deep. She blinked and looked away, making a quick retreat down the steps and dashing past the pomegranate tree into one of the gardens.

The Lord of the Dead looked down at his

hand, feeling a faint tingle from where he had grasped hers. Normally, he made the best decisions, patient and wise in his ways. Yet with this alluring goddess, he had acted rashly several times. Rather than ask Demeter about a proper courtship, he had used the incident with Ares as an excuse to hide in the shadows and claim his bride in a quite... forceful way.

And now it was easy to see the result of when one added Zeus's insensitivity and Demeter's over-protectiveness of her child. He knew he could not hide from Demeter forever, and now Persephone's anger and confusion at the entire situation made him feel entirely unsure of just how he should proceed – a dilemma that he had not found himself in for a very long time.

oOo

In the tropical garden, Persephone was in an atmosphere that was as close to the upper world as possible. She could play in and even drink the water, and the plants were lush in variety and composition. The sky was gold-tinted with blue at the edges, making the atmosphere feel even more warm and cheerful. It was one of her favorite places to go when she wanted to be alone.

She shed her clothes on the sand near the pond and climbed the rocky outcropping that led to the waterfall. As she gazed down at the pool, she felt the thrill that she always did before she jumped. There was that moment that for an instant seemed like forever, as she propelled herself, a fleeting sensation of being frozen in mid-air before starting her descent.

Her body sliced through the water before she surfaced, flicking her head and flipping her wet hair over her shoulder. She rose from the water, her hair becoming almost straight as it plastered down her back. When she called for Cloe, the shade appeared with a towel.

Rather than use actual dead souls as servants, Hades preferred these shades. Without minds or mouths of their own, the shades' presence were unobtrusive and inconsequential. They materialized as he needed them and disappeared into nothing when dismissed. The Lord of the Dead truly was a secretive person, and Persephone had to admit that she was flattered at the fact that he would share some things with her that he had never done with anyone else.

She let out a quiet huff as she rubbed her face with the towel before rubbing her hair dry. Hades had been so earnest in his apology, and it had been all too easy to be tempted to forgive him, but Persephone had many things to consider. She was willing to forgive him, yes, but not without something in exchange. Something that was real and tangible...

oOo

Elysium was, as always, a cheery place. A gaggle of women darted by, all of them wearing spotless white chitons with various lavishly hued girdles and sashes, flowers adorning their locks.

Men chased after them, apparently engaging in a game of good-humored tag. Persephone sat in the grass silently, watching the cheerful scene before her. In the simple attire she had chosen, it was easier for the Queen of the Dead to be able to fit more easily in with the residents of Elysium.

She rose to her feet, wandering along a path as she politely declined the offers of fruit from the people with baskets laden with produce. Everything looked so good, and after having tasted the pomegranate, Persephone was undeniably curious as to what everything else tasted like.

Before she realized it, Persephone wandered into a different area, one that was taken up with dye vats, weaving looms, and various textile-based paraphernalia. It reminded her of her mother's dyeing room where Demeter had similar items but on a smaller scale. There were looms such as she was familiar with, with modest-sized frames. Further along one side of the room were looms of considerably larger proportions, far larger than anything she had ever seen her mother work with.

The yarns in the many baskets she saw neatly arranged and stacked by the looms were far finer than the linen or wool her mother had ever created. Some of the yarns really were little more than thin strands, as fine as spider's silk. On some of the looms were halfway-done projects using such exotic material, revealing themselves to be the satins and silks of many of the dresses in her wardrobe.

Despite her usual aversion to the weaving craft, Persephone was actually fascinated with what was going on here. Some of the fabrics were plain, of just one color, but the vibrancy of the hues and the quality of the materials more than spoke for themselves. Others were clearly the products of creative minds, bearing all sorts of fanciful images and designs woven into the cloth. Everybody in Elysium moved at their own pace, but it was clear that they were all enjoying their work – whether it be collecting the ethereal fruit that grew in Dis, performing music or theater, or even doing something that was ordinarily a chore in the world of the living, including this weaving. Some were quickly creating row after row, working at an efficient pace, others sat in front of their looms, toying with different colors or trying to figure out how to illustrate a pattern they had just conjured in their minds.

Persephone noticed with some surprise that a good amount of the people here – perhaps one in nine or ten – were male. She had never seen a man at the loom before as weaving was considered woman's work, and in most of Hellas – though the rest of the world was no exception – the roles of a man and a woman were clearly defined. But here, the men stared at their projects with as much interest or concentration as any of their female peers, and their work was the same in quality.

Several occupants of the studio glanced over at Persephone and would acknowledge her with a brief nod or a quick, friendly smile, but the pace of the activity continued. She walked along, silently perusing the projects being constructed around her before coming to the dye vats again. She paused as she watched several women argued over one particular tub, its contents – from what she could see – the color of pomegranate juice.

The women were talking about what to add, this plant or that or to just leave it alone. Suddenly, the far right of the four women looked up, taking notice of the newcomer.

"Hey, you! Come here, we need your help." The woman was middle-aged but attractive, her thick dark hair tied back with an indigo-colored sash that matched her ankle-length peplos. Persephone felt an odd surge of familiarity as she stared at the woman before approaching the quartet.

The woman pointed to the tub that they had been arguing over. "We're trying to decide if the color needs any change. I think it's fine, Calirhoe here thinks it needs more blue, and Bucea and Halie says it needs more red. What do you think?"

Persephone let out a sigh as she looked at the tub. Pigments always looked much darker in their dye form, so it was sometimes hard to guess how they would look on fabric. "Have you already dyed something?" she asked. She was shown a clothesline nearby with several strips of various dyed cloths on it. The one the women pointed to was at the far left, and fortunately, it had already dried. The color was gorgeous, and Persephone could see no reason why another color should be added to it.

"It is perfect as is. I would love some clothing made with this color."

"Ha," The indigo-garbed woman grinned good-naturedly at her companions. Persephone shrugged apologetically towards the other women. She had simply said what she thought was best.

"You are new here, are you not?" one of the other women asked. She nodded.

"I am just passing through. It looks like you are having fun here." Persephone waved her hand. She received similar waves from the other women.

"Me and Halie still say it needs more red," one of the other women muttered.

"Then make your own dye and add as much red as you want," another woman responded. Persephone smiled faintly before she felt a hand on her arm. She turned around to see the woman who had called out to her.

"I never got your name?" she asked. Persephone let out a quiet chuckle, though she was reluctant to give out her name or lie. As she studied the woman from this closer proximity, she got the same nagging sense of familiarity as before.

"I did not get your name, either," Persephone replied, quickly collecting herself.

"Oh, of course. Do forgive me for not introducing myself in there. We just got carried away with the argument... my name is Eurycleia."

"That is all right, it happens." Persephone maintained her smile as she processed this new bit of information. Eurycleia. Iasion's mother.

Grandmother...

Now that she knew, she was able to make the connection. She had always remembered Grandmother as old, already worn down by Ouranos's curse before her golden years became truly golden. Persephone had only to recall Grandmother and darken her hair and wipe most of the wrinkles, and here was the result in front of her. A vital-looking Eurycleia, her hands smooth rather than gnarled and arthritis-ridden, and her eyes sparkling with good cheer.

Like at her first glimpse of her dead father, Persephone found herself unable to speak. Yes, Grandmother had been old and all mortals must die, but it would be nice to have a warning before things like this happened!

She didn't want to say *Kora*, nor did she wish to announce the fact that she was Persephone, Queen of the Dead.

"I am... Seph." Persephone replied quietly.

"Nice to meet you, Seph. How long have you been here?"

"Just... a few months, actually. You?"

"Almost two years. Just a few months, you say? You seem rather young..."

"I was." Two years, hmm? Then Grandmother had lived a long life, indeed. She seemed content.

"Oh dear, what happened? Sometimes the transition can be quite... difficult."

"I do not want to talk about it. I would rather hear your story. You seem happy here. How do you... find a job here?" she asked, indicating the white-washed building the studio occupied.

"You just do what you enjoy doing," the older woman explained. Persephone nodded. Grandmother had enjoyed weaving, and she refused to allow arthritis to stop her from doing her craft even if it might be slow or painful. She was that kind of woman, stubborn and determined to do as she enjoyed and provide for her family. Persephone didn't enjoy weaving, but she enjoyed being with her grandmother and aunt, listening to them talk as she spun wool with them.

"There is enough for everyone to do. We do not have to worry about anything being in short supply or going to waste. There is always enough room for everyone, Elysium is like that."

Persephone wondered how Grandmother's reunion was with the grandfather that had died decades ago. Grandmother had spoken of him often enough and what a wonderful father and husband he had been, and how proud she was of her sons, telling them that their father would be proud of them as well if they could see how they had turned out. "What about your family? Do you miss them?"

"Of course I do! But I lived a long life, and saw my sons grow up and have their own children. When I was growing up, it was very difficult with the poor land. I worried for my sons and husband, and he did die. But later on, it was as if a curse was lifted. The land became fertile, and I saw my children have children, and know they have it better than I did. There have been enough joys to make the sorrows bearable."

"Any regrets?"

"When my husband died, life was very difficult for us. I was young and so focused on my own troubles and taking care of my children. I did not take the time to show my husband that I appreciated what he did for us. He became so sick and died, and I never got to tell him how I felt. But he was waiting for me here in Elysium, and I know that later on, my family will join me. Though my son..." A flash of sadness appeared on Eurycleia's face, and Persephone bit her lip, tempted to tell her about Iasion. But that would reveal too much. Let Eurycleia be happy here.

"What happened to your son?" the younger woman asked gently.

"He decided that this place was not enough for him. Oh, he explained to me why, and I suspected, even when he was still alive..."

"Sometimes people feel like they need to start over," Persephone offered kindly.

"Oh, I know. And I do not begrudge him. I was thinking about it myself, but not for a long while yet. I am simply enjoying it here too much and with my husband at my side and nothing to worry about..." She let out a wry laugh before she looked at Persephone. "You are new here and you have been through a lot, I am sure, but just relax and enjoy yourself here. You will figure out what you want to do." She patted Persephone's arm.

"Thank you. That makes me feel a lot better." She was happy to see her grandmother so comfortable.

"Do not hesitate to come back whenever you feel like it." Her voice was warm and kind, just as

Persephone remembered it, even if it was younger and clearer-sounding now.

Persephone actually pondered telling Eurycleia the truth, but hesitated. She had had such a nice time just now, learning a bit about her family – what she considered her real family, at least. Being with Eurycleia made her want to go to the surface world to see what was left of Iasion's family. How were her uncles and aunt doing? Had Eraphus found a wife of his own? And what of her cousins?

She walked down the path, feeling a bit light-headed when she thought about her mother's famine. Had it reached Enna? Were her uncles dealing with a famine? Were they still alive? Her eyes darted around, wary of the passersby. Would she see any more family members, or one of the people she remembered from her childhood?

Why would Mother do such a terrible thing? She had every right to be angry, but to cause people to starve... how could Mother decide that punishing the mortals in such a way for something they did not do could be a wise course of action? She pondered the things she had learned here and what Hades had told her about her position here. She, according to his own word and promise, was Queen of the Underworld, second only to him in power and position. She was the offspring of two old and very powerful gods, and knew that she had yet to explore the fullest extent of her Gift. She wasn't quite sure how, yet, but she was determined to deal with her situation and find a way to get what she – and nobody else – wanted for herself.

oOo

Hades reclined on a divan, feeling no need to hold Court or visit the judges or Kampe. The Lord of the Underworld had tried to distract himself with a ride in his chariot, but he found himself unable to enjoy the thrill of moving at breakneck speeds with the wind rushing through his hair. A trip to the library showed that he was unable to focus on reading, finding his mind wandering away from the letters in front of him. All he could think of was how he could earn her forgiveness. He had been more than willing to allow a reunion between mother and daughter, only Demeter was so damned stubborn and Zeus insisted on avoiding the blame. The truth was, everyone was at fault.

Except for Persephone herself, of course. She was only the innocent victim of a mother's over-protectiveness, a father's careless goodwill, and of course, his own decisions.

He looked up suddenly when the door to the terrace opened, admitting Persephone before she closed it quietly. Her hair looked a bit mussed and wind-blown, but it made her no less alluring. He swallowed thickly as he remembered the events of the night before, how incredible it had been, the delight he had gained from seeing how much she had enjoyed it. Whether she hated him or not, he would always be hers.

She rubbed her arms, and he raised his hands, offering her a warm embrace. She glanced at him

97

for a moment, seeming as if she might reject him. To his surprise and relief, she moved forward, letting him wrap his arms around her. He tugged at his cloak, draping it around her shoulders and pulling her down to sit with him on the divan.

Persephone kept her hands in her lap, but let him place his head on her shoulder. She closed her eyes, savoring the warmth that radiated from the fire and his body. It was just what she had longed for, the embrace of a warm body, to reassure her that she was still alive in this dead place.

Finally, Hades lifted his head and looked down at her. He was silent, but his expression remained open. His hand reached up to touch her cheek.

"Persephone, this situation has come about because of the rashness of several people, myself included. None of it is your fault, and you do not deserve to be 'punished' for anything."

"So if I were to make certain requests – ones that I do not deem unreasonable – would you grant them?"

"Certainly, love."

"Do you understand why I was so upset?"

"Much as I hate to admit it... yes. I am sorry for ever hurting you. I might be a mighty god, but I am also a man in love. And for an old god like me, love was something completely new and unexpected. I could not bear losing you, so I did something foolish." He hung his head in shame.

"Oh, Aidon..." Persephone reached up to touch his face, feeling him lean his head into her hand. A quiet sigh escaped her throat as he pressed his lips to the inside of her wrist, gently grasping her forearm.

With a quiet *whoosh*, a shade appeared before them. It spoke in its breezy, almost inaudible wispy voice. Hades frowned and nodded before sitting up, gently easing Persephone against one of his arms.

"We have a visitor," Hades muttered as he rose to his feet. "Hermes bears a message for both of us."

Persephone stared at him before he retreated to his bedchamber to get dressed, refusing to appear before guests as anything less than the mighty Lord of the Underworld.

She took a moment to process the news. What would Hermes say when he saw her? What was it he had to tell her? The pomegranate seeds weighed heavily upon her memory, and she swallowed before she hastily retreated to her room to prepare for Hermes's reception.

Chapter XLIV

oOo

"Hermes is fast, but it will take some time for him to travel through the Underworld and back," Rhea said as she reached out towards her daughter. "Please come with me. There is something I need to tell you... and an apology is also owed." Given the state of Demeter's mood, it was not surprising that the mention of an apology should catch her attention so quickly.

As they waited for Hermes, Demeter let her mother lead her to a shaded place to sit. As she did, she stared off in the distance, thinking about what she would do or say if Kora had eaten the food of the dead. Such a thought sent her heart pounding in a fresh surge of panic, and she struggled to calm herself. It was no use thinking about that unless it happened, and she hoped that her warnings to Kora were heeded.

"Demeter, I am truly sorry about everything that has happened. I did not mean to seem so uncaring before about your troubles. I did not fully understand the situation because Zeus would not talk about it to anybody at first."

"As if Zeus has ever been quick to admit his mistakes," Demeter groused. Her mother smiled wryly.

"That is no secret." She reached out to pat her daughter's hand. "I know that our relationship has never been very close, but I want you to understand that I *did* try to find you. Your father...

he was insidious in the use of his Gift. A few of my brothers and sisters helped me look for you, and we had to be careful lest he learn of our efforts. The magic used to hide you was devious indeed. I do not know how he did it, but he was always clever with his Gift. None of us understood the full extent of it."

"No one understands the extent of Hades's Gift, either." Father had not been an easy adversary, and he had been the most formidable of all the Titans. His own brothers and allies feared him, for he had used his Gift in a cunning way to enhance his own strength. Even now, nobody was fully certain just what Kronos' Gift was, because it had never manifested itself in obvious ways like some of the abilities that other gods possessed. Logically, she knew that, but seeing her mother dote on Zeus sometimes brought up stirrings of fierce resentment.

"I accept your apology. And no one could have predicted what Kronos would do." It was cruelly ironic that the Titan who stood up against Ouranos because of the latter's tyranny should become a tyrant himself. Zeus couldn't be called one, but the mistakes he often made certainly had repercussions that could have been avoided with common sense. "Does this mean I can count on your support?"

"Indeed." Rhea bowed her head in acquiescence. "I know you are afraid that your daughter might have eaten some of the food of the dead. If she has, that does not mean that it's all over. A wrong has been committed, and Zeus *must* right it, however much it might cost him. I am not the only one who feels this way, and rest assured, if need be, the rest of the Olympians will lend their strength to your cause. Many of those who supported Zeus now regret it deeply. You have made your point, and we have all seen, heard, and *felt* it." Rhea's tone was solemn.

"But..." she continued, "Whether or not your daughter is able to come back immediately, this famine needs to stop. It has gone on long enough, and too many people have died already. There is not a god or mortal in Hellas who does not know your grief and wrath. End it now, for not only our sake, but your own."

Demeter took a deep breath. Inwardly, she knew that what she had done was wrong, to lash out at so many mortals. Her wrath had blinded her, and still did, to an extent. The more Zeus had tried to ignore her and avoid the situation, the hotter her rage burned. If she continued down this path, Hellas would be ruined. As it was, the country hovered on the brink of destruction.

oOo

The Lord of the Dead smiled in appreciation as his Queen approached him, clad in a black velvet gown with a minimal amount of silver jewelry on her head and wrists. She climbed up the few steps and seated herself in her throne, draping her right arm across the armrest. Her clothing was of a modest cut, but by the gods, she was still alluring, her gown revealing a glimpse here and there of her shoulders and arms, her shapely neck emerging from the folds of the black material.

"Are you ready?" he said in a soft, playful voice. He had kept Hermes waiting while he took his time to prepare; a bit of waiting would be a needed experience even if it would be viewed as an ordeal by the younger god. Persephone nodded, and Hades lifted his hand. A shade led Hermes in, a warm cloak draped across his lean form, the wings on his sandals folded neatly against his ankles.

Hermes approached the royal pair with increasing disbelief. This *couldn't* be Kora. It was impossible. This graceful, beautiful woman before him seemed almost alien. Her skin, having long lost its tan, was now as pale as cream, causing her dark hair and lips to stand out in sharp contrast. Right now, her eyes were dark, almost gray as she stared at him calmly, dressed in an elegant gown of black, diamonds glistening here and there. Though the gown obscured her cleavage, the curve of breast and hip was unmistakable. This was not the nymphet he had encountered... was it?

"Welcome to the Underworld, Hermes. It is nice to see you again, though I wish the circumstances could have been better," the woman on Hades's left said in a voice that was deeper but unmistakably familiar. So it *was* Demeter's daughter. But gosh! He quickly collected himself and bowed his head respectfully.

"I bear a message from Zeus. If Demeter's daughter has not yet eaten the food of the dead, she must be sent back to the surface world immediately. He is very earnest to resolve this matter with Demeter."

Persephone tensed, knowing she was doomed. Hades nodded slowly, tapping his chin. Tightness wound around her throat and chest as it always did when she felt especially stressed out. She was about to turn to Hades with a questioning expression when his words cut through the silence.

"She was adamant about not eating anything down here," Hades stated, rising from his throne. "I will let her go back with you, but first I need a word with her. I must say my farewells."

"Uh... certainly." Hermes stood there as Hades pulled her away from the messenger god. With a wave of his hand, a shadowy veil fell over the couple, swallowing up all sound so that he could speak as he wanted without his nosy nephew listening in. Had he excused himself to go to another room to speak to Persephone, Hades knew that Hermes would have just sneaked over to the door to listen. Having a private conversation with his wife in plain view was a small way of taunting the ever-inquisitive Hermes. Call it petty, but even the solemn god had to amuse himself at times.

Hades turned so that his nephew saw his back, and took Persephone's hands into his. He knew that his statement had surprised her, but he was well aware of his wife's need, and what Demeter was doing above. The Lord of the Dead was an astute man, and knew that refusing to let Persephone go – however much she was bound to him – would be detrimental to the Goddess of Spring herself and the world above. He was not as selfish as Demeter was being right now.

"Persephone, your fate is bound to mine now and forever, no matter what happens. I release you to go home to your mother and help her set things right. You can say your goodbyes to the surface world then. I give you this reprieve from your existence as my queen because I love you." He smiled faintly, raising her hand and pressing his lips to the back of it. "I do hope that when you are asked questions, you will remember me as a kind master, and look forward to seeing me again."

Persephone nodded slowly, thinking of her life down here, all the opportunities and challenges, and with a man who loved her and vowed that he would be hers forever. "How much time do I have?"

"Hm." He frowned contemplatively, trying to think of what would be a reasonable amount of time. A week? A month? How long ago had he brought her down here? Goodness. It was already past mid-autumn, though on the surface, the early winter that had already settled into most parts of Hellas said otherwise. He was almost surprised at the passage of time, but then, time here in Dis had a different definition.

"I will come for you on the winter solstice. Tell your mother what you will, and I will speak with her as needed. Whether or not she knows or approves, I will be back for you, and this time, if she tries to use her Gift again so destructively, I will personally intervene."

"Yes, my lord. Thank you. For giving me this opportunity." Her pulse quickened as she thought of setting foot on the warm earth again, of feeling real sunshine on her skin, of the life that pulsed through the soil.

"I love you," Hades said as he looked down at her, his heart in his words. Persephone blinked back tears and looked down as he caressed the back of her hand with his thumb. "I will miss you more than anything, but I will be content in knowing that we can never be truly parted." Demeter could do her damnedest to hide Persephone, but now with the unbreakable connection they shared, he could find her at any time.

She reached up with her hands to grasp his shoulders, tugging at them. He bowed, feeling her lips press against his own, surprised at the passion he felt behind the kiss. He lifted his arms, wrapping them around her and hugging her close, already missing the warmth of her body.

The Lord of the Dead had his back to Hermes, but through the shadow-barrier, the younger god could see them locked in a tight embrace.

Persephone gently pulled away, and Hades dropped his arms as he dispelled his magic. He grabbed her hand before she could go to Hermes, and squeezed it. She looked back at him, seeing the sorrow and yearning in his eyes.

"Goodbye, Aidon." She squeezed back before she descended the steps.

o0o

Persephone led the way to the river Styx, Hermes following close behind her, keeping at her left side. He seemed at a loss of what to say, and she was glad for the silence. She could see the surprise in his face at her grown appearance, and wondered how Mother would react.

When they arrived at the deck, Kharon did not turn her away from the boat, and in a surprising gesture, graciously helped her into it with great courtesy. She leaned against the side, staring at the churning eddies of onyx-tinted water. Hermes impatiently tapped his fingers against the seat, and she glanced at him. She could feel his nervous energy, and suspected that it was not entirely due to his impulsive nature. He didn't seem to like being down here, and his frequent glances at the other side of the riverbank revealed his eagerness to be out of this dark place.

Not that she could blame him. She was finally to go back home after months! She could feel the quick beat of her pulse, and almost wished that Hades hadn't let her go, since it had been so unexpected. She was so excited, almost *too* excited.

Once they reached the other side, Hermes practically leaped out of the boat and seemed about to reach for her as if he wanted to tug her along, but he controlled himself. Though Hades had quickly let his prisoner go without any argument, the Messenger God had the feeling that it wasn't over and that his uncle had something planned. But whatever it was, hey, Hermes would be no part of it. That way, Demeter couldn't blame him if something went wrong. It was one time where the young god was able to rein in his curiosity and silence his questions before they could be asked.

"Come, your mother is waiting for you." He offered his hand to her as he located the opening in the rock that led to the surface world. She stared at the hand for a moment before taking it. As they climbed the winding steps, the glimmer of light at the top beckoned her and she focused on it, propelling herself towards it, barely noticing that Hermes had also picked up his speed.

"Ah!" she gasped softly as she emerged from the opening. She was surrounded by hard, rocky ground, but it was still the world of the living, however dreary it was at the moment. She frowned as she stared up at the gray sky, feeling disappointed that there was no clear rays of sunlight to cheer her up. The ground looked frightfully barren, and she recalled her visions of a starving world.

Even though the sky was cloudy, she still had to squint, her eyes adjusting to the light of the surface world.

"Yea, I always need a little time to adjust after going to Hades," Hermes commented. She nodded.

"... How have you been?" he asked tentatively. She shrugged.

"I am doing well, thank you. I do not doubt that everyone has their own theories about what happened to me down there, but I really am fine. I was never abused. You can say that to anyone who asks you." Though she had only met a couple of other gods besides her immediate family, Hades's commentaries on their extended family gave her an idea of how to deal with them. "I would very much appreciate it if you repeat that like it is without adding any of your own twists to it or making things up." Hades had warned her that the gods often exaggerated stories as they passed them on. As she said it, she stared at him levelly, her lips set in a tight line.

"Your mother is at Olympus. I will take you there, but you do need to hold on," he said as he extended his arm after a moment of silence. She seemed so calm and regal as she expressed herself. He wanted to tease her a little, like he often did around anyone else, but he found himself intimidated by her attitude.

Persephone let him hook her arm around her waist, and she wrapped her arms around his neck as he shot up into the air.

The experience was more thrilling than terrifying for her, and she wondered if Hermes felt the same way every time he flew. The air was brisk, and she was glad she had brought her cloak with her. It matched her gown, the thick velvet keeping her warm as the air around them thinned.

Mount Olympus came within view, and she saw that the dark stone was patch-worked with white and green around its peak and parts of the upper slopes, making for a sharp contrast to the dull colors of the blighted countryside. The buildings became clearer as they drew close, and their destination was a modest-looking house on the west side of the peak. He landed easily, his steps practiced as he made contact with the ground and gently eased her down.

"Where are we?" Persephone asked as she took note of her surroundings. There were several comfortable-looking houses within view amidst well-maintained gardens.

"Your mother wanted me to bring you to our grandmother's house, so..."

"Kora!" Persephone's head snapped in the direction of her mother's cry, seeing Mother rushing towards her with her arms outstretched. Before she could respond, she found herself crushed within a bear hug.

After several moments, Demeter finally, let go and placed her hands on her daughter's shoulders, her face awash with a mixture of joy and confusion. This was her daughter, doubtless. The bond that mother shared with child was a powerful one, especially for a woman who loved her child as fiercely as Demeter did her own, but within her embrace, Kora felt so different. She was considerably taller, and that was not the only physical attribute of her that had changed.

Slowly, she released her daughter and took a step back to look. The girl – though this was hardly the form of a girl – was modestly clad in a soft black material that was exotic to Hellas. Only her head, neck, and hands were visible, and the older goddess frowned as she saw the smooth plane of her daughter's cheekbones and the slender hands. If Kora was here in the surface world, she must have starved in the Underworld, and it showed even with what little of her body was visible! That would soon be remedied, because this child was the offspring of the Goddess of Bounty! She would make all of her daughter's favorite foods and bring a healthy flush to that woefully pale skin.

Her brother was not here, Demeter noted wryly. Good riddance, she would deal with him later. Right now she had to help her daughter recover from her ordeal in the Underworld!

Demeter glanced at Hermes sharply. "Did Hades have anything to say?"

"He said that she was very resistant against his attempts to feed her."

"Anything about me?"

"Only that he never wanted to hurt you and had no malice in his heart."

Demeter scoffed at Hermes's statement. "Very well. I will be taking my leave now."

"What about Zeus?" Hermes asked. Surely Father would want to talk with the girl that was the source of all this trouble.

"After what he has done? Hardly."

"Very well, Aunt." He could see that her mind was made up. "You are going back to Eleusis, right?"

"Yes. Not that it should concern you or anyone else." Her tone made it clear that she was in no mood for visitors.

"... Understood." He quickly bowed before flying off.

"Eleusis?" Persephone asked as she raised her

eyebrow.

"It is where I have been staying. We will live there until I decide what to do next."

Just like that, Persephone thought with disappointment. *Not asking me what I might want or if there's a place I'd prefer to be.* She could see the tone that Mother was setting for their relationship, and she did not like it. However, she knew that an argument right now would just make things worse. She would see what Eleusis was like and judge it on her experience.

After all, she was a full-fledged Goddess, aware of her divine heritage. She was young yet and didn't know how her own Gifts might fare against her mother's power and experience, so she maintained her own counsel. She was about to ask Mother what she thought would be an innocent question that would keep her mother amicable when she saw an older goddess come within her line of sight, from behind Mother's left. The resemblance between the two older women wan't immediately apparent, but Persephone noticed the similarity in the shape of their noses and lips.

"Demeter! Oh, how wonderful!" This woman's eyes were warm and friendly, and her hair was a rich, dark auburn, more brown than Persephone's own and barely touched with silver at the temples. Persephone had wondered why her own hair was its particular shade given the two different colors of her parents' own, but now she could see where she had gotten it from.

"Kora and I were just leaving," Demeter said politely as she turned to her mother.

"So soon? Without a hello for my granddaughter?"

"Her time in the Underworld has been an ordeal." Demeter waved to her daughter, indicating the delicate, hollow cheeks and pale skin.

"Some ambrosia and nectar will take quick care of that!" Rhea offered. Her daughter nodded.

"I already have some. I must take her home so she can rest."

Rhea frowned slightly, but quickly smiled. Before she could speak, her granddaughter spoke.

"I should go home with Mother so she can take care of me, but I would be more than happy to see you again soon." She flashed her grandmother a winning smile that made her appear radiant despite her paleness. Rhea smiled again, this time more warmly than before, relaxing as she saw how friendly Kora seemed to be. Though Kora did seem pale, she didn't seem frightened or abused, confirming her feelings that her eldest son, despite his unorthodox ways, was not a cruel person.

Hopefully she would be able to hear Hades's side of the story soon. "I would like that very much." Rhea reached out, offering her hands. Kora did not hesitate to mirror this gesture, placing her hands in her grandmother's proffered palms. Usually, Rhea could read someone's aura and discern their Gifts and emotions. She sensed a bit of anxiety and nervousness, but no fear or loathing, or anything else that would cause her to feel alarm, and she sensed a similarity between

Kora and Demeter's gifts. However, part of Kora's Gift remained a mystery. There was no doubt that she was a full-blooded goddess, though. Demeter would not reveal her daughter's paternity, but it was clear to the elder goddess that no mortal was involved in her siring.

Rhea turned her attention to her daughter. "Go, take care of her. You both need it, but please come back soon."

"Hm." Demeter nodded.

"Good-bye. It was nice meeting you," Persephone waved as her mother led her away.

oOof

Rhea smiled as she waved back. As soon as the pair was out of sight, she hastened to her son's villa. She had ordered Zeus to go home and stay there, hence his absence at the reunion between mother and daughter. She hadn't wanted Zeus to be there if Hermes came back with bad news.

Her son was sitting outside in his private garden. Much like the garden outside the throne chamber, this one contained roses. Zeus considered himself a rugged, masculine man – and no one else could deny that he was – but he did have a soft spot in his heart for roses and often used them to woo whoever he was enamored with at that time. He especially liked white or gold roses, and at that moment he had a deep yellow one in his lap as he idly plucked its petals off one by one.

He looked up as she approached, and raised an

eyebrow in inquiry.

"You will be pleased to know that Kora is back with her mother. The curse on the earth is undone, so we all have a lot of work to do."

Zeus closed his eyes, shoulders slumping in obvious relief. "Where are they?"

"Did you expect Demeter would want to see you?"

"No. But I was hoping to see... Kora."

"Mmhm." Rhea nodded as she sat down in the nearest empty chair. It was well-made and comfortable, just like all the furniture on Olympus. If Hephaistos didn't make it, then one of the Cyclopes did, and nobody could question the quality of their work. She leaned against the padded backrest as she stared at her son. She had been doing a lot of thinking ever since the whole affair had been brought to light, and made careful note of Zeus's comments and actions concerning said matter.

Since she had managed to spirit Zeus away from his bloodthirsty father, she had the opportunity to get to know her youngest child after being denied this opportunity five times with her other offspring. After placing him in the care of several trusted nymphs, she visited him as often as she could without rousing Kronos' suspicion. The nymphs had been kind to him and treated him well, but later, Rhea wondered if he would have been better off being raised by trusted men – Cyclopes, perhaps, or one of her sympathetic Titan brothers – but in the end, she suspected it wouldn't have made much of a difference either way.

Having gotten to watch him grow up, Rhea became aware of his flaws as well as his strengths. He might not be cruel or capricious, but as she knew all too well, he could be careless and irresponsible.

"I need to ask you something, and I want total honesty. Do not try to change the subject or shift blame," Rhea stated as she regarded her son with a steady, calm gaze.

Zeus stiffened visibly at his mother's pointed words, his fingers stilling around the rose. He loved his mother and had a close relationship with her, but sometimes she could make him uncomfortably aware of his own weaknesses.

"Is Kora your daughter?" Rhea tightened her jaw as she saw her son's immediate reaction. He quickly averted his gaze, his fingers nervously plucking and ripping petals with more fervor than before.

"So that is why Hades approached you." She stroked her chin as she studied her son, "What happened between you and Demeter?"

He shrugged and mumbled. She rolled her eyes, shaking her head.

"She did not know it was you?"

"Not at first, no."

"And what appearance did you take?"

"Her lover."

Her daughter had a lover? That was surprising, since Demeter didn't seem to care much for the attentions of men, much like Hestia or Athene.

"And who is this lover?"

"He was a mortal she was living with. He died years ago, but I swear I had nothing to do with that."

"Did you become jealous of him?" she asked dryly.

He looked away again, taking a few moments to answer. "I... propositioned. She said no. After a while, I spied on her and saw her with him."

"Oh, Zeus." She set her lips in a tight line, her disappointment all too clear. No wonder Demeter didn't want Zeus around her daughter. Though she was still upset with her daughter for the curse she had placed upon the earth, there was no way Rhea could begrudge her fury with a god who could be frustratingly obtuse at times, especially because with this revelation, she now realized that her daughter had been holding onto her anger for a very long time, and justifiably so. It was almost a miracle that Demeter hadn't lashed out years earlier. Right now, she could not help but feel disgusted – she loved her family, but she certainly wasn't going to condone or support any of this kind of behavior.

"Listen to me." Her voice was sharp and tight, "You have created a huge mess here, one that will take a long time to clean up. I expect you to do *everything* you can to help, and I will be watching you carefully to ensure that you do. I also expect you to stay out of trouble. Do you think you can manage that?" She was unable to hold back a touch of sarcasm at that last sentence.

"Yes, Mother."

"Good. In the meanwhile, stay in your house unless you are out there helping."

"But, Mama..." Generally, Zeus called her by the proper title of 'Mother', but he had called her 'Mama' as a boy, and still did when he wanted to appeal to her. It had been too long since he had enjoyed the attentions of a pretty goddess or nymph, and a weak, starving mortal woman just didn't offer the same experience as a willing and healthy one. He had offered food for company a few times when he had been getting desperate and in the mood to rut, but they were far more focused on the food than giving him a good time, and since a god had to restrain himself with mortals especially during sex, he gained minimal pleasure from these exceedingly few encounters.

"No buts. Keep it in your tunic. *It* has caused enough trouble."

Damn. It was uncanny how Mother seemed to sense what people were thinking at times.

"Yes, Mother." he replied dully. He knew that if he tried to sneak away, she would somehow know, and just come back to nag and scold him, and was one of the very few women who could actually frighten him. She could be worse than Hera sometimes.

"Good boy." She rose from her seat, patting him on the head before she left.

oOo

Eleusis was a far cry from the barren landscape that had haunted her nightmares, and

118

the land was rich in the flow of life-energy. Better yet, it was a city; a city filled with more people than she had ever seen in her whole life! Persephone had been afraid that Eleusis would be some sort of isolated place like the place where she and Mother lived before. Enna had been a quiet, idyllic valley with a homey town surrounded by a thick barrier of unspoiled land, and she would have been happy to see another village, but this was better.

Persephone started to tug off the homespun wool cloak that her mother draped across her head and shoulders, but with an impatient tut-tut, Demeter tugged it back up. A surge of irritation welled up from deep within, for all she had wanted to do was get a clearer view of the city, and this stupid cowl obscured much of her vision.

Mother wasn't giving her any time to appreciate the sights, sounds, or smells of this new place. She had been silent most of the trip, which surprised the younger goddess since she had expected to be bombarded with questions of her captivity.

Finally, she was ushered within a palace that while nice in its own way, paled before Hades's own impressive domicile. A couple of servants bustled about outside, one with a large basketful of laundry. From what she could see, the palace was built around a courtyard as the homes of the more wealthy often were, and she immediately recognized Mother's handiwork in the well-tended gardens.

She could not help but wonder what Mother

was doing here. How had she come to live with these people?

Suddenly, a cheery voice rang through the air in greeting. Persephone lifted her head high enough to see the source of the voice. The woman at the top of the stairs that led from the courtyard looked approximately the same age as Mother's physical appearance, or a bit older. She was a handsome woman, her black hair streaked with gray, her pose proud and sure.

"Welcome back! Is that your daughter?" the woman asked, tilting her head to one side.

"Yes. This is Kora. But right now, we need to be alone."

"But of course. Will you be joining us for supper?"

"We will see."

"Very well." Metaniera bowed her head as the pair passed. Persephone wanted to talk to the woman, but she was rapidly ushered along again.

They ended up in a modestly sized but comfortable room that bore obvious signs of Demeter's touch. What surprised her most was a cradle near the hearth, cozily lined with clean blankets. It was empty at the moment. In one corner sat a large and comfortable bed with several blankets that were also the product of her mother's efforts.

"Who was that woman?" Persephone asked.

"She is Metaniera, the Queen of Eleusis. She rules with her husband, Celeus." Mother explained as she closed the door. That made sense, given the fact that stood with the assurance of a woman confident in her power.

When Persephone pulled the hood from her head, Mother didn't stop her.

"Sit down," Demeter gestured to the seat next to the hearth. Persephone was glad to sit down, so she did, and watched as her mother started a fire, using her Gift to focus warmth to create a spark. Mother could not generate or manipulate fire, but with enough concentration, could form the beginning of one. As she waited for her mother to bring the fire to her liking with a combination of kindling and several logs, she slid the wool cloak off her shoulders. After getting used to the fine materials that Hades kept her clothed in, the wool felt rough against her neck. She loosely folded it and draped it across the side of the chair as she pondered what she would say to her mother.

"Well." Demeter rose to her feet, wiping her hands on her skirt before she turned to face her daughter. She had been silent on the way home because she had been brimming with so many questions – too many of them – and was so overwhelmed to see her daughter again that it was easier to just hold her tongue.

Now that they were in Eleusis, the place that had been home to her for the last couple of months, she felt more relaxed. Celeus and Metaniera had been such wonderful people even before they knew she was a goddess.

What should she ask her daughter first? It seemed almost hard to believe that this pale and wan woman was the sweet little girl from a summer long gone.

"Mother?" Like everything else, Kora's voice had changed, becoming smoother and almost purring in timbre.

"Yes?"

"I am hungry."

Demeter could have laughed if the situation wasn't so serious. Of course, food would be the first thing Kora needed after starving for so long in the Underworld. She was relieved by this distraction, and hastened from her room to fetch some food for her child.

In no time, there was an array of food in front of her daughter from stew to fruits and vegetables to bread, and fresh goat milk and cheese. Persephone wasted no time getting started, and Demeter watched silently as she ate. She was a bit quick at first, stuffing food into her mouth in an unladylike manner, but given the fact that she had been trapped in the Underworld for months, she could hardly be blamed, so her mother did not scold her. Demeter was just relieved that her daughter was safe, and she smiled when Kora downed the last of the milk, blowing out a contented 'ahh' sound as she sat back.

"That was good?" Demeter asked.

"Delicious! It has been too long since I had anything to eat."

"Hmm." Demeter frowned as she nodded, thinking of the dreariness of her brother's domain. "I suppose Hades did not think to offer you anything to eat."

"Well, he did offer the food of the Underworld, but it was not the same as the food we eat. I could feel it."

"Of course, it is the food of the dead! He should have known better!"

"Mother..."

"How could he do this to you, to me? What was he thinking, taking you to that... unnatural place?" Demeter knew that death was part of life, but living things didn't belong in the Underworld any more than dead things belonged in the sunlit realm!

"Mother..."

"Do not worry, I will see that such a thing does not happen to you again! It was bad enough what Ares tried to do to you, but then Hades had to go and..."

"Mother!" Kora's voice was firm, and given its mature timbre, it had a startling effect.

"...What?"

"I know you worried for me and missed me. I missed you too, but Hades is not like Ares. Yes, he did kidnap me, but he was never cruel to me. He never... forced me, or even *tried* to."

"Ever?" Demeter's disbelief was all too apparent, but Persephone had been fully prepared to deal with her mother's inevitable negative opinion of Hades.

"Ever," she repeated firmly as she stared at her mother. "I know you are angry with him and you deserve to be, but I would be lying if I said that Hades was a poor host. I don't want you thinking things that are untrue. Be assured that he has treated me with respect and dignity while I was there."

"Hm." Demeter frowned for a moment before she quickly collected herself. "Well, the important thing is that you are back with me, where you belong."

Inwardly, Persephone sighed. Hades was a man of his word, and she dreaded telling her mother about the inevitable.

o0o

Persephone stood next to the tub in her underwear as her mother heated the water to a temperature she deemed appropriate.

Demeter glanced up at her daughter, motioning to the pale silk tunic she wore under the dark gown she had been clad in moments earlier. She was disturbed by the physical changes that were apparent under the thin material. Kora had been kidnapped in the form of a barely pubescent girl. The metamorphosis was startling, and Demeter gestured impatiently, wanting to get her daughter in the water and wash away all traces of the Underworld. The water was scented with a few herbs that Demeter used when she wanted a purifying bath, and she had scattered flower petals, adding a delectable fragrance to the crisp, earthy odor of the herbs.

Persephone backed away, folding an arm across her chest shyly.

"I can undress and bathe myself, Mother." She was in no mood to be scrutinized by her mother, and was determined to set some boundaries in their relationship. After what had happened to her in the Underworld, she knew she would never have the relationship she had with her mother in the past. It could mean a good thing if Mother would treat her like an adult, but if Mother saw her experience with Hades as a reason to shelter her further...

Well, Persephone would have none of that. She breathed out slowly, eyeing her mother calmly.

"Is there something you are trying to hide from me? Has Hades done something to your body?" Demeter's tone became tight. *Gods!* Persephone fumed inwardly. Was she going to assume the worst about Hades in everything now?

"No! He has never harmed me." She squared her shoulders. "I know you are angry with him, but do not think that he has ever hurt or mistreated me. I already told you that."

Demeter stared at her daughter for several moments. The girl didn't seem hypnotized, her gaze was clear as she stared back. The older goddess did not sense any sort of evil magic or binding spells woven around her child, but this change bothered her more deeply than she cared to admit.

"A person who captures you and holds you prisoner can hardly be considered a good host," Demeter sighed as she rose. "I need to discuss our living arrangements with Metaniera." She retreated from the room, and Persephone silently bowed her head in gratitude at her small triumph. Perhaps eventually, Mother *could* understand...

She removed the last of her clothing and lifted

a leg, frowning to herself as she felt the warmth of the water. There was once a time where this warm temperature had been enough for her, and it was what Mother used for herself as well. But now, after having enjoyed the luxuries of hot springs and the soporific steaminess of Hades's bathtub, the water Mother had prepared for her felt downright cool. She lowered herself into the water, letting out a low groan as she glanced at the petals floating around her knees and breasts.

Despite the early winter that had ravaged Hellas, Eleusis maintained a mild winter, many plants and even crops continuing to grow well past harvest time. Its nights did get chilly, and a crisp breeze blew in from the open window.

Heat. Persephone knew that heat in one form or another was a gift that several gods, such as Hephaistos, Helios, or Hyperion, possessed. She wished she had such a Gift so she could heat up this water to her liking.

She closed her eyes, staying still so she didn't feel the water. She missed the Sun and the heat it would envelop her in, giving her skin a healthy tan that her mother encouraged. *Well, there's one thing Mother and I can definitely agree on*, she thought wryly. The sun was a life-giver, nurturing all life in the world, even night-dwellers. From such a simple form of energy, more complex energies could gain their strength. Plants and animals alike were able to convert this into life-energy, to keep themselves happy and healthy. The flow of energy was what kept the surface world vital, each and every living creature great or small part of the same web of life.

Now that she was back here, she was happy to feel the flow. It had been almost overwhelming being around mortals, even if her interaction with them was brief. Tomorrow, she looked forward to getting to know them better, particularly the princesses that Mother had mentioned. It had been a long time since she had had mortal peers, and she hoped that she wouldn't intimidate them too much – she saw how Metaniera had obviously deferred to Mother. She would just enjoy herself here and worry about Hades later.

Persephone focused on the pulse of vital energy surrounding her, feeling reassured by it, almost like being wrapped in a warm blanket. *Hmm.* She opened her eyes, looking down at the water. All humans and animals carried warmth within themselves, and even plants. Heat was heat, and didn't she have all of that pent-up energy from not being able to use it in Hades?

She closed her eyes, focusing on her energy. It felt almost like a kernel, tight-knotted and full of the latent energy she had to suppress before. *It shouldn't take much power to heat up this much water...* She imagined it radiating from her, a controlled amount of energy pulsing... *Just a bit...*

Ahh! Persephone let her head loll back as steam rose from the tub, bringing with it a sweet, clean smell.

o0o

Since she was connected to the Earth,

127

Demeter had been able to choke off the natural flow of energy so that plants could not grow. With her daughter returned, she undid her powerful curse. Truth be told, it felt nice letting go, because to maintain such a curse took a great amount of power and concentration. Between that and being angry at Zeus and Hades, she hadn't had much focus for anything else.

She still needed to decide what to do about her daughter and herself. So far, she had found her stay in Eleusis to be satisfying and rewarding. The city had been struggling before, and without her intervention, it might have been wiped from history. Much as she had done for Iasion and Enna, she did for this city and its rulers. Its people were grateful, and now the city's worship belonged to Demeter much like Zeus was master in Olympia. No mortal could survive without a harvest, so the residents of this city – and the refugees that would remember and tell of the great famine – would remember her generosity and fury for centuries to come.

The island she had previously occupied was no longer a safe place because now everybody knew of its location. Would it be prudent to hide Kora elsewhere or keep her here in this city? The princesses would be appropriate company. Hmm. Not a bad idea, really...

Demeter returned to her room. She had already designated its adjoining chamber as her daughter's room, previously used as her private meditation room and where she would sometimes take Demophon. She would be able to keep her daughter close and ensure that Hades didn't have any lasting influence on her.

The faint moisture of steam enveloped her face as she entered her room and closed the door, sniffing at the fragrance in the air. It bore the familiar smell of herbs, but the steam confused her. She approached the tub, seeing Kora's head lolling back in relaxation, her knees loosely spread and just above the surface of the water. Even under the warm, cheerful glow from the fire, Kora's skin still looked unnaturally pale, further emphasizing the color of her nipples and pubic triangle. Demeter quickly looked away, silently cursing her brother. Why would Hades do something like this? Did he find it amusing?

"How did you heat up the water?" Demeter asked as she bent down to pick up the silk undergarment, amazed at the sheer softness of the fabric. Almost unnatural, really. Unbeknownst to her, Underworld silk was finer than even silk in the surface world, so she was close to correct in her thought.

"It was not warm enough, so I decided to add a little more heat." She shrugged as she casually crossed her arms over her chest.

"I have always heated it up the same way for both of us."

"I just wanted more heat." The younger goddess stared back at her. Irritated by this defiance, Demeter frowned, but set her jaw as she draped a towel across the stool, still holding onto the silk.

"Do not take that away, please. I want to sleep

in it," Persephone said. Her mother stared at her as if surprised.

"This thing comes from Hades, there is no reason for you to keep it. I have some nice things for you to wear."

"It is comfortable, and I like it." Her heart was pounding, but she remained still.

"Is it? It is too slippery, this fabric cannot be real."

"But it is. It comes from the cocoons of worms. The threads are very, very fine and -"

"Kora!" Demeter always said her name in that tone when she was especially irritated, such as when her daughter kept asking her questions or insisting on going outside when she should be at the loom, weaving or spinning.

"I have *worried* about you for *months*, and when I finally get you back, you are telling me that you want to keep something from the *man who kidnapped you!*"

Persephone let out a defeated sigh. "I am sorry, Mother." She did not want to go to bed in a fight, so she decided to simply drop the matter. She would be going back to Hades soon enough anyway.

"There there, it's all right." Demeter quickly changed moods, her shoulders slumping in relaxation as she smiled. "I will get you some warm and comfortable things, and you can have a snack and go to bed. Tomorrow is a new day."

"Yes, Mother." Persephone *was* tired, so she didn't argue with her mother's bedtime command. If anything, her discussions – and arguments –

with Hades had taught her how to deal with certain situations, and she felt better equipped to voice herself to Mother than she had ever before. There were times to fight and other times to simply be silent or retreat.

Having grown under Demeter's power, the dates and grapes she was given after her bath tasted robust, and she could practically taste the warmth of their traces of vital energy. After starving herself for over four months, she could eat! Her obvious enthusiasm and gratitude for the food clearly improved Mother's mood, so Persephone remained cheerful, using the food as an excuse to not speak or answer Mother's questions.

oOo

Demeter glanced down at her sleeping daughter one last time before leaving her room. Now that Kora was safe and asleep, she felt confident about leaving Eleusis and using her Gift in other parts of Hellas. The curse was gone so that everything could grow again, but growing took time, and Hellas simply did not have the time to wait for the next harvest. She would have to cast a different sort of magic so that things could grow quickly as she brought the earth to a temporary summer.

Eleusis remained cloaked under her protective magic, and Demeter went on to the nearest cities to feed their starving denizens. Other gods were at work as well, using their own Gifts to restore life to Hellas.

Persephone groaned softly as she stirred awake, blinking at the influx of sunlight that filled the room. It had been so long since she had woken up to light – real, actual sunlight – and she was disoriented for a moment. The linen she was on top of was coarse compared to the soft silk and velvet sheets she had grown accustomed to, and after living in a palace made of black marble, the warm hues of the clay and earth around her was jarring.

She swung her legs over the side of the bed, feeling the slightly cool floor under her feet and looked around, her heart pounding a bit harder than usual as she took in her surroundings. When she was in the Underworld, she had ached for the surface. Yet now here she was, missing the dark surroundings to which she had grown accustomed – and even fond of. The dark and elegant architecture, the splendid wall hangings and decorations, the large and soft bed where she had spent many happy nights with Hades...

Aidon, she reminded herself gently. Aidon, the name she whispered into his ear during their intimate times, or when they were alone, basking in one another's presence. *Aidoneus*, Lord of the one of the few and mighty provinces of Dis, the King of the Hellenic Underworld, and a deity that even the other gods feared. One of the proud few of the small group of chthonic deities; a group that

Persephone herself was now part of. She thought of Hades's earnestly uttered promise, and let out a slow exhale.

She rose to her feet, feeling disoriented, as if her limbs were now different. With a frown, she looked down at herself, wondering why she should feel so awkward in her own body.

Her limbs weren't long and graceful. Her breasts and hips were gone. In fact, her body was entirely devoid of all traces of womanhood. Quickly lifting the hem of the tunic she had slept in – a considerably looser fit than the night before – her horror increased as she saw that she hadn't been mistaken. Everything she had gained in Dis was now gone. With the awareness and clarity that she had gained in her time away, she could feel her mother's magic wrapped around her, stifling her.

It was bad enough that Demeter had blighted Hellas with her wrath to get her daughter back. Once the Harvest Goddess got her daughter back, that simply wasn't enough! No, Mother had to turn her back into the way she thought her daughter should be!

For so long, Demeter had maintained her hold on her daughter, trimming the branches so to speak, as if Persephone was another plant to take care of and protect, like a little flower.

Persephone remembered the pomegranate tree in Hades. She was like that tree – lush, grown, inviting yet mysterious. She had thrived in a way she had never thought she would, and Mother refused to see that. Without even asking her daughter how she felt, she had seen fit to return her to this... cursed physical state of perpetual girlhood!

Examination of the chests along the wall revealed girlish clothing, chitons and tunics in the style that she had worn a decade ago. There was not one single womanly accoutrement to be found – no jewelry, mirrors, or other paraphernalia that she had become accustomed to in the Underworld. And more embarrassingly, in another chest were remnants of her childhood – a stuffed doll, clay toys, a little spinner, things that she had abandoned a long time ago. Now it was obvious that Mother had stored all of her daughter's castaways.

There was also wool, various colored yarn, skeins and other things needed to do weaving. Persephone had never cared much for this, and Demeter knew it. She had spent much of her time on the island weaving and making cloth, using good linen along with soft and fine wool, using rare and vibrant dyes provided by Mother, but the quality of the material didn't increase her passion for the craft.

Her mother was always insisting that weaving was a vital art for every woman to know and to take in with passion. A woman might have other interests, but household arts was a huge priority, even to a goddess who also loved the outdoors, and Demeter often used Nature as inspiration for her designs. Persephone saw it as it was; something to keep her obedient and occupied.

Persephone touched her face, feeling how soft

it the angles of her face were before she looked down at her flat chest.

An outraged shriek escaped between her lips.

Chapter XLV

oOo

No! No! *No!* **Gods, no!** Persephone didn't think she could ever get any more furious than when she realized that Hades fed her the pomegranate seeds, but the seething, boiling fury that threatened to choke her off rivaled than any anger she had ever felt in the past. For so long, she had eagerly anticipated womanhood. In Enna, she had seen older girls grow into women, and had been impatient to see these changes in her own body. Becoming a woman meant she would be treated like one, so as she entered her thirteenth summer, she anticipated these changes.

After several more unchanging summers, her envy of the nymphs grew. After a while, she just stopped paying attention to her body, and then it had all come upon her in a rush in the Underworld. It had been a bit scary but exciting. She liked how Hades looked at her blossoming curves, encouraging her body to catch up with her mind and true age all the while treating her as an adult despite how she looked.

She felt light-headed as she considered all the progress she had made, only to have it wiped out in one night while she was not even aware of it!

Barely a moment after she was able to fully register what had just happened to her, Mother rushed into the room, her eyes wide with concern, having heard that terrible shriek.

"Kora! What is wrong? Did you have a

nightmare?"

"Worse! Look!" She gestured to herself, tugging on the too-big tunic.

"Have no worry, there are plenty of clothes that fit you." She gestured to the chests her daughter had just rummaged through.

"No! Not that! I mean, this!" She motioned to her nonexistent curves, her hands making a sweeping gesture along the sides of her body.

"Oh, *that*." Demeter flicked her hand dismissively, "I removed Hades's influence from you. You are as you were before he kidnapped you."

"I do not want to be a little girl!"

"This is for the best, Kora."

"No, it's not! I like the way I was... the way I *should* be!"

"Should be? Do not be silly. Now, get dressed, and I will get morning supper for both of us. Then I can properly introduce you to Celeus and Metaniera, and you can meet their children."

Ugh. She certainly didn't want to be introduced as Kora, the perpetual girl.

"No. I am not letting them see me like *this*."

"There is nothing wrong with the way you look." Resolutely, Demeter turned to the chest closest to her and opened it, pulling out a few articles of clothing. All of it suited for a child, of course.

"Yes, there is! I am not a child!"

"You are *my* child. Now get dressed."

"No."

Demeter's jaw tightened visibly, but

137

Persephone squared her shoulders.

"Kora, I know you have been through a lot, but I will *not* tolerate disobedience." She used what Persephone had always called the 'most-serious' tone, the kind that had guaranteed obedience in the past. Mother used it very rarely, so when she did, Persephone knew that she had to obey or face punishment.

Then again, she was no longer little Kora despite what she might look like right now.

"I will not tolerate being treated like a child," Persephone replied calmly, in that slightly deep but lovely voice that she had grown into, managing it despite the reversal of her physical form.

"Mother knows best." Demeter maintained her most-serious tone, placing her fist on her hip as she glowered down at her daughter, stunned by this defiance. What *had* Hades done to her?

In response, Persephone closed her eyes, balling her hands into fists as she shut out her mother's voice. She could feel the constricting magic around her tighten even more, and her heart pounded as she considered the possibility that Mother might actually make her look even younger.

Oh hell no. That was *most certainly* not going to happen! She concentrated with all her might, feeling her energy pool up within and expand, her latent power surging through her veins. It filled every fiber of her being, threatening to overwhelm her, needing more room as it struggled against the confines of her small form. The pressure increased from outside as Demeter concentrated her own energy, and Persephone felt almost as if Mother was trying to squeeze her into a small package. There simply wasn't enough room, and she started to panic, feeling claustrophobic within her own body.

Make room! With a fresh surge of energy, she pushed against the invisible force trying to restrain her, allowing her power to fill the small form she inhabited. *Make everything bigger. More room!* She imagined it pulsing under her skin, filling her almost as instantaneously as an explosion, and a pained cry tore itself from her throat as she collapsed to her knees.

Persephone shakily rose to her feet. She felt light-headed, but her body was *right* again. Looking down, she saw that she had curves where they should be and her graceful limbs stretched out from her torso; she was just as she was meant to be. When she focused on her mother, she noticed that whatever had just happened put her mother through a great shock as well. She had her palm pressed to her forehead, her other hand against the wall for support.

"Never.... *ever* do that to me again." Persephone raised her chin as she gazed at her mother. "I stopped being a child a long time ago, though you refused to see it."

"How can you want to be like this after what has happened? Ares tried to force himself on you and Hades kidnapped you! I am simply trying to protect you!" Of course, Demeter would not admit that it was more than just that. She had lost Iasion, and did not wish to lose another loved one.

"I do not need to be treated like a child for my protection. I can take care of myself." Persephone was calm and assured. She thought of the incident with Ares. Now that she knew she was a goddess, she understood certain aspects of her Gift more. Being able to heat up her own water last night had been an exercise in exploring her abilities.

Hysterical at this sudden, unexpected development, Demeter involuntarily lashed out with her magic, trying to bind her daughter into her previous form again.

To apply her Gift, Persephone had to create a mental image. She did so when she wanted to coax a plant to grow, and it had been an effective technique to focus against Ares or to protect herself from the Styx. As she felt the fresh assault of her mother's power, she envisioned a defense, something that would hold fast against the binding attempt. She imagined extending some of her own power to create a bodysuit that would keep anyone else's magic from reaching her body. It was inspired from when Hades would wrap her body in his shadows. To her surprise, the armor she saw inside her mind was black even though she had imagined forming it from her own glowing life-energy.

When she looked down at her hands, there was no visible trace of any protective coating whatsoever, but she could feel it, encasing her in a snug but comfortable embrace, her own life-energy separated and insulated from Mother's own by these invisible shadows.

It made her feel safe. With this invisible shield, Persephone barely felt the magic that was trying to assault her form. It was as if the dark energy surrounding her was swallowing, even *converting* Mother's magic into energy for her own use, feeding her defense. If she knew of an appropriate word, she might have used 'recycling'.

"Stop that, it will not work." Her voice snapped Mother out of her frenzied state, and Demeter blinked.

"How did you..." She didn't mind letting Kora use her Gift to help plants grow. Gods needed to use their Gifts in one way or another, but she had never taught her daughter anything other than how to nurture plants.

"It does not matter *how* I did it." Persephone looked down at her hands again. "I may be your daughter, but I am not a child. Furthermore, I am a Goddess in my own right."

"Goddess? You?" Demeter had never counted on Kora finding out.

"I know my paternity."

"Iasion was your father!" Demeter automatically replied. It was almost the truth, for Demeter absolutely refused to acknowledge Zeus as Kora's father after what he had done. Her husband had loved Kora with his whole heart; why deny him the happiness of having a child? She had tried to have more with him, but apparently her own power inadvertently overwhelmed his seed, an unfortunate occurrence that was often the burden of female divinities. Iasion was Kora's father, this she had repeated to herself so many times that after a while, she began to believe it, except for her moments of greatest self-doubt, regret, or anger.

"I will always consider him as such, but I know who sired me." It made sense, since Hades told her that Zeus had given his blessing. Why would he do that to just anyone? Why would Hades go to him in the first place? At least Zeus had wanted her to join the ranks of Olympus. Goddess of Spring, not a bad idea. Of course, becoming the bride of Hades made her uncertain as to how that would work out. "He is to be blamed for this..." Persephone gestured a loose circle in the air with her hand as she tried to say the most appropriate word for the situation. Mess? Mishap? Affair? Matter? "Situation." That was the most neutral word she could muster up.

"Who would tell you such a thing?"

"Well, he did give Hades his blessing... Had I had a different father, Zeus would not have bothered to see me back then. I remember him asking me these questions and granting me a wish. Hades only confirmed it for me."

"No, no, no...." Demeter muttered, starting to shake her head, trying to deny the fact that Kora now knew the much-abhorred truth.

"Oh, worry not. I love Father. I will always feel that way. After what Zeus did to you, and knowing what he has done to others... I cannot say that I am thrilled to acknowledge my paternity." She shrugged and flipped her braid over her shoulder, revealing the elegant planes of her neck and jaw. "But the fact remains."

"Kora..."

"No." Persephone shook her head. "Kora was the little girl. She is no more. I am Persephone."

"I will not call you that." Demeter was indignant, wondering where the hell Hades got the nerve to give Kora a different name. Kora's physical appearance matched her true age, but the sudden change unnerved Demeter. She would always be Kora; she refused to let her brother's machinations change that!

"Very well. You do not have to *say* it, but I will not respond to Kora, and I will inform everyone here that I am Persephone." Persephone was furious at what Mother had done to her, but was resolved to stay calm. If she threw a fit, as she sorely wanted to right now, Mother would just have an excuse to think of her as a child, and she just didn't feel like fighting again.

"I am happy to be up here with you, but I cannot and will not be treated like a child. I am a grown woman. Now... these clothes are not appropriate for a woman. I am going to need something else..." Silently, she opened a chest, lifting out the largest pieces of cloth and laying them next to her pins.

"I would like some privacy when I get dressed, please." Persephone lifted her chin before raising her eyebrow, the way Mother had done to her so often in the past. It was the first time she had ever done it... and it felt *great*. Mother stared at her levelly for several moments before retreating from the small chamber.

A thick linen cloth the color of freshly turned

earth made up her skirt, ending just below her ankles. A green rectangle in a cheerful verdant hue and woven with red poppies made up her knee-length chiton.

"Cloe?" she called out, having gotten so used to having the ethereal servant around to help her with her hair. Persephone smiled sheepishly as she realized that Cloe would not be able to appear here.

Without Cloe, she had a hard time with her hair, but she managed by herself and braided it before wrapping it in a sash and tying it in a bun. The result was practical and attractive, and she patted it with her hands to make sure she had done decently. There was not a mirror to be found, but she wasn't vain enough to be concerned about it right now. There was one thing she did need – sandals. All the ones in here were child-size. With some improvisation, she fashioned suitable footwear from what had been meant to be a pair of winter booties.

She wanted to refrain from asking Mother for everything she needed. If Mother was to see that she was an adult, she would not run to her every time she did not have something that Mother purposely kept from her.

Besides, she was hungry. Well, she was certain that Mother wouldn't try to keep food from her!

She pulled back the drape that covered the doorway to her room, seeing Mother sit in one of the chairs, staring off at a spot above her daughter's shoulder.

"Mother?" Persephone asked with obvious concern, approaching the older woman.

"What did Hades do to you?" Demeter asked as she slowly turned her focus to her daughter.

"He did nothing. I am the way I want to be. Hades encouraged me to be myself. I am still your daughter, and I missed you when I was in the Underworld. I missed the sunshine and the flowers and *life*! I have longed to return to the surface world so many times, but I must be myself. I am not a little girl, and stopped being one a long time ago. You just refused to see it or let my body grow."

"Look at the attention being a woman has gained you! Need you be reminded of what happened with Ares? I kept you well-protected. You never lacked for anything."

"You never gave me *freedom*. You tried to keep me a child forever after you took me from the home I knew and loved. Now I am wise enough to be able to protect myself. You saw that just now when you tried to make me a girl again. And I made it so that Ares couldn't do it to any other woman. Should any god – or man – ever try *anything*, I can easily defend myself. My safety is no longer an issue."

Mother and daughter stared at one another for several long moments. Demeter clenched and unclenched her jaw several times.

"Yet Hades was able to keep you captive."

Persephone refused to be swayed by that answer. "Had he captured you, you would be unable to escape, as well, and you know it. I noticed it right away, there was no life-energy. Hermes could not fly down there. It is no wonder you all dread that realm. I could have done no more than you could, it is not my fault that he is such a powerful God." She gazed at Mother with a measuring expression.

"Out of all the gods that ever took an interest in you – or anybody else – it had to be him. He has never seemed to show any interest in women until now! Why did he have to choose my precious daughter?"

"Sometimes things just... happen." Persephone shrugged. "I learned a lot about myself down there, and so much about so many things, but right now I am just happy to be here, and I intend to enjoy every moment of it. Now, I am very hungry, and I know you are too." She looked around, finding no food items on the table.

"Are we to eat with the family then?" she asked. Mother nodded hesitantly. That had been the plan, at least before the girl broke through her binding-magic. She had already told Metaniera to arrange for seating and dishes for them. She was a mighty deity and could do as she pleased, including skipping meals. As she looked at her daughter, she debated doing just that. But if she did, Kora would know that this bothered her overmuch. She might want to be called Persephone, but nothing could stop Demeter from using 'Kora' in her mind. She refused to let the jackassery of her brothers get any further than she could prevent.

"Wonderful, then!" Persephone reached out to

take her mother's hands, and Demeter allowed herself to be pulled to her feet. Besides, there were others who were responsible for this situation, and her energy would be better expended upon dealing with them.

"Oh, would you tell me their names? It seems only appropriate."

"Certainly." Demeter was happy to focus on a new subject. "You saw Metaniera last night. Her husband is Celeus, and they have six children. The oldest is Triptolemus, almost your age. Then four daughters – Thalassa, Melinoe, Aethra, and Eirene. And a baby boy, Demophon."

"And how did you come to live here?" Persephone was eager to know how Eleusis had come to become a fertile refuge in the bleak landscape of famine.

"When I wandered this earth, I disguised myself as an old woman. The princesses showed me extraordinary kindness, and their family took me in. I was a nurse to their baby, and the people here were so kind that I decided to bless them. The family knows I am a Goddess now, of course, but I do not flaunt it in the city."

"A mortal identity? I like the sound of that. I do not want to flaunt myself."

She doesn't want to flaunt, Demeter thought with relief. Kora was startlingly beautiful, and the last thing she needed was vanity. Right now, her hair was just a bit messy, but enough to give her a more 'human' look, and her garb was modest.

"Yes. Modesty and humility are traits that more people should emulate." Demeter nodded approvingly.

Persephone had a few choice words to say, but remained silent as Mother spoke of the building of the grand temple that they would visit later. The people of Eleusis regarded Demeter as their primary deity. Worship of the other gods had been all but abandoned for the practicality of the mighty Goddess who put food into their very mouths. *She might have fed the people here, but so many others starved...* What was the rationale in that? All these lives for a kidnapping?

Her thoughts were interrupted as they came to the banquet room, where east-facing windows revealed a generous view of the gardens. A quick count of the people seated at the table revealed that the entire royal family was here. Two empty seats sat between Metaniera and the oldest princess, Thalassa. Persephone estimated her to be seventeen or eighteen. Like her mother and sisters, she was raven-haired. She let herself be directed to sit next to Thalassa and did a quick survey of the table's occupants.

Celeus was a man in his middle years, and could not be called handsome, but he had a pleasant dignity to his features that more than made up for it. He bowed his head as she took her seat. Persephone smiled and nodded back. Next to him his eldest child sat, his features a mix of his father and mother's. The four princesses looked like one another from a distance but for their sizes, but upon closer inspection, one could see the subtle but distinct differences in their faces.

The baby was being held by a servant just

behind Metaniera.

"Good morning, everyone. I am Persephone. It is nice to meet all of you. Would you mind telling me your names?" Even though she had already been told them beforehand, she wanted to get an impression of everybody before she shared food with them. Hades had taught her that; how to read someone upon introduction. Of course, she wasn't quite as good as he was, but she had practiced on the residents of Elysium and Tartarus alike.

Celeus introduced himself first, and it went from oldest to youngest. Some of them were curious, others apprehensive, but she simply smiled at all of them. As everybody else ate, she sat back, listening politely, enjoying the food more than the company.

oOo

Oh, gods. How much more of this would Hades have to endure? He had supped alone and then gone to a bed that felt exceptionally cold despite the thick blankets and intense fire. He was still alone when he woke up, and there was nowhere in the Underworld that she might be hiding from him, since she was with her mother!

He almost regretted letting her return to the surface world. He had but to remind himself that he had laid his incontrovertible claim on her and that he was free to come and take it as he pleased. If he truly desired, he could keep her a literal prisoner, kept in the confines of his bedchamber for his sole pleasure. However, watching her grow and become the woman he knew she was meant to be was more rewarding. He enjoyed her defiance and challenge.

This walk wasn't doing much to distract him. He was tempted to go up there, and it had not even been a full day! He was usually so patient, a month should be nothing to a god that had lived for centuries!

"Someone looks sad and grumpy on this lovely day," Hekate said from behind him. Hades stiffened and slowly turned towards his unwelcome companion.

"What is it?"

"Come on, Hades. Everybody knows that Demeter got her darling daughter back. It is about time she did, this has gone on long enough."

"I know. That is why I let her go back."

There was something about Hades's words that raised Hekate's suspicions. "Let her go back?" she repeated. He nodded. She narrowed her eyes.

"Oh, of course. You would not just *let her go*, would you? Not without making sure she would come back..."

He gave her a tight smile, and her eyes widened.

"Did she eat..."

"Yes."

"And I suppose Demeter does not know," she replied tartly.

"Not yet. I figured she would want some time with Persephone before she gets the bad news."

"You are not *still* putting this off, are you?"

"No, no. I have set a deadline." He shook his head firmly. No more postponement. "You must keep this a secret, though." There was clear warning in his tone, and Hekate had no desire to rouse his wrath again. She would wait and see what happened before deciding to get involved, if need be.

"Very well."

"Persephone will return here on the winter solstice. I will talk to Demeter."

"Good." Hekate crossed her arms. "If you and Zeus had bothered to talk to her in the beginning..."

"What is done is done. Let Demeter and Persephone have their time."

oOo

Persephone sat in the weaving room. Even though Metaniera and her daughters were royalty, it was still expected of high-born women to know the arts of the household. A practical woman might rule over a household of servants, but by having intimate knowledge of the chores required for a family's comfort, she was better able to determine and care for the needs of her household.

Demeter certainly hadn't considered her own daughter above the routines that fulfilled the basic needs of those who performed them. The weaving room wasn't quite the place Persephone would have wanted as a place to get to know the Princesses. She would much rather be taking a walk or sitting outside, but at this time of the year after the harvest, women did a lot of spinning and weaving, so this was an ordinary activity even in her old life. It was kind of odd to think of her past as 'old', but she had changed so much that she barely recognized herself.

As some new dyed wool and linen was brought up in a basket by a servant, they went about comparing it with their existing supplies and deciding what kind of pattern or color to use. The colors were vivid, and Persephone could see her mother's hand in the making of the yarn.

The oldest princess – Thalassa, she reminded herself – had a project that was nearly finished. Her color of choice was pale blue, and she had skillfully woven a pattern of leaves and multicolored flowers along the border. Doubtless this young woman liked weaving. The next one was Melinoe, and Mother was especially proud of her because she was now a priestess at the temple. She gave Persephone a friendly smile, so the goddess smiled back. Her loom had a project that looked just started; all she could see was pale green threads.

Aethra and Eirene had smaller looms with plain cloth in them. That kind of linen was generally used for underwear, light clothing, or bandages. She glanced at the youngest Princess, noticing the impatient jiggle of Eirene's foot. *Looks like someone here shares my dislike of weaving*. She smiled at Eirene before Mother filled her line of vision.

"Pick out what colors you want and you can

get right to work." Demeter gestured to the empty loom. Persephone held back a groan before giving the obligatory glance towards the palette.

Barely registering her choice, she reached for the thick bundle of dark purple yarn. She was in no mood for pale hues, and started to thread it into her loom.

"Pick another color," Mother said. Persephone steeled herself against her mother's voice. She wasn't interested in a pattern! All she wanted was a nice purple chiton, since the clothing Mother had left for her were all light or muted colors.

"This purple is lovely on its own and needs nothing to accent it," she replied calmly as she continued her work. She hadn't woven since she came to the Underworld. And why would she, when there was so much to do down there? Even after so long, her fingers still moved nimbly, moving as if on their own as she let her mind wander.

Demeter was about to argue further, but she quieted herself. Kora had made it more than clear that she was willing to fight. She had the power to do so – repelling her own Gift was testament enough of her daughter's strength. Best not to fight in front of the mortals, and over such a trifling affair at that. She wanted Kora to enjoy her time here, so let her weave what she wanted. As long as she was occupied, at least...

"Hmm, so it is." She nodded before returning to her own loom, leaving a slightly stunned Persephone in her wake.

That... was *nice*. It was what she wanted from

Mother, for her to listen to her and actually respect her. As her hands moved up and down the loom, she let her mind wander again, thinking of Morpheus. She had visited him a couple of times to try to understand her dreams better. He was very taciturn and didn't seem to enjoy long visits, but he was always polite and respectful to her. The mortals were not the only ones who suffered from Mother's wrath. Mother had mentioned going to other cities and throughout the countryside to quickly grow food for the starving populace.

Persephone wanted to do her part. She wanted to be a Goddess – not just by blood, but by deed. She had a marvelous Gift, and she would use it. She was practically bursting with it, but she was able to bear with it for a while by expending some of her nervous energy on her weaving and listening with half an ear to the chatter of a room full of girls and women. After getting used to the sometimes-deafening silence in Hades's palace, it was startling – yet it felt good – to be surrounded by so much light and noise.

oOo

After a while, Demeter returned her attention to her daughter. The younger goddess had remained silent while everyone else chatted with one another, her hands moving quickly along the taut yarn, weaving with the quickness of experience. The weave was nice and tight, the threads set up properly. Demeter could find no

154

real technical flaw in her daughter's work, but it was clear that Kora did not have her mind set on the project before her. Her gaze was focused – albeit distantly – at something outside.

Well, it was important to know household crafts, but it was just as important to spend time outside. Some men thought it was better for women to be shut indoors all day long, whether for 'practicality' or 'safety' or 'women's work' or whatever excuse they could come up with. But as a nature-goddess knew, everyone needed to be outside at least sometimes. It was from Nature that mankind gained everything they needed to fulfill their needs – minerals, plants and animals alike for food, shelter, and clothing. And not just for survival, but also for enjoyment. Each of the seasons had its own delights to take in, and she could happily recall many a time she and her daughter had gone out for walks simply to enjoy their surroundings.

She had been hired as Demophon's nurse, but she also spent time with the Princesses, showing them what Nature had to offer. All of the girls were eager to learn what she had to teach, especially Melinoe and Eirene.

When Metaniera's schedule permitted, she would join them for their outdoor excursions. Demophon's illness had been a great strain on the family, but now Metaniera could spend time with her daughters and not have to constantly worry about anything else. It had brought them closer together, and now that Kora was home, she could spend time with her daughter and trust that

Metaniera and her own children could take care of their own family dynamics without her help.

She poured herself a cup of fruit juice mixed with wine, and after a moment, poured one for her daughter. Kora nodded in acknowledgment, but she continued to stare off as she took a sip.

It was almost noonday before Demeter deemed that enough work had been done. Like her daughter, she wanted to go outside. Besides, she still had a lot of work to do in Hellas, and Metaniera and her daughters would keep Kora occupied. Her daughter still treated the others with respect despite knowing that she was a full-fledged goddess. At least Hades hadn't made her prideful or rude, thank goodness.

Demeter rose from her seat and gently touched her daughter on the shoulder. Kora's hands fluttered to a stop, and she gazed up with an open, relaxed expression.

"Come outside with me for a moment."

"Yes, Mother."

Demeter came to a stop in the hallway. It was quiet, with no servant in the immediate vicinity.

"The duties of a Goddess are many. I have work to do, so I must leave you alone. You will have Metaniera and the princesses to keep you company. There are nice areas around the Palace where the princesses like to go to, and you could use one another's company."

Persephone glanced at her mother for several moments, considering. No, she would not object to such an arrangement. She wanted some time away from Mother, after all, so she could explore this world by herself. She could investigate the city and learn more about what had happened up here since her disappearance.

But not right now. She was a goddess too, after all. Her gift was like Mother's, and she wanted to end as much suffering as she could. Why should she sit here and twiddle her thumbs when she could be helping? It would give her a chance to get to know more people, and be recognized in her own right. She didn't want to merely be known as the kidnapped bride whose disappearance was responsible for the great catastrophe that had nearly wiped out Hellas.

"That sounds pleasant... but I am a goddess as well. My Gift reflects yours, does it not?"

"You are young yet, and inexperienced in your powers." Demeter knew that outright saying 'No' would cause an argument with her strong-willed daughter, so much like Kora, she was finding her own way around the situation.

"What better way to gain experience than with an older and wiser person?" Persephone's smile was faint. "Of course, I could just go by myself and see what I can do..."

"You are not going by yourself!"

"You know I am capable of it."

Demeter let out a low sigh. "I do not want you going to those places just yet."

"Because you do not want me to see what you have done to them, do you?" Persephone hadn't been counting on dealing with this question right now, but if Mother was going to stubbornly deny her opportunities and try to hide what she had done...

"Kora..."

With an annoyed hiss, Persephone spun around and stalked off. Just when things had been going nicely, Mother had to be like this again! As she heard Mother's angry demand to stop and turn back, she continued walking, her steps long and fast. She would have liked to spend time with Mother learning how to use her powers and showing her mother what she was capable of, but if she had to do this alone, then she would!

She heard Mother's rapid footsteps, and only quickened her pace, bursting outside and nearly gliding down the stairs.

Demeter was a sturdily-built woman, but she was surprisingly agile, and reached out to grab her daughter's arm. To her utter shock, her hand closed in on thin air – and her daughter was gone. She blinked and looked around, but the gardens were empty.

oOo

Persephone reeled back as Mother glanced right through her, calling out for her.

Mother, I'm right here... She almost said that out loud, and stood still for several moments as her mother continued her frantic searching. *Can't she see me? How can she... not?*

Persephone became aware of a faint, buzzing feeling at the back of her throat. She had been aware of Mother just about to grab her and wishing that Mother couldn't see her. *So I got my wish, huh?*

She let out her breath slowly, focusing on that faint buzz as she pondered her current situation. Where had she gotten this Gift? Was this just a defense against Mother, or was she invisible to others? Seeing Mother look so angry almost caused her to call out and reveal herself, but this opportunity was too good to not explore. What would Mother do when she became visible? She didn't know if it was possible, but what if Mother tried to keep her from using this Gift?

Oh wait, she can't. Persephone had managed to make her body the way she wanted despite Mother's best efforts. She could use her Gift to defend herself, and this new discovery added a new dimension to her possibilities. *Goodness...*

She carefully backed out, not making any noise. Being invisible didn't mean much if people could still hear you...

As she made her way back into the Palace, she recalled what Hades had said about invisibility requiring great focus. He had his magical helmet forged so that it would enable him to use his Gift at an unconscious level without becoming tired or distracted.

As soon as she was in the pantry, which was dark and unoccupied at the moment, she relaxed, feeling the buzzing subside. She slid down to the floor, leaning against a rack that held jugs of ale and wine. She let her gaze wander along this part of the pantry, noticing roots and tubers hanging from the eaves. The place smelled a bit musky, but also of a pleasant mélange of fresh and stored foods. She could smell goat cheese, and was hungry for some.

Well, as long as I'm here... She found a block of the cheese on a table used for food preparation, wrapped up in a piece of cloth. She wrested off a piece, nibbling the cheese and enjoying its powerful flavor. When the chatter of servants alerted her, she concentrated on not being seen. Even if it didn't work, the servants wouldn't dare reprimand her for taking some cheese. They knew that the old nursemaid was really a goddess, and that this was her daughter. Like Metaniera, they understood that she was the reason for their good fortune.

As Persephone stood there holding the cheese, the two old women walked right past her, casually conversing about something one of their grand-children had done. They came back with roots and various herbs and tubers for the midday supper. As they did, she waved to them, her hand mere inches from one woman's eyes. *Not even a flinch.* They couldn't see her!

She left the kitchens, maintaining her focus as she passed the oblivious eldest princess until she came to her mother's room. It was empty, so she ducked into her room and made herself visible again.

That was incredible! Had Hades ever anticipated anything like this? He said that he didn't know what she might be able to do. For a God who knew so much, he knew nothing about her Gift. He admitted that he couldn't even begin to guess what they were, for Gifts appeared in the most seemingly random places. No one knew the Gift of any god when he or she was born. Many of Poseidon's immortal children were sea-gods, and it was true that Gifts could often be inherited. Like Mother, she could make plants grow. After learning of her paternity, she wondered if she would gain any of Zeus's Gifts, but so far, displayed none of his abilities.

Truth be told, invisibility was way better, as Persephone was quickly finding out. No wonder Hades enjoyed it so much. As she sat on her bed, her head lolled against the wall. She still needed to figure out how to get to other places. She couldn't run fast like Hermes, or fly, at least as far as she knew. Mother had this way of quickly moving using the earth, almost like Hades's teleportation. It wasn't just plants that Demeter could control, it was the earth itself, which was why her curse had been so devastating. She could also create violent earthquakes if she willed it.

Persephone needed to get to Olympus. She wanted to confront the man who had sired her, and to gain recognition as a goddess in her own right. It wasn't for vanity that she desired this, it was to show them – especially Zeus – that she wasn't little Kora anymore. Since she was bound to Hades, she was a queen in her own right, companion of the dreaded Lord of the Underworld. A bit morbid, but fascinating nonetheless.

As she heard her mother call out again, she frowned before steeling herself. This had gone on long enough; she had already proved to herself that she could get away if she needed.

She became invisible again before emerging from her room, following the sound of Mother's voice. Demeter was in the kitchen, looking around as the servants did their best to help her. She willed herself visible again and paused just outside, peering in as if surprised to see her mother.

"Mother, here I am!" she called out. Demeter's head snapped in her direction, and she made a beeline towards her daughter. Persephone quickly backed away from the doorway to give her mother a wide berth.

"Where did you go?" Mother hissed.

"I have been here in the Palace the whole time, Mother."

"Where did you hide?"

"I was not *hiding*." Persephone shook her head slowly. "I just needed a few moments to myself. But I came back to you, did I not?"

"How did you..."

"I just did." She shrugged, refusing to elaborate on the subject further. "Look, I have no wish to fight with you. But I do not appreciate being treated like that. I know what you did, Mother. I had nightmares of it."

"... Nightmares?"

"I saw dead and dying people and animals... children crying for their mothers who could not feed them. You lashed out against the world because you lost your child, but you did not stop to think of the mothers who would lose theirs!"

Demeter took a step back. No one had ever...

put it that way to her before. Yes, she knew people were dying, but she had been too angry to think about it.

"I..." She gazed at her daughter. Persephone glared right back, her eyes glazed over with unshed tears, her cheeks rosy with fury as she stood there with her shoulder squared, her fists clenched.

Demeter blinked and slowly turned her eyes away before taking a deep breath.

"Come with me. If we do it together, we can move more quickly." She looked back at her daughter. "Bring a cowl."

Persephone almost rolled her eyes at this, but she quickly returned to her room to wrap one around her shoulders. If anything, she could just give it someone who needed it a lot more than she would.

Chapter XLVI

oOo

The earth shifted and groaned before parting to reveal Demeter and her daughter. Mount Olympus was visible in the far distance, but what held their attention was the city before them. Not one bit of green could be seen anywhere, and Persephone shuddered as she studied the scorched farms surrounding the city. It was exactly like her nightmares...

As the earth smoothed itself under their feet, she cast a quick glance at the remains of yellow grass.

"Will you teach me how to do that?" Persephone asked. Mother blinked and stared at her.

"I mean..." She waved her hand to the ground "When you move us from one place to another so quickly with the earth!"

"You do not seem to have any power over the Earth." Usually, a god's abilities would manifest themselves in childhood, as Demeter remembered fondly. A three-year-old Kora had hated being told that she had to wait until the right time in springtime for the flowers to bloom. She had gone outside, and simply by staring at the tiny little flower-buds and wishing they would blossom, they did. But as far as the dirt itself, she didn't seem to wield any power over this element.

"There must be a way I can move quickly. You and Hermes can do so."

"Each god must use his own Gift the best way he can. I cannot move through the sky like Zeus or through the ocean like Poseidon. You have... unique Gifts."

"I cannot help being born with them, can I?"

"I suppose not. But..." Hades could become invisible, as well. This concern nagged Demeter as she studied her daughter.

"But what?"

"Nothing." She quickly turned away from her daughter. "You can see what has happened here." She was grateful that Kora didn't continue to reprimand her or scold her for what she had done. The younger woman's gaze was calm as she studied the devastated landscape.

"I was unable to use my Gift in Hades. I have a lot of power... stored in me."

"Still, you have never used your power on such a large area."

"Mother..." Persephone tried to not show obvious annoyance. "Like you said before, it will go quicker if we do it together. I will have your guidance, will I not?"

"Yes." Demeter sounded almost sorrowful.

oOo

Skouros lay in bed next to Hypia, his eyes closed as his hand rested atop hers. Three more of their children had died, and they had gone through every single scrap of food, that could be found in the house or outside. This had happened a long time ago, and they had been reduced to eating things that they would have ordinarily disdained in the past. Skouros would never forget the morning when he caught his wife outside, putting dirt into her mouth. Unfortunately, for just about everyone in Olympia, chewing on leather or braided hemp or eating dirt and clay had become their only options.

There were sordid rumors of parents eating their children, but such an idea evoked only the most utter revulsion in Skouros and his wife. They had gone on as far as they could, and now simply had no more energy to even try living. Both of them used the last of their energy to pull on their nicest clothes before settling down into their bed, pulling up the covers. Once in a while, they would have a bit of strength to talk, and used this to reminisce about the good old days.

Their courtship and marriage, the birth of their first – and subsequent – children and various smaller joys filled their conversations.

However, it seemed that Hypia could now talk no more. Her breathing was shallow, and her hand was cold. When he whispered her name, he gained no response – not even a slight twitch of her eyelids or fingers.

He could barely move. A modern-day doctor would have told him that his organs were shutting down, just like his wife's already had. Even without that medical knowledge, Skouros knew the end was imminent.

"I love you," he whispered, squeezing Hypia's hand and hoping she could still feel it. He stared at her one last time with bleary eyes, seeing not the emaciated woman that was at the very brink of death, but the bright-eyed maiden he had fallen in love with three decades ago.

The high priest of Zeus sent out one last prayer that his patron god might save his remaining children. He had prayed so many times that it was almost out of habit that he did so.

oOo

Distantly, as if she was on the shore of a great sea and seeing lamps on ships in the distance, Persephone saw tiny pinpoints scattered all around Olympia. At first she was unsure of what she was seeing, but focusing on the flow of life-energy, she realized that these were the people that had in one way or another managed to stay alive, though none of them would remain so for long without divine intervention.

Before Mother could speak or give out instruction, Persephone took a step forward, focusing on the overabundance of energy within herself. These people would have to be fed, but if they were too weak to get to the food, then Mother's efforts would come to naught.

Persephone raised her arms, focusing on these tiny pinpoints of diminishing life. She could sense that many of these people hovered upon the brink of death. Rather than focusing on the dead vegetation before her, she turned her efforts to the people.

A vision of a web formed in her mind's eye, and she connected all of the people on it, like stars connected by silk threads. She expanded this web, seeking out every last living being she could find, feeling her will stretch out in countless gossamer strands, refusing to give up until she was confident that she had located every creature – human or animal – within a sizable radius.

The process felt slow to her as the strings expanded and branched out to find everyone, as it had taken great concentration to accomplish such a task, but in reality it took no more than several seconds.

With the network in place and everyone connected, she did not hesitate to move through the next step. Her power burst from her, filling the pale threads with a radiant golden light. The entire web was suffused with almost unbearable brilliance for a glorious, fleeting moment before it dimmed, the rich life-energy flowing towards all of the flickering lights that formed the base of the intricate arrangement.

Demeter could only stare as she felt the intense outpouring of power from her daughter. The landscape remained barren as the Goddess of Spring collapsed to the ground.

oOo

Skouros remained still, peacefully resigned to his own death. He and Hypia had led good lives, doing the best they could. They had reared their children with a firm but loving hand. They were charitable towards poorer neighbors, and Skouros had used his power as head priest of the temple to see to it that the poorest citizens of Olympia need not go without the most basic necessities of life. The kingdom of Hades was a mysterious place, but the Elysian Fields was the assured future of those who had led good and honest lives. Granted, his tenure as a mortal was not as long as he would have liked – it was his fondest dream to see his children have children of their own – but who could defy the will of the gods? Hopefully Hades would be a kinder – and more attentive – master than Zeus or Demeter.

The house was silent. He could not even hear his own breathing. The peace was.... actually *nice*. Death in battle was considered great, at least to Ares and the Spartans. However, Skouros simply could not imagine meeting his end in such a way. It was much more pleasant to just lie still and focus on the silence that surrounded him. There was nothing to be afraid of.

Suddenly, he was filled with an almost searing sensation, like light pouring into his flesh. His body arched off the bed violently. He gave out a strangled moan as his muscles relaxed, slowly lowering him back to the mat.

"Skouros?"

After resigning himself to death, he was certain that he would only hear his wife's voice again on the other side. When he opened his eyes, his surroundings were the same. Was it like this in Death, waking up to a place that looked just like his own? Was he not to be judged and sent to his appropriate place in the Underworld? His thoughts were interrupted by a hand touching his cheek, and he turned his head to look at Hypia. She was gaunt, but no longer fatally so.

His joints ached a bit, but he was surprised to find himself able to move with fair ease. His vision was no longer bleary, and after staring at his beloved spouse for several moments, he softly uttered her name.

o0o

"Kora!" Demeter cried out. She hadn't used this name to try to annoy the younger woman; it had been an entirely instinctive action on her part, especially when it seemed as if Kora was hurt.

She rushed to her daughter's side, patting her cheek and juggling her shoulders gently before taking her into her arms.

"My darling child..." Demeter looked down at her daughter's pale and wan complexion. Fortunately, they were both goddesses, and Demeter knew exactly what she needed to do. She could transfer some of her own life-energy into her daughter and restore her. Her hand slid down her daughter's chest, feeling the beat of her heart. It was even and steady, not too strong or weak. She took a deep breath before Persephone's eyelids fluttered open.

"No. Save your energy for them." She nodded towards Olympia.

"But..."

"I just need rest. Let me be. Make the plants grow, Mother."

As her daughter spoke, Demeter became

aware of the fact that despite the barren landscape, the presence of death was no longer so overwhelming.

"Go on." Persephone nodded wearily.

oOo

Skouros shakily sat up, feeling light-headed.

"Are we dead?" he whispered. Hypia glanced at him and shrugged.

"I think we are alive." She placed her hand on her chest. "The dead have no need for beating hearts."

A powerful clash of emotions percolated within Skouros as he assessed his situation. He had been resigned to death, and now, apparently, he had been yanked back to the world of the living. His vital signs were a bit weak, but he was able to climb off the bed with relative ease.

He didn't want to go through the process of starvation again. It had been agony at first, but when he passed the critical point, there was no longer any pain. The final stages of starvation, much like that of hypothermia or drowning, was peaceful as the body started to shut down, cutting off pain receptors in its course.

It had been at least several days since he felt hunger pangs, and he silently cursed his stomach when he felt its empty rumble. Better to be dead than go through this again!

Skouros walked to the window, pulling back the drapes. He gasped softly when he saw green. The gardens had been picked clean weeks ago, yet there were plants blossoming and growing right before his eyes! Little green shoots reached towards the sky, becoming taller and stronger as their leaves opening to drink in the heat of the sun. Hypia joined him at the window, watching as the plants started to flower. The variety usually only seen in spring also made itself apparent, daffodils, crocuses, lilies, and many other flowers vying against one another for space and sun.

In the vegetable garden, the flowers budded, blossomed, and wilted in a matter of seconds as their true crop grew into visibility, their stalks impressive as they stretched upward, needing no support or trellis. A flash here and there revealed carrots pushing the dirt from around them, topped by clusters of thick shoots. The olive tree that sat in one corner of the courtyard gained an ever-increasing load, growing many branches since most of its old ones had fallen off due to not receiving any nourishment and being used for firewood. In the blink of an eye, olives appeared, growing bigger than any Skouros had ever seen.

Vines tumbled over one another as they spilled across the crisscrossing walkways of the courtyard, revealing a bounty of peas and cucumbers.

Bare patches of dirt were overcome by thick grass, and soon enough Skouros's courtyard became a veritable cornucopia of flowers and fruit, regardless of what time of the year each individual plant grew. The sweet odor of honeysuckle alerted Skouros to the fact that the pillars holding up the veranda roof were being quickly overtaken by the flower, its vines wrapping around the carved wood. The odor of dill and mint wafted over from Hypia's herb garden, which just like everything else, was overflowing.

The almost non-existent strawberry bush – *Melissa loved strawberries*, Skouros thought sadly – was now clustered with berries bigger than his dead child's fist.

As if in a trance, he slowly drew from the window and walked down the hall, calling for his remaining children to come outside. He was not sure if they had been given the same... rejuvenation, for lack of a better word, that he and Hypia had just experienced. He did not bother to check that they had risen out of their beds as he walked outside. He would bring food to them if he had to.

The smell of myriad flowers enveloped him, and he stood still for a moment as he examined the greenery. His steps were slow and measured as he approached the strawberries.

The fruit certainly feels real enough, he mused, plucking one from its vine. When he brought it to his lips, he sniffed it for a moment before sinking his teeth into the sweet treat.

"Father?" Skouros turned around to see his youngest surviving son. Menaus was on the brink of puberty, though starvation had made him appear much smaller and younger.

"Come on out. Everybody! There is plenty to eat!" He grabbed another strawberry, and within several moments, all six remaining members of the household were outside on their knees and taking whatever caught their fancy. Three of his children joined him at the strawberries while Hypia and a fourth were happily tearing open pea pods. Alinoe, their only remaining daughter, was pulling carrots out of the dirt – she had always liked carrots – and was munching on one after having quickly brushed earth off it.

After eating several handfuls of the most succulent strawberries he had ever tasted, he finally went to the gate. He was hesitant to open it, and nobody had left the property in the last couple of weeks. Gingerly, he placed his palm on the cool wood of the bar.

His shoulders sagged in shock and relief when he saw that the road was lined on both sides with tall shoots of grass. The farms he could see had the same abundance that his own garden did. In the distance, he heard surprised and delighted cries, and over the next few minutes, he saw people on the farms, surveying what had happened and grabbing at least several mouthfuls of food as they did so.

He turned around to see his wife.

"It is the same out there. Everything has grown back."

Hypia let out a slow groan of relief as she closed her eyes for a moment and nodded.

o0o

Persephone barely moved, wiggling around a bit as she felt the grass grow around and under her. It formed a lush carpet, and she was tempted to simply fall asleep.

A shadow passed over her eyes, blocking the sun. She opened her eyes to see her mother looking down at her. Persephone quickly pulled herself up to a sitting position, glancing around at the changes that Mother had effected onto the countryside. It was a veritable paradise compared to the barren hell that it was before, and the sight filled her heart with relief and joy.

"Are you well?" Mother asked.

"I will be, as soon as I eat." She felt drained from the spectacular feat she had just performed, and was just now aware of being ravenously hungry. As she looked up, she noted that Mother didn't look particularly surprised.

"Do not worry. You can eat all you want when we go back." As the older goddess scooped her daughter into her arms, Persephone offered no argument, wrapping her own arms around her mother's neck.

oOo

Hades leaned against a tree, invisible to mother and daughter as they each used their Gift to revive Olympia. When Persephone fell, he had nearly been unable to restrain himself from rushing to her side and taking her into his arms and comforting her.

He had promised himself that he would give her this month to enjoy the upper world and her reunion with her mother. He wanted to show himself, but feared how Persephone might judge that. Yes, she enjoyed his presence, but did she desire a reminder of her bond with him at this time?

He watched quietly as Demeter lifted Persephone into her arms.

oOo

Many mortals considered Zeus the mightiest of the Gods, but Demeter's famine had shown him just what he could not do. His Gift had been valuable when it came to fighting Kronos's Titans. A well-placed lightning bolt could stun a Titan and enable his brothers and sisters to close in and subdue said Titans. And he had gotten into a few fights with his own sons or siblings. Ares himself had to be brought down with lightning bolts several times when he became so lost in his blood-lust that he could not be reasoned with.

Nobody could deny that a lightning bolt was a very effective weapon, but it could not grow food or do a single damned thing to feed mortals. He was just happy to see Olympia green again. Ever since the famine had started, the prayers from Olympia had been almost unceasing. Skouros had served him well for years and he was one of Zeus's favored humans. When Skouros prayed for food to feed his children, Zeus had been forced to turn away in shame. In the beginning, he had been able to add food to the temple stores for Skouros and anyone else who might need it, but as food ran out everywhere, even the mighty ruler of the gods had been unable to locate this basic and much-needed commodity, and to raid food from other lands would rouse ire of the other god-clans.

At least it's all over. In the last couple of days, most of Hellas had been restored to its former vitality. Even in areas where Demeter had not yet been able to attend, the land was still healthy, because the nymphs had been doing their own part to rejuvenate the countryside, now freely able to use their abilities in the absence of Demeter's curse.

The nymphs still disdained him, though. It would be a while before he got into anybody's good graces, so he had taken to being alone – just like Mother had told him to, anyway – when not helping the mortals.

He took a swig of the ambrosia before setting the flask back on the table. There was still plenty to be considered. He was surprised that Hades had given Kora up so easily – hadn't his older brother said that he intended to keep the daughter of Demeter as his Queen?

"You have a visitor, my lord." Zeus looked up to see Hebe.

"Who is it?"

"Hades."

What? Zeus quickly collected himself and nodded, waving his hand in assent.

Hades was a somber figure encased in a flowing black cloak, his expression unreadable as he came to a stop before his brother. Despite the fact that the Lord of the Dead was the elder sibling, he looked younger than his other brothers, and Zeus would sometimes note this with curiosity. His eyes were dark, his stare penetrating as he focused on the younger deity

"What brings you here?" Zeus asked, inclining his head in a slight bow.

"Perhaps I came here to visit you out of brotherly concern." Hades's tone was openly dry, and his lips formed an almost indiscernible smirk.

"Have you come to ask me for Kora again?" Zeus asked, in no mood to put up with his brother's attitude.

"I do not need to. She is already mine."

"There is someone who would disagree with that. We have all known her displeasure. Do you wish to provoke it again?"

"Of course not. She may have increased the number of my subjects, but unlike most of the Olympians, I am not concerned with how many people worship me." He shrugged, giving his surroundings a cool glance.

"What do you really want?"

"I will get what I want soon enough."

"Does it amuse you to speak in riddles?"

"To be honest? Yes."

I should have known he would say that, Zeus groaned inwardly.

"Just remember, what is done cannot be undone."

"What is *that* supposed to mean?" the younger sibling asked, not bothering to hide his frustration.

"You will find out soon enough."

"Do not jest with me."

"I have better things to do, little brother. I am

simply telling it as it is. All will be revealed in due time – meanwhile, you have a lot of work to do still. Is our darling sister on speaking terms with you?"

"No," Zeus muttered. Rhea had told him to stay away from Demeter for the time being, and he had been all too happy to do so. He was of course curious to see Kora, but his fear of his sister outweighed everything else. "I still do not understand why you wanted her. Look at all the trouble it caused."

"You are scolding *me* for the trouble?" Hades asked. Demeter hadn't initiated her curse until she discovered her youngest brother's hand in it. Hades had been more than willing to talk to her, and had been close to, but Demeter had somehow found out where her daughter was and went to Zeus. Now, how had she found out?

Hades was usually able to figure things out quickly, but this was something he had been puzzling over in the last couple of months. The most plausible thing he could think of was that she had been given the information. But by whom?

"Do I need to remind you of the fact that it was your own callousness that set Demeter in her fury?"

Zeus crossed his arms and looked away.

"I had merely thought to come up here and visit with you, and I am not responsible for you bringing up the subject of Persephone."

"Her name is Kora," was all Zeus could offer, remembering Demeter's insistence on that name.

179

"Her name... is *Persephone*." Hades's tone was steely as he glared at his brother. Zeus blinked and took a step back.

"Kora does not suit her. She is an extraordinary woman. Not that you would know."

"Leave me alone."

"Very well then."

When Zeus turned around, his brother was gone.

oOo

Persephone sat next to the fire in her mother's room, comfortably full after the meal Mother had put together for both of them. Demeter also had a ravenous appetite, and Persephone made note of this. Before, Mother had always disappeared to do her duties, never allowing her daughter to see firsthand what she was capable of. She would be gone for days, but this hadn't been an issue when Iasion was still alive.

A casual observer might have thought that eating was a competition between the two of them. Mother had assembled a feast that could easily feed Metaniera and her family, yet between the two of them, the platters and bowls were quickly emptied of their contents. She was hungrier than she had thought, and apparently Mother suffered the same consequences of using her Gift in such a widespread way.

Persephone used this quiet time to assess the events of today, especially what she had done in Olympia. She didn't know where the idea of the web had come from. It had simply seemed like a natural way to connect the dots, to make sure that no living thing that remained in Olympia was left out of her healing magic.

Having used her Gift in such an incredible way, the thought of returning to the Underworld filled her with apprehension. She let out a quiet sigh as she fiddled with the corner of her tunic.

"Is something the matter? Have you had enough to eat?"

"Yes, Mother." Persephone kept her gaze averted.

"Something is worrying you." Demeter's tone was patient and gentle, and Persephone looked up at her. *What can I say?* How best to approach the subject of her inevitable return to the Underworld?

"Well...." She took a deep breath, slightly reassured by her mother's encouraging nod. "I was just thinking about Hades, and..."

"Why dwell on such unpleasant matters?" Demeter asked. "It is over."

"That is not what I meant. I just..." She looked at the fire. "I was treated kindly down there. I bear no ill will towards Hades."

"You should! He kidnapped you!" Mother was getting worked up again, much to Persephone's horror.

"Well, yes, I was angry about that, but..."

"There is no more reason to speak of him."

After hearing the anger in her mother's tone, Persephone quickly fell silent. Maybe another time, but definitely not right now. She wouldn't have even brought it up if Mother didn't ask her these questions!

"I suppose not," she replied acquiescently, "I am full from all that wonderful food you gave me. I need some fresh air, so I will go sit in the garden."

oOo

Being alone in the garden had given Persephone some time to think. She knew she had to tell Mother the truth about Hades. But how could she do so without sending her dear mother into a rage? It was one thing to have nightmares, but she had seen the bleak surroundings of Olympia up close, giving a terrifying dimension to her nightmares. She could never forget, *ever*.

She wanted to enjoy her time up here, but it was hard to do between Hades's promise and Mother's anger. Couldn't a compromise be made? Despite Mother's concessions, it was clear that the older goddess had made up her mind about some things.

Well, so has Hades. What about you?

oOo

Persephone let her mother fuss over her, tucking her into bed. Sometimes it felt nice to be... mothered. She tilted her face to let Mother give her a good-night kiss. Being tucked in and kissed had been a routine between the two of them, and she actually enjoyed it. Mother certainly did.

She lay there in the silence as Mother retreated from the small room. She wasn't afraid of the dark, especially after being in Dis, but she felt alone. It had been only two nights, and already she missed Hades's presence. It was nice having him to snuggle up with under the soft blankets, or to feel him holding her. Mother had left her with an adequate amount of blankets and warm clothing, but she still felt a slight chill.

She wrapped herself within the blankets, much like a cocoon. It was something she had always liked doing, especially during the winter months. When she was little, Father would make a game of 'unwrapping' her from her self-imposed confinement and be rewarded with plenty of hugs and kisses from his daughter.

But Father was dead, and given his decision to go to Lethe, she would probably never see him again. Hades had been so considerate about the whole matter. His kindness and thoughtfulness made her miss him all the more.

"Aidon..." she whispered fiercely.

oOo

In his bed, Hades stared up at the ceiling. The sky outside his Palace was dark to mimic the night on the surface world, so he knew that by now, Persephone would most likely be sleeping.

The bed was so empty without her. It wasn't simply because she was a fun person to share pleasure with; rather it was her very presence that brought him happiness as he had never known.

183

All he wanted to do at the moment was to simply hold her, inhale her scent and feel her skin under his hands. His home was a darker place without her – figuratively and literally.

Almost as if on cue, he heard his name. He raised his head, looking around in surprise. The entire Palace was entirely devoid of souls – living or dead – yet he could have sworn that he heard someone say his name.

He wasn't given to fits of fancy, and considered himself a grounded person. He wasn't the kind of person to create something out of nothing, and his keen senses told him what he already knew, that there was nobody around who could have said his name or anything else! Yet he had heard the voice clearly, soft, sweet, and sad, full of longing.

He glanced up at the ceiling again, feeling a fresh surge of loneliness.

Chapter XLVII

oOo

Several more days passed as Persephone experimented with her powers. She went with Mother to the ravaged areas that remained, becoming more and more experienced with her Gift. She did not feel as drained as she had the first time, though she still felt weak after each feat and needed to eat lots of food to restore her energy, just like Mother.

Things weren't entirely peaceful between them. Mother still refused to call her 'Persephone' but at least she didn't use 'Kora' either, and there were times when Mother tried to dictate her schedule, like right now.

It was an especially cold morning, with a light snow falling outside. She was eager to go outside and take a walk in the city and escape Mother's constant attention.

"I do not want to weave. Or do *anything* related to weaving." No matter how much Mother might try to ingrain it into her, she simply didn't enjoy weaving as much as Mother wanted her to, and she never would. It might serve as an useful distraction sometimes, but nothing could rouse her enthusiasm for this chore. Mother should go weave with Hestia if she wanted a companion for this task, then. Persephone certainly had heard enough about Hestia's talents!

"Come now." Demeter squared her shoulders. "You have yet to finish your project."

"I will finish it later." She could not help but recall Eirene and her obvious dislike of the craft. The girl had a talent for music and while her mother didn't try to suppress it, it was clear that making her daughter weave – and thus teaching her one of the duties of a proper wife – was more important than encouraging her natural talent, to Metaniera. Eirene was full of energy, and when she wasn't seated, she liked to dance or skip or run. The goddess empathized with the mortal girl.

"No, now. Weaving is important."

"Yea. For you," Persephone muttered dryly.

"What was that?" came the terse reply. Before her kidnapping, Persephone would have been too afraid to repeat herself. This time she repeated her words clearly and loudly.

"I will not be disrespected."

"Neither will I!" Persephone raised her chin defiantly. The pair stared at one another for a moment that seemed to stretch on for eternity.

"Oh, now I am disrespecting you because I simply want you to do a chore?"

"You *know* weaving is not my passion." She didn't mind other chores – sweeping the floor, feeding and tending animals, harvesting various fruits or herbs, cooking, or preserving food for the winter months. She had never had an issue with taking responsibility for chores, but she would be damned if she was going to do something just because Mother said so!

"That does not matter. If everybody only did the things they liked, nothing would get done!"

Persephone didn't even attempt to stop herself

from rolling her eyes. "Hades never made me do it." The words tumbled out of her mouth before she could stop herself, and she flinched slightly at sudden pained expression on Mother's face.

"... Is that so?" Mother narrowed her eyes.

"Yes."

"Well, you are not in the Underworld anymore, are you?" Demeter asked crisply after quickly collecting herself. "Come with me."

Rather than try to argue the matter further, she simply took a deep breath, vanishing from sight. She remained where she was in her seat, silent as open irritation burst forth on her mother's features.

"Are you going to do this every time I ask you to do something you do not want?"

"You never *asked*." Persephone's voice was clear, appearing to materialize from the air itself.

Demeter clenched her jaw. Before the kidnapping, Kora had always been easy to manage. Yes, she could be a bit rebellious at times – but then, that was entirely normal for any child, god or mortal. Usually a stern warning was enough to compel her daughter to obedience. Now, with the newly revealed aspects of her daughter's Gift, it was unpleasantly apparent that she could no longer be compelled to do anything.

When the younger woman suddenly came into visibility again, Demeter was unnerved as she recalled the fact that Hades had done the same thing on several occasions. It was most certainly not unheard of for different gods to share a similar Gift, except that Hades had always used his famed helmet of invisibility... Like everyone besides

Persephone, Demeter was not privy to the fact that Hades was able to manifest this Gift on his own.

"Enjoy your weaving. I am going outside." Persephone rose to her feet.

o0o

Eirene stared at her loom, tempted to just tear all the threads out. Weaving had never been her best talent... or any level of talent, really. Her rows were never tight enough, and it was agony to spin thread or yarn. The repetitive task of weaving the rows, up and down, up and down, up and down made her want to scream sometimes. She found it impossible to sit still for more than a few minutes, and this inevitably gained her a good amount of scolding from her mother. She envied her oldest sister; Thalassa enjoyed it and she always did such beautiful work! Her patience and creativity seemed endless, and Eirene wished there was some way that Thalassa could share some with her.

As much as she tried, she simply could not enjoy the craft. It was so boring, and she bit back a groan of frustration as she finished a row, fiddling with the loose yarn and twirling it around her fingers. Fortunately, Mother was so focused on her own weaving that she did not notice, so Eirene continued to twist the yarn, winding and unwinding it around her fingers or thumbs in a sort of game of cat's cradle.

Thalassa glanced at her sister, but said nothing. It was no secret that the youngest princess hated being in this room. Eirene was such a lively dancer, and despite her young age, had found a natural affinity with music. Thalassa herself was far more graceful with her hands than her feet, and the few times she had tried her sister's flute or lyre, it sounded *terrible*. She had tried to teach her youngest sister a few tricks to improve her weaving, and it was clear that Eirene had tried to apply the information, but she had no more talent for it than her elder sister did for music and dance.

Unfortunately for Eirene, she lived in a time where nobody knew of much less understood such terms as 'learning disability' or 'attention deficit', otherwise her mother would have been considerably more understanding about her daughter's restlessness and energy.

"Eirene, you have barely started and already you are just sitting there and playing with the yarn!" Metaniera's irritation was obvious. The other princesses continued working, not wishing to draw their mother's attention towards themselves; Mother could be formidable when she was angry. She didn't become upset as much as she had when Demophon was sick, but she could still be provoked, especially by her youngest daughter.

Every year, Eirene dreaded the winter months because this meant more time spent in the Palace; and more time under her mother's supervision.

"So sorry I am not the *perfect* princess like Thalassa," Eirene muttered.

"What was that?" Metaniera stared at her

daughter sternly. Thalassa pressed her lips together. Aethra and Melinoe glanced at one another, and the room filled with an uncomfortable silence as Eirene stared down at her hands, twisting the yarn and giving her mother no response.

After several moments, the eldest princess finally spoke. "I will be happy to finish that cloth. I would rather listen to her music, anyway."

Simultaneously, Melinoe and Aethra held back sighs of relief before glancing at their mother and nodding eagerly.

"Very well." Metaniera bit back her irritation and gave them a curt nod.

When Eirene retrieved her lyre and started playing, she found it hard to focus on even that. The only reason she was able to play it now was because of her sisters' intervention, and it was clear that Mother was just humoring them. *Why can't she humor me,* Eirene thought to herself, and her inner turmoil played itself through her music. It wasn't light or graceful, and she could see Mother's growing impatience as she tried to make the music more sweet, but she simply wasn't capable of that ordinarily simple feat at this time.

Persephone strolled along the veranda that hugged the large courtyard before music filled the air. She and Hades would sometimes listen to music or watch dances, and the artists of Elysium were all too happy to put on performances for them. She could feel the frustration and anger in the music that was wafting through the halls of the Palace.

She paused outside the chamber where Metaniera and her daughters were. Her own mother was not with them, since she was currently with Demophon, taking care of the baby so that Metaniera could focus on her duties.

The subtle cues in Eirene's body language alerted Persephone to the girl's discomfort. She also sensed a mixture of impatience, nervousness, concern, and unhappiness from the room's occupants. Over the last few days as she got to know the royal family better, she had picked up a strain in the relationship between Metaniera and Eirene. It wasn't intentional by any means and she knew that Metaniera loved all of her children, but the personalities of the mother and her youngest daughter simply were too different to guarantee a harmonious relationship. In ways, it reminded Persephone of her own conflicts with Mother.

The goddess stepped through the doorway, drawing their attention. Her presence was met with bowed heads and respectful greetings.

"What brings you here, my lady? Have you come to join us?" Metaniera asked. Persephone smiled at her sweetly and shook her head.

"I am here because I need Eirene to come with me."

"What for?"

"You dare question a goddess?" Persephone hated pulling rank and preferred to go under the guise of a mortal when she went into the city, but being a deity did have its advantages. She regarded the queen calmly as Metaniera set her lips in a tight line for a brief moment.

"No, my lady." The matriarch of the family bowed her head.

oOo

It was an especially windy day, but Eirene did not complain as she pulled the cowl over her head. She had been envious of Melinoe since her older sister was now a priestess-in training, and was gone a good amount of the time, meaning that she was often excused from weaving or other chores to go to the temple.

"Thank you for taking me with you!" Eirene said, her cheeks flush from cold and happiness.

"I don't like weaving any more than you do," Persephone replied with a knowing smile as she looked down at the young princess.

"Does your mother not make you sit with her?"

"When I was little, yes she did. I absolutely hated it. She would talk about how wonderful Hestia's weaving was and how all women should learn the craft. But she said it so often it just..." The older woman shrugged.

"You hear it so many times you just stop listening. Especially when Mother does not listen to *you.*"

"Exactly."

Eirene nodded eagerly. It was inevitable that anyone born and raised in Hellas should know the myths of their gods. They could bless or curse you, depending on their mood. She'd never met any gods until Doso revealed herself to be a mighty Goddess. She had always seen the deities as lofty, unconcerned by mortal issues except to get involved when it struck their fancy. After all, look at the state of the city before Demeter intervened, and she had been very aware of the strain in the family due to outside circumstances even though Metaniera considered her too young to explain the problems to.

Though she was only eleven, Eirene understood that gods could be very naughty, though she didn't have a full idea of what 'naughty' entailed. To her, the gods were just stories, since they certainly hadn't proven their existence to the people of Eleusis as far as she could remember. They were apparently concerned with other matters and didn't have time for the mortals that worshiped them, or perhaps they didn't even exist.

Now, she knew they were flesh and very real, and had feelings, like her. Though the older goddess had always been kind to the children of the King and Queen, there was still a distant quality around her that made her nearly unapproachable especially to the girl. However, Persephone was different. She listened and cared. She had problems, just like any mortal!

"I cannot wait to be grown up. Then Mother can not boss me around anymore."

Persephone laughed. But it wasn't the condescending laugh of an adult; rather, it was a warm one of open agreement.

"Believe me, I remember these days... always looking forward to tomorrow, wanting to be

193

treated like an adult, being sick of being told what to do. That day will come for you soon enough." Persephone squeezed the girl's shoulder as they strolled through the gardens.

"I wish that day would come *now*." Eirene had especially hated Abas, since he liked calling her '*little* princess' in a sing-song tone. He was gone, good riddance!

Persephone considered giving Eirene a woman's body. She certainly had been able to do so for herself, and she was able to control her powers through carefully-selected mental imagery. She understood all too well Eirene's frustrations with her mother; it was too similar to her own conflict with Mother.

However, physical and mental age were two different things, she reminded herself. Suddenly gaining a woman's body overnight wouldn't benefit Eirene in the long run, and it wouldn't fix the rampant nervous energy she felt in the girl. What she needed was an outlet for her energy, and not simply her music.

"I have not seen the forests outside of the city. Will you show me around?" Persephone asked.

"Certainly, but we are not allowed outside alone... we have to ask Mother or Father and have guards with us..."

"You have no need for guards when you have a goddess with you." Said goddess' lips formed a grin as she raised her eyebrow. The raven-haired princess stared at her for a moment before her eyes widened in comprehension and delight.

Nobody had come to visit – or bother – her or her daughter in the last few days, and Demeter was glad for that. However, that peace would come to an inevitable end, and she was immediately aware of the presence of another deity on the seventh morning after her reunion with her daughter.

She was outside with her daughter, taking a walk in the woods. This was one activity that they both always enjoyed, so she didn't have to argue with or cajole her daughter to go with her. Persephone didn't seem to be in the mood to talk, but she showed open interest in her surroundings, so Demeter was content to simply walk in silence and enjoy the sights around them.

Yesterday, after giving Demophon back to his mother, she heard from Metaniera what had happened with Kora and Eirene. She hadn't liked that, of course. It was bad enough that her daughter had become willful and defiant, now she was encouraging another girl to do the same! She had always feared the influence of others on her daughter; it had never occurred to her that Kora might be the one doing the influencing!

Rhea was sitting on a stump near the creek that the princesses enjoyed playing at, at least in warm weather. Ice and snow appeared here and there along the curves and bends, though it was held at bay by the churning eddies of the water as it raced over and around stones.

"I thought I might see you here," the elder

goddess said as she glanced at her daughter and granddaughter.

"Hello, Grandmother. I was wondering when I might see you again!" Demeter didn't seem thrilled, but Rhea was buoyed by Persephone's enthusiasm.

"I thought it would be best to allow matters to... settle before I came to see the two of you."

"Hmm." Demeter nodded slowly.

"How have things been here? The temple looks lovely, by the way."

"Things have been going well, since I have my daughter back. And thank you."

Rhea nodded, noticing how Persephone looked healthier after her brief time in the world of the living. Her skin was no longer so pale, though it was still fairly light, giving her a creamy complexion that was further emphasized by the ruddiness of her cheeks from the cold.

"How have you been?" Rhea asked, directing her attention to Persephone.

"I am just happy to be here. The sunlight, the fresh air..."

"I can imagine. If you enjoy that, I think you will enjoy Olympus."

"What?" Demeter furrowed her eyebrows.

"I was thinking that your daughter and I share some ambrosia and nectar at my house. I assure you, you have nothing to worry about."

"You want me to let you take her to Olympus? Without thinking that I might wish to accompany her?"

"Mother," Persephone gave out a small,

patient sigh. "I am a grown woman. I have been looking forward to seeing Grandmother again, and I have shown you that you need not worry about me."

"I will bring her back tonight," Rhea assured her daughter. "I simply wish to know my granddaughter and the newest goddess of the Olympians."

"Is it really necessary to try to put her in the Pantheon? There are already so many, and I do not want her getting mixed up with the troublemakers..."

"She and I will be alone."

"That is what I was hoping for, anyway." Persephone said as she glanced at Rhea. The older woman smiled encouragingly.

"Very well." Demeter could see by the glint in her daughter's eye that Kora was set on going. She certainly didn't want a fight in front of her own mother, and besides, out of all the gods of Olympus that her daughter could spend time with, one could hardly worry that Rhea might be a poor role model. Ever since the overthrow of the Titanomachy, Rhea had acted as an adviser and mediator to the Council. Considering herself both a Titan and an Olympian, she was useful in solving the conflicts that often emerged between different branches of Gaea's immense brood.

"I am counting on you to keep an eye on my daughter," Demeter said sternly. Persephone almost rolled her eyes, but glanced away demurely, giving a nod of agreement.

197

Grandmother's house reminded her of Mother's own, and Persephone felt at ease as she gazed around. Rhea's house was larger, but the construction and furnishings were still simple, offering comfort to make up for its lack of splendor. In the large kitchen, herbs hung from the rafters, and the smell of fresh bread hung in the air. The seats were padded with brown cloth woven through with bright red and orange strands, and the table was covered with a tablecloth of the same color and design.

"Have a seat," Rhea said as she gestured towards the table, and Persephone nodded before doing so. There was already a bowl of fruit on the table, and Rhea quickly fetched some ambrosia and nectar. Persephone remembered how sweet the food of the gods could be, so she took sparing bites and sips, alternating the sweetness with pickled olives that sat in a small bowl.

The younger woman remained silent, figuring that she would wait for Grandmother to start asking questions. How or what Rhea asked her would help Persephone gauge her better and see what kind of person her grandmother was. Hades's disdain for most of the Olympians made her wary of them.

"Would you like to tell me about yourself?" Rhea asked. *Not what I was expecting*, Persephone thought as she studied her grandmother.

"That is a question that can be interpreted

different ways. As it is, I do not think I could describe myself in a way that I would be satisfied with."

"Hmm." Rhea nodded before taking a sip of her nectar. "Has your mother always kept you so sheltered? I am just curious, since my children are usually so happy to announce the births of their children."

"Yes. When my father was still alive, Mother was happier. She did not fuss over me so much, since I already had a family to watch over me, but she did not talk about being a goddess or about the Olympians and we lived like mortals. After he died, Mother took us to an island, with only the nymphs for company. It was like that until Hades..."

"Yet others have found you. Hermes, Ares..."

"Hermes told other gods, and Ares got wind of it. Hermes found me by accident, and he was funny. He tried to tease me, but he left when I turned him down. I know he was not being mean or anything."

"You certainly show wisdom in analyzing the situation like that." Rhea looked pleased, and Persephone could not help but feel a small surge of pride. For this elder goddess to compliment her in such a dignified way!

"I just did some thinking after he left. I always do a lot of thinking," the younger woman replied in frank admission.

"I suppose your time in the Underworld was no exception."

Persephone stiffened as she glanced at her

grandmother. Mother had refused to discuss the subject when Persephone had tried to bring it once more.

"Is something wrong?" Rhea asked.

"Mother absolutely refuses to talk about it."

"May I talk about it with you? Is it appropriate for me to ask you to tell me whatever you are feeling comfortable with, at least?"

"You will... listen?" Persephone sounded mildly astonished.

"I always do."

"You will not tell anyone?"

"Hermes certainly did not get his loose tongue from me," Rhea shot back, wagging her finger. "You have my word."

"What is it you want to ask me?"

"How did he treat you? I was worried, you looked so pale..."

"He always offered me food. He would not let me starve and always made sure I had access to victuals. No matter how many times I refused... but he was a fair host. He showed me that I did not have to be afraid of him. He treated me with much kindness." Persephone had an almost indiscernible smile, and Rhea was surprised to see the glimmer of fondness in her granddaughter's eyes.

"For so long, I have wondered if my son would ever have interest in a bride. He is king of a dread realm, and many fear him. I have always wondered if he might be lonely. He is a selective man, but once he makes a decision, he does not turn his back to it. He must consider you special, and I think I can see why."

"Oh." Persephone drummed her fingers lightly on the table.

"So, I cannot help but wonder why he gave you up so easily. When I begged him to release you, he became angry with me. He has suddenly released you back to your mother. I have known my children for too long to not gain insight into their actions. Hades is not one to acquire something and simply let it go."

Persephone held back a soft groan as she thought of the pomegranate seeds. Nothing had been more juicy or luscious than those seeds, and even after eating all the scrumptious meals Mother or Metaniera provided, she still wanted more of that pomegranate.

"You are correct." Persephone did not elaborate. Rhea sat back with a mild frown.

"You mentioned your father dying." Rhea felt unsure of how to broach the subject about her granddaughter's paternity. "Do you have any Gifts?" She figured that this might be an easy way to turn to *that* subject.

"I think you already know the truth about... who sired me. I just prefer to call Iasion my father since he was the one who loved and raised me until he died. I have only ever known him as my father. Zeus never told me who he really was, so why should I care for him?" Persephone sighed as she stared through the window. "I learned a lot about myself when I was in the Underworld. I have no desire to have any truths hidden from me."

"Very well. Have you given thought about what you want for your future? I sense an independent streak within you, and that you and your mother struggle in your relationship. Would you want a husband and family of your own? Or do you wish to be a maiden goddess like Athene or Artemis?"

"Maiden goddess?" Her lips quirked into an amused smile. Rhea did not miss that.

"Zeus has designated you as the Goddess of Spring, to complement the Goddess of the Harvest, but he has not made an announcement of it out of... respect to your mother."

"Truth be told... I am not entirely certain of what I want. Until Hades kidnapped me, I had not realized just how sheltered I was. Hades really was a kind host. I actually enjoyed spending time with him; he tells good stories and has taught me many things. But I missed Hellas, and I know I belong here. It is part of me and my Gift."

"You are young yet. I will always be here to listen to you and help you out any time you need me."

"Thank you." Persephone was truly grateful, for Rhea seemed neutral, a willing and patient arbiter. Perhaps Rhea could talk to Mother. *No. This is something I need to do for myself.* She still had nearly a month to go before Hades came to reclaim her. "For now, I am just happy spending time with you. I would like to ask you questions about Olympus."

"Oh, I am sure you do. It is only fair, after asking you so many questions." Rhea considered what kind of reception Persephone would gain from the Olympians. She was strikingly beautiful in a way that rivaled Aphrodite's own. To the gods, she would be 'fresh meat' as they vied for her attention and entry to her bed. Come to think of it, she *had* been safer with Hades than she would have been with many members of her family. However, she had the feeling that Persephone would be able to stand her own against the clan.

"But I do have one more question."

"Very well." Persephone shrugged.

"Do you have feelings for him?"

Persephone blinked, biting back a gasp of shock. She quickly collected herself, cocking her head slightly to the side, her gaze thoughtful and distant for a moment. "What if I do?"

Rhea smiled faintly. "Has he shown that he cares for you?"

"Yes." Persephone's response was calm.

"Have you eaten the food of the dead?"

Persephone stared back at Rhea, her pulse racing, her outward appearance exuding quiet self-assurance.

"No wonder Hades let you go so quickly."

Persephone exhaled slowly as she glanced at the window again.

"Your mother does not know?"

Persephone nodded. "How can she know, when she refuses to talk about him or listen to me?"

"I suppose Hades thinks he is doing you a favor by letting you come up here and say your goodbyes?"

"It is better than nothing. He gave me until the winter solstice."

"More than I would have expected. What do you think your mother will do when she finds out?"

"I do not wish to contemplate it. But I know I must. Please do not tell her, I need to do it myself!"

Rhea patted her granddaughter's hand reassuringly. "I appreciate you being honest with me. But yes, you need to tell her yourself." Woe betide the unfortunate messenger, and after the progress she had made with her daughter recently, she was loath to lose the bit of closeness she gained with Demeter.

"And what of Hades? Does he expect you to handle this yourself? I never thought my eldest son would be afraid to confront someone."

"No, he has given me his word that he will talk with Mother. He..." Persephone took a breath as she stopped herself from revealing too much. Rhea had asked for one more question, and it turned into more! "What a mess," she muttered.

"I suppose you could call it that, given what happened up here. Nearly everyone was on Zeus's side when it was first revealed the arrangement he made over you. Now Demeter has more allies than anyone could have imagined. Nature is her will. There is no god alive who is not aware of the fury of a woman scorned. Of course, the cost was great. Many things could have gone better, so it was a mess indeed."

Over the last few days, Persephone had observed her mother. She could see that Mother was stricken by what she had done, especially after Persephone reminded her of all the mothers who had lost their children. Though Mother of course wouldn't admit it, she was deeply sorry about what she had done, her surging anger replaced with regret and shame. Even if Mother would become angry again, she wouldn't curse the earth. Once had been more than enough.

"Has Mother always been so stubborn?" Persephone asked.

"Yes, but it can be very good. She is not someone who is afraid to stand up to Zeus, and that is what he needs. In the beginning of the Olympian rule, even before Athene was born, Demeter assured her own power and the power of the other Goddesses, and would not rest until Zeus acknowledged them and gave them governing roles on Olympus. Kronos never cared much for the opinion of women, and my sisters and I were not allowed to be part of the Titan's Council. But such a trait as stubbornness goes both ways. Be patient with your mother."

"Easier said than done," she replied with a scoff.

"You have been here but for a week. There is time yet, for you and for us and for your mother."

"Hopefully."

"Do not be so sad. I know you will figure something out. You certainly are smart enough." Rhea smiled encouragingly. "And you can always talk to me. I will fill you in with all the things that your mother should have told you years ago... provided you ask the right questions."

Persephone smiled back at her grandmother.

oOo

Since her visit with her grandmother, Persephone spent the rest of the evening with the princesses. A servant amused them with funny stories and jokes before Eirene played her flute and then lyre for them, and Aethra recited a story for them. Aethra was a surprisingly good orator, giving different voices to each character in the story as she told the story of how the mighty sun god Helios's son had wanted to ride his chariot, and begged his father to let him do so. Helios finally relented, but the boy, being inexperienced, rode the chariot too low, its heat boiling away parts of the sea and enraging Poseidon before going on to scorch the rich valleys, rousing Demeter's ire. Finally, Zeus had enough and threw a thunderbolt to strike the boy dead.

Thanks to Hades, Persephone was privy to the truth behind the myths that the people of Hellas told of their gods. Phaeton was a foolish young lad to be sure, but he certainly hadn't boiled away the sea or burned the land like the myth claimed. The bolt sent by Zeus had merely stunned the youth, causing him to fall out of his father's chariot. Mortals believed that the chariot was the Sun itself and that Helios rode it every day to bring light to the world. The gods knew that the Sun was something entirely different, but they let the stories blow out of proportion to gain mythic status. After all, what could be more mighty than a deity who brought the light the mortals needed to survive? It was manifest in the mythology of various races the world over, and gods used this to their advantage, but Persephone remained silent as Aethra continued her telling.

It was a shame that women were not allowed on the stage in Hellas. Men and boys took the roles of females in plays, so Aethra would have little venue for her talent.

Persephone let her mind wander as Eirene started playing again. Sometimes it was impossible to not compare her life here with the one that awaited her in the Underworld. Hades let her do anything she wanted and even though he was fully aware of her femininity in the bedroom, he treated her as an intellectual equal. How many women could say that they had a man who cared for them so? Zeus obviously didn't respect Demeter, or his wife, or other women, and many gods also suffered from this flaw.

She hated to admit it, but she wanted to go back to the Underworld! Even then, how could she ever leave this world behind? She now had a grandmother who was eager to welcome her to Olympus and to help her fit in. There was a frankness about Rhea that she liked. Having such a good experience made her all the more curious to meet the other gods of Olympus, good or bad. Would it be worth it meeting them if she were doomed to go back to the Underworld anyway? Was it worth spending time with Rhea if she might never see her again?

No. That was a silly excuse. That was.... *giving up*. Persephone abhorred the very idea.

oOo

Rhea waited until morning before making the decision to speak with her eldest son. Her granddaughter refused to respond to anything but the name that Hades had given her, and her affection for the Lord of the Dead was apparent despite her self-controlled behavior. There had been nothing about her tone or answers to cause Rhea concern for her safety or mental state.

Last time she had seen Hades, she had angered him, and he had lashed out at her with the coldness that he exuded in his wrath. He might not be happy to see her again, but with this new development concerning her granddaughter, Rhea was willing to risk his anger.

oOo

In the Underworld, Iris's multicolor aura was faded as if the very place itself was sucking the light away from her. In the Underworld, she could not fly, and the most she was able to do was glide a couple of feet above the ground.

Hades sat upon his throne, looking as imperious as he always did when he received a visitor from the upper world.

"What brings you here, Iris?" Hades asked in a neutral, almost disinterested tone. She was a bright spot in the dark room, but her light did not banish the shadows that filled the room, giving her the appearance of a firefly on a moonless night.

"Your mother wishes to see you. She invites you to sup with her, or if you do not wish to go up, she will come down here. She wishes for me to convey that it is urgent and she would appreciate seeing you either way."

"Urgent? Matters have been resolved, have they not?" His last visit to Mother had not gone well, and she had irritated him. She was his mother and he respected her, but he did not feel as attached to her as any of the others did, especially Zeus.

Iris shrugged innocently. "She did not tell me what it concerned. Lord Hades, with all due respect, I entreat you to listen to her. No one summons you on a whim."

"Hmph." He placed his chin on his fist and stared off, as if considering a refusal, but Iris knew better than to beg.

"Very well. Tell her I will be by to see her... sometime later today." He did not specify a time.

"Thank you." She bowed before she retreated from the chamber, the sudden absence of light barely noted by Hades.

oOo

Rhea remained at her house for the rest of the morning and afternoon. She kept food ready despite the fact that her eldest son might not want to eat. If he was hungry, he might be induced to be more talkative. She knew he had a sweet spot for gravy and glazes, so she made dishes laden with the stuff, from honeyed fruit slices to tender pieces of pork and vegetables smothered in gravy made of their own juices mixed with herbs and spices.

It was not until nearly sunset that her son made his appearance. She was at her loom with an eye to the window, but Hades still startled her with his silent entry, almost as if appearing out of the thin air.

"Hades, it is so good to see you! I am so delighted to have you here!" She gave him a warm smile, determined to not have a repeat of what happened last time.

"You are just happy that I did not make you come to the Underworld," he responded dryly as he stood still, letting her wrap her arms around him in a hug. She retreated in a moment, frowning.

"Are you merely here to antagonize me?" she asked softly.

"I am here because you say that you wanted to see me about something important. I have spent enough time up here lately, so I just want you to tell me what it is!"

Rhea looked at him entreatingly before gesturing to the arched doorway. "I... made you some things to eat. I thought you might like them."

"What is it that you have to ask me?" Hades replied, crossing his arms. Defeated, her shoulders sagged slightly before she straightened herself.

"I know that Persephone is bound to you."

"Really now?" he asked, his face betraying no emotion. "What makes you say that?"

"She admitted it to me. She is afraid to tell her mother because Demeter refuses to speak of you. You have put her in quite a situation."

"I have already told her that I will speak to Demeter myself."

"I know. She told me."

"Then what *is* your problem?"

"How do you think your sister will feel to lose her daughter again?"

"I will speak to her. I will take care of it." Hades refused to reveal anything else.

"What of Persephone? Do you love her?"

Hades glanced at his mother, stroking his chin. "Who are you to ask me such a question?"

"So you merely snatched her out of lust, desire? Boredom, perhaps?" She stared at Hades's face, studying it for any little bit of emotion that he might betray. "To spite Demeter?" she asked in an almost-teasing voice.

"Hmph." He scowled at her. "Spite? I would not waste my time kidnapping someone out of spite or anything so petty. Do not waste my time asking me stupid questions."

"I would not ask questions I considered stupid."

"Then you and I obviously have different ideas of what 'stupid' entails." His scowl deepened into a dark frown. "What is done is done, and I will not spend another moment listening to your nagging!"

"Hades, I was not trying to..." He could get so defensive sometimes! She reached for him as he started to retreat from the room. "I simply want to understand what happened between you and Persephone, and why you would choose her..."

"I chose her because I wanted her. Simple as that."

"What about what she wants?" At her words, Hades simply retreated further, ducking out of sight as he left the building. She rushed to the door, refusing to give up. "If you truly care for her, think about what she wants!"

Before she could finish the sentence, he disappeared, shadow swallowing him.

"Ugh!" She slammed the side of her fist against the wall in frustration. It was all too easy for Hades to gain the last word in an argument or making a point by simply disappearing. He certainly wasn't the only god to leave a situation quickly, but his particular Gift made his departures effective. One couldn't compel Hades to do anything he didn't want to.

Fortunately, Hades's defensiveness did reveal to her one thing. If he didn't love Persephone, he would have easily said so. She was for the moment content with this one glimmer of hope amidst his aloof secrecy.

o0o

Persephone laughed as she ran across the sun-dappled snow and grass. It was a warm day, with snow melting in the sun to reveal greenish-brown grass. The air was just brisk enough to keep them cool while the princesses exerted themselves playing a combination of tag and hide-and-go-seek.

Their mothers were occupied, Metaniera holding Court with her husband, and Demeter traveling elsewhere to ensure that the curse truly was lifted in all places and that the damage was repaired. This meant no parental supervision whatsoever, and even Thalassa was happy to get away from inside activities and stretch her legs. Demeter had set up protective magic surrounding the forest so that the princesses would not be attacked. Persephone could sense this magic, but did nothing to disrupt it.

Some parts of Hellas were especially rife with nymphs, but the forest was surprisingly quiet. Persephone could feel the presence of a few, but some nymphs actually preferred to retreat into Nature, not talking to anyone. That was just fine with her, since she had spent half of her life in the company of nymphs and was in no mood for their idle chatter or singing. She just wanted to enjoy herself and play a game and be *alive*.

She hopped over a root, seeing Eirene duck behind a tree to her left. With a mischievous grin, she pranced over to the tree, suddenly reaching around it and startling the princess. Eirene gave out a startled laugh and spun around before Persephone dashed off. She spun around again when she heard a snapping of a branch, seeing Thalassa free herself from a low-reaching limb.

213

Thalassa looked up when she heard running footsteps, seeing her youngest sister approaching her fast. Eirene was nimble on her feet, skipping over roots and dodging branches easily.

The laughter and cries of the five females filled the forest as Hades stood under a tree, watching. Persephone looked radiant, her cheeks rosy from the cold and activity. Her hair was pulled from her face with a pale sash, but it hung free down her back, trailing behind her in flashes of deep red and bright amber as she ran. He felt tempted to snatch her up and make love to her right now.

But at the same time he wanted to continue watching. She was enjoying herself in a carefree game, lovely even in the drab-hued gray-blue and brown clothing she was wearing. The Sun gave Persephone's hair its highlights and glints of polished copper and gold, an effect that the light in the Underworld failed to achieve. He remembered the first time he had ever seen her, over a decade ago, in Zeus's garden. Her hair had the same shine back then, and it was one of the things he had always remembered about her.

Persephone was right. The Underworld, despite the comforts he offered her, was a very different place. A steady diet of Demeter's cooking gave her limbs just the right touch of softness and filling in the hollowness of her cheeks, restoring her to the picture of radiant health.

One of the girls ran past him, coming within several feet but completely oblivious to his presence. He continued watching them play, reaching out several times towards Persephone and having to restrain himself from alerting her to his presence. It was obvious that she enjoyed the company of the other girls, and they all called out one another's names with ease. His breath came out in thick wisps as he tightened his cloak around himself. The coldness of the Underworld was different than that of winter, but he felt it acutely.

Even as twilight turned into darkness, the girls still romped about, aided by the light of the moon. After half an hour, they slowed down, drawing together to form a loose group that trudged back to the Palace.

"I like having you around, Sephie. You are fun to play with." Eirene said as she skipped around the Goddess in circles.

"That is good to know," Persephone responded with a brilliant smile.

I like having you around too, Persephone, Hades thought as he watched them approach the small back gate. As if she knew what he was thinking, Persephone glanced up suddenly, glancing in his general direction over her shoulder. She frowned contemplatively before turning away.

oOo

Persephone reclined in the tub, steam surrounding her as her head lolled back. Had it been her imagining, or did she really sense that Hades was there while she played with her friends? She had felt, just for a moment, before that sensation was gone. She turned her attention to washing herself, and was soon enough having her hair braided by Mother. She was content to let her mother do this for her, and closed her eyes as she felt the comb running through her damp curls.

After her visit with Rhea, Mother had asked her what they talked about. Not that it surprised her, but she wouldn't answer Mother's questions, cutting her off with a simple statement of it being a private conversation. Of course, Mother hadn't liked it, but what could she do? The disappointed parent had given her the silent treatment for the rest of the night, but Persephone simply ignored it. In the morning though, Mother had changed her mood and was pleasant and cheery, even accommodating to her daughter's desires. So Persephone returned that courtesy, polite in her demands, and so far, it was going well.

"Mother, the earth is healed now, and we both have a lot of time on our hands. I was wondering when you were planning to take me up to Olympus and introduce me proper," Persephone asked casually, fiddling with the brush that her mother was now finished with.

"There is no need to rush into that."

That answer did not surprise the younger woman, and she was prepared. "Of course, I am not saying I want to do it now! Just that I would like for people to see that I am not a weak girl, or to have people keep associating my name with Ares's or Hades's own. I want to look them all in the eye and be acknowledged on my own right."

Demeter's hands stilled as she heard these words.

"It is the mortals who worship the gods, not other gods. Are you not happy here?"

Persephone stiffened, but plowed on. "Eleusis is a lovely place and I enjoy the company of these mortals, but I would like to see and meet my family, not just hear the stories about them."

"In due time," Mother replied guardedly, determined to avoid an argument despite her temptation to say 'no'. Determined to not give up, Persephone made a graceful rebuttal.

"What about Athene or Artemis? Or Hestia? Grandmother was so nice and I enjoyed spending time with her! Or would you rather I spend time with Dionysus?" Her eyes twinkled with merriment.

"Dionysus? I am not letting my daughter stumble around drunk with him!"

Persephone laughed out loud. "Mother, I was just teasing! It is not trouble I seek! And the women would have good advice about being a goddess, right?"

Demeter had hoped to keep Kora a little girl, but inwardly, she knew – as much as she hated to admit it – that her daughter would grow up and that her magic could only work on her child for so long. If she was selective about the deities that her daughter spent time with, there was hope yet that Kora would remain aloof to the gods. After what had happened with Ares and Hades, surely the girl's interest in men would have waned.

Demeter nodded. Persephone was satisfied

with that answer, even if Mother hadn't said 'yes'. Hades was right, patience was a virtue... at least, sometimes.

Chapter XLVIII

oOo

"There is no need to be so nervous, Persephone," Rhea said with a reassuring smile as she squeezed her granddaughter's shoulder. Persephone smiled shyly at her grandmother. Another week had come and gone by with a couple more visits with Grandmother, and these were always pleasant. They had talked more about Hades, but there were plenty of other things to talk about.

In some ways, Rhea reminded her of Eurycleia. However, she had only ever been with her first grandmother as a child, and despite Eurycleia's obvious love for her, there was the inevitable age barrier. Here, she was treated like an adult, and as any grown person knew, their relationships with elders were different once they had passed childhood. She still had a few arguments with Mother, but after the first few days of her homecoming, their relationship had improved. Slowly but surely, Mother began to accept the boundaries her daughter established, at least, most of the time.

"You will like Artemis. You both enjoy romping about in the woods, and you are not obsessed with men like some of the other goddesses are," Rhea added with a wry smile. There were so many gods on Olympus – Gaea's immortal brood was impressive indeed – but she thought it best to start with a few goddesses that had proven that they had a good head on their shoulders. And then, a few gods as well, to show Persephone that not everyone was like Zeus or Ares.

"You mean Aphrodite?" she shot back. Rhea nodded. Aphrodite was like no other goddess, and she had quite the impression on the younger gods, and the older ones as well. Persephone was beautiful in her own right, her expressive green eyes and regal features giving her a depth that was lacking in Aphrodite's pretty heart-shaped face and big blue eyes.

"Grandmother?" a new voice called out from the entryway.

"Come on in, we are in the kitchen." Rhea answered. In a moment, a woman with dark brown hair emerged through the doorway, and her appearance fulfilled Persephone's expectations of the Goddess of the Hunt. Rather than an ankle-length dress like most women would wear, Artemis was clad in a tunic that ended above her knees, comfortable-looking leggings completing her outfit. Strapped to her back was her quiver, and Persephone saw the glint of silver amongst the arrows. The younger goddesses appraised one another before Artemis smiled at her.

"Hello," Artemis offered. "So you are Demeter's daughter? I was almost sure you were a story Hermes imagined."

Persephone laughed at that statement. Goodness, Hermes did have quite the reputation, didn't he?

"No, I am very much real, as you can see," she

countered smoothly.

"Good answer. I already like you," Artemis shot back.

"I should hope so."

Rhea smiled approvingly, pleased at the fact that she had made such a good match. "I think you girls will have some fun. Persephone enjoys being outside almost as much as you do."

"You are not afraid of getting your clothes dirty, are you?" Artemis asked.

"Oh, not at all."

o0o

Persephone was amazed by Artemis's unique Gift of talking to animals. She had often wondered what an animal might be thinking, what it might say if it could talk, or if it could understand her if she spoke to them.

Artemis didn't have to wonder about any of that, since she could understand them and make herself understood! It wasn't a flashy Gift, but it opened up a new world for the Goddess of the Hunt. She watched quietly as Artemis chattered and nickered at a deer before it responded with similar noises. Many animals had died from Demeter's curse, and much of what remained was now in hibernation or nestled in warm hiding places.

"If you love animals so much, why are you the Goddess of the Hunt?" Persephone asked. The tall woman glanced at her, a look of faint surprise on her face before she nodded.

"I do not hunt for sport. I rarely use this..." Artemis gestured to her quiver, "But it is part of the cycle of life for living things to eat one another. The wolf is not evil for eating a deer or rabbit. There was once a time, long before I was born, when all man had to clothe himself with was the skin of animals. I must be honest, I am glad these days are over."

Persephone tried to imagine what it would be like when the only options were to kill an animal or go naked. Weaving and spinning did have practical applications, sheep didn't die for the wool that humans gathered from them, and nobody could object to cutting down plants to turn them into fiber.

"You should meet Athene soon. She feels the same way about war that I feel about the hunt. The hunt is to be respected, to be performed only in time of need, and the kill must be done as quickly and painlessly as possible, so the animal does not suffer."

"Hmm." Persephone frowned thoughtfully before she nodded. "Do the animals ask you to not hunt them?"

"Of course. But unlike others, I know when an animal has babies waiting for it to return to them, or a mate. So I am very careful about my prey. It is so much more enjoyable tracking them down or talking to them. I do not enjoy the hunt as much as everyone else thinks I do. The wolf does not eat any more animals than it needs, and neither do I."

After considering that for several moments, Persephone commented on something Artemis had said earlier.

"How do you know what man or animals did before you were born?" Hades had given her many lessons in his private library, she wondered if there was also such a place up here. Perhaps on Mount Olympus?

"The animals tell me."

"What?" Did animals record history, too?

"Humans pass down stories from their ancestors. Why should animals be any different?" Artemis replied casually, as if this should be no surprise.

"Well..." Persephone tapped her chin. True, animals did not read or write, but they weren't the dumb beasts that men tended to think they were. That much she knew. They could feel affection for humans or for one another, and they could feel pain and fear. They used the various tools Nature gave them – claws, wings, fins, tails – to survive and even thrive.

But sharing stories and passing them down? That seemed a bit farfetched, didn't it? Persephone voiced her question.

"Animals are born knowing the things they need. That is something humans do not have. Animals carry knowledge within them, passing it down to their offspring. A mother or sire has only to remind them of what they already know. Deep within, they also carry the memories of not just survival, but of the way things once were."

Now, there was something to think about. "Why do humans not have these memories?"

"Perhaps we once did." Artemis shrugged. It

was something she had pondered before. Young humans had to be taught *everything* – whether it be through actual lessons or by observing others. "However, being born with knowledge leaves very little room to learn new things, which is why humans are so different in their way of living. Of course, animals do not fight wars or play cruel games with one another. They are happy being the way they are."

Persephone considered the animals she had grown up with. The chickens and goats her father tended seemed happy with their lot, giving her friendly butts of their heads or pecking seeds out of her hand. Her cousin's dog could be satisfied with a belly-rub or a firm scratch behind the ears. Sometimes all the animals wanted was to sit or lay in a warm patch of sunlight. They didn't care about wealth or status or anything like that.

"Say, would you be interested in learning how to use a bow and arrow? We would not be shooting at animals, but marksmanship is an useful talent."

Upon seeing her companion's curious and excited nod, Artemis smiled before lifting her arm and removing her bow and an arrow out of her quiver.

"See that knot on the tree over there?" the Goddess of the Hunt asked, pointing in front of her. Persephone squinted her eyes, trying to see just where the other woman was pointing. It took several moments to see the tree Artemis indicated, since it was so far off.

"Yes."

"Watch." Artemis lifted her bow, positioning her arrow. With a sharp *zing*, the silver-tipped arrow soared through the air, hitting its intended target.

The glint of sun off the silvery feathers revealed its location. Before Persephone could comment or give praise, Artemis plucked out another arrow and fired it off with rapid grace.

Artemis bounded off as nimbly as a doe, and Persephone was not far behind. The two arrows were snugly nestled against one another in the tree. Artemis plucked them out and gave Persephone one to examine. It wasn't the first time she had seen a bow or arrows, of course – Iasion's brother had been a fairly adept hunter, bringing home rabbit or pheasant on occasion to augment the food that he and his brother farmed. Eurycleia made the best rabbit stew, and it was always such a treat for the whole family.

The arrow was exquisitely crafted, and obviously not made by a mortal hand. And she had never seen silver feathers before. What kind of bird could boast of such spectacular feathers in its plumage?

"Who made this?" she asked.

"Hephaistos makes the arrow-tips, but I do the rest."

Persephone nodded as she ran her fingers along the shaft, admiring its craftsmanship. Her uncle Esthanes would have envied such an arrow!

oOo

After returning to Eleusis, Persephone thought about what she had been taught and shown. Mortals a few decades older were considered wise and knowledgeable to the younger generation. So a god several centuries older would have a lot to teach her. Hades was certainly proof enough of that. She wondered what kind of valuable insight she could learn from other gods. What could Hera tell her about being a queen? What might Athene say about wisdom or war? Or go back another generation to the Titanesses, Rhea had several sisters, and if they were anything like Grandmother, she was eager to meet them. She had been nervous about meeting another goddess, but she and Artemis had gotten along naturally, as if they were meant to be friends all along.

She's also my sister, Persephone reminded herself. That idea took some getting used to. Growing up, she had been an only child. Now she had to deal with the fact that Hermes and Ares – among a whole host of other gods – were her brothers and sisters. She hadn't revealed her paternity to Artemis, and she didn't intend to. It was lovely having the Goddess of the Hunt as a friend. Why spoil it?

o0o

Persephone was so excited about her new friendship with Artemis, along with her continuing friendship with the princesses that for the time being, she set aside her concerns about Zeus or Hades. She had been isolated even amidst the nymphs for so long that she was determined to simply enjoy the time she had left.

The thought of returning to the Underworld excited but saddened her. She missed Hades and looked forward to enjoying his company again. She genuinely cared for him, and could not imagine any other man as her mate. Yet she dreaded leaving the surface world. She would miss Mother and Grandmother and all her new friends. At least the Underworld wasn't a horrid place like everyone believed it to be.

Eleusis and Mount Olympus were lovely places, but she missed the intellectual stimulation that came from spending time in Hades's library. On the surface world, writing was still fairly new to many cultures, and Hellas was no exception. Stories and myths were passed down orally, and writing was mainly used to keep records. The majority of Hellas's population did not know how to read or write, nor was there any opportunity for them to ever learn. But then, for most people, there was no need to. Farmers and merchants might make marks on pieces of wood, clay or papyrus paper to count how many of this or that they had, and that was all they had need for.

Hades had said that in the future, reading and writing would become more common – and more important as well. He even suggested that somewhere in the future, just about everyone would know this valuable skill. It was hard for her to imagine what Hellas might be like in centuries or even millennia, even though she now knew that she would see the world change just as Hades had done for quite a few centuries.

Such thoughts sometimes boggled her mind, and she was glad for the distractions of daily life. She would explore the city or the forest, visit with Grandmother or Artemis, spend time with Mother or the princesses, or find things to do with her hands like, spinning, gardening, or preparing food with Mother. Cooking was one thing she enjoyed doing with Mother, and those times brought peace between mother and daughter.

Persephone sat in a chair with a basket of pea pods in her lap, prying open the pods with her fingernails and extracting the little sweet orbs, popping one in her mouth here and there. Sometimes they would eat with the royal family, but oftentimes, it was just the two of them.

Mother sat in her own chair, spinning some wool as she stared off with a distant but calm expression. It had been over a week since she had brought up the subject of Hades, and Persephone figured that was long enough. Less than two weeks remained before the winter solstice.

"Mother, I need to talk to you about something important." Persephone tried to sound as light and casual as she could.

"What is it?" Demeter asked, continuing to spin yarn with her spindle. The pair continued working, their hands deftly moving around at their respective tasks, and Persephone welcomed this occupation.

"I know you do not like talking about Hades, but this is important. Please listen to me." She could see Mother stiffen, her shoulders squaring as she took a deep breath, but at least she didn't attempt to close the subject.

"What is it?" Demeter asked again with measured patience.

Persephone took a slow breath, glancing down at the peas for a moment. How best to suggest her inevitable return to the Underworld without sending Mother into a panic or anger? Hmm.

"Before Hades let me leave the Underworld he promised me that he would see me again."

"Absolutely not," came Mother's automatic reply. "After what he has done, he thinks he has the right to see you again?"

Persephone had to bite back a wry smile. "We both know that Hades's word is never to be doubted. If he wants to see me again, he will."

"Not if I stop him."

"You know you cannot." She spoke calmly, trying to project this onto her mother as well. Demeter had stopped making yarn, her task forgotten for the moment as her jaw tightened.

"Do you seriously expect me to just stand aside while the man who kidnapped my daughter seeks out her company?"

"Hades would never harm me. I am not afraid of him."

"*What?*" Demeter was incredulous. Everyone feared Hades, even mighty Zeus himself. "I thought you were unhappy in the Underworld!"

"Yes, the Underworld is a dead place. But that is not Hades's fault. He has always been very kind to me. I do not hate him, and neither should you. I most certainly am not worried about seeing him again." Hopefully if Mother could see that she wasn't afraid of the big, bad Lord of the Underworld, then she might feel more at ease.

Demeter glanced at her for several moments, her furrowed eyebrows clear evidence of her attempt to process her daughter's words and formulate a response. Well, at least she hadn't snapped with 'No!'

"Honestly, I am a lot more angry with Zeus than I was with Hades for kidnapping me. Besides, Hades apologized for kidnapping me. Now, how nice was that of him?"

Demeter gave out a quiet snort of disdain as she resumed her spinning.

"Hades would be happy to apologize to you too, if you let him." Her smile was serene as she continued shelling peas. "He really is not a bad person."

"Then why would he kidnap you?"

"He was lonely." Persephone looked down again, eating several peas as her mother stared at her. To her surprise and relief, Mother didn't say anything further.

Chapter XLIX

oOo

Only a week remained before the winter solstice, and even such a brief period of time felt too long to Hades. He had been sorely tempted to reveal himself to Persephone too many times.

When he saw her romp and play outside with her friends, he was reminded of his mother's words regarding her needs. She looked radiant – eyes sparking, cheeks rosy, her laughter like the sweetest music to his ears. He hated remembering the argument with his mother, or the fact that he would have to confront his sister in a week. Demeter would be angry no matter what he said.

He had many powers, but he could not turn back time. If he could, he would have tried to court her properly, and then the entire mess wouldn't have happened, but what was done was done. He had made promises, and he would fulfill them whether or not he looked forward to it.

oOo

Eirene usually found it hard to focus on things, but she actually didn't mind trying to concentrate as she aimed the arrow at the stump. A few days ago, Persephone had gotten a new bow and set of arrows, and she didn't mind sharing. It was really exciting because Triptolemus alone was allowed to take lessons along with the soldiers and guards, and that made

Eirene jealous. The boys got to do all the fun things like learn how to fight with swords or use bows while she and her sisters were stuck with spinning and weaving, and that annoyed her to no end!

When she complained to Mother about the difference in the way she and her brother was treated, Mother always said that girls had their duties and so did boys and that was how things were. Ugh! That was a stupid answer!

But Sephie was good at getting her out of the weaving sessions she hated. Thalassa and Aethra could weave all they wanted, and Mother was too afraid to defy a goddess. So she could go on walks with Sephie and she didn't care if it was cold or snowing outside. Anything was better than weaving! And it was so much fun having snowball fights or playing hide-and-go-seek with her friend.

"Just take a deep breath," Persephone whispered, standing behind Eirene as she held the girl's arms steady, demonstrating the proper way to hold the bow and arrow. It had been such an unexpected – but wonderful – gift from Artemis, and she was glad to have such a good friend among the goddesses. Despite Eirene's youth, the size of the bow was no great hindrance to its use since it was a bit smaller than Artemis's own bow, and required less force to pull.

"Pay attention that your arm is positioned so that when you let go, the string does not snap against it, because believe me, it hurts!" Persephone had learned the hard way, and had dropped her bow the first time due to the unexpected pain of the sinew whipping against the inside of her arm. Eirene's body was loosely pressed against her own, and she could feel the girl actually concentrating, her nervous energy restrained for the moment.

"Do you have your target?" Persephone whispered. Eirene nodded.

"Good. Now... let go."

Eirene uncurled her fingers, letting the arrow fly. It did not hit its intended target, but it actually came fairly close, missing by a couple of feet.

"Wow! That was close! You did better than me on my first try!"

The princess grinned with relief. Storytelling was popular especially during the long winter nights, and there were quite a few stories of how gods hated to be bested by mortals. Just look at what Athene had done to Arachne simply because the mortal had woven better! But Sephie didn't seem mad at all.

"Would you like to try again?" the older woman asked.

"Yes, please!"

"Well, then!" She pulled another bow out of her quiver and handed it to Eirene. "This time, try it yourself." She took a step back, letting Eirene take her stance.

"Lift your elbow a bit higher... there you go," Eirene heard her friend instruct. Her elbow shook a little, but she took a deep breath, remembering how Sephie had positioned her arms. The arrow veered to the other side of the target – a tree with a large knothole in its trunk – but it did come a bit closer. She remembered the couple of times where she had actually been allowed to watch her brother train with the men. Some of them hadn't been very good marksmen in the beginning, and it thrilled her to know that she was already better than a few of them.

"You said that Artemis gave you this. What is she like?" Eirene asked eagerly.

"She is a bit tall..." Persephone lifted her hand several inches above her own head, indicating Artemis's height. "And slender, but very strong and fast. She doesn't like being inside, and she talks to animals."

"*Talks* to animals?"

"Oh, yes."

"How? Does she make animal noises or does she talk to them with words?" Eirene was a fair imitator of birdsong, and she wondered what the birds meant when they made this or that kind of chirp or tweet.

"She makes the same noises they make. You cannot tell them apart, really, and if you closed your eyes, you would not think there was a human there. And then they talk back to her and she understands them. I do not know how she understands, she just does."

"I would like to meet her!"

"Maybe one day." Persephone smiled. She didn't say 'yes' because she wasn't going to make a commitment for Artemis, as doing so might offend the other goddess. In the meantime, she was content to simply sit against a tree as she watched Eirene pick up another arrow.

oOo

Persephone counted the arrows in her quiver to ensure that she and Eirene had picked them all up before she set it and her bow in her chest. She and Eirene had engaged in a friendly competition, seeing who could get closest to the target. Neither of them had been able to hit the knothole, but some of their shots had come very close. It was something that took practice, to angle the arrow to compensate for different factors like wind or gravity.

With her time on the surface world drawing to a close, she made the decision to see Grandmother the next day. She had been considering what she might say to Zeus ever since she had learned of her paternity and his involvement in her situation. Nothing she could say to him would change her fate, but there were a few choice words she would like to hurl at him. It was intimidating to think of going face-to-face with the mighty King of the Gods, but she had only to remind herself of the abilities that came with her Gift. If he would be upset by the things she had to say, he would find out that she would not allow him to lash out at her.

oOo

Persephone let Rhea serve her ambrosia and nectar along with freshly-baked bread and olive

235

oil to dip it in. After going hungry for so long in the Underworld, she was always happy to eat food that was served to her, whether from Mother or Grandmother or the royal family's servants. Demeter and Rhea were both good cooks, and of course, Celeus and Metaniera had skilled chefs to feed them.

She happily munched on some bread, savoring the taste of freshly-squeezed olive oil. Thanks to the bounty that Demeter had spread through Hellas, everything was fresh, regardless of what season it normally grew in. Normally, strawberries did not grow until it was almost her birthday, but Rhea had a bowl of them next to the bread, and Persephone helped herself to a few.

"I am so happy that you and Artemis are getting along so well. She usually does not like to spend so much time with anyone."

"I could tell..." Persephone replied as she took a sip of nectar. "But you knew I would get along with her, anyway."

Rhea smiled. "I have always been able to match people, though I was blind when it came to Kronos." She let out a quiet sigh. Kronos had been so charismatic and handsome that she found herself dazzled by him.

"Was he truly so awful? I mean no disrespect in asking this as I have only heard stories, and we both know they tend to get exaggerated or twisted around."

"Yes, the mortals were not aware of just how despicable he was. If I could have seen into the future and known the monster he would become, I never would have married him. That is the curse of hindsight. He was actually much worse than the stories make him out to be. I am just grateful that Zeus has not turned out that way, despite all of his flaws."

"Speaking of Zeus..." Persephone folded her hands against the table. "I need to talk to him."

"Hmm." Rhea nodded slowly. She had been wondering when her granddaughter would bring it up. It had surprised her that Persephone hadn't demanded to see Zeus once she was free of the Underworld.

"I want to see him now."

Rhea considered checking to see if Zeus was in a meeting or frolicking with a nymph – though she was more certain of the former than the latter because the nymphs were still shunning him – but she decided against it. This was important, and it was obvious that Persephone had waited for a reason. So what if it inconvenienced Zeus, he had caused enough trouble for everyone else!

"Come with me, dear. Let us waste not a moment," she said as she rose from her seat, extending her hand. The young deity's pulse quickened in anticipation as she considered the fact that she was about to see her biological father, a man she had not seen in over a decade.

Grandmother's footsteps were quick but steady as she strode down several lanes. Mount Olympus was built so that the center of the settlement was a large, public area with the Meeting Hall at one end. Surrounding it on three sides were the private homes of various deities, tucked away along the peaks and set aside luxurious gardens, whitewashed walls, and sumptuous homes and courtyards, accessible by quaint lanes laid out with an eye-pleasing mixture of marble stones.

Zeus's home was silent, and Rhea did not sense anyone's presence there. However, she would not give up until she found her youngest son, wherever he was.

oOo

The King of the Gods was holding court with several other male gods, trying to meditate an argument over dominion. It wasn't the first time that the gods had argued over provinces or worshipers, and it certainly wouldn't be the last. Oftentimes a god would do a great favor for a city or village, and worship would inevitably shift into his favor, displeasing whatever deity the mortals had formerly paid homage to.

Though Ares had Sparta, he also wanted other cities to worship him. To him, war was a noble pursuit, the ultimate exercise in strength. A man who was able to command an army and lead them to victory usually gained Ares's favor, more so when the battle was bloody. He preferred to leave strategy to the mortal generals and enjoy the heat of battle.

The village around Delphi was too peaceful for Ares's taste. Because of the Oracle, Delphi was a popular tourist location, visited by people making pilgrimages from distant provinces to hear her words. Kings of mighty city-states would visit the Oracle, coming to Delphi in elegant processions. Commoners and poor people would come on their own two feet, spending what little – if any – resources they had to hear her words. The residents of Delphi had a thriving industry in catering to their visitors.

Of course, the Oracle was not the only fortune-teller in Hellas, but the Delphi priestesses had the highest reputation in the land, being blessed by Apollo himself and having a good record of making uncannily accurate – if sometimes vague – predictions. Even if one was not lucky enough to see the mighty Oracle herself, her acolytes were adept at making smaller predictions or giving advice.

Ares didn't care for predictions. He thought it was stupid, and a waste of time to try to figure out what would happen in the future. As far as he was concerned, the future was affected by what happened in the now. To hell with the mystical mumbo-jumbo.

It was this attitude that caused him and Apollo to stand before Zeus. Ares had been in Delphi, trying to stir up trouble and cause the men who lived there to take up the sword as their cause rather than serve the Oracle. Of course, Apollo would have none of it, but Ares refused to listen much less cooperate with his brother.

"Ares." Zeus stared at his warmongering son with a stern expression. Ares had already tried to instigate enough trouble during Demeter's famine in a desperate attempt to save his city from starving to death. Now that the Spartans had enough to eat again, he quickly became bored and turned his focus elsewhere. No matter how many times the God of War was reprimanded or punished, he simply could not stay out of trouble!

"You have been told time and time again in the past to leave the other gods alone. You have an entire city that has dedicated itself to your worship. If you like fighting, do it yourself. Hellas has been through enough already, and the last thing it needs is some war that does not even make sense!"

"Who cares if it doesn't make sense! War is war!" Ares scowled. Apollo and Zeus both glared at him, and Helios and Dionysus merely shook their heads.

"One would think that a few centuries would temper your bloodlust, but apparently not." The King of the Gods gave out an exasperated sigh. All too often he had considered physically restraining his son in some way by chains or keeping him in a cell. He was certain that Hephaistos could create something that could effectively restrain Ares, but that seemed like such a drastic measure. The only people in his family that actually had to be incarcerated were the Titans who had turned against their brethren and helped Kronos terrorize Hellas. They had to be dragged into Tartarus by chains, and there they remained for eternity under Kampe's watch.

Would such a punishment be effective on Ares? At this point, it seemed like it was all that Ares might really respond to. Zeus absolutely hated the idea of having to do this to anyone, especially his own child, but he had his other children – and the rest of the family – to think about.

"Perhaps a few years in Tartarus would teach you the error of having such an unbridled temper."

Apollo inhaled sharply, and Ares's jaw dropped open. Zeus had never threatened anyone with a sentence in Tartarus! The other gods stared at Zeus, but none of them objected. They had all been victims of Ares's aggression in one way or another, and were glad to see the God of War be put into his place.

"No, no, no!" Ares shook his head frantically. It was exceedingly rare that he felt cornered. He had never been to Tartarus, but everyone knew it was a terrible place. Damn Apollo for telling on him. His brother was a weakling, anyways. Apollo was a pretty boy who would rather sing or tell stories than fight, and Ares didn't consider him a real man.

"No?" Zeus set his lips in a tight, grim line. "You fear the idea of spending some time in Tartarus? Then behave."

"But..."

"No buts! I have been too lenient in the past. I am tired of it. Sparta is your city. Nothing else. If I hear one single word about you trying to take other cities as your own..." His words cut off into ominous silence as he glared at his son.

Apollo smirked at Ares as he crossed his arms.

Suddenly, Rhea strode into the grand chamber, closely trailed by another woman. All eyes turned towards her for a moment before focusing on the younger woman.

Zeus stared at the redheaded woman, barely remembering to keep his mouth closed because he had come far too close to letting his jaw drop. Whoever this goddess was, she was stunning, and it was clear from the reactions of the other gods that they felt the same way he did.

Persephone was conscious of all the attention given her, but she maintained her dignity, appearing to give none of them any notice even as she studied them out of the corners of her eyes. She was clad in a deep blue chiton – a gift from Rhea – and her hair was pulled back with a matching sash. Her clothing was very modest, leaving only her head, neck, and forearms exposed.

As she glanced in Ares's direction, she raised her chin haughtily, staring at him coolly. Despite what he had done – or at least, attempted to do – she wasn't the least bit afraid of him. She narrowed her eyes at him for a moment before glancing at the others. Even though she had never met them, she recognized them from the statues Hades had in his spectacular sculpture garden. There was Helios and Apollo along with Dionysus. Having heard the argument before she entered the hall with Rhea, she quickly surmised that they were here to support Apollo. The trio appeared friendly enough, and she gave them a polite nod.

"Mother! What are you doing here?" Zeus asked with a smile, trying to figure out who the new goddess was. She looked familiar and he was certain he should know who she was, but he was unable to identify her.

"Your audience is urgently needed, and I see that you have resolved the matter with your son, so his presence is no longer needed." Rhea glanced at her nephew and three grandsons. "You are dismissed."

"Wait a moment, you can not do that..." Zeus stiffened as his mother casually dismissed the rest of the gods as if *she* were in charge.

"You will *not* 'wait a moment' me!" The elder goddess' tone brooked no argument as she glared at him.

"Come," Apollo whispered, nudging Dionysus. Generally, Grandmother was a sweet-natured person, but the whole of Olympus knew that she was a formidable figure and not to be crossed when she set her mind to something.

Her marriage to Kronos had been a harsh experience, and after his overthrow, she was determined to not be pushed around by anybody else ever again. She chose to not be on the Council of Twelve, feeling she needed no recognition as part of an elite, but she managed affairs with a firm hand and was a respected figure.

The gods were curious about the newcomer, but they figured they would be finding out who she was soon enough. With respectful inclines of their heads, Helios, Apollo, and Dionysus bade farewell to Rhea and retreated from the chamber. Ares lingered, but a stern wave of Rhea's hand caused him to slink away.

Silently fuming at being embarrassed by his mother in front of his sons and this pretty goddess, Zeus nonetheless held back a scowl as he regarded the two women.

"What is it that is so urgent?" he asked.

"You ask me what is so urgent when you do not recognize who stands before you?" Rhea asked, gesturing to her companion. Now that they were alone, Zeus had a better chance to study the newcomer. The hair was much like Rhea's own, only redder, and the green eyes were very familiar.

"Kora?" Zeus whispered with genuine shock. Last time he had seen his daughter, she had been a pretty little girl, but he had never imagined that she would grow up to be so beautiful.

"I was wondering if you would recognize me since you saw me but twice in my life," she commented.

Refusing to be shaken by her sudden appearance, he smiled in his charming way. "Do forgive me, dear daughter, but your mother was determined to not let me be your father. I do hope you are not too angry with me for respecting her wishes. Fortunately for us, we are gods, and have endless days to make up for lost time."

Persephone turned to her grandmother, ignoring Zeus for the moment. "Would you mind too terribly if I were to wish to converse with him privately?"

"Oh, not at all." Rhea patted her granddaughter's shoulder before giving her a reassuring smile and leaving.

"Make up for lost time? Are you *serious*?" To Zeus's surprise, his daughter actually sounded offended. He could not possibly imagine *why*.

"What is the matter, Kora?"

"My name is *Persephone*. And you talk of making up time when you gave Hades your blessing, knowing you might never see me again!"

"Why worry about that? Hades has let you go. I am the one who ordered him to release you!"

"And if he had not let me go?" Persephone stared at him levelly.

"Why worry about such things? It is all over!"

"Because not considering such things is what caused the disaster in the first place."

"Ko- Persephone, I never intended you any harm. Hades promised he would treat you well. Has he?"

*Yes he has, but that's beyond the point... **idiot!*** Mother had called him idiot several times, and it was all too apparent why. How fortunate that she had been raised by a much more worthy father figure!

"That is not what I asked," she replied calmly, reining in her fury.

Zeus held his smile as he rose from his throne. "Persephone dear, please do not be angry with me. I only acted in your best interests. Hades gave me his word, I never would have given my blessing to a man I thought would mistreat you."

Demeter and Rhea had both commented on his charm and affability and she remembered her first meeting with him and how kind he had been, but Persephone would not be swayed.

"And you did not think that I would have something to say about that?" As he moved closer, she took a step back. It was all too obvious that he wanted to hug her or pat her arm in an attempt to pacify her.

"What was the point?"

"What was the point?" she repeated with open incredulity. "It did not occur to you that I might appreciate some input, or even a warning? Hades appeared out of nowhere to snatch me away! I thought I was going to *die!*"

"Oh, my! I truly never intended to cause you any distress." Zeus offered in his most placating tone, shaken by the reminder of the fears that had been stirred on the fateful day Hades had come to him for his blessing. "I truly am sorry. But things have worked out, haven't they? Look at you, you have grown into such a lovely woman! More than fitting to be the Goddess of Spring!"

Not for long, Persephone thought bitterly. As soon as Hades reclaimed her, she would sit by him as his queen. There was no spring in the Underworld, how could there be when there was no life?

"Do you understand what you have done to me?" she demanded. "After your son attempted to rape me, you thought it would be appropriate to give me away to another man?"

"Hades did not hurt you, did he?"

"Hnkkk!" Her cheeks were flushed with rage as she gritted her teeth, choking back a frustrated hiss. "Are you always this stupid?"

Zeus's smile froze. "I will not be insulted!" He had dealt with enough abuse from his large family during the famine, and was still being shunned by the nymphs. Kora – Persephone, whatever the hell she wanted to be called – was returned to the surface world, why was she so hostile? He might enjoy the company of women, but they baffled him as much as they had ever. A father arranging marriage for his daughter, that was nothing new! It had been done since the time of the Titans, for god and mortal alike, and not just in Hellas. Most women were generally acquiescing to gender norms, having been raised into them.

"It is the truth!" Persephone snapped back, her voice rising. "You gave your blessing to Hades without telling Mother or me, or letting me any say in the matter whatsoever! You have not seen me for over ten years, and you just... gave me away!"

"I am your father, and I know best!" Zeus responded firmly, wagging his finger.

"My father! You never were my father! You are just someone who tricked my mother into letting you stick it into her!"

"Silence!" The hairs on his body were standing on end due to the sudden influx of static electricity in the room, something that usually happened when he started to get angry, a precursor to his Gift flaring up.

"You cannot tell me what to do!"

"I am King of the Gods, and you will bow to my authority!" Small bursts of lightning crackled around him.

"You are unfit to hold such authority!" she screamed back at him, her normally verdant eyes taking on an amber tint as her rage increased.

"You may be my child, but I will not brook such insolence!" He made no attempt to stop his Gift from manifesting itself, allowing lightning to dance around his body in an attempt to kow her into obedience.

"I do not acknowledge you as my father!" She refused to be intimidated by what she was seeing. Had the two not been in such a heated argument, she would have enjoyed the visual effect of the electricity arcing and rippling along his form "The man who raised me respected me more than you ever did! He was more of a man than you will *ever* be!"

That was it! With a sudden roar, electricity burst forth from his body, filling the chamber. Before he could process anything, he found himself knocked back by an unseen force.

o0o

Rhea respected Persephone's request for a private meeting, but she did not retire from the building itself. That proved to be a wise decision once she heard the shouting that burst from the throne room.

She dashed into the room just in time to see her son fly into the air, lightning trailing in his wake like a madly zigzagging comet's tail. He hit one of the pillars with a definitive thud before

248

sliding down it.

"Persephone!" Rhea gaped at her granddaughter. She could feel the energy rolling off Persephone in thick spikes, and she could almost swear that the room was darker, as if Persephone had actually sucked some of the light out of the chamber. Her granddaughter stared at her for several moments, visibly shaking.

Zeus groaned softly, but Rhea ignored him as she rushed to Persephone's side.

"Persephone!" Rhea reached out to squeeze her hands. The younger deity offered no resistance.

"I am done," Persephone whispered in an almost inaudible voice. "I want to go home."

"Very well." Rhea lifted a hand to cup her granddaughter's face, seeing tears brimming in her eyes.

oOo

There was no mistaking the cold fury in Rhea's face as she stalked towards Zeus's Palace with long, rapid footsteps. The Hall was empty, her son having slunk away while Rhea returned Persephone to Eleusis. The door to his private residence banged open as Rhea charged in, seeing him sprawled out on a divan and drinking from a flask.

"What the hell is wrong with you?" she snarled. He jerked upright and stared at her.

"Me? She was the one yelling at me!"

"She had every right to!"

"She insulted me and my authority! I am King of Olympus and her father! And you dare scold me for refusing to tolerate such insubordination?"

"You sit on the High Throne by the grace of your brothers!" Zeus's contribution to the overthrow of the Titanomachy was not greater than his brothers, so he actually didn't have any particular bragging rights. By the Hellenic birthright rules, it was Hades who should have taken the High Throne since he was the eldest son, but he chose the Underworld instead. Poseidon was much happier in the sea, and the thought of living up high on a mountain did not appeal to the ocean deity at all. So by pure default – often termed as luck – Zeus had gained the throne.

"I am King nonetheless!"

"That is not an excuse for being so thoughtless!"

"Mama..."

"Hush. I am very disappointed in you. You have made many mistakes in your life, but lately, the consequences of these mistakes have come with great cost."

"I did not mean to..."

"Whatever your intentions were, the result is the same. You simply do not think enough when you make certain decisions. You have made many good decisions, but also plenty of bad ones. I keep hoping that the consequences of such errors will instill some wisdom into you, but you still fail to seek the counsel of others. I want to see you succeed as King of the Gods, but you cannot do it on your own."

"But..."

Rhea raised her hand in a gesture for silence. "No excuses. If you want to avoid more unpleasantness, remember that a king can only rule effectively if his subjects are happy with him. Before you act, talk with someone with more sense than yourself." She raised her hands, and he thought she would strike him, so he flinched back. A quick burst of energy came from her upraised palms, but to his relief, she didn't focus it on him, apparently letting it dissipate into the air. With a haughty sniff, she spun around and retreated from his house.

Oh, hell. Zeus picked up his flask – a mixture of nectar and wine – and wandered into his garden. Sitting among the roses always helped him feel better.

The flask dropped to the grass, liquid sloshing out of it as Zeus stared in horror at what remained of his private sanctuary, realizing just what his mother had done. His beloved rosebushes were nothing more than skeletal bushes, blackened leaves scattered around them. All of the roses had wilted, the grass littered with dried-up, colorless petals.

Chapter L

oOo

Apollo and Dionysus were taking a walk through Olympus, discussing what had happened with Ares and who the beautiful woman was that had been with Grandmother. Naturally, Apollo was delighted with the outcome of his meeting with Father. He was convinced that his brother was incorrigible and should have been sent to Tartarus on the spot, but the God of War had been frightened by Father's words, so he should at least keep out of trouble for a while.

Apollo had learned from experience that even if Ares might be compelled to behave, it never lasted too long. Nearly every god on Olympus had quarreled with Ares in the past over one thing or another. It actually seemed as if Ares *enjoyed* the fighting, and clearly that was part of the problem.

He nodded at something Dionysus said before both of them noticed Rhea stalking towards them, her lips set in a grim line. Her displeasure was apparent in the set of her shoulders and the briskness of her pace, and for a moment Apollo thought she might be displeased with him. However, she strode past them, and he let out a quiet sigh of relief before he called out to her.

"Grandmother! Is something the matter?"

Rhea paused and looked over her shoulder. "Yes, something is the matter, but you need not concern yourself."

"Why should I not be concerned when my

grandmother looks so unhappy?"

Dionysus nodded in agreement. Rhea smiled knowingly. Like his father, Apollo could be charming, but he tended to make fewer mistakes than the older god.

"Ahh, your father can be stupid sometimes."

"We know it," Dionysus commented. "Perhaps a drink with us would make you feel better?"

Rhea let out a short laugh. Nobody could deny the relaxing effects of Dionysus's wine.

"Thank you, but not right now. Perhaps later."

"Any time! Just let me know."

"You think a good drink solves everything, don't you?" Apollo teased his younger brother.

"Well, not with Ares because we know how poorly he handles alcohol. But it does work for most everything else."

Apollo laughed, and Rhea could not help but smile again.

"I do have one question," the God of Light said as he turned towards his grandmother. "Who was that woman with you?"

"I should have known you would ask..." She considered simply not answering the question, but realized that by doing so, she wouldn't be much better than Zeus or Demeter when they tried to keep secrets. "That is Demeter's daughter."

The pair of gods stared at her for a moment.

"Her?" Dionysus asked. The general expectation was that Demeter's daughter would look more like her mother. "She is beautiful! Aphrodite will be jealous!"

"There is no need to get ahead of yourselves, boys." Rhea used the term 'boys' whenever she wanted to remind the gods to behave or scold them. "A few hundred years has passed since Aphrodite came to Olympus and you made so much trouble vying for her attentions. You are much wiser now, are you not?"

"Yes, Grandmother." Apollo nodded. Still, it excited the gods to think of a fresh new face on Olympus; it had been so long since a new god or goddess joined their ranks.

"When can we meet her? She will be coming back to Olympus, right?" Apollo asked.

"Persephone will come to Olympus when she feels like it..." came the evasive response.

"Oh, come now! Surely you will introduce us to her! You know we'll be kind to her."

"All the while trying to woo her," Rhea responded dryly. "Persephone alone will decide who she will meet... if she wants to meet anyone."

"You will put in a good word for us, dear grandmother?"

"Perhaps. You would not want to seem *too* eager, would you?" With a knowing expression, she turned away from them and continued walking.

o0o

Persephone sat on a rock in the Eleusinian woods, her chest aching with racking sobs. It certainly wasn't as if she hadn't expected an entirely satisfactory reunion with Zeus, but for him to act so... blasé about what he did to her hurt more than she thought it would. Was it so hard to understand that his daughter might want some say or even a warning after his agreement with Hades? How come she meant so little to him? And then when confronted with a daughter who would not bow to him, he had tried to force his authority on her!

As she recalled just why she was so angry, she broke into a fresh spate of sobbing. Damn him!

"My lady?" she heard a concerned voice ask. She raised her head to see Triptolemus standing beside a tree, maintaining a respectful distance. He was clad in a heavy himation, but a quiver was visible, peeking out of the thick wool at the back of his neck. As she wiped her face with her own wrap, she heard the sound of quietly crunching snow. The prince and his men must be out for a hunting party, she deduced. He had his head inclined in a bow out of respect for her position. Over her time in Eleusis, she had taken notice of him. He was respectful and humble, gracious to his parents and sisters, and deferential to the two goddesses living with his family.

She had also sensed unhappiness within the young man. He was next in line for the throne and though he was intelligent and capable, Persephone had the feeling that he had no desire for the crown.

"Why do you weep, Goddess? Is there something I can do for you?"

Persephone managed a wavering smile. At least Triptolemus was more considerate than

Zeus. He would be a good king, whether or not he liked the crown.

"Only if you could allay the source of my tears!" She sniffled softly, swiping her face again with the edge of her himation. "I thank you for your kindness."

"It is my honor."

She took a slow breath before managing another slight smile. She could see the admiration in his eyes and while it flattered her, she did not return the feeling. Of course, even if she did, what kind of relationship could she offer him? She was going back to the Underworld in a week!

"I will be all right. I simply want to be alone."

"As you wish." He backed away to join his men.

oOo

The weaving room was empty, afternoon having faded away into evening. However, Persephone found out that her night-vision had become especially acute, and she had no difficulty in continuing her project. She was glad for the privacy as she readied her loom, making sure the warp threads were weighed down enough. It'd been a few days since she weaved. She hadn't yet seen Mother, and didn't want to talk to her at the moment.

The weaving provided her with an useful distraction, and *could* be somewhat enjoyable when Mother was away, so she could work at her own pace and select her own color and pattern.

Having secured all the warp threads, she chose the colors she needed for the weft threads, wanting to do a rainbow so that the cloth was red at one end and violet at the other, and continued her task, enjoying it more without Mother looking over her shoulder. She was already done with the red and orange, and was now using two different shades of yellow. Her hands moved on their own as she thought.

Zeus had already proven himself an unfit father and there was no real reason to confront him again unless she wanted to provoke him further. She had been a bit scared when he made lightning because it had been an impressive sight, but she had only to envision a barrier between him and herself, and look at how well that had worked! At least there was one thing to be happy about. She became more and more confident in her Gift.

"Hello?" she heard Mother call out. She raised her head, seeing her mother's form silhouetted in the doorway.

"Yes?"

"What are you doing in here? There is not even a lamp lit!"

"I can see very well."

"Really?" Demeter's tone was doubtful.

"Really." Persephone smiled before she realized that her mother could barely see in the room. She rose from her seat, approaching the other woman. "I simply wanted to be alone, that is all."

"Are you well?"

"... Yes. But I am hungry."

"Good, because it's nearly supper time."

oOo

Whenever Demeter and Persephone joined the royal family for supper, Eirene took a seat next to the her friend when she could. She couldn't help but feel more comfortable around Sephie, because Mother simply didn't seem to understand her – or want to. Eirene often felt out of place in the family, even among her own sisters. Being Princesses seemed to come to them naturally, but she didn't like all the expectations that were set upon her.

Demeter had Demophon in his lap, feeding him bits of meat or vegetables from the yummy stew she had made for everyone. The recovery of her little brother was nothing short of a miracle, because before she came, everyone knew he was going to die though nobody wanted to admit it. Mother and Father had made sacrifices to the gods, but they had not answered. Now he was walking – even running – and his limbs and cheeks were round and rosy. He already had a few teeth, and he chewed on whatever Demeter gave him before opening his mouth for more. His nurse was attentive, taking care to not give him pieces that were too large.

"Can I feed him?" Eirene asked. Demeter smiled and nodded, so she plucked a pea from her bowl and lifted it to her brother's mouth. He clamped down on her fingers, and she laughed.

She could see how happy Mother and Father were that he was alive and well. After eating several more pieces of meat and vegetables, he started to fuss, reaching with his little plump hands for a dish that bore sliced fruit. Everyone laughed at that.

oOo

Persephone sat in the bathtub, her hands on her knees as her head lolled against the edge. Mother had a loom in her room, so she sat in the corner weaving designs of leaves and fruit against a light green background while her daughter bathed.

When she was finished with her bath, she grabbed the towel that sat on the stool next to the tub, holding it up to cover her nakedness as she rose from the water. Nakedness among the same gender was a normal thing, as men and women often bathed publicly with members of the same sex. She had done so with the princesses a few times in the bath room, but Persephone felt shy about her nakedness even in front of other women. Mother's initial reaction to the changes of her body made her especially hesitant to bare her flesh.

Mother barely glanced her way when she retreated to her own room to get dressed. When she came out, the tub was empty and propped against the wall. It took little effort for Demeter to merely lift the tub and pour the water out of the window with her divine strength.

Persephone glanced at her mother's weaving. It was no surprise that Mother had incorporated plants into her design, it was her favorite motif.

"You told me you would talk about what was bothering you," Mother reminded her as she next to the fire. Persephone stared at the dancing flames before she looked up at her mother.

"I... talked to Zeus."

"... Oh." Mother's stare became intense as she waited for details. "Well, how did it go?"

"Not so well."

Mother didn't look too surprised. "Really..." she commented in a deadpan tone.

"I remember the first time I met him. He was so kind to me and so... friendly. I could not understand why you did not want to associate with him. I wondered about that for a very long time."

Mother sighed quietly and nodded.

"He made his agreement with Hades without consulting me or even warning me. I asked him why. He just... acted as if it were nothing. He thought it there was nothing wrong with it because Hades promised him that he would not hurt me. As if that was supposed to make it all just fine, to decide something like that as if my feelings did not matter at all."

Demeter groaned softly as she rubbed her temples. "That is but one of the many reasons why I did not want to acknowledge him as your..." She choked on the last word.

"You do not have to." Persephone's smile was wry. "I certainly refuse to consider him as such. I

260

even told him that Iasion was more of a man than he could ever be."

"You said that?" Demeter asked with shocked delight.

Persephone nodded as she grinned. "I also called him stupid, and told him that he was unfit to hold the authority of King of the Gods!"

Demeter almost couldn't believe it. Her daughter, her sweet, little daughter had said that to mighty Zeus himself?

"What did he do?" Demeter asked in a hushed whisper.

"Well, he tried to make me submit to his... *authority*." She emphasized the last word in a mocking tone. "He had the lightning... it was all over his body..." With her hands, she gestured at how the electricity arced along his body, and Demeter nodded, having seen it several times before.

"But I... pushed. Like when you tried to make me a little girl again. I just... would not let it happen. And then bam! He flew up in the air!" She swept her arm up to emphasize her words. "And then he hit the pillar and slid down to the ground."

The older goddess stared at her daughter for a moment before she let out a burst of cackling laughter, tears of mirth streaming down her cheeks in no time. Persephone blinked and looked at the other deity. She had never seen Mother like this before! Of course, they had laughed before, but Mother had never looked so... delighted. She rocked back and forth, still screaming with laughter, and in no time, her daughter joined in, their shrieks of amusement pouring out of the chamber and echoing down the hallways.

oOo

Demeter had been stunned to hear of her daughter standing up to Zeus. After her daughter went to bed, she stayed up late, well into the night as she pondered what had brought Kora to this point. When Kora had resisted her magic and kept her form as a woman, Demeter had felt angry at it and furious with her brother.

Over the last three weeks, Kora had shown no ill effects from her time with Hades. To be sure, they had their fights, but her daughter was not spiteful or belligerent even if she was rebellious at times. She was not depressed or withdrawn, either. Aside from her matured body and a surprisingly strong manifestation of her Gift, Kora was little changed. She enjoyed the same things she had before, and also displayed the same dislikes that she had always had.

Considering that Kora had been a captive in the Underworld – what a dreadful place! – she seemed to not be affected in any worrisome way. She didn't lord her newfound power over mortals or use it to antagonize her mother. And she had actually been able to resist Zeus's power and gotten away with calling him stupid!

Demeter laughed quietly to herself as she recalled how Kora had described the encounter. She had also been able to put Ares in his place.

Given that, she could not help but be curious as to how her daughter had handled Hades. Was that why Hades had been willing to give her up?

Initially, she had fretted over her mother's involvement in Kora's life. She had kept her daughter sheltered for so long without any interference from other family members that it took some getting used to, but Kora seemed happy.

As much as she hated to admit it, she could see that Kora had matured into a woman she could be proud of. However, that knowledge also made her sad. After losing Iasion, she was loath to lose her daughter. Thank goodness at least Kora wasn't interested in boys.

oOo

The princesses were outside, enjoying a warm day. The air was mild enough so that they barely felt the chill, but it was cold enough that the snow didn't turn to slush. Thalassa was happy to leave her weaving and enjoy some fresh air – her beloved weaving would be there when she came back – and such nice days like this were rare at this time of the year. Eirene hadn't needed to be told twice when Persephone said she was going out, joyfully escaping Mother's irritated glare. Persephone played with them for a while, but she decided that she wanted to be alone.

The shouts of her friends became distant as Persephone wandered between the trees, her cloak wrapped tightly around herself. Since her confrontation with Zeus, her relationship with Mother had only improved further. Before, it was as if Mother was treating her as an adult only grudgingly. However, her mother now actually seemed proud of her, and she was particularly fond of hearing the story of how her daughter had defied Zeus. Persephone had actually repeated the story several times, and it never failed to put a smile on Mother's face!

As she looked around, she realized that she had wandered further than ever before. This part of the forest was unfamiliar to her, though she could hear the bubbling of the river off to the right. She could simply follow it back, but she decided to press on further. Mother had cast her magic over a large area, and Persephone wanted to find the limit of it.

Suddenly, she was aware of a soft nickering, and turned her head. Horses? Such creatures were rare, and would be so in Hellas for a while yet. Celeus didn't have any horses, and she wondered if there were wild horses in the forest. This was definitely worth investigating, so she veered off to the right. After taking just a few steps, she saw the glint of the sun on a glossy black coat and gave out a soft gasp as she became aware of a familiar presence.

In front of her were the first horses she had ever seen in her entire life. They had looked imposing in the gloom of the Underworld, but here they looked downright fierce, their fur shiny under a sun that Persephone was fairly certain they had not seen in a very long time if ever.

Their harnesses glittered with the polished onyx and hematite set into them. The chariot they were attached to had a dull leaden gleam, its workmanship perfectly illuminated under the early afternoon sun.

It wasn't the winter solstice already, was it? As she quickly counted off the days, she realized with mild shock that it was indeed! The horses raised their heads in her direction, and she took several steps back before she heard his voice.

"Now, now, my love. You know better than to try to run off... we both know what will happen."

Chapter LI

Feeling lightheaded, Persephone slowly turned around to see Hades leaning against a tree trunk. She acknowledged that she missed his company, but she was surprised at how strongly she reacted to the very sight of the God of the Dead.

"I know. I was just... startled." In response, Hades nodded slowly.

He was as handsome as ever, clad in a long black tunic with matching himation. His thick hair was tied back loosely, illuminating his regal features in the afternoon light and bringing out the blue in his eyes. As she made eye contact with him, he smiled at her, and *oh*, how that made her heart flutter!

She noticed that he had a pomegranate in his left hand, already open and displaying its seeds like a cluster of glittering rubies in the sunlight. It was hard to not miss the sharp flashes of light on the facets of the seeds as the sun shone on them.

"Aidon..." Her breath came out in a soft mist. It would not be until later that she realized that the horses did not have mist coming from their mouths like anyone else who would breathe this cold air.

"Seph..." His smile grew wider as he beckoned her closer. As if of their own volition, her feet moved forward, closing the distance between them. He raised his other hand, drawing her into a tight embrace. How often had she simply longed for his embrace, to snuggle up to him as his powerful arms wrapped around her? She closed her eyes for a moment and let out a quiet sigh, savoring his physical closeness. Even when she had been lonely and missing him, she had no inclination to seek attention elsewhere. The thought of being with another man – even when she knew they would be all too eager to give her the attention she wanted – simply didn't appeal to her. Not even the thought of bedding devastatingly handsome Apollo or accepting Dionysus's invitation excited her even just a little bit.

Hades inhaled the sweet scent of her body as he rested his chin on the top of her head, thrilling at the warmth of her body.

"It has been far too long, Persephone," Hades whispered as he ran his fingers through the thick waves that cascaded down her back. She remained silent as he continued to touch her lovingly, caressing her arm and shoulder.

"I thought we might enjoy a treat." He had already eaten several seeds, and he brought the pomegranate within her sight. She lifted her head and stared at the fruit for several moments as if unsure of whether it was safe to eat. Finally, she slowly lifted her hand, plucking a seed out of the husk. She brought it to her lips and sucked it off her fingers, her eyes closing in an unmistakable sign of pleasure.

"Mmm." Persephone took several more seeds, savoring their sweet and tart flavor. Mother had offered her pomegranates to eat, of course, and she had a delicious recipe for pomegranate bread, but the surface-world fruit was nowhere near as divine as the mystical pomegranates from Hades's tree, and she sucked the juice off her fingers.

She drew away from Hades, and he let her go.

"Is something the matter? Are you not happy to see me?" Hades asked, his voice almost teasing.

"I have missed you," she admitted.

"Not as much as I have missed you." He smiled again, and she returned this with a faint grin.

"So... you have come to take me back to the Underworld for good."

"Is it such a terrible prospect?"

"What about my mother?" Persephone asked, evading his question.

"You know I never break a promise."

"It will be terrible news for her." Persephone was grateful that she hadn't given up on the subject of Hades and that Mother wouldn't find his return a surprise. But to have her daughter actually taken away again...

"She would not be happy seeing you with any man. So you need to think about what makes *you* happy." He looked at her hopefully. "I do hope you are happy with me."

Persephone was moved by the sad longing in his eyes, and blushed as she looked away. Suddenly, she felt a hand stroking her cheek, and she shivered. His touch was intoxicating, whether an intimately arousing caress or a gentle, innocent trailing of his fingers along her face or arm.

268

A sudden laugh alerted them to the nearing presence of the princesses. She saw the flash of light pink from Thalassa's chiton and the dark brown of her woolen cloak. Hades narrowed his eyes before she squeezed his arm.

"They are my friends. Please do not do anything to them!" she asked, remembering Cyane.

"Because you have asked it of me, it shall be so." He touched her face again to reassure her.

"Persephone!" Thalassa called out before she came to a sudden stop, staring at Hades. Eirene trailed behind her, her eyes widening as she took notice of the newcomer. Thalassa had never seen a man as handsome as the person Persephone was with. He was so tall and regal, his chin lifted imperiously as he glanced at her and her sister.

Persephone took a step forward. "Thalassa... Eirene... This is Hades."

A sudden look of fear appeared on their faces as they regarded the Lord of the Dead before Thalassa quickly collected herself and bowed.

"You honor us with your presence, Lord Hades."

In imitation of her older sister, Eirene quickly bowed before the two of them glanced at their friend questioningly, waiting for a cue. Persephone turned back to Hades when he grasped her arm.

"We will be going now. At least they will have an interesting story to tell their children." He flashed a knowing grin before he nodded briefly to the princesses.

269

"*Now?*" Dismay flashed across her features. "But what about Mother..."

"Your mother will be furious either way. Let her have her hot anger before I speak with her. There is still plenty of today left, and I will speak to her before the moon hangs high in the sky." Their voices were quiet enough to keep their conversation private from the princesses.

"What the..."

"Ah, but I keep my word, as I always have."

"And leave them to be the messengers of bad news?"

Hades tilted his head as he glanced down at her before he nodded. "Then, something that will protect them and prove your safety?" he suggested. She was tempted to protest, perhaps run off, simply to defy him. Considering that she had eaten the pomegranate seeds, he could have simply denied her the chance to come up here, and antagonizing him might cause him to continue to be more of the stern and cold-hearted King of the Dead that everyone was afraid of.

She drew away from him and approached her friends. "Send Mother my love and inform her that I am safe. Tell her that Hades will see her before the moon is at its peak. I shall miss you. Tell Melinoe and Aethra I will miss them as well." She touched Thalassa's shoulders and pressed her lips to the maiden's forehead, imbuing some magic into it.

Eirene wrapped her arms around her friend's middle. "Sephie! I don't want you to go!" she whispered, not wishing for Hades to hear and be offended. Persephone gave out a faint, sad smile as she stroked Eirene's dark curls.

"You may have my bow and arrows."

"Really? Oh, thank you! Thank you!" The girl grinned as she received a kiss on her forehead. She still didn't want Sephie to go, but Sephie had already told the princesses a few things about Hades – one of them being that the Dark God was not to be trifled with, but also that he could be fair. She glanced at him over her friend's shoulder, and he gave her a slight but kind smile.

As Persephone rejoined her Lord, she turned back and waved to them. Hades offered his hand and helped her onto the chariot, standing behind her as he flicked the reins. The horses sped across the river before the earth opened, swallowing them as the girls watched.

oOo

It seemed as if they were engulfed in oblivion before color and light burst before them, revealing the Sea of Eternity on their left side as the chariot made its way along its shore. The sky was the color of sunset's rainbow hues, the colors more saturated in the atmosphere of Dis. These colors were reflected in a fierce display of scattered flashes of seemingly infinite shades of blue, magenta, red, and gold on the surface of the water.

Well, at least Hades had made the effort of a pleasant homecoming. She relaxed, leaning back into him as he wrapped one arm around her middle. The chariot sped along the sand, swaying gently from side to side.

After a while, they arrived at the Palace, pulling up beside the pomegranate tree. Hades smiled and lifted the partially eaten pomegranate from a fold in his cloak. Without the sunlight, they didn't glisten as fiercely as before, and looked more like thick drops of blood.

"The Palace has been very lonely without you, Persephone." He took his hand and led her up the stairs

"And where are you taking me?"

"I thought we could relax together. Perhaps have some supper, or take a hot bath. How about sitting by the fire? Or I could take you to bed..."

Persephone chuckled softly at his last suggestion. Though she and Hades had a relationship where they could respect one another intellectually, she could not deny that she enjoyed the carnal aspect of what he had to offer her.

"All are sound ideas. But I must be frank – I ache for you." Already her insides warmed in anticipation. "I want... need your attention. I have been... lonely."

"Oh, darling. Let me remedy that, hmm?" He set the pomegranate on the table and scooped her up into his arms.

Persephone was gently tossed to the bed before he sat down and took her foot into his hands, firmly tugging away the thin straps of leather that held her boots up. He was slightly impatient, tugging the cords and trying to remove her boots as quickly as possible. Once that was accomplished, he was quick to divest her of the rest of her clothing. She was compliant, even helping him with the pins that held up her chiton.

In a short time, she was naked before him, an utterly enticing sight as she posed provocatively for him. He growled softly as he quickly stripped himself, standing before her with passion burning in his eyes and thrillingly visible between his legs.

A searing reminder of her arousal ached afresh at the sight of the glorious male before her and spread through her loins and belly. His gaze was dark and penetrating as he lowered himself to the bed.

"Is there anything you would like to start with?" he asked, running his fingers along the side of her foot. She shuddered and unconsciously jerked it away, she was simply too sensitized right now for foreplay and only wanted him to couple with her.

"Please... No games. I just want you."

Hades draped himself across her, one hand sliding down to touch her most intimate areas. He rubbed his finger along her ready opening, hearing her soft whimper as he slid two fingers inside to ensure her preparedness. She was oh so snug but hotly slick, her muscles clenching around them as she wiggled around.

He drew his hand away and brought slick fingers to his mouth, savoring her essence and aroma. There was the natural musk, of course, and the familiar flavor of dark sweetness. The taste was fleeting and intoxicating. He had missed it.

"So many times I have longed to feel you

273

inside of me since I left the Underworld..." She let out a quiet sigh. She didn't obsess over him, no. But sometimes she could not help but be reminded of him, and this would cause her to reminisce their time together and what had happened just before she returned to the surface world. It was impossible to forget just how intimate they had become, and how much she had missed that. "Take me, Aidon. Make me yours..." she added in a seductive purr, one that she knew would arouse him further.

"I have longed to hear your invitation." Hades kissed her forehead before he lowered himself between her joyfully spread legs. The Dark God had but to place the tip of his aching manhood inside of her before he plunged down smoothly. She whimpered his name as she felt his hilt pressing against her, and he wrapped one of his arms around her before placing a kiss on her cheek, remaining still to allow her to simply enjoy it.

As he lowered his head to nuzzle her neck, she lifted her hands to his head, running her fingers through his hair. His other hand reached down to gently massage her breast. This lasted just a few moments before she wiggled against him, clenching hard.

He let out a low groan of approval before he pulled out and thrust back in. She helped him begin a steady pace by clenching around him, but soon enough, they were moving against one another fiercely. Suddenly Persephone pushed Hades to the side before climbing on top of him, grinding against him with an almost frantic pace. Hades grinned and allowed her to maintain dominance for a while, liking how she moved against him so enthusiastically. Her gyrations were driving him wild, and he thrust up, baring his teeth and growling at her, which would cause her to snarl back at him. As much fun as it was to ravish her, he enjoyed being on the receiving end.

When he finally stopped thrusting, she collapsed on the bed. Hades grinned slowly before flopping down on his back. He was tempted to rouse himself again, but decided to let her rest. She didn't fall asleep, but stared ahead quietly. He spooned up to her loosely before resting his hand on her hip, and they stayed like this for a short while before Persephone rolled over to face him.

He reached out to brush a thick, stray lock away from her face. Persephone looked up at him.

"I am hungry." Hades stated cheerfully before rising out of bed and pulling on a loose robe. "Is there anything you are in the mood for?"

Persephone merely shrugged. He raised an eyebrow but summoned a shade and told it to bring up several different kinds of food. He turned back to her.

"Would you like to eat at the table, or shall I feed you in bed?"

Persephone considered her options and whether or not she would eat the food.

"I will sit with you." She rose from the bed. "I would like a robe, though."

Cloe whisked into existence, carrying a deep green silk robe.

"I had almost forgotten what it was like to have such a servant," Persephone commented as she took the robe. The Eleusinian Royal Family had servants and they were commanded to respect the two goddesses, but Demeter and Persephone generally preferred to be alone when they were not doing something with the family. Cloe also pulled her hair up with a matching sash.

The shades set the table with a limited banquet consisting of dishes familiar to Persephone, some of them done with a twist to liven up the recipe. The rich smells filled the air, as real as any scent on the surface world, and she took a deep breath as she stared down at the dishes.

Even though she had missed Hades deeply and the freedom she enjoyed here in the Underworld, as well as her newly discovered Gifts, her first Gift remained an essential part of her being. Already she felt an inner part of herself panic and rebel at the sight of the food, the lack of life around her an unshakable fact. On the surface, life had flowed freely around and through her.

Right now, she could easily ignore that. It had been but a couple of hours, after all, but she knew that over time, it would wear down on her. She could not use her Gift down here to nurture things like she could above.

"Is something wrong?" Hades asked with concern as he glanced at her, pouring her a goblet of wine, noticing that her plate was empty as she sat there, her arms on the armrests. There was clearly something weighing heavily upon her mind. Her gaze had been downcast, but before she spoke, she raised her eyes to meet his.

"My lord, you wish for me to be happy, do you not?"

"Of course. Why ask such a question?" How could he remedy the hesitation and sadness he saw in her eyes?

"Hades... I am bound to you forever. I am now part of this place just as you are." She inhaled slowly, drumming her fingers soundlessly against the armrests, "But I also share a connection with the world above. The food you eat clearly does not stop you from leaving the Underworld, even though you are bound to it."

"Already you think about going to the surface world?"

"I *do* like it here, but I share my mother's Gift. I need to nurture life. I need to feel the sunshine on my face and the pulse of the earth under my feet. I will be everything you want me to be – wife, queen, and mate. I would give myself to you freely, but I honestly do not feel that it is too much to ask for to be able to spend some time on the surface world."

As he listened to her, he considered the times he had watched her play and frolic outside. She looked radiant and happy under the sunlight and fresh air. It was like that he had first seen her and fallen in love with her.

Persephone stared at him, regarding his silence with apprehension.

"Yes," he agreed. She opened her mouth, about to argue with a ready answer, when she realized what he had said. 'Yes'. Was he merely indicating that he had heard her or... was that agreement of what she had said? He wasn't going to say 'no'?

"You are correct. I would not be a good husband if I was not considerate of your needs." He maintained an even gaze. "You were waiting to ask me that, weren't you?"

She nodded slowly. A smirk flashed across his face before he bowed his head in acknowledgment.

"You can return to the surface world in due time. But for now..." He gestured to the dishes. She stared at him before cutting herself a slice of feta bread. She could almost taste it before it touched her lips, because the scent was so heady. *Mmm*. She hesitated before it touched her lips, remembering how afraid she had been to eat for over four months.

"You promise?" she asked before she prepared to bite into it.

"You have my word." he assured her.

How different things would have turned out if she had been able to negotiate this before! Well, what was done was done. Her lips parted, and she sunk her teeth into it, almost overwhelmed by its perfect flavor. It was warm, fresh out of the oven and baked with just the right amount of herbs and cheese, with honey and olive oil for dipping. There were also chunks of vegetables floating in a thick broth that she could not resist trying. Everything tasted so wonderful! After sampling the bread and soup, she found herself helping herself to the various dishes, savoring each bite and the various ingredients in them.

There was something about Underworld food that made it... *tastier*, and it was not simply the expertise of the Underworld's chefs who had many years to refine their art and had access to a plethora of ingredients that were not available when they had been alive. She stared down at it for a moment, trying to figure out what made it so different from surface-world food, and decided to ponder that later so she could just appreciate the food.

Hades smiled as he watched her enjoyment. It had always bothered him to eat in front of her when she refused to eat, and now apparently that was a concern of the past. The pair continued eating at a leisurely place, each of them pleased with their own recent victory.

Chapter LII

oOo

Persephone licked her fingers clean of the last bit of crumb and juices from the meal she had just shared with Hades before taking several sips of her wine. She leaned back in her seat, remaining silent as he continued eating. Her eyes were focused on the wall in a thoughtful gaze.

As Hades continued eating, she occasionally picked up her wine to nurse it, enjoying the light honey flavor. His eyes moved along her body as she reclined on the plush divan. The robe had fallen open just a bit, revealing a welcome peek at the shadowed area between her breasts.

The promise he had made her meant he would have to see Demeter tonight, but as he studied her, he was reminded of how much he had ached for her during her absence. There was still plenty of time left in this day that he might put off the inevitable confrontation with his sister so he could enjoy Persephone's charms. Setting down his plate, he glanced at her with a smirk. After a moment, she noticed him.

"What?" She raised her eyebrow as she glanced at his lips, thinking of them kissing along her body. She was learning how to read his smirks, becoming familiar with the different ways he would tilt his lips up or down and deducing what it was that he wanted. She tilted her chin up by a mere fraction of an inch before leaning over to set down her wineglass.

"Well, I would like continue with ensuring that my bride has a proper homecoming."

"Oh, Aidon." She flashed a grin before she thought about the fact that he had called her his bride. He had said that things were different in Dis, but it just didn't feel right to be called that when they hadn't made some sort of vow to one another. She had seen several marriage ceremonies at neighbor's houses when she was still living in Enna. There would be a banquet the day before, at the bride's house, and another one the day after the wedding, at the groom's house. Family members and friends prepared a feast, and the bride and groom would have a procession to their home – perhaps a room in the groom's parents' house or a house he had built for his wife and future children. Worship was also part of the ceremony, especially for the bride who would pray to Hera, the patron goddess of wives. They would also pray to others, depending on who they personally worshiped and what they were asking for.

For a warm and happy hearth, women prayed to Hestia. For protection in childbirth, Elithya was called, though young wives would also pray to Artemis for this protection as it was said she assisted her mother in the birth of her younger twin brother, Apollo. And of course, Demeter was petitioned to, to bless the fledgling household with her bounty.

"I was never properly courted. How could I be a bride?" she asked. Hades actually looked confused, as if he had never considered such a matter before. He was quick to recover himself, and shrugged.

"You now eat the food of your own accord. You come to my bed willingly. You wear the crown I put on your head. Do I not give you every honor a man would give the woman he loves?"

Persephone hadn't meant to bring this subject up now, especially after having he had agreed to let her have time on the surface world, but as long as he talked about it, she would just go with it. He didn't seem angry or offended, and she knew this was a good sign that he would at least listen to what she had to say.

"It is not that I do not feel cared for. It is just..." She paused, trying to find the words that best expressed her thoughts, "I would like an occasion to acknowledge... and even celebrate our marriage."

"Celebrate?" He sounded interested, and she smiled.

"Is having me as your wife not worth celebrating?"

"Well, we could have a banquet and invite our friends. Perhaps Erebus will come."

Persephone smiled and shook her head. "That is a good idea for the post-wedding banquet and I am all for it, but that's not quite what I meant. Has it occurred to you that Mother would wish to be involved in this?" She wasn't certain of how her mother would feel, but if Demeter had a hand in the ceremony, she might feel better about her daughter being with Hades. But it wasn't just for Mother, but for herself. She wasn't sure if Hades considered it silly, but she wanted an official ceremony, and personally, she felt that it would be good for him.

"Huh." Hades frowned thoughtfully. It had never occurred to him that she might wish for a wedding ceremony. She did have a point about wanting to celebrate, but why a ceremony? She was already his queen, crowned by him.

"Besides, it would give us both a chance to impress the other gods."

"I did not know you were concerned about such matters."

Persephone laughed softly. "The gods of Olympus fear you. You are the dread Lord of the Underworld and ruler of souls. Even Zeus himself acknowledges your power though he will not admit it."

"That is correct." His smile was filled with pride at her words... which was just the effect she intended. Hades might be taciturn and wise, but he was not above a few caresses to his ego, just like any other male.

"If I am your Queen, should I not be acknowledged as such by these same people?" She remembered the admiring glances of Apollo and Dionysus, and even Helios. The apprehension in Ares's expression had filled her with no small amount of smugness.

She wanted Zeus to see her as a queen and show him that she was not simply one of his many offspring. She didn't plan to tell anyone of her true paternity – she would work on her reputation through her own merit – but she wanted Olympus to know her as Persephone, not little Kora.

Hades could not think of a good reason to argue. There were plenty of reasons he could make up, to be certain, but none of them suited Persephone.

"You want me to show you off to our family?" he asked with a grin.

"You will be the envy of the others."

Hades sat back as he laughed quietly. Everyone feared and respected his power, but during all these long centuries, he had never boasted of a lover or affair. When dressed up in her finest, Persephone truly was a sight to behold, though she was just as comely in plain, homespun garb. He could not help but envision himself among the Olympians with Persephone on his arm, having his brothers, cousins, and nephews admire what could never be theirs.

"They will envy me, indeed. There is no Goddess like you, and none could ever compare. I truly am the Rich One."

Persephone grinned before she rose from her seat and approached Hades, placing her hands on the sides of his face and giving him a deep kiss.

Her kiss was light and fresh, tasting of fruit and a deeper, underlying sweetness. He moaned against her lips, his hands reaching up to her sides. She gave out a quiet coo of delight when his hands slid down to squeeze her rear end, and she wiggled against him with a knowing smirk.

o0o

When Demeter heard what Thalassa had to say, she became livid. The princesses cowered from her, their heads bowed, their mouths silent in an obvious attempt to not draw any attention from the goddess. She wanted to explode; such was the anger boiling within her.

She was supposed to just sit around and wait for Hades? Hah! He might not be here for her to lash out at, but she knew exactly who she could vent her wrath upon; and he fully deserved it.

With a rumble and whoosh, she was gone from the room, and the girls did not lift their heads for several seconds, holding still as statues. Only when the room was fully silent did Thalassa raise her head. She slowly rose to her feet, wondering what it would be like with Persephone gone. Demeter had blessed Eleusis, and Thalassa knew they were lucky to be spared from the blight upon Hellas.

She silently prayed such a disaster would not repeat itself.

oOo

Since his confrontation with his mother and daughter, Zeus had been unusually subdued. He still held Court, but he was usually quiet, and his suggestions or ideas actually seemed more thought-out. He eased off his attempts to seduce the nymphs that lived on Olympus or in Hellas.

He spent much of his free time reminiscing about his childhood and later being discovered by the elder siblings he had never known he had. The overthrow of the Titanomachy had not been easy, and took over a decade before the clash of the Titans ended. During this time he had gotten to know his siblings – some of them better than others, of course – and learned of his father and what he was doing to the people of Hellas.

After Kronos was brought down by the combined efforts of his children and their Titan allies, the Olympians settled into a golden age. Mortals no longer had to worry about abuse from Kronos or his allies. Metis had been his first serious relationship, though that had failed in a way he had never expected it to. Then Mnemosyne, and nine lovely daughters, though he had cheated on her a few times through the relationship. And of course, there was Hera; the only woman to be his crowned queen. He missed watching his children grow. The thrill of these golden years had faded, leaving behind the inevitable hubris that came from decades or centuries of rule by a dynasty. It certainly seemed that he had been making more mistakes lately, and he made a conscious effort to avoid trouble. This change was noticed by some, but they did not consider it unwelcome.

He spent some of his time in the quiet mountain valley where he had been raised, hidden away from Kronos. He noticed over the last week he had not been in one bit of trouble, and it actually felt good. The absence of female companionship helped to somewhat clear his mind.

He had even managed to get Hera to agree to

have supper with him. Like most of the other gods, she had been displeased with him over the whole Hades-Persephone-Demeter affair, but she had been friendly to him today. She had even volunteered to cook supper for him, telling him that her nymphs would simply carry everything over to his house. That certainly suited him, so he was all too happy to accept.

"I was going to have my servants cook, but you always make such wonderful food, I would rather have what you can make! I look forward to it, but more, your company."

Hera had smiled brilliantly at him, and as he watched the nymphs bustle about the table, setting the food and dishes down. He had considered having it in his rose-garden, but unlike Rhea, he could not command plants to grow, so he was stuck with them until she would undo the damage.

Zeus was tempted to flirt almost out of force of habit with the nymphs that worked for his wife. It had simply taken some introspection to come to the conclusion that flirting with them would not be the wise thing to do to the woman who had just cooked dinner for him. He glanced at a spot on the wall, focusing on someone only when Hera came into the room, looking as well put-together as she usually did.

She had on a peacock-blue tunic with matching gold and lapis jewelry, and he smiled in appreciation at her efforts. He truly enjoyed looking at her, and was happy for this opportunity. Perhaps she would even come to his bed tonight, and they could reminisce about the old days afterward. Their marriage went in ups and downs, with periods of conflict – mainly due to Zeus – followed by times of him wooing her back and being able to enjoy having her as a wife before his eyes strayed elsewhere in an unending cycle.

He poured her a glass of ambrosia, doing everything he could to be charming. From the warm smile on her face, it was obviously working.

A startled cry from one of the nymphs outside alerted him to the fact that this wonderful evening was at risk of being ruined. Quickly excusing himself with a promise that he would be back as soon as possible, Zeus rose from his seat and rushed to the front door just in time to see Demeter take wide, angry steps across the yard, the grass and trees withering in her wake.

"Demeter!" Zeus exclaimed in a shocked hiss, lifting his hands up to halt her progress. "What is the matter? I thought everything was resolved!" He could not think of anything he might have done recently to incur her wrath, unless Persephone had told her what happened between the two of them... *Oh, shit.*

"Persephone is gone! Hades has kidnapped her again!"

"WHAT!" Zeus's obvious surprise caused Demeter to still for a moment.

"Yes! He kidnapped her while she was playing with her friends!"

"I... well... I really do not know how I can help you here..."

"Tell Hades to give her back, like you did last time!"

"Well, yes, I can do that, but..." Zeus stilled as he remembered Hades's words during their last meeting. His older brother hadn't stated outright that he would take Persephone back to the Underworld, but as Zeus remembered – and considered Hades's words, he was overcome by the sensation of his heart sinking into his stomach. *Oh, no...*

"Of course, I will be more than happy to send the message to him!" Zeus said, quickly collecting himself so that his astute sister wouldn't be able to norice any cues he might involuntarily give her.

"None of this would have happened in the first place if it wasn't for you!" Demeter raged.

Well, that might have been true, but it was beside the point, and...

"What is going on?" Hera asked as she appeared in the doorway.

"Nothing, dear wife. Would you go back to our supper and just relax, and I will join you in a short while?" He shot her his most winning smile. He had to hold back a cringe as she crossed her arms, glaring at him.

"I asked you what is going on." She held her stare at him for a moment before turning to Demeter.

"Hades has kidnapped my daughter again."

"Zeus!" Hera put her hands on her hips, doing a wonderful imitation of her sister's hostile glare.

"Look, I had nothing to do with it, I swear! I thought she was safe with her mother and that everyone was happy! Truly!"

"Well, apparently Hades wasn't happy," Hera replied tartly.

o0o

Persephone sighed in pleasure as she lay on her stomach against the thick, velvety blankets, Hades's hand languidly rubbing her back and rear end. The kiss she had given him had been responded to eagerly, and soon enough they had been pawing at one another, their immediate need for one another only escalating with every moment.

She was appreciative of every loving caress to her naked body, and was content to simply lay there in the afterglow of another heated lovemaking session. It was exciting to see the usually reserved Lord of the Dead as a man filled with burning passion that was focused solely on her, and oh, how she welcomed it! This time around, he had been much fiercer, and she had simply egged him on, liking the sounds of his growling or feeling his hungry touch.

She smiled faintly as she glanced along Hades's chest and shoulders, seeing the bite-marks she had placed there. Hades wasn't the only passionate one in the relationship...

When he lifted his hand away, Persephone sat up and started to wiggle off the bed.

"Where do you think you are going?" Hades asked in a sly tone. As she stood up, she turned to face him as she flipped her hair over her shoulder.

"Wherever I want," she responded cheekily, and he laughed. "Seriously though, I need a bath. And the day draws nearer its end. You have something to do." She raised her eyebrow before exiting the bedchamber.

One of the things she had missed about the Underworld was Hades's spectacular bathchamber. The water bubbled up as she approached it, creating soothing jets that massaged her body as soon as she lowered herself in the water. Even the wealthiest and most powerful king in Hellas did not have such a marvelous bathtub, and she reveled in the churning heat as she floated in the water, closing her eyes.

When she felt a gentle touch on her forehead, she opened her eyes to see Hades waist-high in the water.

"Could not bear to be alone, hmm?" she asked with a smug purr.

"Perhaps." His grin was playful.

"How did you ever manage to survive an entire moon without me?"

"It was not easy, I assure you." He leaned down to press his lips to her forehead before he pulled away and sat down, the water now just below his chin.

"But you still sneaked up to the surface to watch me," Persephone replied as she righted herself, sitting at the opposite side of the tub. He glanced at her with a light smile, making no denial of her accusation. They sat together in companionable silence, letting the bath cleanse and soothe them.

A shade appeared, talking to Hades. He nodded and whispered something before dismissing it.

"How can you understand what they say?" Persephone asked. He shrugged.

"I crafted them to serve me. Thus, I gave myself a way to understand them."

"And what did it say to you?"

"Inquisitive, are we?" Hades shot back, but he did not sound annoyed. "I have just been informed that your mother is on Olympus, harping on Zeus." He climbed out of the tub and picked up a towel. "I might as well go up there now."

What about me? Persephone thought as she glanced up at him. As if in silent reply, he picked up another towel and held it up. She rose from the water and he wrapped it around her. She stood there as he rubbed her body with the towel, enjoying his treatment.

"When you dress, put on a crown or whatever else you feel makes you look like a Queen."

She glanced up at him with mild surprise. "You really want me to come with you?"

"But of course. Your mother will not be satisfied with anything I say."

"That is true," she responded dryly.

In her room, Persephone reacquainted herself with the things she had left behind. She touched the various sparkling jewels that Hades lavished her with and ran her fingers along the luxurious robes and gowns in her wardrobe. What should she wear to Olympus! Goodness! She knew that with the right outfit and accessories, she would make quite the impression. What should she wear? Should she bedeck herself with jewels or go for an understated appearance? With so many choices, it was near impossible to decide what to wear!

Finally, Persephone chose fine black linen for her chiton and deep red velvet for her himation, draping it across one shoulder. For jewelry, she chose a gold necklace and armbands set with rubies that looked like pomegranate seeds. A matching crown and rings completed the set, and Cloe swept her hair up with several pins, showcasing the graceful planes of her neck.

When she emerged from her room, she was rewarded with an open smile of appreciation from the Dark God. He had dressed himself in black and blue with onyx-studded silver accessories. Having seen the clothing of the few gods she managed to glimpse on Olympus, she knew that she and Hades would make quite the pair.

"I am nervous," she whispered. He stared at her for a moment before nodding slowly.

"Why?"

"Well..." She let out a quiet sigh. "I am worried about Mother. She was so happy to have me back..."

"No happier than I am to have you here." He held out his hand, and she took it.

o0o

Hades had considered simply appearing in the throne room, but decided against it, bringing

Persephone to the gate that opened into the grand city of the gods. It was already evening, so the sky was dark, but illumination was provided by enchanted street lamps that had been crafted by the Cyclopes ages ago. That and the natural light of the moon and stars provided a peaceful ambiance to the lavishly built city.

The shadows cast the royal pair in an alluring but mysterious silhouette. Hades's pale skin was almost white, and even Persephone's recently gained light tan was subdued.

From the lights that shone from the Great Hall, Hades surmised that Demeter had brought other gods to hear her complaints. There were a couple of latecomers, and Hades slowed down a bit as he saw Rhea and Hestia. Hestia looked like a younger version of her mother. Her face was unlined, but her eyes were old, and the extreme modesty of her appearance added to her mystery – only her face and hands were visible under the cowl she wore.

"Hades. Persephone." Rhea's subtle gaze reflected her admiration at the way her eldest son and his queen had presented themselves. Hades inclined his head in a polite bow.

"Grandmother, how wonderful to see you again. And Hestia, I am so happy to finally meet you." Her warm smile won one from Hestia. "As much as I would like to acquaint myself with you further, there are pressing matters we must attend to. However, I would very much like an invitation from you later."

Hestia nodded before Hades swept toward the

doorway with his arm, indicating that the others go first. Rhea went forward, and Hades looked down at her.

"We will not be parted. You know it as well as I do."

She gave a brief nod before he took her hands and squeezed them. "Know that I love you always." He pressed his lips to her knuckles several times.

o0o

Even though Zeus swore up and down that he had nothing to do with Persephone's second disappearance, most of the gods had sided against him, demanding that he take action against Hades. He tried to explain to them that he hadn't endorsed such a thing, nor had he been told of it. He did not mention Hades's hinting at taking Persephone again because he knew that would destroy what little case he had to defend himself.

He had simply thought it best to not tell Demeter of Hades's intentions in the first place because he knew she would just say 'no'. When he had tried to argue this, he was sneered at for being a coward and even his own brother and sons were surprised that he hadn't even deigned to inform Demeter or Kora of his blessing or Hades's intentions. What was done was done! When the hell would this be over?

Hera, who had not an hour ago been laughing at his jokes and even responding to his flirting, assumed the role of the injured and rightfully angry wife she had taken so often in the past.

"All I can do is ask Hades to bring Persephone back... again. I cannot do more than that." Zeus had his palms forward as if begging as he stared at his sister.

Hermes stared at his father with disbelief. He liked Persephone and found her refreshing. She challenged him, and even if she wouldn't bed him, he didn't think any less of her. Her presence and attitude commanded respect, much like Hades's own. All Father could do was dither about, trying to avoid blame. Well, not that he could be blamed, but he wasn't even trying to find a solution!

"Are you *serious*?" Hermes asked incredulously. "You will not offer Persephone any real help, but when Perseus went off to kill that Gorgon, you had us lend him our things! I gave him my winged sandals, Hades gave his helmet, and Athene gave her shield! Then after killing the Gorgon, you arranged a bit more help for him so he could defeat the leviathan and save Joppa!"

The death of the leviathan was a sore spot for Poseidon, who felt he had been justified in sending the beast to terrorize the residents after Cassiopeia's insulting boasts. Feeling betrayed by his brother, Poseidon had gone over to Demeter's side.

Hermes continued, "Now he is a king, and it is because of you! You did what you could to help him and his mother, but when Demeter and Persephone needed your help, you do *nothing!* You let all these people starve to death, knowing that you could have ended it at any time!"

There was a stunned silence in the room for a fleeting moment before murmurs of agreement rose up like a tidal wave.

"My son is a king, as is befitting a son of mine. But Persephone is a queen! You can hardly say that she's worse off than Perseus, when her husband rules over the realm of wealth!" Zeus said, trying to quell the tide of angry chatter.

"You are missing the point!" Hera commented acidly, throwing her hands up in exasperation. She could tell by the glint in her husband's eyes that he did see the point, but in his usual fashion, he was trying to avoid it by pointing out the fact that Demeter's daughter was far wealthier than Perseus could ever be. Why couldn't he ever just admit his mistakes without having to be pushed to it?

"I have been your son long enough to know your weaknesses and mistakes, but you went too far with Demeter." Hermes crossed his arms.

"Hermes has an excellent point. You did everything you could to help your son, but when your sister was looking for her daughter, you did nothing even when you knew all along where she was! When Demeter finally found out where her daughter was, you still did nothing! When the people of Hellas starved, you did nothing!" Athene's eyes glinted sharply as she issued her words. As Zeus's eldest child as well as being the Goddess of Wisdom, the gods often looked to her for advice even if she could be quite acerbic at times.

However, in this case, her frankness was welcome. Even the few who remained on Zeus's side could not dispute the veracity of her statement.

"You had no business making such a decision about Persephone in the first place," Artemis was quick to add, coming to the defense of her friend.

"I am King of the Gods! It is my responsibility to look after the clan!"

"Fine job you have done of that," Hermes muttered. Those nearby chuckled at his words.

"You will do anything to help your own son, what a pity you cannot show the same concern for other people's children." Hera reminded her husband, irritated that she had been so close to letting him into her good graces again.

"I have an idea," Athene said, giving her father a disdainful glare before looking at her siblings and cousins. "Since Zeus is clearly incapable of helping and he does not seem to even want to, how about we just focus on Demeter and assist her? We helped Perseus, and I am sure we could figure something out if we worked together."

Demeter nodded in gratitude as several gods spoke in agreement. Athene smirked snidely at her father. Her relationship with Zeus was strained, to say the least. Of course, it didn't help Zeus's relationship with his daughter that he had mistreated her mother, and even centuries later, Athene harbored bitterness towards her father. Nobody who knew the real story of Metis could blame her.

Rhea came forward, studying the gods that had gathered in the chamber. Most of the major deities were here and quite a few others, including Titans, were also here. News had quickly spread through the clan after Demeter started screaming at Zeus, and nobody could resist a spectacle.

"Excellent idea," Rhea said as she nodded at Athene. "I am confident everyone here appreciates your suggestion, but it will not be needed."

"What?" Athene raised her eyebrow. Rhea merely smiled before turning towards the entrance to the throne room. Two figures could clearly be seen advancing through the short hallway, and shocked whispers filled the room when people realized who they were. Instinctively, those nearest the doorway stepped back, giving the Lord of the Dead and his consort a respectable berth.

All eyes fixed upon the pair before Demeter cried out, rushing forward and taking her daughter into her arms.

Chapter LIII

oOo

Persephone felt crushed in her mother's embrace, but bore it as she hugged back. After a few seconds, she gently wiggled away and looked around the room, seeing all the attention that was focused on her. She'd never been in a room with so many people in it, much less divinities, but she managed to square her shoulders as she gave Zeus a fleeting, disdainful glance that was not missed by quite a few onlookers.

"Rarely if ever do I get such a reception such as this," Hades commented as his gaze swept around the room before he returned his attention to Zeus and Demeter. "So good to see the two of you again."

Demeter frowned and grabbed her daughter's arm, tugging her further away from Hades. Hades was tempted to pull her back, but restrained himself.

"Hades, what is the meaning of this?" Zeus asked.

"That answer is very simple." Hades looked from Zeus to Demeter. "I have come to settle things once and for all." He held out his arm towards Persephone. Demeter yanked her daughter away from the proffered hand. He regarded her calmly.

"Sister, I can understand your wish to keep Persephone. You are her mother and love her. However, she is grown, and is now my queen."

"Absolutely not!"

"Mother..." Persephone firmly broke free of her mother's grip. "I am not a little girl. I do not need protection." She looked at Hades. He stood there, giving her an encouraging nod.

"I have no more desire to be parted from Hades any more than he wants to lose me. As he says, I am his queen."

"See!" Demeter shot at Zeus with indignation, "He has put her under his spell!"

"Everything Persephone says is of her own volition. I have done nothing to quell her spirit." The Lord of the Dead studied Demeter with a steady glance. "Your daughter has nothing to fear from me. *Nothing*. I am not worried about what she might say, for she is no more a liar than I am." His tone was firm with the fierceness of his honesty.

"Why not ask Persephone herself?" Rhea interjected. "Zeus and Hades made their plan without consulting anyone. Demeter wishes to keep her close. Still, no one is asking Persephone what she wants, or what she thinks." She stared at Demeter and Hades. "She is a grown woman and I have become very familiar with her. I am delighted to have her as my grandchild, and have come to know her as a wise person."

"Yes, but..." Demeter started, but Hades cut her off.

"Persephone, do you consent to be my queen and wife?" Hades asked. She smiled before nodding.

"I do. And I am honored."

"Any god would be honored to have you as his bride." Hades's smile was brief, but Persephone read the pleasure in it.

"No... no!" It had been so wonderful having her daughter back, and Demeter could not believe she would lose her again! Why did this have to happen? How could it have happened?

Most of the other gods could only stare in shock. After all that had transpired, it seemed surreal that the daughter that Demeter had raised such a furor over would *choose* to return to the Underworld. Having gotten to know Persephone, Artemis was surprised she would want to return to the gloom of the realm of the dead.

"How could you do this to me, Hades?" Demeter demanded.

"I did nothing *to* you. I acted with no malice towards you. I simply wanted Persephone, but I am very sorry for the pain I have caused you."

"You say you are sorry, but here you are, taking her again!"

"I allowed Persephone come up here because I knew she needed the time with you."

"*Allowed*?" Demeter was clearly offended.

"Persephone had already eaten the food of the dead before I sent her back to you."

A shocked clash of mutters rippled through the Hall, and Zeus cringed, knowing that this fact meant an end to further debate. If Persephone had eaten the food of the dead, that was it. Nothing could ever change that.

Mother looked so stricken that for an instant, Persephone regretted eating the food Hades had offered her. She hated how all of the other gods gawked at them, treating Mother's pain like a spectacle. *Let us be alone. Give us the privacy we need*, she thought to herself as she closed her eyes.

"Persephone?" The shock was evident in Hades's tone, and the young goddess opened her eyes, gasping softly when she saw that she was alone with Hades and Demeter amidst seemingly endless darkness. No wait, not quite alone. She saw a faint silhouette of the other gods, as if she was gazing at them through a veil of black silk.

"You did not..." She stared up at Hades. He shook his head.

"I just wanted us to have privacy, and..." As she spoke, the shadows faded away, revealing them to be in a place she remembered from a decade ago – the garden she had first encountered Hades. How did she... Her mind reeled with the implications of what she had done and how this might be applied to future situations. She just had to understand what it was first, but right now she had more urgent matters to attend to. She glanced at Hades before going to Mother.

"Mother, you have not lost me forever!"

"But you have eaten the food of the dead! After I warned you so many times!"

"I remembered that for four months. I refused to eat anything Hades offered me..."

"Why would you give up, then? Did you think you might never be rescued from that dreadful place?"

Persephone looked away, feeling Hades's

intent gaze. She had allowed Hades to feed her those seeds.

Quick footsteps brought her attention to the presence of Zeus striding out of the Hall. Demeter spun towards her brothers, glaring at both of them.

"Damn you! Damn Hades!"

"Demeter, you know that Hades is not a cruel man. Persephone would have told us, asked us for help. Can you not see she is happy with him? Remember the prophecy."

"What prophecy?" Persephone asked, her voice edged with keen interest. Hades raised his eyebrow, sharing her curiosity.

"Don't tell her!" Demeter flared. "I will not have outside forces determine my daughter's fate!"

"Demeter..." Zeus sighed.

"No!" the Harvest Goddess cut Zeus off, raising her chin to him. Persephone stepped forward, raising her hand for silence.

"The Fates merely tell us what will happen. Their word is inviolate." The Queen of the Underworld's voice was filled with calmness and confidence as she spoke of the three – who were also one – manifestations of the mysteries of the universe. "Regardless of whether we fight against them or accept, our destinies are fulfilled. Ouranos told Kronos that his offspring would rise against him, just as he and his Titan brethren had overthrown their heavenly sire. He sought to avert that prophecy and cast his children into a pit to seal them away for what he thought would be eternity. Yet you escaped and fulfilled the prophecy."

Demeter stared at her. Persephone continued.

"When I was in Hades, the Fates summoned me and issued a prophecy of their own for me. I fought against it, yet it has come to pass. Please, I would like to know what the Fates told you about me."

"That you were radiance, and many men would desire you. That you were born of the earth and the heavens, but Death would take you," Zeus replied before Demeter could stop him, so awed by this elegant, collected goddess who stood before him, as regal as Hera in her own way; and mysterious and alluring. Her eyes were a shade of clear green-blue, full of wisdom and cool aloofness. Hades was silent, pondering the revelation. He and Persephone *had* been fated to be together, after all.

A sad smile crept across Persephone's lips before her gaze shifted over to Demeter. "Mother, I know you love me and you want what is best for me. Do not worry that I am unhappy. I am honest when I say that the Underworld is a good place for me, and Hades is the best husband I could ever have."

"Kora, I am your mother... am I never to see you again? I lost the man I loved, now am I to lose my child to Death as well?"

"My name is Persephone. I stopped being a little girl a long time ago."

Zeus swallowed. He remembered when Hades had notified him of his decision to have Demeter's daughter as his wife. The King of the Gods had been afraid that her time in the Underworld would change her... and it did.

"Zeus, do you remember when you bade Mother to bring me to Olympus? You gave me a wish back then and said I could use it anytime."

"Yes. You did promise her one thing she desired," Demeter whispered, staring at her daughter before glancing at Zeus for a moment. "Daughter! Use that wish to make Zeus annul your union with Hades!" she said in a desperate, last-bid effort to keep her child.

Zeus stilled as he heard Demeter's words. He had never considered the consequences of giving his children wishes. They had been children, their wishes innocent and easy to grant. Even though Persephone hadn't immediately acted upon his offer, he had been fairly certain she would act upon it soon after. Days turned to weeks and then years, and Kora had been all but forgotten until the ugly confrontation with Ares.

"Yes." The Queen of the Dead tilted her head to one side, tapping her chin. "You know, back when I was newly captive, I remembered the wish that you had given me. I challenged Hades and said that surely you would not allow this to happen to your own daughter. Not the little girl you were so kind to, the one who had smiled at me so warmly and asked me how I was." Her voice had taken on a light timbre, sounding much like when she was a little girl, sweet and pure.

Demeter was now staring at Zeus, open resentment smoldering within her eyes.

"There is one thing that I learned I could count on from Hades. Honesty. Not once has he told me a lie. I did not want to believe that you would be so... careless. You didn't even bother to pay me a visit and tell me of this, at least. You still owe me that wish."

"I cannot..." Zeus started to shake his head. He hadn't sworn by the Styx, but a promise was still a promise. He would lose face before Demeter and Hades as well as his own daughter, along with anyone else he had granted a wish to, especially given this situation.

"I could demand that you annul the union and take me away from Hades. After all, I am here on Olympus, aren't I? I am certain you could prevent Hades from forcibly removing me from this place. You are after all, King of the Gods, and a father's duty is to protect their children. Here, I am protected, yes..?" The last line was spoken in a knowing tone, a drawl to the yes that made it clear to Zeus that she knew differently.

You know better than that, my love. Hades thought as he stroked his chin. Oh, wait. She was baiting Zeus, wasn't she? Oh ho. This should be fun to watch, and he observed the conversation in gleeful silence.

"You owe her that much." Demeter leaned over, growling into Zeus's ear. Zeus was distinctly uncomfortable under the gazes of his daughter, brother, and former lover.

"Demeter, no... this is Hades we're talking about."

"He goes too far!" the Harvest Goddess

retorted hotly.

"I could demand that you protect me and keep me here. It would be a fair request," Persephone said. Zeus did not even realize he was holding his breath as his daughter continued, "But oh, that would displease Hades. And Death is not to be trifled with." She raised her chin with just the right amount of haughtiness, "He would make his wrath known. It is within his power to take Olympus as his own, and crown himself High King. To be Lord of the Upper and Lower Worlds, no god has ever had that awesome responsibility! And since it is I that he has chosen to rule at his side, so would I be queen of both worlds!"

"Indeed. I did say that I would lay the world at your feet," Hades intoned from behind the others. She looked over her shoulder, giving him a brief but warm smile.

Demeter merely stared at her daughter, stunned after this short monologue. Never would she have imagined she could ever hear such lofty words from her own child, the girl she had raised to be modest and humble! However, she had to admit that it was pleasing to see how nervous Zeus had become.

"When I was in the Underworld, I was certain that I knew what to use my wish for. I have changed my mind, since I do not need to use it at this moment. I will hold onto it for the time I need to call upon you for a favor... and you *owe* me greatly. Never forget that." She gave Zeus a pointed stare before she turned to her mother.

"Mother, I know you do not want me to go back, but I must. I care for Hades, and I want to be with him."

"My daughter..."

"Hades treats me well. He is not unmindful of my needs. I told him that I wanted a real wedding ceremony, and I want you to be part of it."

Demeter stared at her daughter, conflicted over the request. It felt good to be asked to be part of her daughter's ceremony, it was her role as a mother, anyway! It had infuriated her to no end that Zeus and Hades had excluded her from their decision regarding her own child!

"A superb idea!" Zeus said, happy for the distraction. "I will hold a fine banquet! It will be quite the affair! It is not every day that my oldest brother marries - "

"No." Hades stared at his brother, his tone flat with disapproval. "The last person I would see about hosting my wedding would be you. I will not have my ceremony turn into one of your rowdy affairs." He looked at Demeter. "I do believe that my sister has better ideas for her daughter's wedding."

"I will not endorse this union!" Demeter shot back. Hades took a deep breath before Persephone spoke.

"Mother, it would mean much to me. I understand if you do not want to do it now, and we can postpone the ceremony until you are ready, but I would really like you to be a part of this. I *want* to be with Hades."

Demeter stiffened as she heard her daughter's

words.

"You would rather be with him than me, your own mother?"

"I love you. It is not that I never want to see you again or spend time with you, but I am not a child. I enjoy being Hades's companion. I really do." She moved forward to touch her mother's shoulders.

"How can you stand being in the Underworld?"

Hades glanced at mother and daughter before he spoke. "You would be surprised. You and Persephone are alike in a few ways, but you are also quite different. There are certain things in the Underworld that amuse me, and she is able to enjoy them with me. Being King comes with its comforts and privileges. However, I have agreed to let my bride have some time on the surface world. She is a grown woman, after all, and needs no more supervision from her husband than she does her mother." Hades and Persephone shared a smile with one another.

"How much time?" Demeter was quick to ask.

"That is not for you to ask," Hades replied, refusing to let his sister try to dictate Persephone's time. "You and I have something in common. We both love and want what is best for Persephone. I truly am sorry for the grief I have caused you, and I have no wish to cut you off from your daughter forever, but you *will* refrain from making any demands of me... or her. Is that clear?" Hades didn't wish to be so harsh with his sister, but he had to make it clear to Demeter that he would not tolerate any attempt on her part to manipulate the situation.

"Persephone wants a wedding ceremony, but we will not do it until you are ready and willing to participate. Is that fair?" he asked. Demeter stared at him silently before moving her attention to the other deities.

"I can have a say in the location and other things?"

"Certainly. Persephone says she does not want a ceremony on Olympus. She wants it simple and said she thought you would feel the same..." Hades shrugged and gestured towards his bride, who nodded in agreement.

"I need to think about it," Demeter muttered.

"Take your time. You can come speak with me any time," Hades offered.

"Last time I tried to reach you, Styx pushed me back."

"Only because you wanted to take Persephone away, but as long as you come in peace, Kharon will be happy to ferry you."

"Of course I wanted to take her away. Would you expect any less?" came Demeter's terse reply.

"No." Hades brought his hand up. "I do not want a fight. I came up here in peace, to talk to you myself. You can see that Persephone is well. She wants you to be part of her life, and I will not deny her that, but if you attempt to be disruptive..."

Demeter bristled at the use of that word. Her, *disruptive*? After what Zeus and Hades had done? As hot-tempered as she might be, she could be patient. She would figure something out. Her daughter still had her wish, after all.

"And I am to go back to Eleusis alone?" she muttered. Persephone's expression softened.

"You *will* see me again, Mother. And Hellas needs you. Eleusis needs you." Persephone turned towards Zeus. "You will not meddle in my affairs, or Mother's. I will have my wedding ceremony on my terms."

"Olympus is such a grand place for a party! You cannot mean to tell me that you would rather have it elsewhere? I can make it a glorious affair..."

Persephone turned her back to him, hooking her arm through Hades's own and leading him through the garden, ignoring Zeus's protests.

"Wait, you can not just walk away...!"

"Oh, shut up," Demeter snapped at Zeus before she followed her daughter.

o0o

As the other gods talked about Hades and Persephone, Aphrodite was besides herself with envy. Persephone was beautiful, and it seemed to be all the men – and some of the women – could talk about. It would be a good thing if Persephone was stuck in the Underworld, she had eaten the food of the dead, after all! Then Hades would have her all to himself, and the other gods would never see her again!

She crossed her arms with irritation as she overheard Dionysus say how beautiful Persephone looked all dressed up as a queen, though he added that she looked just as lovely in plainer garb!

"The right amount of jewelry or expensive fabrics can make anyone look less ugly!" Aphrodite said acidly. Dionysus grinned at her.

"Jealousy is not becoming of the Goddess of Love and Beauty. Besides, she does not have the snotty expression you often do. She actually looks *friendly.*"

Several others chuckled, and Aphrodite blushed angrily. "You certainly were not complaining the other night, were you? Oh, the praises you sung of my beauty..."

"I am not complaining about Persephone, either..." He grinned at her.

"They are coming back!" someone whispered excitedly. The chatter died down as Hades and Persephone walked into the light from shadows that had surrounded the garden. Hades was aloof, glancing at his family as if they bored him. Persephone had to bite back an amused reaction as she took notice of his attitude.

Zeus and Demeter came up from behind them before the shadows faded away under the light of the brilliant lamps. The gods stared at the quartet expectantly.

"The situation has been resolved," Hades announced as his gaze moved along the throng. "I must make one thing clear. Persephone is my queen, and she will be treated with the same respect as I am. I expect no less." His gaze lingered on several faces, namely Ares and Aphrodite's.

He turned to his brother and sister. "I came up here to talk with you and resolve this matter. Now that it has been done, I see no further reason to stay."

"Leaving so quickly?" Zeus blinked in surprise. Hades nodded.

"It has been a long day." It was all the Dark God felt he needed to say. There would be time later for Persephone to become more acquainted with her family. He could see that she had made quite the impression on them, and he wanted to leave them with that. He looked at Persephone, and she nodded with agreement. As she turned, she caught Aphrodite's gaze and held it, instantly recognizing the Goddess of Beauty. Well, she certainly fit the title.

Hades was right, her beauty is only skin-deep, Persephone mused as she caught the veiled animosity in Aphrodite's glare. She lifted her chin, staring back levelly.

"I will see you soon, Mother." Persephone gave her mother a reassuring smile before Demeter drew her into a tight hug. She smiled to herself, taking comfort in the warm embrace, and hugged her mother back just as fiercely.

oOo

Since they returned to the Underworld, Persephone was quiet and contemplative. She declined to share some wine with him, but she did not seem upset. She retreated to her room, coming out in a plain, comfortable robe. She settled into bed, staring at the fire that burned cheerfully amidst the shadows in the room.

"Are you well, my love?" Hades asked, concerned that the talk on Olympus hadn't brought her satisfaction. Demeter hadn't agreed to a wedding, but she at least no longer tried to fight Hades. The Lord of the Dead was more than willing to give her the time and space she needed. Hopefully after a visit or two from her daughter, his sister might be happier about the whole affair.

"Yes, my lord." Persephone continued to stare at the fire as Hades gently brushed his fingers against her cheek. He could not help but be impressed by the way she had used her Gift to ensure privacy for their discussion. It truly was fascinating, and he wanted to ask her about it, but he held back his inquiries.

"Are you certain? Is there anything I can do for you?" His voice offered promise if pleasure if she wanted it. She smiled and shook her head.

"I just want to sleep."

"Mmm. Very well." He didn't sound angry, or put-out at the least. "Pleasant dreams."

"You too. Good night, Aidon." She continued to stare at the dancing flames until her eyelids fluttered shut. Hades let out a contented sigh, placing his hands behind his head as he stared up at the ceiling, listening to her steady, peaceful breathing. Before long, he let himself relax, comforted by the warmth of her body next to his own.

Chapter LIV

oOo

Persephone stirred awake, feeling luxurious fabric against her skin. For a moment she was disoriented, but the familiarity of her surroundings rushed back to her in a pleasant cascade of memories. The drapes were halfway open, letting in gray light. She could tell by the particular tint of light that it was early morning in the surface world. Hades didn't have to change the sky for her, but he had arranged this to make her more comfortable. For someone who had kidnapped her and had such a fearsome reputation to both mortals and gods, he had certainly proven to her how sweet he could be.

He had proven that again with the agreement they made the night before.

She glanced to her left, seeing him deep in slumber with the blanket up to his chest, one hand resting atop it and the other arm splayed along the comforter. She remained where she was, not wishing to leave the warm snugness of the bed. Even in here, there was an almost indiscernible chill in the air, everywhere as it always was.

With a quiet sigh, the Queen of the Underworld burrowed deeper into the bed as she wiggled towards Hades, pressing her body to his. It was nice just lying there with her head nestled against his shoulder, his bicep snug in the softness of her chest. She stared off thoughtfully as he slept.

She felt content. She had been so anxious about returning to the Underworld, but having secured the right to go up to the surface world, she would still be able to enjoy the warmth of that world, and down here she had a man who treated her like his queen, and much more than that. His vows of undying love and unwavering loyalty reassured her.

Her thoughts were interrupted as he stirred awake. She raised her head to look at him, and as he opened his eyes, she saw a smile of delight on his face. He certainly looked happy to have her here; would he feel this way every morning from here on?

"Seph..." His voice was a soft rumble as he reached up to touch her face and hair. She was here with him, at his side as she was meant to be. His wife, queen... mate. Her mere presence, even if she wasn't touching him or paying him any special attention, brought about a feeling of contentment he could not put into words. As he shifted around, he realized that he was awake in more ways than one.

With a playful growl, he rolled over and climbed on top of her, smiling faintly down at her. Though Persephone was by no means petite, Hades was still able to pin her easily. He was broad-shouldered and nearly seven feet tall, his form blanketing over hers as he looked down at her. Despite the fact that he was almost one and a half times her weight, she did not shrink back from the formidable deity. She wiggled against him, savoring the warm bulk as she slid her hands into his robe, running her palms up and down his chest.

o0o

When Demeter came back without Persephone, the royal family was especially careful around her. Fortunately for them – and everybody else – the Harvest Goddess did not strike out at any innocent bystanders. At least not this time around. Demophon was healthy enough to not constantly need care, so she had spent most of the last few days by herself, roaming various regions of Hellas to distract herself from her daughter's absence.

She went back to the valley where she and Kora had gone to live after Iasion's death. The house was quiet, a layer of dust covering everything. All of the furnishings were well-crafted, having been created for her by the Cyclopes a long time ago, the quality of their work evident in the fact that the furniture had lasted for so long in such wonderful condition.

Two looms sat at one side of the common room where the windows faced south and west. The projects on both of the looms were not finished. They had not been given any attention since the disappearance of her daughter, so the bright colors of the yarns were subdued by the dust that coated it.

"Oh, Kora..." She sat at the table, ignoring the dust as she placed her face in her hands.

"She does not like being called that." Demeter

looked up at the source of these words, blinking in surprise as she saw her mother. Rhea approached the table, sweeping the dust off a stool with the edge of her cloak before sitting down.

"What brings you here, Mother?"

"I know you needed someone to talk to. I would have come earlier, but I sensed that you needed some time away from us."

"Thank you." Demeter's tone was dry.

"I know you miss her, but at least you know you will see her again." Rhea was thankful that Hades was being considerate of Persephone's needs.

"Only when Hades says so." She let out a frustrated sigh. The compromise Hades had made mollified her only a bit. There would be no wedding ceremony until she participated in it, or so her daughter said. She considered telling Hades she would never give her blessing, but she knew it would make no difference to him. Her daughter would never be truly free of the Underworld because she had eaten its food. "He has left me no option."

Rhea nodded slowly. She did think that Hades was being harsh with his sister, but then she also knew that Demeter was overprotective of her daughter, not that she could be blamed. Demeter had as much to learn as Hades did.

"I know it was difficult losing your husband." Rhea hesitated before she continued, "Have you considered finding a lover? Or adopting a child? You need something to nurture."

Demeter stared at her mother, her lips set in a

319

tight scowl. "I am not as mercurial with my affections as so many of us are."

"And they could learn much from you. But while you were searching for your daughter, did you not nurse a dying baby back to health? You are the Goddess of Bounty, and it is not just your own child that should benefit from that. You drew away from the world when you married that mortal and raised Persephone with him."

"I saw no reason to remain on Olympus."

"I understand. But things have changed. You made quite the impression on everyone, even the older ones. You have been gone from Olympus for too long. I have missed you, and you would be welcomed by many."

Demeter did not speak, and Rhea wisely decided to mirror that silence. It was clear her daughter needed time to think, and Rhea had never been one to press a matter at the wrong time.

"My home is always open to you," the older goddess said as she rose from her seat and squeezed Demeter's shoulder.

oOo

Persephone wasted no time in reacquainting herself with the Underworld. She paid visits to the friends she had made – Hekate, Nyx, Kampe, and Hypnos – and was happy to resume her role as Queen of the Underworld. When she had been on the surface, the only Underworld deity she was able to see was Morpheus, since she could visit him in her dreams. Despite the fact that Hellas was renewed and the mortals had a bounty of food like nobody ever had before, their dreams were still filled with sorrow for the misery they had been through and the loved ones they had lost.

Elysium had plenty of people who lost their lives due to Demeter's wrath. Some had been killed for food, others had simply crawled off to die, and some had even killed themselves to escape their own pain or seeing their loved ones dying. There were mothers who had given all their food to their children at the cost of their lives, something that inadvertently renewed Persephone's bitterness towards her mother. She tried to not dwell on that, for in this idyllic afterlife these people had better lives than they had as mortals, but it still wasn't right.

She could not help but feel that her mother needed to be punished in some way. Not for being angry at what had been done to her, but for how she had expressed it, inflicting so much needless suffering on completely innocent parties. She found herself swinging between wanting to see Mother again and avoiding her entirely, especially after having been lied to for so long and trapped in the body of a girl when she was well past the age of being one.

She pushed these thoughts out of her head, determined to not dwell on such negativity as she approached the large building that held the weaving studio. It did not take her long to find Eurycleia. The other woman did not immediately register her, but after a few words, her eyes lit up with recognition.

"I was wondering if you had gone off to Lethe. You were nowhere to be found!"

*Well, I **did** go to Lethe, but that's beside the point...* "Well... I... it is not something I wish to discuss." Persephone knew she would need to tell the truth sooner or later, but she couldn't do so now. "I just had to do something important. But I missed it here."

Persephone could see the curiosity in the other woman's eyes, but Eurycleia nodded slowly and silently before she spoke. "Remember that dye you liked so much? I have a bolt of linen for you. I had been saving it for you."

"Oh, thank you!" She had nearly forgotten about that.

"I will give it to you later. For now, I am in the mood to enjoy a hot meal. Would you like to come with me?"

"Certainly." Persephone smiled. Food never ran out in Elysium, and even though a dead soul didn't *need* to eat, it was still a comfort for them to have food available. Some people liked to cook, so they had no end of ingredients to experiment with, and were always happy to prepare food for others to keep themselves occupied. Others liked to eat, and enjoyed the various flavors, whether it be familiar ones from their mortal lives, or new ones that the limited locales of their previous lives did not offer. It felt good for her to not reject the food anymore. No longer did she have to feel her mouth water at the exquisite foods Hades tried to offer her and turn her head away from it, or to smell all these delicious aromas and wonder if the food did indeed taste as good as it smelled.

oOo

Persephone woke up to feel Hades scramble out of bed. She stirred and rolled over, lifting her head to stare at him sleepily. Shades appeared to give him raiment and accessories, including a crown. Apparently he had someone important to meet. But who?

"Aidon?" she asked softly. He turned to look at her as the shades pinned up his chiton and draped a matching himation across his shoulder in their usual efficient manner.

"I have been summoned," he replied. Persephone knew that no one could *summon* Hades; he merely decided if he was in a generous enough mood to honor a request to see him. A quick glance through the window revealed that it was still night, and Persephone wondered who might be visiting, and why Hades was willing to entertain them at this hour.

"Who is it?" she asked.

"Merely some important business. Just stay where you are." He approached the bed and tucked her in. Feigning cooperation, she snuggled into the bed and closed her eyes. As soon as he was out the door, she quickly slipped out of bed and pulled on a robe before turning invisible. She hadn't revealed this Gift to Hades as she wanted time to explore her abilities more fully. Besides, it would be nice to surprise him.

She caught up with Hades as he strode to his throne room, and he showed no indication that he suspected her presence. But she wasn't fooled, Hades was good at masking his thoughts. If she was able to sense him when he was invisible, it wouldn't surprise her if he did the same. Still, she continued to follow him, keeping a respectful distance.

She bit back a startled cry when she saw her mother. She remained beside a pillar as Hades sat on his throne. Next to him, her throne was conspicuously empty.

"Welcome to my kingdom, sister." Hades's tone was neutral but without a trace of hostility or aloofness. One wouldn't think that he had just been roused from his sleep.

"I have no desire to remain here for long. I need to see my daughter," was Demeter's curt reply. Persephone tensed, wondering what Hades would do. Hades wouldn't try to keep this meeting from her as Mother had kept so many things secret in the past, would he?

"I shall not prevent you from doing so. But I would like to talk to you first." Hades wanted a private conversation with his sister without his younger brother around to make an ass out of himself like he had before.

"What is it?" Demeter asked, her gaze wary as she regarded her older brother.

"I really am sorry for how... things turned out. It was never my intention to hurt you. I had been planning to tell you where your daughter was, and that was my intention from the beginning..."

"Then why did you not?"

"Why do you think?" His voice remained calm, but Demeter could hear an edge of rebuke in his tone. "You refused to allow your daughter to be in the company of men. Of course, with certain... events that had transpired, I could hardly blame you for that. Still, I knew you would not allow me to court her. You would not want her with any man, much less one who lives in a dead realm." He shrugged. "So the only recourse I thought was possible was to kidnap her."

Hades could feel the anger building up in Demeter. The Goddess could be truly frightful, as she had proven with the famine. He was fully prepared for this, and continued, "In hindsight, it was not a smart thing to do, but love can drive one to do things they did not think possible, hm?"

Demeter had fallen in love with a mortal and all but withdrew from Olympian life so she could enjoy a peaceful existence with him in Enna. She had never thought it possible to love anyone since she had never found anyone she cared for so deeply. Iasion was the first time she had ever felt what she knew she could define as love. It made it all the more painful when he died, and she almost envied Zeus who was able to move on easily when one of his mortal lovers died or he became bored of them.

"I regret all the pain I have caused you. I truly do." Hades's expression became kind – a rare instance indeed for the Dark One – as he leaned forward. "Even though Persephone eats my food, I have no desire to cut her off from the surface world. It would be cruel to you and to the woman I love."

"You truly love her?"

"Of course I do. I do not make a habit of kidnapping maidens. Persephone is the only one I have ever wanted as my mate. Our brothers would tease me, telling me that I needed a companion in this dark world. These words never affected me until the first time I saw your daughter."

"Why her? Out of all the women in the world, why my daughter?"

"Why love Iasion?" Hades countered. Demeter opened her mouth, but nothing came out.

"I have never treated Persephone with anything but kindness. Be assured that I never forced myself on her or kept her confined. I ensured that she had all the comforts she could want."

"So you consider yourself a good host?"

"Yes," Hades replied wryly. He was silent for a moment before he spoke in a firmer tone, "I would – and could – never harm her. I desired her very badly – and still do – but I always treated her with dignity and respect. She is worthy of nothing less. I *earned* the affection she has for me."

"It is hard to imagine that she could enjoy being with you."

"I can understand that. I expect no special favors from you. We have always respected one another, and I desire to maintain that. Do not think of me as her warden. Think of me as a man who loves her with all my heart."

Demeter tensed, but remained silent as she

pondered his words.

"Would you like to speak with Persephone?" Hades offered.

"Will you give us privacy?"

"As you wish." Hades gave a nod before he rose from his seat. Persephone ducked behind a pillar, turning visible before she emerged from the shadows. Surprise flashed on his features for a moment before he smiled at her.

"How nice of you to join us. Your mother is here to see you." He stepped down from the dais and gave them a quick bow of his head before he left the throne room.

"Were you there the whole time?"

"Yes, I followed him. He does not know what I can do."

"... Really?" Demeter raised her eyebrow. Persephone smiled and shrugged.

"Women have their secrets, do they not? So how have you been?" It was nearly a fortnight since her return to the Underworld. She had actually been thinking about asking Hades to let her go to the surface world. She had practiced the varying aspects of her Gift as she tried to find out what other abilities she might have, while she was by herself.

"As well as any mother could be in these circumstances, I suppose. Is everything Hades says true?"

"To the last word. He will be a good husband."

Demeter let out her breath before she spoke. "I dread the thought of you having a husband."

"So you tried to keep me a little girl forever."

"Could you blame me?"

"Yes!" was Persephone's blunt reply as she narrowed her eyes, letting some of her old resentment bubble up, "You would not even tell me about the monthly courses so when it happened to me, I was terrified, not knowing what was happening to me. For so long I waited to grow up, to have a body like the nymphs. How I waited and hoped... and you never would talk to me about womanly matters. There were so many times that I was angry and frustrated with you because you refused to actually listen to me or talk to me as if I were anything more than a stupid little child... sometimes I even felt like I hated you."

"I am sorry." Demeter quickly looked away.

"The words of the Fates have been fulfilled despite your efforts to circumvent them."

"I know." The older woman shook her head slowly. "At least Hades has been kind to you."

"I would not wish to be with him if he had ever been cruel to me."

"I am not yet ready to help you with the wedding. I need time."

"Certainly." Persephone shrugged acquiescently.

"I was thinking we could do it on the spring solstice, unless another date suits you."

That was nearly three months away. Persephone was mildly surprised, but relieved that her mother wouldn't be giving her a hard time. "I think that is a wonderful idea, Mother. That gives us plenty of time. And I was thinking that Grandmother could help. And Hestia, if she wants to."

"I think she will. She enjoys cooking, and I have always liked being with her."

"Sounds good to me."

"I would like you to come back with me. I miss you."

Persephone had to bite back a laugh. Of course Mother wouldn't come down here just to leave her daughter behind! And she *had* been missing the other world. But first...

"Is that all you have thought about since my return to Hades?"

"Would you expect me to simply forget you?"

"Of course not! But I hope that is not the only thing you have been worried about..." Persephone's tone and expression was pointed. "The mortals have been through so much. They were punished for a crime they did not commit."

"I know. I have already decided what I am going to do. I would like to show you."

"Very well. I need to talk to Hades."

Persephone found him in the banquet room, looking especially lonesome amidst all the empty seats at the long table. He held out an arm as she approached him, and drew her into his lap.

"Aidon, I would like to go to the other world with Mother."

Hades's expression revealed no surprise, though he did look a bit sad.

"Just for one day?" she asked as she touched his cheek, surprised at how much his sorrow affected her. "I will be back in time for supper and bed."

He nodded slowly. "I know you want to go... there because you enjoy the surface world and you love your mother. I do hope that you will come back here because you enjoy it here, and also..." He was silent for a moment and she regarded him with an inquisitive glance.

"What is it?"

"It is my sincerest hope that you come back to me because you love me. If not now, then one day."

Persephone quickly looked away as she felt her heart flutter rapidly and her cheeks warm.

oOo

The journey back to the surface world was quiet. Whatever it was that Mother had planned, she wanted to show it first instead of merely telling, and that was just fine with the younger deity. Mother looked uncomfortable sitting amidst the souls of the dead in Kharon's boat and kept her cloak wrapped tightly around herself.

Eleusis was just as Persephone remembered, but instead of going to the Palace, Demeter took her to the temple. It was early morning, and the priestesses were just beginning the morning rituals. Persephone recognized all the priestesses, including Melinoe and Kalia. She did not miss how the priestesses regarded Demeter with rapt attention, always ready to listen to whatever she might say.

Despite the winter weather, the morning atmosphere lacked biting chill, so the coldness of the air was refreshing. Demeter led her daughter into the inner garden and dismissed the priestesses.

"Years ago, when I first came to Enna, the people there were miserable. They had to put every bit of effort into the land just to survive, and sometimes that was not enough."

Persephone nodded slowly, already knowing this story, but patiently waited for her mother to get to the point.

"I not only removed the source of their suffering, but showed them better ways of farming that would yield more – and better – food. It is my intention to share that knowledge with the rest of Hellas. When I was looking for you, I saw farms that were not managed as well as they could be. I could just make Hellas overflow with food until the end of time, but that takes a great amount of energy, and it would simply cause the mortals to become lazy. I can teach them some of my techniques, so they can earn a better bounty for themselves. But my priestesses..." Demeter smiled faintly.

"What?"

"My more powerful secrets, I reserve for my acolytes. You know that Melinoe is... special."

"Yes." Persephone sensed a trace of a Gift in the princess.

"She is not the only one. I have been working with her and the other priestesses, teaching them how to feel and use magic. They cannot do what we are capable of, but with enough training, they can harness some of the magic and use it for the benefit of the people. Apollo has his priests and priestesses at Delphi, trained in the ways of clairvoyance..."

"And you will have your own order of priestesses, trained in the ways of Nature?" Persephone asked. Mother smiled.

"Women have always had a greater affinity for Nature than men."

"Is that why nymphs are women? I've never seen a male nymph."

"Yes." The minor male gods were not called nymphs, and tended to be gods of rivers, lakes, caves, or deserts, unlike their sisters who preferred more verdant surroundings. There was the occasional male who deviated from the norm, but that was rare enough that most people would never see a male nymph in their lives. Persephone pondered what she had just learned about her mother's intentions. All in all, it wasn't actually a bad idea. She couldn't think of any criticism for this plan.

"These women are chosen to learn certain secrets. I cannot remain in Eleusis forever, but these priestesses will use their knowledge and magic to bless the city."

"Eleusinian Mysteries." The words tumbled out of Persephone's mouth, reflecting the first thing that came to her mind. Demeter glanced at her with a mixture of mild surprise and open approval.

"Eleusinian Mysteries. I like the sound of

that."

As she had not eaten morning supper, Persephone was happy to sit down with Mother and eat. It was interesting noting the difference between Underworld and 'real' food now that she had the chance to actually sample and enjoy what Hades had to offer her. While Underworld food had more flavor – almost too much sometimes – food grown here on the surface world had life in it.

Food in the Underworld didn't grow. It was... simply there. Even the animals that provided the meat weren't real in the sense that they were living, thinking creatures. Underworld meat was merely mystical substance given a certain flavor and appearance to suit Hades's desires.

When she ate the food Mother gave her, she could feel its life, where it had come from, where it would go. The seeds would actually grow and bear fruit, and left too long, would go to seed and then decay. She looked down at the lentil stew thoughtfully for several moments before dipping bread in it.

"Is something the matter?" Demeter asked. Persephone smiled and shook her head.

"Just thinking about how Underworld food is different from this."

"What is the food like?"

"It looks and tastes the same as what we eat." Persephone was tempted to describe how tasty it was, but since Mother couldn't and wouldn't eat it, she didn't see the need to go into detail.

"Really? There is nothing special, like how we have ambrosia and nectar on Olympus?"

"Uh-huh. There is no special food." *Except for the pomegranates from Hades's garden, maybe, since I know how special the tree is to him*, but Persephone saw no reason to comment on that.

oOo

After nearly half a month in the Underworld, Persephone was keenly aware of the difference between the two realms, though it didn't bother or overwhelm her as much as before. After returning to Hades, she didn't feel so afraid or distressed at the lack of life down there, and conversely, when she came up here, she didn't feel the surge of relief she had experienced upon her first return to Hellas.

It was early afternoon, and she still had several hours ahead of her. She was at the moment roaming the Eleusinian countryside alone, thinking about what to do next. Familiarizing herself with the rest of her family was her top priority as long as she was here, but she didn't want to rely on Mother or Grandmother for transport. Now that she knew she was not barred from the surface world, she was more determined to know her clan. How could she get around on her own, unaided?

When there's a will, there's a way, she reminded herself. She had but to apply her Gift...

or first, figure a way to do that. Visualization was an excellent way, as she remembered. As her mind meandered its way through possible ideas, she could not help but recall the Fates and their cosmic tapestry. In some ways it resembled a spider web, one that spun out for eternity with an infinite amount of threads. She would never forget the sight of the tapestry for as long as she would live, and the thought of threads going on forever boggled her mind.

Hmm. Like just any woman across the world, Persephone knew of the importance of threads. It mattered not what they were made of − thick woolen yarn or leather cords to slender linen strings or thin, delicate strands of silk. One could even say that without these threads, civilization would not exist.

She had used the idea of threads to make it easier to share her Gift with the dying people of Hellas. The concept had just come to her naturally, and now she could see it spinning off into something else...

Persephone turned towards the Palace, envisioning a thread that started from her hand and stretched all the way to the Palace walls. If she could somehow... reel herself in, or slide along it, and...

A startled gasp penetrated the silence when Persephone found herself a couple of feet away from the wall. She placed her hand on it to make sure she wasn't dreaming.

I did it! I really did it! She felt almost faint from the thrill of her discovery. *I can go anywhere I want!*

Persephone tested her new ability several times, trying varying distances. She appeared in her mother's temple and the Palace with the same success. Hekate had told her that she needed to find her own way of doing things. The Goddess of the Crossroads had but to imagine a road opening before her to lead her wherever she wanted. Having walked down a couple of these paths with Hekate, she now had a better understanding of her powers. A thread worked for her just as well as paths did for Hekate, or the darkness for Hades, or the earth for Mother and Grandmother.

Would it work over a long distance? Well, there was one way to find out...

o0o

More often than not, Athene often went amongst the mortals, whether as a goddess or in disguise, but she had elected to spend this afternoon on Olympus, visiting with Artemis. Despite having different mothers, Athene and Artemis got on very well. Though they had different interests, they had enough in common to agree on most things, like how especially stupid and/or useless men were, and how better the goddesses were off without them around. What had happened with their father and Demeter certainly was proof enough of that.

However, they were not as inclined towards gossip as some others were, and often amused themselves by playing games or making up riddles. Sometimes Athene would weave as her sister talked, like right now.

"Hello?" Athene heard someone call out as a firm but polite rapping filled the air for a long second. She raised her chin, shooting the other goddess an inquisitive glance.

"That's Persephone," Artemis commented as she rose to her feet. "Should I invite her in?"

The older woman gave a brief nod. "This should be interesting," She followed her sister.

Persephone stood in front of the gate. Generally, gates were made of wood and sometimes rope with the rare exception of iron or brass when one could afford it, but the ones on Olympus were beautifully wrought metal, swinging on proper hinges just like the ones in the Underworld. Each gate was unique and matched the personality and identity of its owner, making their homes more identifiable. She had gone to the nearest gate to knock. Nobody was home, but at the second a nymph was there to answer the door. Persephone declined to leave a message.

Upon seeing the fourth gate, it was easy to guess whose home it opened to. Athene's had carved marble owls on either side of the opening, and the gate itself looked like silver, slightly tarnished. The first had been black iron, the second brass, and the third gold, so this darkly gleaming silver seemed to fit the stately-looking goddess she had glimpsed during her last visit to Olympus.

Spreading through the design of the entire gate was an olive tree, branches and roots visible, mirroring one another. Set amongst the branches were cabochons of peridot and emerald of varying shades of chartreuse and green, representing the olives Athene so loved.

After she knocked, she waited for several moments before Artemis emerged. Athene followed, and Persephone lifted her hand in greeting as they approached the gate.

"You have come just in time for lunch," Athene said as she regarded Persephone with an even gaze.

"Really? How nice!" Persephone entered after Artemis opened the gate. She did not miss the way Athene was appraising her with her stare. The younger woman stared back just as coolly, and Artemis bit back a smile.

"Pardon me for asking, but how is it that you are up here? I thought you were trapped in the Underworld," Athene said. Everyone knew that Persephone had eaten pomegranate seeds, many said that Hades tricked her, a few said he raped her, others said that she had simply been so hungry that she gave in to temptation. Not one person thought that Persephone would eat the food of the dead on her own accord.

"I made an agreement with Hades for some time in this world."

"So he permits you to visit Olympus?" Athene asked sardonically. Artemis frowned faintly; Athene had the habit of teasing or baiting a newcomer as a way of testing them and gauging their reactions.

"*Permit?* Oh, no. He is quite easy to manage

when one knows how to treat him." Persephone smiled mysteriously. It had taken a while, to be sure, but her growing intimacy with the Lord of Death also brought greater understanding. She had seen him angry and sad, and knew that she could rouse either emotion from him with choice words or actions. Yet she didn't want resort to provoking him and they were both so much happier for it.

"Oh, really?" Artemis flashed a grin. "The mighty Lord of the Underworld, managed, you say?"

"Hades is Hades, but he is also a man." The red-haired deity was calm and confident if a bit flippant. She knew people would wonder about her relationship with Hades, so she had already decided how she was going to be about it. No bragging, just short and simple truth without unnecessary details. "I never got the chance to really meet or know the other gods before, so I am eager to make acquaintances." *And some friends*, but Persephone refrained from saying it because she didn't want to sound *too* eager.

"How come your mother did not show you before?" Athene asked bluntly as they entered the house.

"She did not want to raise me amidst the Olympians. With what has happened, I hardly wonder why."

Athene snorted quietly. "I can see the logic in that. Though that did not help any when Hades kidnapped you."

"Right you are. However, things did not turn out too badly for me."

339

"For you? What about Demeter?"

Persephone shrugged. "That was not my fault. If I could have escaped the Underworld and stopped the famine, I would have. But, Zeus..."

"Yes, yes. We all know. Sometimes I wonder how I can be related to such a man," Athene replied. Artemis grinned and nodded in agreement.

"Just be glad that our Gifts are our own, and not given to us by our parents. No one could call him the God of Wisdom, hm?" Persephone asked.

Athene was intelligent and at times caustic, but she was not above well-timed flattery. There was a sparkle of pleasure and approval in her gray eyes.

"Makes you wonder what it would be like if Hades was High King. The gods would not get in so much trouble!" Artemis commented.

"Imagine Father sitting on Hades's black throne! Surrounded by all that gloom, the only women around already dead!"

"It might have done Zeus some good," Persephone added dryly. "But I did not come here to bitch about men."

"So you will not be regaling us with tales of married life?" Athene asked.

"Oh, please. There are so many topics that are more interesting than that!" she shot back lightly, responding to the gray-eyed woman's challenge.

o0o

Metaniera could sense Demeter's sadness as

they worked in the weaving room. Demophon played with clay animals on the floor. He was full of energy, often running around and laughing. Celeus would chase after him with his eyes twinkling, a smile on his face, moving like someone half his age, but right now Demophon was ready for a nap, his toys on the blanket that had been spread for him. As he played quietly, the women weaved. After what had happened with Persephone, Metaniera was unsure of Demeter's next course of action now that her daughter's fate was decided.

She glanced at Demeter several times before she finally spoke.

"We have enjoyed having you here, not merely as a goddess, but as... a friend. You have blessed us in so many ways. We are forever in your debt. I know you miss your daughter. Would you like to have Demophon as your own child? He enjoys your care, and you are a wonderful mother."

"You would be willing to give him up?"

"He is happy with you, and I see the fondness in your eyes when you look at him. I know my son would be in good hands. After all, what good mother does not want the best for their child?"

A wistful smile appeared on Demeter's lips.

"You have made me feel welcome. It has been a while since I felt so honored. I am happier here than I am with my own family. And the Mysteries... Anyway, Triptolemus does not wish to stay here. He wants to travel the world. He has the deep yearning for it, so I will put him under my protection. As he travels, he will teach the farming secrets I wish to share. Demophon will be your heir. The reign of your husband will be a long one yet and you will live to see Demophon become a father. I will stay here until spring." There was Persephone's wedding to prepare for, and she was loath to leave Eleusis so soon. She would enjoy some more time here before leaving with Triptolemus.

The queen let out a sudden squeak of joy before quickly collecting herself. She had seen the wanderlust in her son's eyes. Triptolemus would be unhappy as King, though he would bear the crown out of filial piety. Serving Eleusis should be more than that. She also wanted Demophon to be happy, but she wished that for all of her children, which was why she would not allow her daughters to be wed to men they did not like. And now this, knowing that she and her husband would share a long and happy life yet, seeing her children and grandchildren grow... and just the year before Demophon was going to die, and her city was being threatened, her daughters about to be forced into marriage... Oh! This change of fate was all so wonderful!

"Goddess, we are infinitely blessed by your presence. We delight in your presence for however long you wish to stay. My hearth is yours."

oOo

Oftentimes, a deity's power would take the

form of a tangible object. For some, this made it more effective for them to wield their magic or utilize it in certain tasks. Sometimes such objects were formed so that mortals could actually see the power being used, or to benefit from the deity's magic in a more practical way.

Kharon's boat served such a purpose. It acted as a ferry and barrier alike. While mortals and gods saw Kharon as the ferryman of souls and nothing more, he actually had a far greater purpose; keeping dead people from leaving, or keeping live souls from trespassing to Dis before their time. People focused on him being a ferryman, thus underestimating his powers and abilities, and that was just how he wanted it. His boat went back and forth endlessly, bringing souls to the other side. What people never thought about was that once you went across, there was no going back.

Many a soul had indeed tried to escape, but Kharon's powers, just like any of the other underworld deities', was inexorable. He could deny any living person passage to the Underworld, or prevent them from leaving. The gods of Olympus never knew just how much they relied on Kharon to give them a safe journey in or out of the Land of the Dead. No one would ever suspect that the simple boat depicted in the artwork of the Underworld and in stories was representative of something much more.

Persephone stared out at the waters, silent as Kharon ferried her. The ethereal oarsman was a very taciturn person, and the Queen of the Dead welcomed the silence.

Just looking at the Styx made her feel cold inside, yet she was unable to look away. She had faced two rivers of Hell and had only come out stronger for it.

When the boat came to the pier, the cloaked oarsman gracefully helped her out. She regarded him with an appreciative nod before going on her way.

In the endless depths of the river, Kharon was aware of the goings-on of his boat. Live souls had a different feel to them, and he solemnly regarded Persephone as she had boarded the vessel.

Of course, the ferryman did not focus his entire self on the task the dead souls set to him. To do so would drive him insane through sheer repetition. Persephone barely had his attention, and in a moment, all thoughts of her were banished as he felt icy teeth nibble along his ear. The chill only enticed him.

Everyone else was terrified of the abyssal cold, even Persephone. He allowed himself to get lost into it.

o0o

Hades said that he was going to come for her shortly after sunset, but Persephone decided to surprise him. Even as she spent time with her mother and other goddesses, Hades's parting words weighed heavily upon her mind. She was content to let everyone else do most of the talking, finding it a good way to learn about others.

When she tried to use her Gift to return to the Underworld, she was surprised when it didn't work. It left her at the bank of the Styx, but would go no further. For some reason, she could not make her 'string' penetrate the barrier between the Kingdom of the Dead and the land of the living. *Hmm, I wonder why that is.* Still, she waited patiently for the boat before being helped into it by Kharon.

Upon arriving at the Palace, she summoned a shade to take her to Hades. He was playing with Kerberos, throwing a branch and having the dog chase after it. Despite his frightful appearance, Kerberos could be puppy-like at times when being played with by people he recognized and liked. The dog yelped and bounded towards her, stopping just short and giving a friendly bark, offering her the stick. She took it and threw it, and he retrieved it before bounding back to Hades. Hades tossed the branch so hard it disappeared from sight, but the dog went after it. Persephone knew from previous experience that the dog always found what Hades threw.

"Have I forgotten the time?" he asked as she approached him.

"No, I decided to come on my own. I do not *need* to be fetched."

"Oh, but I have such fun fetching you." Hades said with a winning smile. Persephone smiled to herself and looked away.

"Oh, very well, you can do it next time!"

o0o

Despite Hellas's fairly mild climate compared to the lands of the North, Mount Olympus could become cold. Hades was thankful he did not have to deal with the cold wind as he stared at the fish that moved about in front of him, a transparent panel of crystal separating him from the ocean.

Despite the rarity of his visits to the surface world, Poseidon's palace was one of Hades's favorite places to go to. Yes, Dis had the Sea of Eternity, but only in the world of the living would the oceans teem with life. He enjoyed the spectacular view that could only be found in his brother's palace. Very few mortals ever got to see the sea this way, and he smiled faintly as he touched the cool surface of the panel, watching a school of multicolored fish swim by and the play of refracted light on the coral reefs.

"You really like looking at that, don't you?" Poseidon asked with a bemused smile as several Nereids bustled about to fill the table with a banquet.

"I will admit that it is a very good reason to leave the Underworld," Hades answered as he turned and approached the table once the nymphs retreated from the room. He noted with approval that his brother had made sure many of his favorite items were on the menu. He did not like when people gave him things just to curry favor, but he wasn't about to object to having his palate catered to.

"It is almost hard to believe that my older brother is soon to be a married man!" Poseidon commented after a while. Hades smiled and swallowed his bite.

"I almost wonder if it's a dream, that I should have such a woman at my side," Hades replied easily.

"That's how I felt when I married Amphitrite. Still do."

Hades raised an eyebrow. It was known among the gods that Poseidon, like his younger brother, did not have a monogamous relationship with his wife. The Lord of the Seas did not miss this, and smiled at his brother.

"I can assure you, my wife fares much better than Hera."

"She is unmindful of your... activities?"

"Just as I am unmindful of hers."

Hades nearly swallowed his fish too quickly. He collected himself before staring at his brother with a curious expression. "I do not understand this. You speak of her with love, and I see how she looks at you." When he arrived, Amphitrite had been there to greet him, and she and her husband regarded one another with respect and unmistakable affection. "Yet..."

"After so long, sometimes you want to try... something new. I was confused at first, to be honest. I love and desire my wife as I always do, but sometimes I find my attention caught by a pretty maiden here and there. I tried to fight it, but then I noticed that my wife's eye might wander, too. We talked about it, and decided to take new lovers for ourselves. Afterward, we came back together and... I actually enjoyed my wife more."

"How is that possible?" Hades asked before he took a long swig of wine.

"You know how you have a favorite food? You enjoy it often, but if you ate it all the time, why, you would tire of it! If you eat something different, you appreciate your favorite more."

"I would think a woman would be more... meaningful than food." Hades leaned back on his divan. He simply could not imagine ever being bored with Persephone. She had effectively ruined him for all other women.

Instead of pressing the matter and encouraging him to enjoy the pleasures of other women like their younger brother doubtlessly would have, Poseidon shrugged. "Everyone is different. I love my wife more now than I did before. Our relationship is happy because I do not hold her to a different standard than I would for myself. I have found that *that* is the key to a successful relationship."

"I will toast to that," Hades intoned, raising his goblet. Poseidon grinned as he lifted his own.

o0o

Persephone stared down the neck of the flask that Dionysus had just passed to her. Having tasted all sorts of exotic wine in the Underworld, she was able to discern most of the ingredients, but there was also ambrosia in there, the sweetness balancing the high alcohol content.

She took a large sip, feeling the burn as it slid down her throat. Promptly, she passed it back to

Dionysus. She could see how such a beverage could cause the revelries and orgies that Dionysus was so famous for, and resolved to be especially careful about anything a god might offer. In front of them, several nymphs entertained them with a boisterous song and dance, and she could not help but laugh and clap her hands with the beat.

As she did so, Dionysus stared at her admiringly. She had eschewed all jewelry and opted for a deep purple chiton, looking more like a nymph than Queen of the Underworld. Many a god had tried to capture her attention, but the bride-to-be of Hades remained impervious to the attempts to seduce her. She might tease and even flirt back just a little, but she was ever elusive to anyone who tried to claim her.

"Have some more!" Dionysus stated as he tried to pass the wine back to her, but she shook her head.

"I think not."

"Afraid of getting a little drunk? Worry not, you are in safe hands!"

"Safe?" Persephone gave out a small snort. "With the way you are looking at my leg..." Said limb was visible through the side of her chiton, draped across the grass gracefully and terminating in a slender bare foot. Instead of tucking her leg under the skirt, she jiggled it enticingly. If the gods were going to try to hit on her, then she would tease them right back.

There was less than a month left before the spring solstice, and despite the fact that it was now widely known that she was to be married to

Hades, the other gods still thought that they could gain her attention, and more. Successfully wooing Hades's bride-to-be would be no small feat, and some saw this worth risking his wrath.

Dionysus made a playful grab for her ankle, and she laughed before rising to her feet, dancing away from him.

"That is not fair, teasing me like that!" he commented with a good-natured pout.

"Oh, but it is so much fun." Persephone grinned at him. "I know that you and the other gods have made a game out of seducing me... or at least, attempting to."

"Game?" He sounded surprised, and she grinned at him.

"You think I am not aware of what you and your brothers say? You compare me to Aphrodite, and you also like the challenge of knowing that I am to wed Hades."

"Oh, but you are lovelier than Aphrodite!" Dionysus replied eagerly, quickly regaining his composure, "And you are charming, betrothed or not. Is it our fault you are so alluring?"

Persephone had used flattery on Hades to get her way with him, but she was not immune to its effects, and smiled in pleased approval.

"Perhaps if I were not already with Hades, I might consider your suit. But as it is, I am already committed to someone else, so that's that," she replied matter-of-factly before giving a pointed shrug.

"Who says you can not have more than one lover?" Dionysus retorted smoothly. "After all,

Hades is a cold realm. Do you not ever feel the need for... warmth?"

Persephone didn't deign a response, and merely rolled her eyes. Suddenly, laughter burst out from behind them.

"Try all you want, Dionysus," Apollo said as he looked at them. "She will not be wooed with the most honeyed words or extravagant gifts."

"I do wish you would find better things to do." Persephone shook her head slowly. "I was excited to come to Olympus so that I could meet the other gods. When I was little, I imagined it to be a wondrous place. However, Mother had few nice things to say about it." Her gaze was cool as looked around. Apollo tried to stare her down, but she squared her shoulders. "Dionysus invited me here, and I thought that I would accept the invitation and have a nice time. That is hard to do when my hosts are more focused on being amorous than hospitable."

"You are right. Please sit down," Dionysus waved a nymph over with a platter of treats. "Enjoy yourself, and Apollo can play his lyre while the nymphs dance to it."

"That is better." Persephone sat back against the tree trunk. She was content to watch the nymphs dance, there certainly were enough pretty faces – and bodies – for the gods to appreciate. She laughed and clapped her hands, accepting a bit of wine from Dionysus as Apollo wrestled with Hermes. She sensed that it was partly because they wanted to impress her. She certainly didn't mind watching them wrestle, though no man's body other than Hades's own could make her feel a sensual thrill.

oOo

Aphrodite was bitter about Ares's impotence. She missed the way he would pound her into the bed – or against the wall or to the floor or on the grass or across a table... almost anywhere, really. He had a primality to his sex drive that she was irresistibly drawn to despite the fact that she could have just about any other lover she wanted. After Ares's 'misfortune', she had wasted no time in finding other outlets for her desire, but as always, her yearning would inevitably return to her rugged, handsome God of War. In this aspect she was a lot like her father, having one favored lover above all others, though Ares was considerably more forgiving than his mother regarding her affairs.

She had even tried to get Ares to marry her, but despite her charms, the God of War would have none of it, disregarding the fact that he had already fathered a child upon her. It figured that the only man she would ever consider marrying – Hephaistos certainly as hell didn't count because Father had arranged the marriage – would not complete the matrimonial tie with her.

Aphrodite was one of the few who knew who the real culprit was behind Ares's impotence, and it made her hate Persephone all the more. It was bad enough that the Queen of the Dead was her rival in beauty, but the fact that Ares had taken interest in her only irritated the Goddess of Beauty all the more. Yes, Ares had had other lovers in the past, but that was just fine with her because nobody could ever be as beautiful as she! But to know that she had shared Ares's desire with Persephone, oh, how that galled her!

For several centuries, Aphrodite had the uncontested title as the loveliest goddess in the entire Pantheon. Even her enemies and detractors had to acknowledge her beauty. Ever since Persephone had been revealed to the other gods, it had been 'Persephone this, Persephone that, how nice, kind, lovely, charming, sassy, clever, cute, she is!', and that got really old after a short while.

After being vaunted for her beauty and grace for so long, Aphrodite was totally unused to having any serious competition even among the other attractive Goddesses. She had been stewing over this ever since Hades and his bride came up to Olympus. Oh yes, that was another thing that absolutely vexed her. When she had tried to seduce her handsome uncle, Hades merely regarded her as if she was only a slightly amusing child – more annoying than amusing in his eyes – and his deadpan stare caused her to wilt in such a way that she had actually questioned her own beauty and Gifts, which was an uncomfortable position for her. Yet with Persephone he had been enamored enough to kidnap her and cause all that trouble!

At least that little upstart was stuck in the Underworld most of the time. She lifted her chin, looking in the mirror as she slowly turned around, admiring the elegant girdle around her slender waist and the way it emphasized the curves of her chest and hips. Despite her distaste for Hephaistos, she was happy that her lame husband was good for *something*.

She knew that Dionysus and a few of the other gods were having a private party, thanks to her doves – 'a little bird told me' gained literal meaning in these instances – and she was bored. Sometimes she might decide to grace the gods or mortals with her presence if she was in the mood to be so generous.

o0o

The charming smile on Aphrodite's face froze as she heard Persephone's laughter, and she approached the grove to see the younger goddess clapping her hands as Apollo and Hermes danced with a pair of nymphs while another nymph merrily plucked the strings of Apollo's lyre. Dionysus sat next to the Queen of the Dead, a recipient of a brilliant smile from her.

Wonderful. Just wonderful, Aphrodite thought darkly. She had been thinking about her rival, and here she was! Ugh. For someone who wasn't even on the surface world often, Persephone certainly had a way of leaving a lasting impression. *Much like her husband-to-be*, Aphrodite thought sourly.

"Look who is here!" one of the nymphs called out. With the attention turned to her, Aphrodite widened her smile, flipping her hair over her shoulder as she sauntered closer to the gathering.

"Boys, I am hurt. You are having a party, and you did not think to invite me?"

"Well..." Dionysus shrugged, grinning sheepishly as he silently cursed her presence. Already he could feel the tension between the two goddesses and knew all too well how capable Aphrodite was of vindictiveness. "This party just... happened. I invited Persephone along, and then Apollo dropped by to visit and eh..." He shrugged again.

"I should be going home," Persephone said as she started to get up from her seat.

"Oh, do not leave on her account!" Dionysus grabbed her wrist gently. "You are my honored guest."

"Oh, let her go home. I doubt Hades would appreciate her being here, anyway," Aphrodite gloated, delighting in the fact that she could drive Persephone off. If she could keep doing that, then she just might get used to the fact there was a new goddess in the Pantheon.

"Ha!" Persephone's eyes flashed as she looked at the older woman. "You are one to talk! What would Hephaistos say about you being here, huh? Do not talk to me about wifely duties when you are incapable of performing yours!"

Both women heard a sharp intake of breath from several of the onlookers. However, Aphrodite refused to be cowed. Despite her official status as a married woman, she had never truly considered herself a wife, and wasn't as bothered by this sort of scolding as most other women would have been.

"The little one thinks to tell me what to do, hm?" Aphrodite placed her hands on her hips. Persephone calmly mirrored this gesture before approaching Aphrodite.

"Who is little?" Persephone retorted. She was actually a couple of inches taller than the Goddess of Love, and to punctuate her statement, she reached up and patted Aphrodite on the head. From behind them, stifled laughter penetrated the quietness of the grove.

"Just go home before you embarrass yourself," Aphrodite replied sweetly, swatting away the other woman's hand.

"You know, I normally would, since I *do* have a very nice home to go to, but I will admit that it is amusing to make fun with you."

"You do not want me as an enemy," Aphrodite hissed, her azure eyes seeming as cold as ice.

"...I thought you already were."

Surprise was plain on Aphrodite's face at this flippant response. She quickly recovered herself and grabbed Persephone's arm, leading her away a short distance so they could have more privacy. Dionysus started to approach them, but Persephone shook her head and winked at him.

"Who the hell do you think you are? First you take away Ares's potency, then you come up here and think you can usurp me! You are Queen of the Dead, not of the gods!" Aphrodite said in a quiet but fierce tone.

"I have never tried to lord my status over anyone, but I refuse to be pushed around. As for

Ares..." Persephone uttered the name as if she were talking about a bowel movement, "He attempted to rape me. I merely rectified the situation and gave him a much-needed punishment."

"Ugh, don't remind me. It would have been better if he had no interest in you," Aphrodite retorted.

"Finally, something we can agree on," was the wry response.

"Perhaps we could work something out..." Aphrodite was now smiling sweetly, but the younger woman saw right through the facade. Still, she was curious as to what the Goddess of Beauty had in mind.

"What would that be?"

"I only ask that his potency be restored. In return, I would welcome you to Olympus with open arms, and give you my alliance, and I would also see to it that Ares does not bother you."

"No. I am in no mood to do either of you any favors."

"At least restore Ares! He will never bother you again. No man should be without his -"

"Silence yourself."

"Don't tell me to be quiet!" Aphrodite snapped, her pretty features twisting into a dark scowl.

"I will do as I please." Persephone started to turn away. As she did, she felt a hand grab her arm, this time manicured nails digging viciously into her skin. Almost unconsciously, her Gift reacted to the assault, driving the older woman back with a sudden spike of dark energy that sent Aphrodite sprawling onto her rear end.

"Do not ever touch me again, or ask anything of me unless you are prepared to pay the price. And the man you *love* so much..." 'love' was uttered in a biting, sarcastic tone, "is much better off as he is, and I know the women of Hellas would agree with me."

"You cannot do this to me!"

"I can. And I will." As Persephone said this, the shadows around them thickened. "If you want to go crying to your father about this, just keep in mind that I already put *him* in his place as well." Her voice was edged with cold triumph. "Any and all mischief you try to wreak on me will be repaid a hundredfold. Do not make the mistake of thinking that I will not." Despite the sunny day, it looked as if twilight had suddenly encroached upon the grove, plunging it into semidarkness as Persephone spoke, every word of hers heard by the gods as well. She hadn't displayed this sort of power to the gods before, but figured that now was as good a time as any to show it to the others if she was going to do it to Aphrodite.

The boys – despite her age, she considered them as such, especially compared to Hades – might have backed away from her for the time being, but she knew that if she did not make her message clear, they would just start acting the same as they had before, out of habit. Some habits really needed to be broken...

"She truly is the bride of the Dark One." Apollo whispered. Having heard that, Persephone looked in his direction, though without anger since she knew he had meant no offense.

"Who I am mated to does not define who or what I am."

oOo

Hades was waiting for her as she crossed the Styx, and she smiled at him as he held out his hand to her. She was almost surprised at the immense comfort she took from the feel of his hand wrapped around hers.

"You look pleased with yourself," Hades observed as they walked along the path.

"Oh, I am." Having been so sheltered for most of her life, Persephone still found the use of her Gift to be exciting.

"And what could it be that pleases you so?" he shot back with a smile of his own. Persephone let out a short, quiet laugh before she explained what had happened with Aphrodite and how she had used her powers to prove herself.

"That reminds me of Ereshkigal."

"Who?" The name sounded familiar to her, but having learned so much from Hades, she found it difficult at times to keep track of it all.

"The Queen of Irkalla."

"Oh! Yes." Hades wasn't the only realm in Dis, after all. Irkalla was the Underworld of the people who lived in the Levant, to the east. "I have never met her."

"You will, in due time. It is important for the rulers of the realms of Dis to know one another, for we all share a great responsibility."

"Why do I remind you of her?"

"She is beautiful, and keeps to herself. But her power is so great that the other gods fear her."

"Sounds more like someone I know than myself..." she replied, tapping her chin lightly. Hades laughed.

"There was a time when she became greatly angered, but the other gods thought lightly of her. However, like you, she proved she was a force to be reckoned with."

"What happened?"

"She fell in love with one of the gods, Nergal, and seduced him when he visited the Underworld on a mission. She wanted him to stay with her in Irkalla, because it was a fearsome place and she was lonely."

"Again, sounds like someone I know..."

Hades smirked down at her before he continued, "Nergal saw what he did as a mere dalliance, a night of pleasure, and left Irkalla, seeking refuge with the other gods. They laughed at her, and this roused her wrath so greatly that she threatened to throw open the gates of Irkalla and unleash the dead onto the earth."

"What happened to Nergal?"

"He was sent back to Irkalla."

"Seems like you death-gods have similar mating habits," Persephone teased. Hades growled in mock dismay.

"I do not hear you complaining about it!" he retorted.

"Hmph." She feigned displeasure as she

crossed her arms.

"I think it is time for supper."

"I am hungry, but I would like to take a walk with you first. In your garden, I mean." All playfulness was gone from her voice. Her confrontation with Aphrodite and the other gods and the words exchanged had caused her to do some thinking about her relationship with Hades.

"As the lady wishes." He offered his arm, and she wound her own around it, enjoying the feel of his strong forearm under her hand.

oOo

The King and Queen of the Underworld were in one of Hades's favorite gardens; a thickly forested atmosphere with plenty of ponds and quiet streams amidst canopies of weeping willows and hanging moss. Most would consider it gloomy, but Hades liked it and Persephone found it tranquil if a bit eerie. However, with Hades at her side, she felt comfortable.

"I have been thinking about what you said to me a while ago. About love," Persephone said softly as they walked along a thin path.

"Oh?" Hades looked down at her, his expression hard to read.

"We might not have had the most auspicious start in our relationship. I never would have thought that someone who snatched me could actually care for me or feel for me the way you do. At that time, I thought I would simply enjoy what you had to offer and make the best of my time here until I managed to find a way out of here, but I found myself caring for you more and more."

Hades smiled at this admission.

"When I was away for that month before the winter solstice, I missed you so much. I was lonely at night without you holding me. Mother refused to talk about you, and I dreaded the thought of never seeing you again. I honestly did not think I would feel the way I did. I cannot imagine life without you."

"Persephone..." She was moved by the warmth she saw in his eyes.

"I love you."

For a man who was cynical and considered himself above emotional weaknesses, Hades actually found himself feeling lightheaded when he heard that. He had desired to hear these words for so long, even before he kidnapped her, but he knew that forcing her to say these words would be a hollow victory. "I love you too," he replied before he pressed a kiss to her forehead. He placed his hands on her shoulders and gazed down at her, his face set in a rare expression of unguarded happiness.

Chapter LV

The scent of various foods hung in the air, emanating from Demeter's kitchen and the additional firepits that had been set up for the wedding feast.

Demeter was pleased with the wedding plans. Persephone would not have Zeus's input in her wedding day, and had asked her mother to step into the role a father would traditionally assume at his daughter's wedding. Thus, instead of having the customary pre-wedding feast on Olympus at Zeus's house, they were having it here on the island.

This wedding would be different in some ways from the ones mortals had. Normally, after the wedding day, another feast would be held at the groom's house. However, given the location of Hades's home, the Olympians were relieved to not receive invitations to the Underworld. Rather, Hades intended to have his feast with the Underworld deities, while the Olympians would have the pre-wedding feast for their own celebration. Demeter wasn't one to complain and since her daughter had already expressed her approval of this plan, there was nothing more to be said on the matter.

To accommodate the tables and furniture, a large, grassy area had been flattened out with some earth-shifting, making the plateau totally level as if it was one of the marble floors on

363

Olympus. However, instead of being hard, Demeter had ensured that a thick, even layer of grass grew across the entire clearing.

Tablecloths and decorations had been tastefully arranged, thanks to Hera. One could see the regal goddess's touch in the way the tables and divans had been set up, down to the smallest detail of color and design, and she also had a hand in the preparation of the banquet. Though Rhea, Hestia, and Demeter were skilled cooks in their own right, none of them could rival Hera when it came to creating an elegant atmosphere. Persephone had been the one to petition her for her help, and Hera welcomed the opportunity to make herself useful.

Traditionally, the bride's parents made the arrangement for the wedding, but Persephone refused to play a passive role. She had gone to many gods for help, both as a way to make them feel included and as an opportunity to get to know them better. Artemis was honored to hunt down some animals for the banquet, and Dionysus had been all too happy to contribute wine upon Persephone's request. Poseidon was charmed by his niece and graciously provided some of the sea's bounty for the feast, and Apollo and the Muses accepted Persephone's invitation for them to sing or provide music. Demeter was surprised, but could not help but be pleased with how well – and humbly – her daughter established a role for herself within the family, especially after she saw how everything had been set up.

Even though the wedding was not on

Olympus, the atmosphere was just as beautiful, many of the gods found it a refreshing change. Persephone remembered her mother's words about making an impression on her family and asserting her role.

o0o

Persephone looked fresh in the attire that she had chosen for today. She would have two different outfits; one for today, and one for the wedding ceremony tomorrow. She had carefully pondered her options, deciding what colors she would wear, what accessories, and the like. For today, she set aside the jewelry she wore in the Underworld. Today was the first day of spring, and she would dress for her role as the Goddess of Spring. It was now widely known among the Olympians just who she was and what role she would have. She bore the unique distinction of being a deity of both the Kingdom of the Dead and the realm of the living. Right now, she would embrace and welcome spring. It was a happy time of the year for god and mortal alike.

She adorned her hair and neck with flowers; bright yellow, blue, and purple petals highlighted against her skin. Her tunic was silk, and dyed to create an umbra effect, going from warm blue at the hem to cheery pinks and oranges in the middle and sunny yellow at the top. Her ankle-length chiton was a deep and vibrant green, matching the current shade of her eyes and giving an appropriate backdrop to the lighter colors of her tunic. She opted to go barefoot, wanting to enjoy the feel of living grass under her soles.

As she stepped outside, she was encountered with greetings, several goddesses going to her side immediately and their male counterparts eyeing her with open admiration. Quickly scanning the scenery, she saw that over half of the guests had already arrived. Mother was already chatting animatedly with a trio of them.

Everything looks wonderful. She had already thanked everybody for their help, but she intended to do so again after it was all over. She had been a bit intimidated by the thought of asking Hera for help, but then she thought of it as a meeting between two queens, and that had helped. The casks of wine were nearly overflowing, though Demeter had them placed out of sight, not wanting people to start getting drunk right away. It was something Persephone heartily agreed with. All the food was set out, some of it in covered dishes, and the goblets and plates Hephaestus and the Cyclopes made gleamed with polish under the afternoon sun. In a short while, it would be time to eat, and she looked forward to sitting at the head table alone with Hades.

Persephone listened to the compliments the gods sent her way with measured patience. She knew that by resisting their advances, she was only making herself more enticing, but that could not be helped.

"What a lovely party you have here, Persephone." She turned around upon hearing the lilting voice of the Goddess of Love. Aphrodite stood several feet away, her hands resting lightly on her hips.

"Good to see you too, Aphrodite." Persephone replied casually, making no effort at sweet small talk. They had so little in common, and she was put off by the older woman's vanity, especially after observing how Aphrodite interacted with other people. Hades certainly hadn't been exaggerating in his tales of the Goddess of Beauty!

"What a... charming setting you chose for your little wedding," Aphrodite said as she waved with a slender arm that was adorned with gold arm- and wristbands. It was clear that the other goddess had adorned herself to garner as much attention as possible, but Persephone chose to not comment.

"This place is charming, is it not?" Persephone asked, refusing to be put down by Aphrodite's subtle jabs, "But I certainly would not call my wedding little! I am delighted to have so *many* people share my happiness!" she said, grinning at her rival. After hearing just who was getting married, many a god had been eager to accept their invitations out of simple curiosity. Of course, the Olympians had been invited, but she had also added the Titans and Cyclopes to the guest list, giving her a chance to familiarize and make friends with the senior members of Gaea's brood. All together, the number was more than most gods had ever had at their own weddings. That number sometimes felt daunting to her, but she reminded herself that it would be over soon enough.

"Indeed. There has not been a wedding as big as this for... well, a long time." Iris said as she approached Persephone, extending her hands in greeting. Persephone smiled at her and took her hands, returning the gesture. "And everything looks so wonderful. I will not be forgetting this for a long, long time! And you look so radiant!"

"Thank you, Iris."

"You know, seeing this almost makes me want to have my own wedding. *Almost*." Persephone turned around with a smile, seeing Bia. Being the Goddess of Force and Power, Bia certainly didn't fit the usual standards for a Hellene woman. Her fierce attitude and personality would not bow her to most men, and she was one of few deities who could hold her own against Zeus or Ares. The younger goddess glanced at Bia's biceps and broad shoulders. Anyone who would try to have this mighty goddess for a wife would be in for a dear challenge unless he was very, *very* patient and submissive, or just as stubborn as she was..

"Only *almost?*" Persephone replied playfully. Bia laughed and playfully punched her arm. Persephone's eyes twinkled with merriment as she noted Aphrodite's displeasure at not being the center of attention or compliments. It was *her* wedding, after all!

oOo

Hades chose to not reveal himself right away

when he came to the scene of the impending banquet. The odor of food cooking over the fires mixed with the chatter of various deities filled the air, and he glanced around, secure under his helmet of invisibility. Many were already seated while others were walking around. Nobody would eat until he made his appearance.

Persephone was surrounded by several Muses, but she stood out amongst them in Hades's eyes. Stealthily, he wove around the guests, and his bride lifted her chin, glancing around before she looked in his direction. He smiled under his helmet as she maintained a steady gaze. It was almost like a game to them, with him becoming invisible and trying to approach her without her knowing, or seeing her react to being touched or teased by an unseen hand. She said something to her companions before pulling away from them and walking off in the opposite direction, briefly looking over her shoulder.

She entered the house, ostensibly for a moment of privacy. As soon as he was in the room, he lifted his helmet as she watched. He placed it in her outstretched hands as he looked down at her. It was an interesting visual effect, to see this colorful maiden with flowers in her hair holding a helmet that resembled a horned skull.

"Good afternoon, my lady." Hades regarded her with an affectionate smile. She performed a slight curtsey. Amidst the cheerful, homey surroundings of the room, he was an especially imposing figure, clad in his usual color choice of dark hues. In her time living with him, she rarely ever saw him in light colors, and that was only when he was alone with her. Like her, he had chosen a more understated outfit, opting for a dark blue tunic that terminated at his elbows and a black cloak and breeches.

"Looks like everyone who was given an invitation took it," he commented as he glanced through the window.

"It is not every day that the Lord of the Underworld gets married."

"You know many people are simply here out of curiosity."

"I do." She shifted the helmet to one hand, resting it against her hip as she touched his shoulder with her free hand. Curiosity was inevitable, so she had planned this wedding with that in mind, working on creating the best impression on her guests.

"I cannot wait for this all to be over, and then I will have you all to myself," Hades grumbled.

"It is just today and tomorrow. What are two days to a man who has lived as long as you?"

He chuckled softly. Most men simply wanted a submissive wife, but he liked the fact that she could argue well.

"Let us go outside. I am hungry, and no one will eat unless you do. Just as you commanded." She looked up at him. Hades had left most of the wedding plans to her, trusting her decisions, but he had been very firm on several things.

"I never want to see you go hungry." He reached out to stroke her cheek, remembering all too well her self-starvation.

Hades was aloof as others greeted him, nodding politely and saying a word here and there as he deemed fit. He had seen enough weddings to know what was expected of a groom, but he found some of the comments from the other gods grating, such as back- or shoulder-slapping and compliments on having such a lovely bride, and a few bawdy jokes. The cold glares he directed at those who tried to tease him caused even the most raucous of the men to wilt. He knew that some speculated on how long he would remain faithful to Persephone before finding another lover. If there was one thing that Hades absolutely hated, it was being compared to his brothers.

Persephone would not be an oft-cast aside bride like Hera, nor would he give her any reason to seek attention elsewhere like Amphitrite. When he saw his youngest brother approach him, he stifled a groan but did not retreat into the crowd.

"How are you on this fine day?" Zeus asked, trying to put his hand on Hades's shoulder. The older god jerked away, in no mood to tolerate any more touching than he already did. He was well aware of Zeus's attempts to have his input in the wedding. The younger deity certainly liked weddings, especially those of his own children, and always made them grand affairs. Hades knew it rankled him to be shot down at every opportunity by his sister, daughter, or brother.

And yes, Hades enjoyed knowing that! He shrugged as he regarded his youngest sibling.

"As well as can be, I suppose," he replied, deliberately sounding nonchalant about his wedding.

"I know you are usually not so excited about anything, but you should show more enthusiasm! This is your wedding, after all!"

"I will act as I please at my wedding," he shot back coolly.

"Are you not happy to be marrying Persephone?"

"I am giddy," Hades stated this in the most deadpan tone he could manage, which was no great feat for the Dark One.

"Haha! Um..." Zeus's laugh quickly died as his older brother maintained his blank expression.

"I do believe you have waited long enough to eat."

"Er... Yes?"

"Then sit down." Hades turned away with a dismissive gesture.

Demeter did not attempt to bite back a smile as she saw how Hades had effectively wilted Zeus's ego. Well, the King of the Gods would re-inflate his ego soon enough – he always did – but it was always satisfying to see the confident deity in a moment of uncertainty.

Demeter had amassed a staff of nymphs to help with the food for the wedding, and she gave them the signal to bring the food to the tables and open the casks of wine.

o0o

Nobody could deny that Hades and Persephone made a striking couple. He looked especially somber next to her, his appearance as Lord of the Dead further emphasized by the fact that his bride looked every bit the personification of the Goddess of Spring.

Persephone noticed him fiddling with the hem of his cloak and rested her hand on his arm. They were seated alone at their own table. It sat upon a dais overlooking the other tables, and she was happy to have the privacy, though at this point their guests were too busy paying attention to the food or one another to intrude upon them.

"Here, try these stuffed dates Hestia made. They're simply wonderful!"

Hades raised an eyebrow as he looked down at her, holding back a smile as he took the proffered treat. She was right – they *were* good. The stuffing was made of mashed-up fruit, nuts, and honey. Hestia had always had a flair for creating unique and fun recipes with ordinary food.

After he had eaten his fill, he reclined on the divan. The banquet was not to be the entirety of today's wedding activities, since there would be dancing. Ugh. He wasn't a fan of it, but Persephone wanted to have some fun.

There were quite a few gods skilled in the arts of music and dance, so after being given a signal by Demeter, they rose from their seats. Persephone sat back and let them start things off, pleased to be able to witness such skill. The stories told of Apollo and his lyre were not mere myths, but Terpsichore's skill on her own instrument was a close rival, and her song accompanied his beautifully while she danced, for she was also the Muse of dancing. Thalia started dancing with her sister, doing it in a funny way and eliciting chuckles from the audience, and the rest of the Muses provided entertainment in one way or another with their voices, hands, and feet.

In no time others were dancing merrily around the bonfire while the melody of flutes and drums joined the music produced by the lyres.

"Will you dance with us, Persephone?" Hermes asked, extending his hand towards the dais. She looked over her shoulder at Hades, and he nodded faintly.

"Just know that I will be watching you, Hermes. And everybody else," Hades stated, his gaze intent as he regarded his bride and the messenger god. "I trust my wife, but I am well aware of the thoughts you have." It was rumored that Hades had mindreading among his Gifts, but the God of the Dead did nothing to discourage this rumor. If his astuteness was seen as mindreading, then let it be a lesson to them.

"Yes, Uncle," Hermes replied, bowing his head before Persephone followed him off the dais.

Hades was momentarily amused when he saw a barely repressed frown on Aphrodite's face as Persephone twirled around with Dionysus, leaving a lingering odor of flowers and spring along with a mysterious trace of sweet tartness in her wake, an alluring scent that caused the males nearby to give her notice. Persephone was dressed modestly, yet no one seemed to notice the cleavage Aphrodite was proudly displaying. The three Graces that often accompanied the Goddess of Beauty were now dancing around Persephone, and she spun around with them as well, laughing with them.

Aphrodite glanced around before she noticed his distant stare. He had been glancing at a tree behind Aphrodite, but she mistook it as interest. When Hades realized she intended to step up on the dais, he silently summoned shadowy tentacles to bind around her ankles. He flashed a cold smile at her before shaking his head and leaning across the table, whispering in a tone meant only for Aphrodite's ears.

"Persephone wants her wedding to be a happy occasion. You will behave as an honored guest, or there will be consequences. And no, your magic is not working on me. It never has." He could sense that she was trying to use her Gift to charm him – he certainly wasn't the first married man nor would he be the last she would try to win over – but he had been impervious to it, even upon his first encounter with her. Yes, she was beautiful, but when she tried to seduce him, it actually brought up a deep sense of revulsion. "Now, go sit down and be a good girl."

He leaned back, smugly satisfied, and watched his bride dance.

o0o

Persephone lay in the small bed as she stared at the lamp. She didn't feel as nervous as most brides would on the night before their wedding, yet she could not help but feel a little apprehensive. When she was younger, she had imagined how her wedding might be, or what kind of man she would marry. After Father died and she realized that Mother was keeping her in the body of a girl, she inevitably wondered if she would ever have the chance to marry.

"Persephone? Are you asleep?" Mother whispered as she stood in the doorway. It certainly had taken her mother long enough to accept that name, though Persephone had been patient with her. For a couple of months, Mother hadn't used any name to refer to her, merely calling her 'daughter' or other neutral names.

"No, Mother."

Demeter slid into the room and sat at the foot of the bed. Persephone pulled her feet up to make room, as the bed barely accommodated her as it was. It was the same bed she had slept in since Mother had moved them here. She couldn't wait to go back to the spacious bed she shared with Hades, but she was willing to bear her current surroundings for the night.

"Did you enjoy yourself today?" Demeter asked.

"Mmm-hm. Everything was wonderful." The younger woman propped her head up on one elbow. Demeter had to admit that she agreed. Despite a few young deities becoming drunk and stirring up trouble, Persephone handled herself well, and it was a delight to see Aphrodite become flustered as she tried to get a rise out of the Goddess of Spring. Though Demeter would not boast of it, her daughter *was* strikingly beautiful, even more so than the Goddess of Beauty, and it wasn't just maternal pride that said that. At least Persephone didn't let it get to her head.

The season of spring was a relief to many, the fresh, warm air refreshing after being shut up in their homes all winter long. Persephone was definitely a breath of fresh air in a figurative sense to the Olympians.

It could be worse. She could be stupid, vain, petty, or cruel. And there are plenty of men worse than Hades. It was these thoughts that gave Demeter comfort as she contemplated how much her daughter had grown. It had been so upsetting at first after Persephone returned from the Underworld for the first time, all grown-up and defiant.

"Are you nervous about tomorrow?" Demeter asked gently.

"Not really. I know who my husband is and I know exactly where I am going and what I can expect. Not many brides can say that."

Well, there was one positive thing about her daughter growing up, Demeter mused. She had developed an enjoyable sense of humor, and the older woman could not help but laugh a bit. It was too bad Iasion was not around to see this. He would have been so proud to see how his daughter turned out.

She had been dismayed to learn that he had gone to the Lethe River, and knowing of his reason did not make it less painful. She did not blame him, and if the positions had been reversed, she probably would have done the same. Still, it hurt. Would she ever see him again? Would she know him if they countered one another in the future?

"There is one thing I am curious about..." Demeter tapped her chin.

"Yes?"

"Have you and Hades talked about having children?"

Persephone let out a slow breath, looking down at the blanket for several moments.

"Is something the matter?"

"No. It's just that life cannot grow in the Underworld. Hades explained it to me."

"You mean that you cannot..."

Persephone nodded. Demeter bit back a frown. "And what do you think about that?"

"I am not certain. I do not want children right now, but in the future...well, I do not know."

"Yes." Demeter hadn't wanted children at first, and it was several hundred years before she became a mother. It had been a wonderful experience for her.

"Do not worry about it. Really." Persephone wished her mother hadn't brought up the subject. "I am happy with Hades." She wasn't simply saying that to placate Mother. She was a powerful goddess in her own right, Queen of the Underworld and the Goddess of Spring. She could enjoy both realms. How fortunate that she had been able to bargain with him! Would any other god have been so agreeable?

o0o

The clothing she had chosen the day before represented her role as Goddess of Spring, but her attire today reflected her status as Queen of the Underworld. She was garbed in black silk sprinkled with tiny diamonds that glittered like stars. Accompanying her clothing was a diamond-studded silver crown and matching wristbands. The effect was almost startling, especially to those who had seen her as the Goddess of Spring, but she was no less beautiful.

Attached to her crown was a veil of the same fabric, only thinner, lending a mysterious air to the Queen of the Underworld. She could feel many pairs of eyes on her – many looking at her with admiration, a few with jealousy – but she kept her focus on Hades. He had clothed himself to complement her attire, wearing black and deep blue-purple with silver accessories.

She smiled at him, her expression visible under the gauzy material that covered her face before she looked up at her mother. Demeter's hands were strong and warm, and Persephone took comfort in the gentle squeezing that her mother was giving around her hands. When she was little, she had always been comforted by Mother's embraces, and even now, she continued to feel the same way.

"Lord Hades, I give you my daughter to protect and keep," Demeter stated. These words were purely ceremonial and fathers usually said something along this vein when giving their daughters away. Persephone would not even consider having Zeus say these words. It was her way of showing her displeasure for the trouble he had caused, and besides, he had not been a father figure in her life. So why should he assume the role of one at her wedding? Perhaps later on, she would get to know him better and familiarize herself with the man who had sired her, but right now, she preferred to focus on more important things.

"I accept her with pleasure." Hades held out his hands, and Persephone gently slid her own out of her mother's grip, the older woman reluctantly yielding. Persephone smiled at her mother reassuringly before giving Demeter's hands a squeeze. Before Hades could take her hands, Demeter suddenly pulled her into a fierce hug.

Hades waited patiently for Demeter to relinquish her hold on her daughter before taking Persephone's hands.

Hera glanced at the couple wistfully, seeing a long and happy future ahead for them. She wished she had been able to see her own future with Zeus, but he had charmed her so well that if she had any bouts of prescience regarding the matter, she hadn't paid attention to them. *Well, I was young and stupid, not fully trained in my powers*, she reminded herself. Nonetheless, she wished Hades and Persephone the best. Faithful, lasting bonds were rare among mortals, and even more so among the gods.

"Ah, this reminds me of our wedding day." Zeus whispered into her ear. Since Kronos had been deposed, it was Rhea who had given Hera away at their nuptials.

"But this marriage will be happier than ours has been," Hera shot back in a pointed whisper. Out of the corner of her eye, she saw his dejected expression. Ever since that night when he had come for dinner and tried to seduce her, she had given him only cold aloofness. She knew that she would eventually warm up to him, because they did care for each other – though Zeus could be really terrible at showing that oftentimes – and he could be so damned loving, but she was determined to put that off as long as she could. Besides, it was fun to see him grovel and try to win her favor. He still had a long way to go before she would consider intimacy with him, and she was going to make the most of it.

Hades's chariot awaited the royal couple, and the Lord of the Dead led his bride to it. In the glow of the sunset, the couple made a striking image of light and shadow. With a bow of his head to Demeter, he climbed into the chariot and flicked the reins, the horses galloping off.

o0o

Instead of going to the Underworld, Hades honored his wife's request to take a ride through the woods. Like Persephone, he could feel the difference between the world of the dead and the living. The Underworld was so... quiet, compared to this forest with its animal noises and the rustling of leaves as the wind blew through them. For one who spent most of his time in the

Underworld, stimuli like these were sometimes overwhelming. At least the sun had just gone down, because he was especially sensitive to light.

"Let us stop here." Persephone said as she squeezed his hand. Obligingly, he tugged the reins, signaling for the horses to stop. She squeezed around him and stepped off the chariot. The forest was beautiful under the light of an almost-full moon, the grass taking on a rich emerald hue. To her right was a patch of daffodils, deep gold under the muted light, and here and there were crocuses where there were small clearings in the forest. She had always loved spring and seeing the flowers and plants bloom after being dormant all winter.

Hades stepped off his chariot, glancing at her with curiosity. He wanted to return to the Underworld, but it was so peaceful here that he figured he would oblige her for a while. As he turned around, he realized that Persephone was missing. Now, where had she gone off to?

"Seph?" he called out. A soft giggle met his ears, and he turned in its direction. There was a rustle of undergrowth, and he darted off in that direction. He had always found it so easy to chase and capture her, but this time, she remained elusive, baiting him on with a giggle or whisper of his name.

"Damnit! Where are you?" he asked with a playful growl, catching a whiff of her scent. He could hear her footsteps, but she remained out of sight, and he knew that it was more than just the shadows that hid her. Critically, he scanned his surroundings, looking for any hint of her presence; a glitter of diamonds in the moonlight or her skin against the darkness of her clothing and surroundings.

"You will just have to come and find me, Aidon!" Her sing-song voice came from behind him, and he spun in her direction, only to be confronted with the sight of the forest and nothing else. He could sense her presence... so where the hell was she?

As he stepped forward, he felt something grab hold of his right ankle. He looked down, and was shocked to see that it was a shadowy tentacle. *What the...*

His left ankle became restrained in a similar manner, and when he raised his right arm, another tentacle wrapped itself around his wrist, and he was lifted into the air, a foot above the ground. How was this even possible?

"Persephone?" His remaining free limb was quickly bound as well.

"Yes, my darling?" Her voice purred out from behind him, and he twisted his neck to look over his shoulder. Again, he saw nothing. If she was able to summon these shadow-tentacles, was she able to conceal herself with shadows as well...?

"Where are you?"

"Right here." She appeared to materialize out of the thin air. She casually strolled along the grass until she was directly in front of him, a faint smile on her lips.

"Seph... you... how did you..." He tugged at the binds with his right wrist. They were slimmer than the tendrils he summoned himself, but their similarity was undeniable.

"Oh, I discovered this while exploring my Gift, seeing what I was capable of..." She became invisible again, delighting in the surprised expression on his face before she reached out to undo the brooch that held up his cloak. Folding it loosely before setting it aside, she commenced to remove his tunic, running her hands along his muscled arms and chest and listening to the quiet groan of pleasure that escaped his lips.

"Release me!" he asked as he twisted against his bindings. He was certain he could break free of them on his own, but he was curious about what would happen.

"Oh, I will. In good time, that is..." Her hands slid down his belt, tugging it open before sliding his breeches down his legs, leaving the material pooled around his ankles. He was a handsome sight, bound and nearly naked. She could see why he enjoyed binding her and having his way with her. Well, turnabout was fair play, wasn't it...

He arched towards her when he felt her rub his groin, massaging his private parts through his loincloth. He bit back a sudden gasp when his right nipple was tweaked, and he looked down as the invisible hand rolled the hardened nub between its fingers.

"Persephone..." He twisted against his bonds, but they would not release him. Her name issued from his lips again in a heated whisper when he felt the unmistakable sensation of lips on his chest, licking and lightly biting his nipple, causing him to harden further, the loincloth feeling all too confining for him.

Her hands slid along his body freely, and his eyes would follow the sensations, trying to see her despite the magic she had cast upon herself.

"Enjoying this, Aidon?"

"Perhaps..." He would not give in so easily.

"We will see about that..." He felt the tug on his loincloth, and let out a quiet, relieved sigh as his erection sprang free of its confines.

"Is that all for me?" Persephone's whisper was velvety, and he nodded.

"You know it is..." He shivered in his binds as her hand cupped his sac, massaging it. "Unbind me so I can ravage you good and proper..."

"I think not, my love. Tonight... you are mine." She became visible again and looked up at him, her gaze penetrating as she studied him. As much as Hades strained against his bindings, she was able to maintain her hold on him more easily than she had thought.

She summoned several more shadow-tentacles, binding his limbs more firmly as well as his middle so that his weight was more evenly distributed, ensuring his comfort, because she intended to keep him like this for a while. Nobody would interrupt or stumble across them; she had made sure of that.

"Put me down!" Hades demanded, trying to not laugh. Everyone else was afraid of him, so it was quite an experience to be bound and at someone's mercy.

"Do not tell me what to do, or I will bind your

mouth too..."

"You are enjoying this, are you not?"

"Perhaps." She placed her hand on her hip, regarding him with an open grin. "The sight of you bound up like this is very arousing to me..." Lifting her hands, she removed her veil and crown, setting it on top of his discarded clothing. His pulse raced as she slowly undid her chiton, revealing a white tunic that barely ended below her upper thighs. The silk was so thin that her erect nipples were visible.

"Mmm..." He gazed at her with open admiration. However, she did not remove her underwear, much to his disappointment.

She closed the distance between them, pressing her chest against his stomach. His erection was now flush against her stomach, and he brought his hips forward, making his desire clear.

"Not so fast, Hades... what makes you think you can have your pleasure so soon?" She flashed an impish smile at him before backing away. With a flick of her wrist, the bindings widened and covered his entire body up to his neck in the same kind of shadow-suit that he had her in before. His head lolled back as he closed his eyes when the shadows started rubbing his cock and balls.

A sudden hiss escaped his lips when he found his nipples vigorously rubbed, and it felt as if there were a hundred fingers teasing him all over his body, focusing on the sensitive areas that Persephone had discovered through her intimate sessions with him.

"Seph..." He brought his head back up only to have it drop forward. Unconsciously, his hips were rolling forward, his manhood aching from the slow, steady pressure the shadows were applying to him. "Please..." He felt near bursting, but the slow treatment continued, the sensation of a finger rubbing the slit in his penis keeping him near the edge.

"All is fair in love and war..." she commented glibly, massaging her breasts to tease him. Her hands slid down to her thighs, tugging up the hem of the tunic. Just as her womanhood was about to be revealed, she lifted her hands. The usually guarded and taciturn Lord of the Dead's face was an open book for her to read, frustration mixed with enjoyment and pleasure as he wiggled around in his confines.

Well, no wonder Hades enjoys doing this to me! It was thrilling to hold her lover captive, to push him to the brink and tease and please him, and have him plead with her and moan her name in a way that aroused her even further. Her cunt ached, and she could feel the wetness against her inner thighs. As he watched, she lifted the hem again, this time revealing the thatch of dark red hair at the apex of her thighs as she started to finger herself.

"Damnit, Seph... Can you not see... and feel how much I need you?"

"Yes, I can." She fingered herself slowly, not bothering to mask her pleasure as she lifted her chin and closed her eyes, whispering his name.

"Let me go!" Hades demanded, feeling

overwhelmed by all the touches, fighting against his bonds. She opened her eyes and looked at him.

"Uh-huh, I warned you..." She flicked her free hand, and shadows crept up his throat to cover his mouth. "Now, I am going to try a little something that Hekate told me about..." She turned her palm upward, wiggling her fingers. Hades let out a muffled moan and arched as he felt a 'finger' prodding his rear end, rubbing against his sphincter.

It slid in, and was no thicker than Persephone's finger, but he wiggled furiously against this unexpected sensation. He knew of men taking other men or boys as lovers, but he had never explored such arrangements. It wasn't painful, but it definitely felt weird, and... Oh! He bucked in surprise as it pressed against an area in the front of his previously unexplored cavity, frissons of pleasure radiating from the area.

"Women and men alike have two spots for pleasure – one on the outside, one on the inside. You are very familiar with both of mine..." Her head tilted to one side as she shot him a knowing smile, "but I have only been familiar with one of yours. That hardly seems fair now, does it?"

Hades could only offer a stifled moan in reply as she started to massage that inner spot in a gentle way, compounding the pleasure gained from the attention to his private parts. After the initial shock, he realized that it did indeed feel nice, though at this point all he wanted was release. His sac felt almost impossibly heavy, and he let out a whimper that was audible around his gag. Unconsciously, he was swaying his hips in response to all the touching to his nether-areas, and she smiled as she took note of this.

She continued her treatment, delighting in the noises he made and the way he was twisting around. His gag disappeared, and he took a deep breath before moaning out her name.

"Seph... Please." This delightful torment seemed endless, and he was not sure of how long he had been like this until he looked up at the moon. It hung high in the sky.

"Please what?"

"I need you. Please, let me have my release. I *ache* for you..."

"I know." Her expression softened, and he found himself being lowered to the ground gently, facing upwards as she kept him spread-eagled. She leaned over him and placed her finger at his throat before tracing down his chest with it. The shadows opened up as if she were cutting it with her finger, revealing his chest and stomach. She continued downward, revealing his throbbing manhood. He could smell her, and his cock twitched as he caught a whiff of her arousal.

She stood up and pulled her tunic off over her head. Under the moonlight, her skin looked white. Without preamble, she straddled his face.

"Before you can have your release, I need mine. You were so much fun to watch..."

Hades obligingly stuck out his tongue as she lowered herself onto his waiting mouth, letting out a low sigh as she felt his tongue wiggle into her.

"What a good husband you are..." she purred in approval as he continued to lavish her with his mouth, leaving nothing unattended. Since he could not use his hands, it took a little more time getting her off, but he continued his ministrations, feeling her grind against his face as she neared climax. He was rewarded with a mouthful of sweet, musky essence as she cried out his name, shuddering and continuing to grind around a bit. He wasted no time in cleaning her, his tongue probing her and causing several pleasant aftershocks to radiate upwards to her stomach and down her thighs.

Finally, she climbed off him, panting quietly as he stared at her with satisfaction. She took several moments to collect herself before she climbed on top again, this time straddling his hips. She grasped his organ gently with one hand, holding it steady as she guided herself down it.

He let out a contented hum, gazing up at her with a lazy grin as she started to rock herself in a slow, careful rhythm. Before he knew it, she had picked up the pace, and he was thrusting his hips upward, matching her fierce rhythm with his own. A primal growl escaped his throat as he neared his climax, and this only spurred her on, her breasts jiggling as she ground herself against him fiercely, her eyes glinting with pure desire.

He gritted his teeth before letting out an impassioned roar, bucking upwards as he achieved his long-sought-after release, bucking around almost uncontrollably in the throes of his orgasm. She was nearly thrown off, but held onto him, wrapping her arms around his neck as she pressed her chest to his, savoring the feel of his release.

She could feel his faint trembling, and nuzzled him lovingly as she placed kisses along the side of his face.

"Mmph... would you please unbind me so I can hold you?"

"Well... since you asked so nicely..." With a lazy wave of her arm, all of the shadows disappeared. He lifted his hands, running them along her back as he breathed in the scent of her hair.

He didn't think he would enjoy this so much, but there was a certain sort of relief in letting someone else have control. For once, he didn't have to make decisions or be in charge of anything.

She wiggled around as he reached down to playfully squeeze her buttocks. As she did, she became aware of the fact that he was aroused again.

"Up so soon?" she teased.

"Well, I *am* a god..." He rolled them over so that he was on top as he looked down at her.

"That is not something I will forget any time soon."

"Good, because I am *far* from done with you!"

o0o

The couple lay in the grass, supine in the aftermath of their pleasure. Persephone idly plucked up a daffodil, running its petals along her face as she listened to Hades's breathing. Tonight had been like no other, the surface world adding a new set of background to her experiences. The night air had a certain quality to it that the Underworld atmosphere was lacking, with the scent of flowers and grass, and she also enjoyed the feel of grass against her skin as Hades pounded into her mercilessly, or when he had her propped against a tree, the bark rubbing against her nipples. She even teased him by binding him again and trailing flowers along his body, lightly stroking different areas with silken petals.

Hades paced an arm across her middle as he dozed peacefully, eyes half-lidded as he looked at her. She touched his face, her fingers sliding along his features as she felt his breath on her throat.

Being tuned to the earth's energy, Persephone sensed it waking just before the sun started to rise. She stroked his hair as the sky started to lighten. Hades stirred and sat up, starting to get dressed.

"What's the rush?" Persephone asked languidly, stretching out.

"Daytime is upon us."

"You are not afraid of a little bit of sun, are you?"

"I gave you your wedding night as you wanted it. However, the night is over," Hades replied, evading her question.

"When was the last time you saw a sunrise?" she challenged as she wrapped her chiton around herself loosely before she walked off, climbing up the small slope to be greeted by a view of the beach and sea. He trudged after her and saw the ocean illuminated by the light of dawn. He looked down at her, seeing how entranced she was as she sat there in the swaying grass, leaning back against a tree. He smelled the ocean, noting a briny tone that was lacking from the Eternal Sea. It was almost overwhelming, all these odors in the air, trees, flowers, the wet sand...

He took a sharp breath when the sun peeked above the horizon, a sliver of light startling him. It had been at least several decades since his last sunrise. He shielded his eyes, dazzled by the sun's reflection on the ocean even as it climbed higher, the sky brightening further.

He felt her hand on his, and he allowed her to tug him down to the grass. The light prickle of grass blades was an unfamiliar sensation to him, and he ran his palm across the living carpet. His skin looked white under the sunlight, and he turned to look at her, seeing how the sun illuminated a pale tan. Her eyes sparkled, and Hades found the contrast of illumination and shadow on her body to be fascinating. The colors surrounding her were so vivid...

Hades leaned down to place a kiss on her lips, and felt her hand slide up his throat to hook around the back of his neck.

"You truly are the Goddess of Spring," he whispered as he looked down at her. Even with the black cloth wrapped around her middle, there was an undeniable glow around her that did not come from just the sun.

"It gladdens me that we could come to such an agreement."

"I fell in love with the Goddess of Spring. I am loath to lose her," he admitted before he leaned in for another kiss. As she leaned into his embrace, he stood up as he slung her over his shoulder.

"Unhand me, you brute!" she cried out in mock dismay, lightly flailing her fists against his back. He walked to his chariot, flicking his hand and using shadows to pick up their discarded clothing and accessories off the grass.

"I think not, my love. You had your time in this world, now it is time for mine." He gently released her, and she slid down his front as she landed on her feet. He let out a yawn before taking hold of the reins. Persephone was just as passionate as he was, and he could not deny the fact that she had given him a thorough working-over. Not that he was going to complain, of course...

oOo

"Would you like a bath, or do you just want to go to bed?" Hades asked as he carried her up the steps to his Palace.

"Mmm... Bed." Right now all she wanted to do was recover from their long, passionate night.

"As the lady wishes." He approached the bed and lightly tossed her onto it before climbing in the bed after her.

"Welcome home, wife," he whispered

contentedly as he rested his head against her shoulder. She gave out a sigh of approval at these words as he cuddled up against her. She stroked his hair, studying him through half-lidded eyes. It had been an interesting – and at times, tumultuous – journey to become the bride of the Dark One. However, she was pleased with the end result.

"Home sweet home, indeed. Sleep well, Aidon." She closed her eyes, basking in the warmth of his body.

Epilogue

oOo

Though Persephone was content in her dual role as the Goddess of Spring and the Queen of the Underworld, there were still a few things to be looked after.

She looked around the forest, seeing how vibrant it was, with the scent of greenery and flora wafting through the air in a natural, invigorating perfume. It was not yet summer, but even in the shade, the air was warm. After being in the Underworld, this setting almost felt too hot for her.

The pond where Hades had snatched her had changed very little, the grass around the edges now more overgrown than before. It was thick under her bare feet as she padded to the water's edge and knelt down. As she contemplated what happened here the year before, her gaze dropped, seeing her reflection in its tranquil surface.

Cyane had been her best friend since Mother brought her here to the island in what almost seemed like another lifetime. She knew many things about the world and often was candid, subverting Demeter's gag order on certain subjects to quell Persephone's curiosity – out of the older goddess' earshot, of course. To leave her friend formless like this, simply because she had tried to help a friend who was being kidnapped in front of her, would be doing this loyal nymph a grave disservice.

"Cyane?" Persephone whispered. Having known the Naiad for so long, she immediately recognized the nymph's presence. Yet no form appeared, and the only response she got was a rippling of the pond's surface. How could she forget how she had seen Cyane's body melt away, flesh quickly liquefying until it was indistinguishable from the water?

Assured that her friend was paying attention, Persephone closed her eyes and channeled her power into the water. A tendril of water rose from the pool and grew larger as it thickened, creating the form of an attractive young woman. Cyane's body defined itself further as finely formed fingers grew from her hands and her facial features became apparent even as the sun shone through her body. Details quickly became apparent, like her ears, eyelids, and nipples.

"Kora? Is that really you?" Cyane asked. Her tone had a bubbly undertone, but her voice was sweet enough to make her words clear.

"Yes." Persephone held out her hands, shivering as cool water surrounded them. Cyane was ethereally beautiful, shaped in every detail a human female could be, yet she was no longer a creature of flesh. She almost looked as if she were made out of glass, light shining and refracting through her curves.

Cyane looked down, noticing that fact, and curiosity flickered through her features before she lifted her hands to touch her face. For nearly a year she had been formless, unable to speak or cry out, or even to crawl out of the pond and make her presence known.

"What is this?" the Naiad whispered as she examined herself. Persephone had been wondering what to say, but since the nymph had always been so honest with her in the past, she figured anything less than the truth would be unfair.

"When Hades stripped you of your flesh, it died. I have been able to give you a new form, but it is no longer of bone and blood."

Cyane would never forget what Hades had done to her, but now she could talk again. She had despaired at being lost and forgotten, never to have anyone hear her pleas for help. After seeing Kora snatched away by the God of Death, she had imagined all sorts of terrible things happening, what kind of horrors there must be in the Underworld, and not being able to do a damned thing about it! She had tried so hard to communicate with Demeter, but to no avail.

The nymph no longer had flesh, but after being virtually imprisoned in her pond with no means of communicating with anyone, she wasn't about to nitpick at the gift her friend had just given her.

"Thank you, Kora! Thank you for not forgetting me!"

"How could I forget my best friend?" Persephone smiled as Cyane approached the edge of the water with her arms held out. She let Cyane wrap her in a tight embrace, ignoring the water that was now soaking through her chiton. It actually felt nice amidst the thick, balmy atmosphere.

When Persephone contemplated her role as Queen of the Underworld and what she had gained since becoming Hades's lover, she could not help but recall the prophecy that the Fates had issued to her. She hadn't wanted to accept it any more than Mother had for the prophecy regarding her daughter, but as time revealed, the word of the Fates was inviolate.

She could not help but be curious as to what her future would hold. Would she always be Queen of the Underworld? Would her relationship with Hades last? Were there to be any conflicts or serious trouble in her future? What if she received a terrible prophecy? Despite her morbid thoughts, her curiosity was overwhelming, so she gave in to these urges and paid the mysterious trio a visit.

Her excitement was edged with trepidation, but she knew that the longer she put this off, the more curious and anxious she would become.

The tapestry was as she remembered it, the threads ever-moving and shifting, reminding her of currents in a river. Klotho sat on the floor cross-legged, with spindle and distaff in hand. Persephone could not help but wonder what the cosmic material Klotho was spinning would feel like in her hands. Was it warm, or cool? Was it as soft as it looked?

The youngest aspect of Fate was adorned in black, making her pale thread stand out in sharp contrast. Lakhesis wore gray, and Atropos was clad in white.

"We have been expecting you," Atropos intoned. *Why doesn't that surprise me*, Persephone thought wryly.

"There are many questions on your mind."

"You would have us tell you what the future holds for you," said Klotho.

"Yes. What you told me before... it has come true, but then, we all know that. Yet I must know more. Will you answer my questions?" Persephone asked.

"Yes, if you ask rightly." Persephone wasn't sure which one of the Fates had said it, since they all sounded the same.

"What does my future hold?"

"As the seasons go on from winter to summer in an eternal cycle, so will you."

"Gods are born and they die, but you transcend the forces of life and death, which very few can claim."

"The love of your lord is something you never need fear losing."

Well, that is good to know, Persephone mused as she heard the last statement. In her short time as a full-fledged deity, she had seen and heard enough of the tumultuous relationships that deities could have with one another or with mortals. She eyed Atropos as the elder aspect of Fate cut several threads.

"How do you find the time to maintain all these threads?" Persephone knew that there were countless living beings in the world, and after all

400

her experience with weaving, she couldn't imagine spinning, measuring, and cutting thread for each and every one of them.

"We exist outside of time," came the singular response.

Outside of time? Persephone suddenly realized that even though she couldn't feel life in this... place, wherever it was, she also couldn't feel any lack of it.

Atropos beckoned to her, and Persephone drew closer, letting the Fate situate her in front of the grand tapestry that told the history of the universe and everything within it. There were no definable boundaries, and the pattern was ever-shifting, causing her to feel a bit dizzy. What was she supposed to be looking at?

Atropos lifted a slender, bony hand and pointed to a spot. Persephone narrowed her eyes, seeing the threads of colors swirl around and shift before they slowed down, revealing a bit of black. *What was it?* She brought her face closer, focusing on that one area before it all came into focus.

She could see it clearly – a black thread with a golden-rainbow glow – intertwined with a slightly thicker black thread that glowed deep blue and indigo. Though the Fates did not explain who these threads were supposed to represent, she knew immediately who they were for. Her eyes followed the threads, finding the beginning of her own thread, its end hanging separately from the indigo thread and touching a glowing golden-green one, representing the beginning of her life and childhood. As she followed the twist of her thread and Hades's own, she could see no end of them. She looked back at the Fates.

"No one can violate the Great Tapestry."

"But it is how you meet your fate that determines your destiny."

"Rather than let circumstances overcome you, you overcame them."

She stared off thoughtfully, seeing countless threads within the design. Instead of turning Hades away, she had come to respond to his attention rather than spurn it - even though their relationship was not without its fights – and was now his queen and a powerful goddess in her own right. What would have happened had she continued to stubbornly resist Hades? If she had refused to embrace her new-found Gifts and instead used her time to pine for things taken from her, how would she be seeing the Underworld right now? Would she have ever seen the surface world again if she let bitterness dictate her actions?

She had gained far more than she thought she ever would, simply by being open to new things. As she was about to speak, the tapestry vanished from sight, and when she blinked, she found herself back in the Underworld, in the same exact spot she had been when she left, on the terrace overlooking Hades's private garden.

She descended the steps, approaching the flowers that Hades surrounded the garden with, their black-blue petals reflecting a dark iridescent sheen. It was easy to remember the first time she had seen one, when Hades placed it in a clearing of grass for her to find as she romped around the woods, oblivious of her fate. She reached down to touch one, feeling the silken texture between her fingers and thumb as she realized that the color was a match to the glow of Hades's thread.

His eyes are also the same color, she mused as she plucked up a flower.

oOo

"Aidon..." Hades heard a whisper as he lay in bed, waiting for her to join him. He looked up, but the room was empty, and his lips curved in a faint smirk.

"Come here..." He patted the area next to him, "There's no reason to hide from me."

"Really now?" He still couldn't see her, but her voice was closer.

"Of course, my dear." He patted the bed again, his tone dropping to a seductive rumble. "What do you have to be afraid of?"

"Oh, I don't know..." Persephone replied teasingly, drawing closer but maintaining her invisibility.

"Oh, come now." His tone was playfully chiding, and he heard a quiet chuckle before the shadows melted away, revealing the fact that his wife was wearing a crown and matching collar braided of his favorite flower and nothing else. The blue-indigo hue of the petals was a rich contrast to her deep red hair and pale skin, and Hades found this incredibly alluring. He had never imagined that she would use his flowers in such a way... and he certainly had no objections.

oOo

Going back to Enna was a bittersweet experience for Persephone. She had deliberated over what she would do. Would she appear before her cousins, and how would she explain herself? Or should she let them be, and leave them to enjoy the rest of their mortal lives in peaceful bliss? Though Demeter was long gone, the valley that had once been blighted by Ouranos's thirst for vengeance remained prosperous, the goddess' residual magic keeping Enna safe.

Thinking about how much she had missed Enna and the resentment she had felt when her mother uprooted her from her childhood home spurred Persephone to return to the place of her birth.

Eurycleia was long dead, but her family lived on, now spanning five generations – something that was unheard of during the valley's centuries of blight. Having grown up with her cousins, it was funny to think of them as grandparents. Her uncles were now old men, sitting outside with a couple of other elders, sipping ale from mugs and watching their great-grandchildren run around and play games. Iasion's brothers had grown up amidst extreme hardship, and despite their age, would never forget their tribulations, giving them a greater appreciation for how idyllic their lives had become. Their children had grown up without having to worry about where their next meal would come from or if there would be enough firewood for the winter.

Persephone was tempted to make herself visible and say hello to them, but she wasn't sure if they would recognize her. Everyone seemed so happy, so she was content to stand under the shade of a tree – one of the trees she had played under with her cousins – and watch Iasion's family.

What would things have been like if her father hadn't died? She almost wished that Atropos had cut the thread of one of his brothers instead, but that was a petty thought. Death was death, no matter who it affected.

She watched as Alestis – now a dignified and gray-haired matron – emerge from the well-kept house with a platter of dates and pita bread, setting it before her father and his guests.

Enna had changed since she had been here last. What was once a village was now a prosperous town, bordering on a city. The buildings around the marketplace were larger and more impressive, and more houses dotted a landscape that was as verdant as she remembered it. The richness of the soil and vegetation ensured a healthy and prosperous population, and given time, this village could become a city-state as mighty as Thebes, Athens, or Sparta.

In the grandchildren and great-grandchildren, she could see her uncles and cousins. One youth bore a striking resemblance to Iasion, and the surge of love and memory she felt was bittersweet.

Satisfied that Iasion's family was happy and safe, Persephone was comfortable with returning to the Underworld, but she knew that she would be coming back to this place.

oOo

It had been nearly a century since the death of her husband, and Demeter still remembered him as if he had only been alive yesterday. She had had a couple of lovers through the years, and did remember them with affection – especially Triptolemus – but she had never truly loved anyone as she did Iasion.

The people of Eleusis had been faithful supporters of her rites, performing them every year with the priestesses she had chosen. The original set had all died except for Melinoe, who was now an ancient crone, and head priestess of the order for the last few decades. The order was made up entirely of women... until now, potentially. Melinoe had detected a Gift in the youth that stood before her. He was tall and broad-shouldered, nearing twenty. Normally, men would not be allowed to join the Eleusinian Mysteries, but long ago, Demeter had ordered that anyone – male or female – with a Gift should be brought before her, and Melinoe had always obeyed her patron.

If Demeter deemed fit, then Isokrates could become the first priest in the order. She had been priestess for so long that the thought of a male among their ranks was still a strange concept to her, but it was the goddess' decision.

She felt Demeter's presence even though she could not see the goddess, and led the young man into the inner courtyard. The grass was warm under her fare beet, and when she came to a stop, she wiggled her toes into it. Lately, with her advanced age, she found sandals bothersome and went barefoot whenever the weather permitted.

"Goddess, I bring you Isokrates, for your consideration." She bowed, feeling the creak in her spine as she did so. She righted herself, seeing the rustle of the leaves, and smiled slightly. Though her body was riddled with the infirmities of old age, her eyesight remained clear. She shuffled back into the temple.

Men had the capacity to be born with Gifts as well as women did, but the nature of their Gifts often ran in a different vein. This was clearly evinced among the Olympians when one compared the feminine Gifts to the masculine.

Demeter immediately recognized a connection to Nature in this man's Gift – sometimes exceptions to the rule were good – and it pleased her. With the proper training, this man could be an excellent priest. She would have to test him, of course, to make sure he had the dedication and right kind of attitude needed for such an honored role.

There was something oddly familiar about Isokrates, though Demeter knew she had never met this man before. She studied his face, taking in the particular features that comprised his expression. His traits were typical of a Hellenic man, with dark hair and eyes and a modest tan from the time he spent outside in the fields, and he couldn't be considered handsome or ugly, just plain-faced. Her attention moved to his eyes, and she felt a shiver pass through her very soul as she looked past them.

Could it be... Yes, it was! Love and joy surged through her, and as if Isokrates sensed it, he smiled.

oOo

The city of Rome sat snugly on the Italian peninsula, a sprawling metropolis that exceeded any of the city-states that had existed in Hellas at the height of its power. Though writing was not as prevalent as it would be over two thousand years later, the Latins now had a well-established alphabet and system of writing that enabled them to keep records and communicate better with one another. Persephone remembered a time where important messages were brought by runners who had to memorize the exact words they had been given, and now these runners often bore scrolls.

It was not until after the fall of Ilion – what would later be known as Troy – that the Hellenes developed and took advantage of the written word as much as they could have, giving rise to epic sagas like the *Iliad*, *Odyssey*, or the *Aeneid*, among other great classical works of literature. The myths of the gods, the legends of the heroes and the chronicles of kings were also written down, preserved for the rest of time even if not necessarily truthful or accurate.

While Classical Greece was rebuilding itself after the dissolution of Mycenaean Greece and the destruction of Troy, Rome was establishing its own destiny, borrowing much of its early culture from Hellas and Tyrrhenia but eventually developing its unique identity.

Romans took what they found useful and innovated upon it, creating an empire that would last for centuries, eventually conquering Aigyptos and Hellas among other lands, spreading in all four directions in a way that no country had ever before. In its time, it truly was the mightiest empire known to man.

"Last time I saw these seven hills, there weren't nearly as many people," Hades commented as he stood atop the highest hill, looking down at the city.

A thousand years ago, the thought of living for a century boggled Persephone's mind. She would listen to Hades's stories about the Titanomachy and how the Olympians had defeated the old order and enabled Hellas to prosper under the new. When she had first seen the grand cities of Hellas, ruled by powerful kings, she had a hard time imagining that they had once been tiny villages, and before that, great expanses of plains or woods yet to be populated.

Now having seen how much the world and its people could change through centuries, she had a better understanding of how things happened, but it was still overwhelming at times to think about how things had once been, or what they could become. She had seen this place in Romulus's time, and wondered what the founder of Rome would think about the empire it had become.

"It is almost hard to believe that this would not exist without Ares or Aphrodite, hm?" Persephone asked with a sly smile as she glanced at her husband.

"Who would have thought that their affairs could bring around something of value?" he remarked with a half-smile, "Although I have no doubt that lots of people would have been happier if your sister hadn't offered such a prize..."

The Trojan War had brought about the end of an era in Greek history. With Aphrodite's offer of the most beautiful woman in the world – a woman who was already married to the King of Sparta – in exchange for a golden apple, she unwittingly exacerbated what had been meant to be a harmless joke by her daughter, Eris. With her thoughts set on an immediate reward, Aphrodite triggered a devastating chain of events that destroyed an age.

But even as the Goddess of Love was in a large part responsible for the destruction of Ilion, she had also contributed to the duration of the survivors of the ruined city. Her son, Aeneas, born from an affair with the mortal Anchises, led what was left of the Trojans to settle in what would later become known as Italy, calling their colony Alba Longa. Aeneas's line became the rulers of this settlement, and generations later, Ares would play his own part in the fate of these descendants of Ilion.

The God of War had been forced to be chaste for several decades before Persephone would restore his potency – after much groveling and favors – but not without the codicil that if he attempted to force himself upon another woman, she would punish him with permanent chastity. Thus far he had actually managed to behave himself, and when Rhea Silva – a daughter of Aeneas's line – caught his attention, she was a willing recipient of his desire.

Rhea bore twin sons whose names would be remembered through the history of the West. They were unaware of their divine paternity, but had inherited much from Ares, including a tendency to fight. Not knowing his own strength, Romulus slew his twin by accident before going on to found Rome.

Many of the Greek gods integrated themselves within this new kingdom, taking on new names, just as they had done in Tyrrhenia, where Hades and Persephone had been worshiped as Aita and Fersephenai, and now the Romans knew them as Pluto and Proserpina. Ares and Aphrodite were quick to embrace their roles as Mars and Venus, two of Rome's most prominent deities, and their names were often used even after the inevitable fall of the Roman Empire.

Just as Rome was more advanced than Hellas, the gods had advanced, some more than others. Under his new identity of Jupiter, Zeus was more thoughtful and wise. He still made mistakes now and then, but he made a lot less of them. Ares and Aphrodite also tended to make less trouble, focusing their energies into more productive ways. The Trojan War had a sobering effect on the Goddess of Love especially, and in her Venus aspect, she was considerably more loving and patient than her former persona. Mortals had but decades to gain wisdom, but sometimes it took a god centuries.

Persephone laughed at her husband's statement. "A long time ago, I never could have imagined it. Makes you wonder what will happen next, hm?"

Hades touched his wife's face, rubbing her chin and cheek affectionately. "Only time will tell."

oOo

The plantation filled most of the valley, its well-groomed lots filling the landscape with a patchwork of various colors. The lots were interspersed with whitewashed and neatly maintained buildings that hosted a number of activities.

Toula marched towards the cart at the end of the lot with a basket full of olives. One thing she liked about the job that it was never the same year-round. A couple of months ago, she and the other workers had harvested grapes, and now it was time to collect olives. She had always liked working outdoors, so she considered it the perfect job for her. Several of her siblings and cousins also worked here, because the company that owned the farms employed many people in the neighboring town.

The town had languished due to its isolation and a sagging economy before the company set up base here. The jobs created paid well, and many young people – or their parents – were able to afford going to one of the larger cities, like Athens or Thessaloniki, so they could attend university. Every worker here was also able to take a certain amount of the product the company generated, to share with their family or friends. The village had also become a small tourist attraction, and her aunt had set up a bed-and-breakfast business a few years ago. Sometimes the visitors liked being given tours of the plantation or the caves that sheltered the wine production. If not for the company, more people would have left the valley because it was so remote, and in today's world, many considered remote villages outdated.

Some people said that the valley was almost magical, because its bounty was so delicious and abundant. The Christmas bonuses that came in the form of generous packages of food were never turned down, and Mother always said that after the company set up here, she wouldn't consider getting wine or olive oil anywhere else. Toula and her brothers and sisters had grown up eating these products, and she couldn't imagine consuming anything else.

The smooth rumble of an unfamiliar-sounding engine caused her to lift her head, peering at the road under the brim of her hat. Trucks came and went on a regular basis, but what she saw was a car that was closer than she had thought it would be since its engine was quieter than the company's vehicles. It was a finer car than she had ever seen in her life, its polished ebony surface gleaming in the afternoon sun. It drove past her and stopped in front of the largest building in the compound, and the back door opened to let out a tall man in a black suit and deep blue tie. His long hair was as black as the car or his attire, and was pulled back in a thick ponytail.

Sunglasses and a dark gray fedora hat obscured most of the upper half of his face. He was too well-dressed to be a worker, and Toula wondered who he was. Was he one of the company's international buyers? A glint drew her eye to the cane the man was carrying, the handle of it having the appearance of a polished skull.

The field workers had been taught to leave such visitors alone unless instructed otherwise, so Toula continued her way to get the olives pressed.

oOo

Ms. Kory sat in her office, going through the paperwork and tallies. Every year was profitable, and she really should expect no less, but she liked looking at all the numbers, especially since she was unable to be here every day like most other bosses could. Several crates of various products sat in the corner of her office, bottled or jarred and bearing the company label and logo on them. The flavor of the food grown around here was like it had been in her childhood, deep and rich, each kind of fruit or vegetable bearing just the right fullness of flavor.

Though this place was no longer known as Enna and much had changed, it still felt like home to her. When she had come here a couple of decades ago, the valley was nearly deserted, people trickling out through the years to seek their fortunes in the larger cities. Europe had been through much in the last few centuries, including a lion's share of wars. Borders shifted and disappeared, and the history of Greece had been turbulent. Things had become more stable over the last few decades, but the march of time had inevitable effects.

She had been especially fascinated – and sometimes mystified – by the technological advances of the last century. The Renaissance had been glorious, but could the great thinkers and artists of that era have ever envisioned a television or phone? The stylus was replaced with a quill, and then the typewriter, and now computers. The city-states of ancient Hellas and even the sprawling urban centers of the Roman Empire and Byzantium paled before the glittering metropolises of the current era, the densely populated complexes attracting people just as they had done in ancient times. Modern life had a way of doing that to people, and those that were left had borne the brunt that was typical of small towns or villages in this era, something she had seen the world over.

However, modern living had also enabled her to create her own company – something that would have been unheard of for women in ancient

Greece – and the valley was revitalized, just in a different way than her mother had done so long ago. The goods her company produced were all organic, and demand was high. Thanks to her powers, the farms need never worry about drought or blight, so business was steady. Of course, she had to learn how to run a business, which required more than it did in ancient times. Learning how to use a computer had been so frustrating at times; Hephaistos had a much easier time with the infernal machines and had helped her to understand them. Dealing with all the paperwork required – tax forms, employee benefits, compliance and safety guidelines and the like – caused her to want to pull out her hair at times, but with patience and determination, understanding of these things came within her grasp. Sometimes she longed for a simpler time, but progress did come with its complications.

She lifted her head when she heard a gentle rapping on the door, immediately recognizing the presence of her visitor.

"Come in!" she called out, keeping her eyes on the papers and computer, feigning perfunctory interest in her guest. She bit back a smile as he drew the blinds closed before sitting down in one of the chairs in front of her desk. He took off his hat and sunglasses, placing them at the edge of the desk as he regarded her silently for several moments.

Hades leaned back, studying her as she made a show of examining her paperwork. She had done very well, but then, he would expect no less, and she looked every bit the professional she was, clad in a green silk suit with her thick hair pulled back in a bun.

"How can I help you?" she asked as she looked up at him, her face and voice neutral, the gleam in her eyes betraying her delight at his presence.

"Mmm... I think you know the answer to that, my dear." Hades's voice was a soft purr that sent a pleasant shiver up and down her spine, causing a faint tingle in her fingers and toes. He could be so damn sexy when he wanted to, and he was an especially fetching sight in the well-tailored suit he wore.

"Oh, now I am a mind-reader?" she shot back lightly.

"You never needed to read my mind to know what I want... or *need*." His gaze told her of just how fierce his need was, and her lips curved up in a smile.

"How about some refreshment?" she asked. She pressed a button on her phone. "Theresa, bring up some bread, plates, and cutlery."

"Right away, Ms. Kory." It was standard practice with prospective clients or buyers to let them sample her products, and it wasn't the first time Hades had done so. Within a few minutes, everything she requested was set before her on the desk, and the secretary closed the door behind her.

As Hades started cutting slices of the bread, his wife went over to the crates, retrieving a bottle of olive oil and jars of strawberry and pomegranate jelly.

"I have missed you," Hades stated as he sat back with a slice of bread slathered with jelly.

"You always do."

"How could I not?"

Persephone smiled again, thinking about what the Fates had told her about her relationship with Hades. He was as loyal and affectionate as ever, but the time she spent apart from him also kept the dynamics between them fresh. Absence really did make the heart fonder, and it applied to her as well as it did him. Like her, he had established a company of his own as a diversion, though she was much more hands-on with her own business than he was. She really enjoyed being part of this world, and the challenge of establishing and running a business. Hades had not objected at all when she proposed the idea to him.

As she munched on a piece of bread, Hades idly picked up one of the jars and looked at it, admiring the design of the sticker. A picture of a cornucopia laden with produce dominated most of the label, with 'Cornucopia' emblazoned in deep red – the color of a pomegranate – above it in Greek language and letters, and below it in English. The name was appropriate for a company known for its wine, olive oil, fruit jams and jellies, and vegetable dips and spreads. He opened the jar and slipped his finger inside before licking it clean.

"Don't you know it's rude to eat out of the jar?" Persephone chided playfully. Slowly and deliberately, he repeated his motions, dragging his finger through the sweet substance and getting a larger dollop than before. A faint blush rose in her cheeks as he languidly licked it off his finger, and he winked at her before she laughed and shook her head.

"Whatever am I going to do with you?"

"Love me?" he shot back.

"You're such a charmer."

"I know."

o0o

After being in a quiet, semi-lit room, the sunlight almost felt like an assault on Hades even with his hat and sunglasses, and he was eager to return to the peaceful darkness of the Underworld. His chauffeur emerged from the car and bowed as he opened the door for Persephone.

"Good to see you again, Kharon," Persephone stated, and the almost-skeletal man smiled faintly. Like Hades, he wore sunglasses, and wore a black suit and chauffeur's hat, though both of them know and respected him as much more than a servant. Kharon did not always accompany Hades to the surface, but once in a while he would come up and enjoy some time in the surface realm before returning to Styx. Once Hades was in the car, Kharon closed the door before going back to the driver's seat. The windows were tinted and the air conditioning on full blast, and Persephone shivered slightly from the cold.

Hades took off his jacket and draped it around her shoulders, wrapping his arm around her. Her head lolled back on his shoulder, and he pressed his lips to her forehead. He knew she needed her time on the surface world, but it was always good to bring her home. Sometimes she would come without any argument, and other times she would tease him and make him chase after her. He never tired of chasing after her.

"Since you are so cold, I will give you a nice hot bath when we get home, hmm?" he asked. She smiled and nodded.

"You always take such good care of me."

"Would you expect any less of your loving husband?"

"Of course not." She smiled at him before looking out the window, seeing several of her employees hard at work collecting olives, Toula among them. In the young woman she could see a bit of Eurycleia and Alestis, especially around the eyes. Many of the residents of the village were distant descendants of Iasion's family. So many generations separated her father's relatives from these people today that a resemblance generally wasn't apparent, so Persephone was always happy to see a bit of familiarity here and there in the faces of the lucky few, especially dark-eyed and -haired Toula.

It was almost hard to believe that she had actually lived this long, or made it this far. Through millennia, many gods died, either on their own or from vicious battles, like the Ragnarok that obliterated many of the Teutonic deities over a thousand years ago. Others simply abandoned their roles as gods and disappeared among mortals.

Her recollections were interrupted as she felt the shift in the air that signaled their crossing from one realm to another. The car rippled before appearing as a boat for a brief moment, the sound of flowing water meeting her ears. Kharon turned to them, the steering wheel in his hands now the long handle of an oar, his body clad in a dark gray cloak instead of the chauffeur's uniform. He bowed before he and his boat faded from around them, the sounds of the Styx going with him.

The jacket that Hades had placed on her shoulders expanded, its texture becoming velvety on the inside as it revealed itself to be part of her husband's cloak. His cane thickened and lengthened, the handle stretching out in the form of a curved blade. The scythe wasn't something Hades had used when he first became Lord of the Underworld, but when the long-handled sickle was first invented by mortals, he took a liking to it and created a modified one for his own use that became iconic as part of the representation of Death.

Persephone looked up, seeing the familiar skull-shaped helmet perched atop her husband's head. His face was visible in the shadow formed by the helmet, and he was smiling down at her faintly. After her time in the upper world, she was inevitably aware of the coldness of the Underworld. No matter how many times she returned to the Underworld and quickly re-acclimated herself to its unique atmosphere, she felt the cold every time upon arrival, but the warmth of the body holding her reassured her in more ways than one.

With his helmet lowered over his face and scythe in hand, his black cloak swishing around him, Hades was quite literally the stuff of nightmares and deepest fears. She had to admit, there was a delicious thrill seeing him in this getup, and he knew it. She could even say he was... what was that word the mortals used today... *sexy*. Even after all the years they had been married, she enjoyed his company as much as ever, and knew her feelings were more than reciprocated. It made every homecoming something to look forward to.

"Aidon..." she whispered. Hades touched her hair with his free hand, burying his fingers in the thick waves that were not quite bound in her bun, before pressing his lips to her forehead. Even now, it sometimes amazed him just how he felt for her. He was supposed to be merciless and cold, lord of a cursed realm, his heart as hard and unyielding as stone. For millennia he ruled over a realm that even gods feared. People hesitated to say his name out loud. Just like in the past, people today spoke of him as a dark and even evil god though nobody believed in the Greek gods anymore. Some things never changed, and Death was one of them. Yet his bride did not fear him, or his power, and a surge of contentment filled him as she pressed her body to his, resting her head on his shoulder.

"Welcome back, Seph."

Nobody had worshiped him or his wife for a long time. The story of her abduction was overly simplified, and she was often portrayed as an unwilling victim and perpetually unhappy queen, hating the Underworld, pining for every spring and dreading every autumn. He was portrayed as evil and cruel, a greedy and selfish man who plucked her from her mother's arms without any thought as to what she might need or want. And so the Greeks had come to blame him for their autumns and winters, and the story persisted even through the modern age. At least the truth was far better – and more interesting – than fiction.

Notes

oOo

The Titanomachy refers to the time where the Titans ruled Greece after Kronos overthrew his father Ouranos. Kronos had eleven siblings who were Titans, including his own wife, and in some versions of the Greek myths, these Titans were forced out of their former godly positions by the Olympians when the Titanomachy ended. For example, Selene (the moon) was replaced by Artemis, Helios (the sun) was replaced by Apollo, Okeanos (the sea) was replaced by Poseidon, and so on.

oOo

The river Styx also had a goddess of the same name; she was one of the many daughters of Okeanos/Oceanus and Tethys, and when the Olympians rose against Kronos and his Titans, Styx was the first to ally to Zeus's side. For her loyalty, Zeus made promises to her binding, which was why it was the custom to swear by the Styx to show the seriousness of your words.

According to the original myths (at least some of the versions) Styx was mated to Pallas, a Titan who was in some myths killed by Athena. With Pallas, she had four children – Kratos (strength) Bia (force/power) Nike (victory) and Zelus (zeal) These four gods were sometimes depicted as Zeus's personal enforcers.

For this story, I thought it'd be fun to have Kharon and Styx together, those two need love, too. It felt more appropriate to me given Styx's position as an Underworld deity, so it felt better to me to pair her with Kharon rather than Pallas. Since Kharon is a son of Nyx and a god in his own right, I decided to extend his duties beyond that of merely a ferryman – I imagine that it would get boring after so long – so like Hades with his shadows, Kharon can extend his will and not be required to be physically present for his duty.

oOo

In one version of the myth, Abas was a son of Metaniera, in others he is simply a gardener who does get turned into a lizard. In another version of the myth, Abas was a gardener in Hades who saw Persephone eat pomegranate seeds and tattled to Hades, and was transformed by Demeter for being such a narc. I felt that being a gardener would suit Abas well and work better for my story, even though I must admit he would make a good bratty prince!

oOo

The kingdom of Tyrrhenia is the ancient name for Etruria, a kingdom that flourished at the beginning of the first millennium BCE as Greece was in its Dark Ages (before the Classical Greece era) and contributed much to the early Roman

Empire. Infact, before 500 BCE, a few Etruscan kings ruled Ancient Rome, and the seventh legendary King of Rome himself was Etruscan before he was deposed prior to the founding of the Roman Republic.

oOo

Those familiar with the Hades and Persephone myth know that she was forced to go back to the Underworld every fall for the duration of one month for every seed she consumed, which ranges between three and seven in the various tellings of the myth. Often, this month for a seed rule was a judgment passed down by Zeus in an effort to placate Demeter and Hades. Rather than force Persephone to traverse between her mother and Hades on a set schedule, I decided to empower her and give her some control over her fate rather than have Zeus or Hades determine it for her.

About the Author

M.M. Kin has been interested in history and mythology since she was young and has been an avid reader for as long as she can remember. Her other interests include hiking, kayaking, and world domination. 'Seeds' is her first work, and she is currently at work on more books.

She can be contacted at ememkin@gmail.com.

Made in the USA
San Bernardino, CA
31 October 2014